Charles C Atchison

A Winter Cruise in Summer Seas

Charles C Atchison

A Winter Cruise in Summer Seas

ISBN/EAN: 9783337252502

Printed in Europe, USA, Canada, Australia, Japan

Cover: Foto ©Andreas Hilbeck / pixelio.de

More available books at **www.hansebooks.com**

A WINTER CRUISE IN SUMMER SEAS

"HOW I FOUND" HEALTH.

DIARY OF A TWO MONTHS' VOYAGE IN THE
ROYAL MAIL STEAM PACKET COMPANY'S S.S. *CLYDE*,
FROM SOUTHAMPTON, THROUGH THE BRAZILS,
TO BUENOS AIRES AND BACK,

FOR

£100.

BY

CHARLES C. ATCHISON.

*PROFUSELY ILLUSTRATED WITH PHOTOGRAPHS, AND
SKETCHES BY WALTER W. BUCKLEY.*

LONDON:
SAMPSON LOW, MARSTON & COMPANY
LIMITED,
St. Dunstan's House,
FETTER LANE, FLEET STREET, E.C.
1891.

LONDON :
PRINTED BY WILLIAM CLOWES AND SONS, LIMITED,
STAMFORD STREET AND CHARING CROSS.

PREFACE.

BEING in failing health and ordered an ocean voyage "at once," one of the three questions—"how, when, and where," was solved for me. The other two I was left to decide for myself, and very trying I found them, for while plenty of books tell you "where" to go, few say "how." Besides, as a rule, such journeys consume too much time or too much money—often both.

The problem set before *me*, was how to make the best use of, say £100, and two months' leave of absence. To begin with, I attacked my task by a process of exhaustion—*this* was too dear, *that* was too long a journey—and thus I winnowed the issue down. So far, judgment counted for something. The rest of the solution was pure luck, look at it how you will. What else could it be in such a quest, to light on a path of roses which, for two months *to a day*, you shall tread in genial company, and under summer skies, *for exactly* £100 ?

Such was my good fortune. And if you are a sufferer from over-work and "beating about" for guidance, as I was, you will welcome even my erratic footprints on health's highway, and will tolerate the minute details which may be of use to others if not to you.

Mind, I promise you just footprints, and no more. In me you have no scientific guide, no travel-stained "globe-trotter;" nothing but a sick man wandering in search of health, and finding it, or at least enough of it to make "life worth living."

My "Winter Cruise in Summer Seas" was undertaken solely in search of long-lost sleep, and health that fled with it; and now that both have been restored to me, I venture to christen my notes with a second name, that is, I think, at once appropriate and fashionable: — "'*How I found*' Health."

AUTHOR.

CONTENTS.

INTRODUCTION.

PAGE

CHAPTER I.

SOUTHAMPTON TO LISBON.

CHAPTER II.

LISBON TO ST. VINCENT.

CHAPTER III.

ST. VINCENT TO PERNAMBUCO.

Leaving the Verde Islands—The "Gulf line"—86° in my cabin—The puzzle lock—"Mouse-trap in three letters"—Fresh fruits from St. Vincent—Dancing on deck—The band—Some of the dancers— Oh! for a Quadrille!—"The rhythm of unresting feet"—Sunday, 2 a.m.—"Meet me by moonlight alone"—Strange bedfellow—Is it a mermaid, or only a dream?—Various theories—The Portuguese certificate—Hypnotism—Pog's mental abstraction—The result— Moonstruck or drunk from the opening of the *port?*—No duels allowed on the *Clyde* on Sundays—"Bull" in your own cabin— Church parade—Service in the saloon—The hymn "St. Alban"— The fo'cas'le chant—Pog's vocal organ—The Yankee in doubt —"J.H.S.": Pog explains—The Purser interviewed—Vessel signalling—Our flags—The little Portuguese town astern—Lucifer matches on board—Fire is bad and shipwreck is bad, but terror is worse—"Fear nothing but fear"—The Irishman's new boots— North German Lloyd steamer homeward bound from the Plate— The Doldrums—Two thousand five hundred miles from home— "When the breeze comes before the rain," etc.—Mr. Courtney —Well-digging—Pumping by horse-power—Ostrich farming— Steering the ostrich—The tarantula—Porpoises—Tropical rain—

CHAPTER IV.

PERNAMBUCO TO BAHIA.

A little joke—" The partners "—Frightened or faithless?—The fox
and the straw—Pernambuco coffee—Cock-crow on board—Sims
Reeves in a crate—A death on board—The crow of ill omen—
"A crow's a crow"—The coffin and the Union Jack—Worse news:
Small-pox on board—Bank Manager, Monte Video—How for-
tunes are made—£115,000 profit—Coasting to Bahia—Catamarans
—Counting the revolutions by beats under the foot—Blue waves
with white caps—Cape San Antonio—The boilers of the *Reliance*
—Half-a-gale—Itaparica—The *Thames* twin-sister to our *Clyde*—

CHAPTER V.

BAHIA TO RIO DE JANEIRO.

CHAPTER VI.

RIO DE JANEIRO TO BUENOS AIRES.

CHAPTER VII.

BUENOS AIRES, ROSARIO DE SANTA FÉ, LA PLATA, ETC.

CHAPTER VIII.

BUENOS AIRES TO RIO DE JANEIRO.

CHAPTER IX.

RIO DE JANEIRO TO BAHIA.

CHAPTER X.

BAHIA TO ST. VINCENT.

CHAPTER XI.

ST. VINCENT TO LISBON.

CHAPTER XII.

LISBON TO SOUTHAMPTON.

ILLUSTRATIONS.

INTRODUCTION.

THERE is wisdom in the multitude of counsellors, but there is also a limit beyond which their further augmentation becomes embarrassing. Advertisements, for instance, are counsellors who leave one more undecided after than before the consultation. How on earth can a man choose with such a heap of things to choose from ? And, worse than all, any little shred of a notion he may have had is swamped in the whirlpool of information.

My thoughts have been led into this channel by a remembrance of the difficulty I found in planning my trip. My first idea, greatly due to Mr. William Clark Russell's charming description of his passage, was to take a run to the Cape. But there were not enough breaks in that trip for me, so I looked elsewhere. The West Indies, Mediterranean, Egypt, etc., all these were weighed in turn, discarded, and—such is our fickle nature—reconsidered, till one got as sick of the voyage before it began as a cook of her dishes.

My plans were in this very chaotic condition, when a friend brought me "The Cruise of the *Falcon*," a voyage to South America in a thirty-ton yacht, by E. F. Knight, Barrister-at-law. This delightful book soon turned my thoughts in quite another direction—to the Brazils and the River Plate.

Thus "where" was very soon in a fair way to being solved, and the doctors having settled that the "when" was to be at once, there remained only the "how."

It had been ascertained that the run to The Plate and back would consume about two months. The next step was to find out the cost, and something about the places touched at, for what I needed was rest of a kind that should be recreative. A long voyage with no stoppages would not serve my purpose.

The Royal Mail Steam Packet Company's route to Buenos Aires, offering variety of experience at the ports visited, pleased me greatly. Vigo, Lisbon, St. Vincent, Pernambuco, Bahia, Rio de Janeiro, Monte Video, and finally Buenos Aires, were tempting sounds to a sick man in London in dreary October. Why, one could rest all day and all night if one chose, and taking sleep as it came, store it away in one's nerves and tissues, and having fed them fully after their long fast, lay by some store in case of further need.

The more I pondered on these things, the better the prospect pleased me of a summer cruise through the Brazils, while England lay wrapped in her mantle of snow. Home for me! if I had been free to choose; and next to that a yachting trip on a grand scale along the South American coast.

From what I could learn from Anglo-Indians and other friends, the *Messageries Maritimes,* whose vessels, starting from Bordeaux, go over much the same ground as the Royal Mail, ran them very close also in catering for the comfort of passengers. Moreover, the Bordeaux route, it was said, offered the additional advantage of an escape from some of the terrors of the Bay of Biscay, though, as some one has aptly put it, " 'tis not the rocky *Bay* you fear so much as the *rocky ship.*"

An important consideration to an invalid on his first ocean voyage.

All this about the Bordeaux route I afterwards found was nonsense. In exchange for the open ocean rollers of the Royal Mail route from Ushant to Finisterre, you have the enclosed, pitching, chopping, food-churning breakers from Bordeaux to the latter cape. If some sort of pedometer could be worn by two passengers, one going by the one route, and the other by the other, it would be found, I think, to record far more shakes from Bordeaux than from Ushant to Finisterre. Smaller and more disagreeable shakes; for the annoyance a wave causes is, I have learned, in inverse proportion to its size. So far then this route seemed "no great shakes."

Another feature of the French route, however, though it was not of moment to me, would weigh with a man in health —the greater variety of experience afforded by the overland travelling to Bordeaux. The point is worth consideration; but to my mind the great recommendation of the French boats was the food. The dainty snacks, so tempting to a fastidious palate; coffee, and a little roll in bed—"roll in bed" is a bit ambiguous, but let it pass—midday lunch, and French dinner at seven or half-past. However, on reckoning it up, I found the French prices for second-class equal to, if not a little more than, the Royal Mail's ordinary first-class, the passage-money for which is fifty guineas to Buenos Aires and back.

It should here be explained that on board the French boats first and second-class passengers use the same dining-saloon, and are treated in every way alike, except as to sleeping accommodation, the first-class cabins being in the best parts of the ship.

So far the pro's and con's of the French route were about equally balanced ; but as my informants were mostly Anglo-Indians, and could only speak from their knowledge of the *Messageries Maritimes* in the East, the question of route was kept open till the last. And it was well it was so, as things turned out, though I barely escaped the proverbial fall that threatens the man " between two stools."

The Royal Mail Steam Packet Company's new ship, the *Clyde*, a magnificent vessel, was announced to leave Southampton for Buenos Aires on October 23rd. This was only her second voyage, her maiden trip having been made but three months before, July 31st, 1890, to the same place. As she was advertised 5645 tons burden, and 7000 horse-power, and was clearly therefore one of their largest vessels, my friends never dreamt there would be any difficulty in booking a passage for me, and so October 20th dawned before application was made at the Company's head office in Moorgate Street. (This well-nigh wrecked me before starting. At least, so I see it now; for though doubtless there are other splendid vessels on this line, as well officered and equipped, to me the *Clyde* is, and must ever remain, *facile princeps.*)

As may be supposed, then, our surprise was great on learning, three days before her departure, that not a berth was to be had. The huge *Clyde*, capable of carrying a thousand people, was full! It will astonish no student of human nature to be told that this news only made me keener to go by the *Clyde*, and nothing else. Ill as I was, even discomfort on that ship seemed preferable to luxury on any floating palace that ever sailed the seas.

Luckily, it was found on further pressing the Moorgate Street officials, that there was just one berth, a top one, as

far as Lisbon—an *ordinary* first-class affair—and thence to
Buenos Aires, there was what is termed an *extra* first-class
top berth, at a cost of £3 15s. more. This or nothing was
all they had to offer.

Here, then, is how the case stood. Should I pay fifty
guineas plus £3 15s. for what seemed like mere disturbance
at Lisbon, or should I, for this was the alternative, wait
till November 4th, and go out in their next vessel, the
Moselle ?

By the way, there was something more than the mere
shifting of cabin at Lisbon. Thereafter I was to exchange
English society for Portuguese. It did seem hard to be
mulcted in £3 15s. extra for *this*. Such close quarters as
three in a cabin with *any* foreigners is disagreeable, but this
was exasperating.

It speaks well, therefore, either for my inherent obstinacy,
or for my intuitive admiration of the *Clyde*, that despite
all these drawbacks, ten minutes' thought settled the
question, and in five minutes more I had paid my £56 5s.,
secured the two short leases of the vacant berths, and
pocketed my ticket to Buenos Aires and back, which included the railway journey to and from Rosario de Santa Fé.

Don't let me be unfair to the *Moselle*. I have since known
many who have travelled by her, and speak as favourably of
her as I do of the *Clyde*. She is some 3000 tons burden, and
has electric light throughout, and, as there were far fewer
passengers, the comfort would have been proportionately
greater. But she was not starting for another twelve days,
and time was precious. Besides, she was going direct to The
Plate, and so the chief attraction, the coasting cruise from
Pernambuco to Buenos Aires, was wanting.

Here let me explain the fares. My outlay of £56 5s. entitled me to a first-class berth to Lisbon, and an extra first-class thence to the end of the voyage out; and on the return journey to a first-class berth only. For the single journey the charge is £35 ordinary first-class, and £5 more for extra first-class. The return first-class is £52 10s., *i.e.* a fare-and-a-half. The return extra first-class is £60.

As a rule the first-class cabins are amidships, and being the inner of two rows have no outlet to the sea. The extra first-class are forward in the bows, and farther removed from the heat and noise of the engines; and as there is but one row of them, the occupants have the undoubted advantage of air through the port. But any one to whom the difference of fare is an object, will find the first-class cabins quite good enough. I should have taken a berth in one of them myself if I could have got it, but I couldn't.

As it may interest some to know exactly how the £100 was laid out, I append a summary of the actual expenditure :—

COST OF TRIP

(*From start to finish*).

	£	s.	d.
Two suits grey flannel at 34s. (trousers and jacket only) ...	3	8	0
Four pyjama suits at 4s. 9d.	0	19	0
Two caps for deck use	0	3	0
Boating shoes (canvas)	0	9	0
Two flannel shirts at 8s. 6d.	0	17	0
Two silk and wool ditto at 10s.	1	0	0
Total cost of outfit required to supplement ordinary wardrobe ...	6	16	0
Return ticket per Royal Mail S.S. Company to Buenos Aires and back (inclusive of rail to Rosario de Santa Fé), *i.e.* "extra" first-class one way and "ordinary" the other ...	56	5	0
Liquor bill (each way £3)	6	0	0
Carried forward ...	69	1	0

					£	s.	d.
		Brought forward	...	...	69	1	0

			£	s.	d.			
Gratuities—Cabin Steward	(each way)	...	1	0	0			
„ Dining Saloon Steward	„	...	0	10	0			
„ Bath Steward	„ ...	...	0	10	0			
„ Boots Steward	„	...	0	5	0			

2×2 | 5 | 0 | = 4 | 10 | 0

Cost of going on shore—		£	s.	d.	£	s.	d.
Lisbon (staying the night) and visiting Cintra	...	1	10	0			
St. Vincent (Verde Islands) and tips to the divers		0	5	0			
Pernambuco	...	0	10	0			
Bahia (staying the night)		1	0	0			
Rio de Janeiro (staying the night)	...	1	10	0			
Monte Video		0	10	0			
		5	5	0	5	5	0

Ten days in Buenos Aires at Hôtel l'Universelle (bed and breakfast only)	5	0	0			
Lunch and dinners at Café Filip opposite hotel ...	2	10	0			
Rosario de Santa Fé—Hotel bill	1	0	0			
Sight - seeing, liquors, travelling, laundress' fees, etc.	3	0	0			
	11	10	0	11	10	0

Rio de Janeiro (staying the night on Corcovado) ...	...	...	1	10	0
Cab and Rail between London and Southampton, each way £1			2	0	0
Dock fees	...	...	0	9	0
Porterage of luggage to and from vessel at Buenos Aires and Southampton			0	5	0
Mementoes of places touched at, say	...		5	10	0
			£100	0	0

Some friends on board had books descriptive of Brazil and the Plate district, and at the Buenos Aires Club there were many similar works, all of which I found both helpful and interesting. For the convenience of such of my readers as may wish to know more of the places visited, I conclude these introductory remarks with a list of the authors whose names I noted, together with the titles of their books so far as I have been able to verify them:

AUTHOR'S NAME.	TITLE OF BOOK.
Gallenga, A. ...	South America.
Hassaurck, F.	Four Years among Spanish Americans.
Herbert, Henry (Earl of Carnarvon) ...	Portugal and Galicia.
Hinchcliff, T. W.	South American Sketches.
Marcoy, Paul ...	Journey across South America.
Mulhall	Handbook of Brazil.
Murray ...	Travels in Uruguay.
Napp, R.	Argentine Republic.
Waterton, C.	Wanderings in South America.

"Farewell!"

A WINTER CRUISE IN SUMMER SEAS.

"HOW I FOUND" HEALTH.

CHAPTER I.

SOUTHAMPTON TO LISBON.

By noon on October 23rd, the special train leaving Waterloo at 9.45 a.m. had delivered us and all our belongings at the Southampton Docks. The usual first-class single fare is 16s. 6d., but on presenting a voucher from the Royal Mail Company, you get your ticket for 11s., and as many return tickets as you like for your friends, at 16s. 6d. each.

It was a bitterly cold morning, and I was glad to find that less than an hour sufficed to pass us all through the docks (at a cost to me of 4s. 6d. only, i.e. 1s. 6d. for each of

B

my three boxes) and put us on board the tender which was waiting alongside the quay.

To reach the *Clyde*, which was lying some two miles out in Southampton Water, did not take many minutes, and before two o'clock we were all lunching on board this comfortable vessel in company with the officers of the ship. Another tender had yet to arrive with more passengers, luggage, and the mails; but no time could have been lost, for by 3.45 p.m. all had embarked; the last good-byes had been said; the bell had sounded for visitors to quit the ship, and as they trooped reluctantly down the gangway to the tender, the signal was given to "weigh anchor."

Sad to see were some of the partings, and I could not help thinking how much more merciful would have been a farewell on the quay, or better still at Waterloo. On such occasions, one is driven either to philosophy or sentiment, and the latter being my besetting vice, my only chance lay in quoting philosophical platitudes, and pretending to believe them. How well I can recall some of the faces of those who were being torn apart by the *Clyde* and the tender. "Ah!" I almost chuckled to myself, "I wisely took *my* farewells at Waterloo. Thank goodness, all *mine* are over!"

And then I fell-to musing thus :—Here are the wealthy bringing their dear ones with them, and so drinking the very dregs of suffering, while that poor nursemaid we saw hanging on her sorrowing mother's neck at Waterloo and kissing her tears away, has got all her troubles over. There she stands, now happy and smiling, as, only to be like the rest, she waves her handkerchief and cries "good-bye" at the top of her merry voice to the tender-full of friends that are drifting away. And there, close beside her, droops her mistress on her young husband's shoulder, sobbing her heartaches in his loving ear. Ah, little nursemaid, you and I are spared all that!

But what's this nasty swelling in my throat, and what are those dewdrops on the baby's dimpled cheek as the little nurse snatches kiss after kiss, and hugs her mistress' bundle of love in a close embrace? Oh, I know; she's cold of course, poor child, and so am I. This comes of not taking my accustomed glass of sherry with my lunch. I'll go and get it. If I were not a philosopher, I could almost wish that some one had come to see the last of *me*. But *I am*.

5 p.m.—The sea is smooth, but there is a good deal of mist in the air which seems freshening. Ominous gulls are following us, and the pilot says an in-coming vessel this morning brought news of a stiff gale in the Bay of Biscay.

Well, I managed to make a fair lunch, and if it should prove to be my dinner, I shall do very well. After all, in the midst of so much that is new—the ship, the people, the busy life, everything—mere food counts for very little.

This fiction was prepared for a possible contingency which most of us foresee, but few express—express in words, that is, for there is a sort of facial volapük language that tells what our lips fain would hide—and hence there is, at first, a solemnity about the demeanour on ship-board, that is begat of fear. A smile may be occasionally indulged, but not repeated too often. It is looked upon at such times as presumptuous, and should such a smiler be seen going to his cabin, the verdict of all would be "*mal de mer*"—with the rider "serve him right!"

I tried a small smile on one portly old gentleman, just to see how he would take it, but it was such a ghastly failure that I had, by a great effort, to keep it there during our few moments' conversation. This device answered, and I could see his stern expression relax, as he gradually became convinced that it was not bravado, but a natural deformity.

But, alas! he found me out soon after. We had chatted rather longer than usual, and, getting tired, I dropped the

little smile I had worn so long, just for a rest. I saw his countenance change, and tried to replace the thing. Too late! I stammered, blushed, coughed, sneezed, clutched at the rigging for support, brought myself up with a round-turn, faced the spot where erstwhile his portly figure had bent to me in patient audience. He was gone!

"*The smile fell off.*"

Here ended my first imposture, and at the time I remember vowing it should be my last. For, I argued, if a man can't sport a small artificial smile like that—a thing one might wear at a funeral—without its falling off like a false moustache, he had better not enter for heavier business.

But I had learnt something from my companion—we were not going to touch at Vigo, as had been announced in the company's itinerary; for, owing to the prevalence of cholera in Spain, if we put in at Vigo, we should be quarantined at Lisbon, where we were to embark some five hundred Portuguese emigrants. From him, too, I gathered the meaning of quarantine. It matters little to passengers not disembarking, though on a voyage every one likes to break the journey, and to see whatever there is to be seen. But to those destined for the quarantine port, the discomfort is great, unless they have a fancy for crowded quarters in a lazaretto, on meagre rations, at from ten to twelve shillings a day, during the period of their quarantine sentence.

5.25 p.m.—Off the Needles. The hull and masts of the *Irex*, a brigantine steamer till they removed her spars, are dimly visible as she lies ashore with a rock through her bottom, at the base of the southernmost "needle," so to say. She has laid here since last Christmas. I am not aware that the remark applies to her case, but, from all I can hear, the festivities on or about the 25th of December have much to answer for.

The half-hour dressing-bell for dinner has just sounded. Black coats, waistcoats, and ties, are *de rigueur*, I find, so I must to my cabin and delve for them. It is a hunt-the-slipper sort of business, this dressing for dinner first day outward bound. No one knows exactly where to put his hand on the things wanted. There are three of you in about seven cubic feet of space, and you have two boxes or portmanteaus apiece. Each has one of them half-full on the floor, and the rest of the contents spread for convenience around him.

"Beg pardon; that's *my* coat."

Where the three men stand, how they get into their own clothes, or into any clothes at all, is a mystery which every one in time solves for himself, but never can explain to another. It's like trying to describe how you got over a five-barred gate when the bull was after you. You've got to do it—that's all you know at the time, and all you can recall afterwards is, that you *did it.*

And now for a confidence that I hope won't go any further. Whether it was the stooping about in the close cabin, or the grim forebodings of the approaching bay, one man on board (I will never divulge his sacred name) forewent the dinner, and I (out of sympathy) kept him company on the upper or promenade deck. He ate nothing, poor fellow; and to avoid the slightest contrast, I did the same. He felt that "we eat a great deal too much as a rule;" that "one good meal a day is plenty."

He submitted a motion, in fact, embodying these sentiments, which I seconded, adding, that I presumed all on board had breakfasted and lunched heartily, and that the man who needed anything more was a guzzler and a cormorant. This was carried amid acclamation. But whether it was the calmness of the sea, or the freshness of the breeze, or the savoury odours from below, suffice it to say, we suddenly agreed upon another motion—we went down, and joined the "cormorants"—late, it is true, but still in time for a snack of pudding, fruit, and a glass of wine, which we took in some vacant seats near the door; and so I had my first leisurely view of the ample proportions of the saloon.

This is situated one deck lower, on what is called the spar-deck. Along both sides of it are comfortably broad, softly upholstered seats. Down the middle, from end to end, runs the main table, to seat thirty people, the Captain presiding at the bows—behind him a fine American organ with sideboards to right and left of it—and the Chief Officer at the stern end, with, at his back, a noble sideboard extending from the starboard to the port entrance.

At intervals, and placed at right angles to this table, on

either side of it, are six smaller tables, capable of seating eight people each. Over the fourth table down from the Captain, the Chief Engineer presides to starboard and the Doctor to port—while the Purser does the honours at the third table on the starboard side. These are the only officers that dine with the passengers in this saloon, the dimensions of which (of the saloon, not the officers) I afterwards found, by stepping it, were forty-five feet by twenty-four feet, the whole being lighted by thirty-two electric lamps of sixteen candle-power each. The ménu may as well be given here just as it appeared on each table.

MÉNU.

Soup.
Ox tail.
Consommé Maccaroni.

Fish.
Cod and Oyster Sauce.

Entrées.
Côtelettes Jardinières.
Pommes de Terre à la Crème.
Poulet Sauté.
Chasseur.

Joints.
Roast Beef.
Boiled Mutton.

Salad.
Mixed.

Vegetables.
Boiled Potatoes, Cabbage,
Baked Potatoes.

Curry and Rice.
Fowl.

Pastry.
Apple Pudding, Madeira Cake,
Jam Sandwich.

Dessert.
Almonds and Raisins, Oranges,
Apples, Filberts, and Figs.

But these details were varied every day throughout the voyage, changes being frequent in the dishes and in the fruits and vegetables which we got fresh at every port we touched. Indeed, this applies to all sorts of provisions, and to my mind it is one of the chief advantages of this trip that no ports being more than five days apart, the commissariat can be constantly replenished.

After dinner, some took "a constitutional" up and down the hurricane or promenade deck, which is nearly 110 yards long, so that eight times to and fro gives you a mile walk.

Others adjourned to cards, in the very fair-sized smoking-room, wisely placed well aft or "abaft the funnel," as the

"The constitutional."

smoking place is called on the Thames boats. Others again, like myself, paired off with a friend for a sit-down, a blow, and a chat. At the time the dinner-bell went, we were off Purbeck Island with the Anvil Light on our—I must try and be nautical —starboard quarter.

It is now 9.30 and we are off the Portland coast. Ushant about noon to-morrow, they say—and then! I must turn in and prepare for it.

October 24th.—Still intent on preparing for the bay, I lay in my bunk till 7.30. Then, after a tepid salt-water bath, I proceeded, also in view of that event, to line my interior with porridge, sole, chop, and fruit. Now, if we reach (suggestive phrase) Ushant before lunch, I am prepared.

"I wish you wouldn't dream so loud."

Of my two cabin companions, the one on the far side was on his way from Yorkshire to Lisbon, the other in the bunk beneath mine was our new consul to the Portuguese capital. My bed was of wire webbing, soft and yielding as a spring mattress, and I think I should have slept well, but for a loud-dreaming companion, whose mind seemed to run all night on anchoring at Lisbon, and whose laboured breathing sounded exactly like the running of the cable.

We tried coughing, singly and together, speaking to one another and to him, shouting, dropping things on the floor, all in vain, for as fast as we woke him up he was off again, and letting go his anchor just the same three minutes after! "Sir! sir! you're on your back again—would you mind turning over?" To which, always in good humour, the poor dreamer would reply, "Thank you, gentlemen, for waking me; I am very sorry. I hope you'll not hesitate to stop me whenever I snore;" and he would turn on his side thereupon, as obediently as a child. But waking another man up does not give you a night's rest, and neither of us slept except in snatches. Our night's rest was more of a *conversazione;* indeed, at many a conversazione I have slept better.

A *conversazione.*

This morning we found, what with luggage loose about the floor, and clothes on the beds and hanging round the cabin in all directions, there was not much space for washing at the nice little shut-up basins, of which, by the way, there were but two for three persons. We all therefore did this part of the business in the lavatories attached to the beautiful baths, which were of marble. For gentlemen there are four of these baths, all of which are fitted with hot and cold water.

It is a lovely morning, sunny, and so warm on deck, that I have to discard some of my London wraps; and the sea is as calm as the Thames at Waterloo Bridge.

I have just learnt the ship's bells. Half-past twelve (noon) is one bell; increasing one every half-hour, four o'clock is eight bells; then come the two "dog-watches" of two hours instead of four, thus making seven watches in the twenty-four hours instead of six. This is done, so as to vary the periods or spells of duty for each man each day. The first dog-watch is from four to six o'clock, which is four bells, and the second is from six to eight o'clock, when, instead of sounding four bells (perhaps to make it tally with the hour), they sound eight. There is no other break, the bells going night and day every half-hour, from one bell to eight bells, with the utmost regularity.

The sounding of them devolves on the quarter-masters, and, strange as it may seem, this simple act requires a musical ear; for, by nautical traditions, a distinct interval must be allowed after every two strokes. Thus, three bells is sounded 1, 2—3; four bells, 1, 2—3, 4, and so on. It not infrequently happens, I am told, that a man fitted in all other respects, fails to pass in this trifling test, and is disqualified. Hence, like the soldier, part of a sailor's education consists in being able to "mark time"—*with his hands.*

"All's well!"

Another ship's tradition requires that, at the half-hour bell, the look-out man in the bows, in proof of his watchfulness, shall pass the word to the bridge "All's well;" and very impressive is this solemn benison, as it faintly floats to you in the stillness of the night. How many a gallant vessel must have gone to her doom, with these brief words, so full of hope, sounding at once her knell and requiem!

It is eleven o'clock, and they have just fetched out the

materials for playing "bull," a game greatly in favour on ship-board—combining sufficient interest, with even more than sufficient exercise. It consists of a sort of huge, sloping chess-board with numbered squares, at which loaded pads are thrown from a distance; and, of course, the highest score wins. What with the throwing, the walking, and the stooping, you find that a little of this sort of thing goes a long way—*and so do you.* If you notice your calves after a few days of this pastime, you will see how very appropriate the name "bull" is.

Noon.—Yonder lies the island of Ushant, with its ominous cape. We are in the Bay of Biscay! whose horrors Sims Reeves' voice has done so much to depict. It is absolutely as calm as a lake! Not a wave has a white crest to it; indeed, there is scarcely a wave to be seen. Rollers, there are, it is true, but as they glide broadside on to the *Clyde* and sweep under her keel, they scarcely disturb the even tenour of her way. At the bulwarks, you can detect, now and then, a faint heave like the sigh of a sleeping swan; but in the saloon she is as steady as a rock.

And this is the great bay of disasters, the sepulchre of a thousand ships! Oh, what a thing fear is! Where is that "portly old gentleman"—we had already dubbed him P.O.G. "Pog" for shortness—who shied so, at my poor little smile? "The Ides of March are *come!*"—"But not yet *gone.*" *Unberufen!* as the Germans say. Long ago, a young German doctor was good enough to explain to me the meaning of this warning word. It was, he told me, an expression deprecative of bragging. "For instance," said he, "if a wasp-waisted lady were to tell me she had never felt any ill-effects from tight-lacing, the monition, *unberufen!* would rise unbidden to my lips, and I should probably add

as a free translation :—'Beware, for all that, my dear madam!
You may burst to-day and die to-morrow!'" A *translation*
for the lady indeed, thought I.   But feeling sure he was
too polite to mean what he distinctly said, I pressed him
further, and was relieved to find that *burst* was only his
pronunciation of *boast*.   *Unberufen!* then, I discovered
(literally, *uncalled for, unnecessary*) means simply *boast not*.

Ah! here comes Pog, and he is smoking—that looks
auspicious; and talking, for him, quite animatedly. Yes,
there's no possible doubt whatever, that was a distinct
smile.   So was that, as he knocked the ash from his cigar—
and rather a loud one. Now, if only he doesn't put the
wrong end in his mouth, we are saved! Hurrah! at last
the ghost of the grim bay is laid! He can laugh now, for
he has looked in the very teeth the spectre that affrighted
him, and found it nothing but a sheet, and a turnip with a
candle inside.

Just see how all the faces have changed on board!   They

"Begone, dull care."

are, I declare, as broad to-day as they were long yesterday ;
and in every corner of eye and mouth, the strings are
loosening that restrain mirth on board a bark that is bound
for the billowy bay. Just a few solos like Pog's to start
us, and very soon we shall all be laughing in chorus.
Henceforth good-bye to care and sorrow, all faces shall
be wreathed in smiles, and as the tropic beauties creep

around us and we float under the summer skies that woo
them into life, our spirits shall expand, and, forgetting for
a time the cold grey of old England, we shall lave our limbs
in the sun-bath of the lovely lands that lie just over there
beyond the seas.

The daily noon-tide notice has just been posted outside
the music saloon. It reads to-day "October 24th. Lat.
47° 36′ N.; long. 6° 3′ W. Run, 273 miles. J. Douglas
Spooner, Capt." I'll have my game of "bull" before lunch.

1 p.m.—"Bull" is a trifle too fatiguing at present for
me; I think the form in which he is served at lunch will
suit me better. Ah! there's the bell—we'll try.

3 p.m.—My place has been permanently allotted to me
in the dining-saloon. Finding a vacant seat at the end
of the Chief Engineer's
table, I modestly took it.
The president of this
table I cannot mention
too soon, for his friend-
ship and hospitality at
least doubled my enjoy-
ment. Let me here record
his name in full—John

A *tête-à-tête.*

Kemp Ritchie. We chummed from the moment I sat down
with him, and before the meal was over he had invited me
to the vacant seat by his side, where I sat the voyage through.
A stout, middle-aged, round-faced, bright-eyed man, with a
heart as big as his body, and a cheery laugh that did more
than "cocktail" or sauce could do, to season the meal.

Moreover, he had travelled much and could spin you
wondrous yarns. He met you in the morning with a
welcoming smile, and his kindly "good-night" had some-

thing so solid in it, so reassuring, that one could have gone to one's berth in the worst weather secure and at perfect peace. There was such strength, too, in his sturdy hand; it seemed almost a part of the giant whose body, far down in the fiery depths below, was busy sculling this leviathan through the sea. The reins of seven thousand horses lay in that hand; no word, no blow was needed, only a touch of that rein, and they walked, trotted, cantered, or galloped, and never once stumbled, or fell, grazed a knee, or shed a shoe!

As I write, friend Ritchie, your seven thousand iron steeds are pawing the ground, neighing, and champing the bit, as once again they sniff the scent of the arena, and gird themselves for another struggle. There is no need to say, " Peace and joy go with you," for they are ever your inseparable companions.

Thanks to this kindly Jehu, I this afternoon made the acquaintance of the engines and learnt something of the grand ship they were driving. Here are some of the dimensions, weights, etc. In length the *Clyde* is 437 ft.; in width 50 ft. Her hold is 33 ft. deep: her draft 22 ft. From the hold upwards, come in order the main, spar, and promenade decks. On the main deck are cabins to accommodate upwards of two hundred first-class passengers, and there is no gangway round. In the centre of this deck is a small dining saloon capable of seating about twenty-five people.

In the fore part of the spar-deck is the principal dining saloon, before described, outside of which runs a broad 6 ft. gangway which is continued aft on either side of the engines.

Here, on the starboard side, are most of the officers' quarters —the purser's, doctor's, chief engineer's, fourth and fifth mate's and second engineer's, etc., while on the port side are the chief steward and his belongings.

Above, on the promenade deck, is the music saloon, corresponding with the dining saloon ; forward of the music saloon is the captain's cabin, commanding an uninterrupted view of the bows ; behind the music saloon the ladies' private saloon, some 12 ft. square, and the first and second officers' cabins athwart ships ; then come the smoke stacks and the smoking-room, of fair size with starboard and port entrance,

In the clouds.

and fitted with round marble tables, chairs, and cushioned seats along each side.

Aft of this comes the main-hatch, on a level with the spar-deck, where the emigrants and so-called "steerage passengers" take the air, though some are allowed in a similar place on the same deck forward of the captain's cabin. Then, further aft, comes the second-class part of the ship, much like the first, but on a smaller scale, and not quite so sumptuously fitted, while from the one class to the other run, on either side of the ship, connecting bridges on a level with the promenade deck.

The *Clyde* and her engines were built by Napier and Sons, of Glasgow, where, upon the river from which she takes her name, her trial trip was made in June, 1890. Her registered tonnage is 5645, and the indicated horse-power of her engines is 7000.

It interested me, and it may interest others to know some of the weights of her gear. She carries 2 bower anchors, 2¼ tons each, 2 Hingley's stockless ditto, 53 and 54¾ cwt., and there are 3 other spare anchors of smaller proportions. Her 2¼ in. stud cable weighs 300 tons, and she has 110 tons of stream chain, etc. The fore and mainmasts together weigh 17 tons, and the mizzen 5½ tons, while the stern frame in which the propeller works adds another 25 tons, and her rudder 10½ tons more. Her propeller, of 4 blades, each 10 ft., has a diameter of 20 ft., giving her a stride or "pitch," I think is the technical term for it, of 30 ft. 6 in.

She is fitted with 10 water-tight bulkheads, 6 of which come as high as the spar-deck; her water-tanks carry 18,210 galls., and she has in all 354 sixteen-candle electric lights. Her complement of officers and crew is 150 exactly, *i.e.* 19 officers and engineers, 36 sailors, 53 stewards, 42 firemen. From another source (for such information is, for some reason, not to be had from those on board) I learnt that on this voyage, after leaving Lisbon, we were carrying 196 first-class passengers, 30 second-class, 576 third-class or steerage, and 28 servants—all told, 830, which, plus the officers and crew of 150, brought up our total to 980.

On my way to the engines I casually met my friend Pog, looking a little "off colour." It seems some one had incautiously mentioned the earthquake at Lisbon, without giving the date 1755, and poor Pog's recent exhilaration was falling rapidly. "It was just the way when I was going to Naples, in 1884," he said; "Vesuvius, that had been quiet for twelve years, must select that very time for an eruption." "Yes," I observed, "I was there and saw it: in fact, spent a night on the summit to observe it."

"Really!" he ejaculated, "what risks some people can run. I can't. Just now I sat down on another man's deck-chair, only for a moment; the leg rest ran out, the back gave way, and I only saved myself, by rolling sideways on to a lady who was sleeping in an adjoining chair. I apologized, but she was very much annoyed; you see, sir, I turn the scale at sixteen stone. She muttered, 'à la

Neighbours. "I just dropped in."

pétard,' which I take it meant, God help me, that I should be blown to pieces. What's worse, I broke my watch-glass, and the minute-hand is sticking into my ribs." A friend tells me that the exclamation which resembles Pog's version of it, in sound but not in meaning, is very commonly used by all classes of men, women, and children. It will not bear translation, but, if any one is in want of an expletive to use to a Spaniard, I can promise him "à la pétard" will be near enough, if only he will emphasize the last syllable.

My visit to the engines pleased me greatly. They were indeed a grand sight—7000 indicated and 1100 registered horse-power, and costing, at the usual rate of £50 per horse register, £55,000. The pace they got out of her on her trial, and with perfect ease, was 17½ knots, and on her first voyage she reached a top speed of 18·8 knots. Worked by a separate small machine in the same part of the engine department, stands the dynamo which supplies all the electric light, and the cautious Ritchie had therefore warned me to leave my watch in his cabin before descending. One visitor, he told me, declining to do so, had his watch-spring magnetised and permanently spoilt. Having gone slowly, stage by stage, down the oily iron staircase, and wended

"The Inferno."

our way round, and into, and through the wondrous engines, we next visited the neighbouring Inferno where, stripped to the waist, sopping wet, and ruddy in the intense heat and glow, the firemen were serving the ten huge furnaces.

It surprised me to find how beautifully the air-shafts answered down here. These men were actually supplied with air as cool, fresh, and abundant as we on deck. But what a sight it was, and what a contrast, this life below to our life above! How many, of the thousands who go down to the sea in steamships, ever behold, or care to behold, their motive power? Why, we might be in a sailing ship, for all one hears, on deck or in a saloon, about the engines. Knots are occasionally mentioned, because the ship's daily run depends upon the speed, and there are sweepstakes and bets hingeing thereupon. And, now and then, you will see a man, watch in hand, counting the screw's revolutions by the throbs they produce in his foot. But he is looked upon as a weird, uncanny person. Pog, indeed, pointed out to me one so engaged, and muttered something about clockwork and dynamite.

Leaving the workers below, and coming up once more among my fellow drones, I noticed for the first time, just outside the dining-saloon, a small drinking-bar. Here can be obtained almost every kind of cocktail, wine, spirit, liquor, beer, aerated water, or lemon-squash; and this, too, is the dispensary for all beverages required in the dining-saloon. Every man writes his own prescription, and the dose is brought him by the steward of his table. The bar-keeper holds these checks and sends them to you in a pile every week or so for payment.

On the *Clyde's* last outward voyage, I heard, the champagne bill alone was £400. The company, I suppose, takes the profit on these sales, and it must be considerable, for, though they of course pay no duty, the charges are much the same as on shore. Not that I begrudge it them by any means; they must get dividends somehow, and it is better that the profit should come out of the wines than out of the fares. Better to tax luxuries than necessaries. But oh, the time some of the young men devoted to "breaking their chests" over that bar.

The glass is rising.

From one of these young fellows, a light-hearted lad, I heard a funny thing about Pog. Finding him, shortly after we had gone below, busily hunting for the minute hand, this young fellow offered his services, and soon, of course, found the thing loose in Pog's waistcoat pocket. Seeing his way to some fun, the finder, without acknowledging the find, suggested a visit to the powerful magnets in the dynamo below. After some demur, Pog consented to go, and as they stood a few feet from the thing, a confederate—to whom the tiny pointer had been passed—stepping forward, with a "What's this?" pretended to pick it off the machine. They tell me Pog's face was a study. For one moment he smiled an astonished smile, and then, fearful what this unknown power might next achieve, was seen making the best sixteen-stone time on record up the slippery stairs, holding on to his money in both trousers pockets all the way.

Poor Pog! What fun we had, getting him seriously to

recount this miracle ("Hey! Presto! It was done in a second, sir!") to every new-comer, while we listened, in agonies from the wrigglings of our guilty consciences, and in horrible fear lest we should laugh, betray ourselves, and spoil all.

During dinner I made the acquaintance of a Mr. Ringer, who had been all over and round the world, and was now bound for Rio on business. I am much indebted to this gentleman for frequent kindnesses and much useful information. To the knowledge of a very well-informed man, he added the rare power of imparting it without making you feel you were being taught. We went to Ritchie's cabin, and yarns were spun.

He told us a strange story of a man he met long ago in Pernambuco, in the grounds of an hotel. They exchanged names, and all went well till Mr. Ringer asked if the other was related to a certain family. Fencing the question, the stranger in a moment or so left abruptly, and they never spoke again, though they often passed each other, and on these occasions it was astonishing to note the number of different suits of jewellery the mysterious stranger wore. A different set for every day in the week—diamonds, sapphires,

"Good mo(u)rning! Have you used—?"

rubies, emeralds, etc., and three or four rings on each finger. Besides these peculiarities he had his nails stained black, "in mourning," as he said, "for his darling wife."

At this time the man wore a long beard, but, many months after, Mr. Ringer was shown a photograph, in which, though there was no beard, he was able to recognize the person by the hands. The outcome of this recognition was, that the man was arrested in Lisbon (where he was lying in quarantine) for a theft of two hundred thousand dollars, and sentenced to ten years' penal servitude.

Also, this evening, I got acquainted with some others at the Chief Engineer's table. My *vis-à-vis* was a Mr. Courtney, who was returning (after a holiday in England) to sheep-farming in the Argentine; and on his left a Mr. Ollendorff, an engineer, a native of Hamburg, similarly returning to Buenos Aires, where he has been settled for some years. (Of both these kind friends I saw much on board, and still more during my stay in the Argentine.)

October 25*th.*—The snoring again spoilt our rest. There is really no excuse for a man, who has a pair of socks to stick in his mouth, monopolizing conversation in this way.

What ideal weather we are getting! No one on board, that I can find, has ever crossed the bay in such a calm sea. Every one is marvelling and cannot understand it. Pog has just come along, letting off one of his malicious little crackers, to the effect that when the bay is like this you may look for bad weather between Lisbon and Las Palmas. The fact is, there's just enough probability about this prophesy to make it annoying.

It is noon, and we are in lat. 42° 44′ N., and long. 9° 32′ W., and the run has been 330 miles.

Ah! there at last are the "Portuguese men-of-war," as the nautiluses are called. How pretty these little pink convoys look in the bright sun! They are to be seen in large numbers, they tell me, in these latitudes in fine weather. They used to be termed Argonauts, from the old classical yarn about the good ship *Argo* and her golden freight. One likes to recall this fact, because it at least lends the respectability of age, to a tradition which scientists

now brand as apocryphal, viz. the sailing powers of the
nautilus. He used to be supposed to put out oars as well,
and so "paddle his own canoe"—but that, one *had* to surrender. Now, the sailing fable must go, too, it seems—but it
is hard to part with this pleasing fiction. Pope believed
both, for he wrote—

> "Learn of the little nautilus to sail,
> Spread the thin oar and catch the driving gale."

Remorseless science, however, sticks at nothing. A
maiden's blush, it tells you, is merely "a sudden expansion
of the minute superficial capillaries"—the nautilus is
"driven by hydraulic pressure"—it breathes by "the passage
of water through its double gills," and "its ejection behind
and over them, drives the little body through the sea."

In appearance, the nautilus is a mass of silver, in which
floats a cloud of most beautiful rose-coloured spots. It is
marked, at one of the extremities, with a semi-circular band
of ultramarine blue which imperceptibly melts away.

5.30 p.m.—As the first dinner-bell sounds, the sun is

Sun-dried Virginia.

dipping into the sea—and,
one by one, the stars come
out to see him sink to
rest. Now he is just gone
below. "Gone below"
reminds me I must do the
same, and dress for dinner.
"How useful the sun is in
many ways"—as I heard

a young lady patronizingly say in a boat, when the sun dried
her hands for her and saved her dainty handkerchief.

After dinner a Mr. Phillips, an Australian, spun us another
yarn. "Just as we were leaving Suez," said he, "a Russian

Count, in high silk hat and puggaree, top boots and silver spurs, and carrying a very small bag, came hurriedly on board, closely followed by two policemen. Presently, the three went together ashore, and anon the Count returned, minus his little bag which had been seized for debt.

"It seems, on the strength of having seen this incident, one of the passengers, a very small man, insulted the Count, who, proud though poor, promptly smacked his face. A challenge followed, as a matter of course, but the challenger took good care the Captain should hear of it. As may be supposed, the thing was stopped—and the fire-eating Count, who was always waylaying and threatening his unwilling antagonist, was bound over to keep the peace. But all to no purpose; the small man still went, he said, in fear of his life; so the Captain, the little man, and I," said the narrator, "held counsel together, and determined to get the Count ashore at Malta, *and lose him.*

"So we did," said the teller of the story. "I managed that. I got him to an hotel, stood him a dinner, and having paid the bill, including, for very shame, his bed for that night, I left him there, hurried on board, and in five minutes we were off. Poor fellow! the last I saw of him, he was waving his hand from the shore as if to stop us. Too late! too late! we were gone!

The challenge.

"Not long after we had started, first one and then another began to miss watches and rings, and the Captain had lost a cash-box and fifty pounds. My jewellery was safe; all I lost was a purse of about thirty sovereigns. As is always the case, those who had lost least seemed to make the most to-do. The Captain and I scarcely exchanged a word on the subject, nor did we trouble other people with our losses. The Purser, knowing of the plan to 'lose' the count, had insisted on his paying his fare that morning, and had given change out of a bad twenty-pound note. But when we three victims went to work-off the few epithets we thought suitable to the little man who had brought all this about, we found he had missed the ship *too.* The Quarter-master had seen him, also, appealing to us to fetch him from the shore.

"There was only one bit of comfort in the whole transaction," said the yarner, finishing :—"To wit, an old friend of mine on board, an omnivorous reader (who, on hearing of my loss, had only remarked 'fools and their money'), found, on going to his cabin, he had lost his gold spectacles. *That was the only piece of sugar in my gruel !*"

"I tell you what, gentlemen," said Pog, who always summed up on these occasions, "in my opinion the men left behind were confederates."

"Nonsense !" we all chorused; and Pog went off, finding no words to express his contempt for our ignorance.

To bed at ten o'clock, to prepare for a tiring day to-morrow. Two hours at any rate before the "cable-layer" comes to bed.

October 26th (Sunday).—Slept much better, owing to a discovery. A friend, hearing of our discomfort, came to our cabin, last evening, with an extra blanket, which he proceeded to roll up like a sand-bag. Then, stripping the delinquent's bunk, he laid this lengthways down the middle and made the bed. The rise in the centre was only slight, but he declared it was sufficient. "And now," said he, with the proud air of a man who has solved a problem, "if that man lies on his back to-night, I'll eat him and the bunk too."

However, we were spared this cannibal orgie, for the patient seemed to hit on the sideways position right off, slept like a top, and so did we.

7 a.m.—We are approaching the Tagus, and on our left is the Rock of Lisbon backed by the Cintra Hills. The coast is lined with groves of orange and olive, through which at intervals glisten, in the morning sun, the white walls of many a charming villa. Presently we enter the river, and are now

Belem Fort, Tagus.

but nine miles from Lisbon. The right bank of the Tagus is crowded with palaces of all shapes and sizes, while the left bank, outlined by an undulating pretty country, affords a pleasant contrast as viewed from the ship, and a delightful prospect, I should say, from the windows on the opposite shore. A little further on we pass the fort of Belem, possessing no particular architectural merit, but interesting, all the same, because picturesquely irregular.

It is 7.45 a.m., and we are anchored off Lisbon, the run

from Southampton having occupied just sixty-four hours.
On a pinch, the *Clyde* could do the distance in fifty-two
hours, or less, but as we had not to touch at Vigo, and time
was therefore less precious than coal, the engines were
slowed down, from their favourite stride of sixteen knots, to
thirteen knots an hour only.   Other things being equal, far

Praça do Rocio, Lisbon.

less coal is consumed in sixty-four hours at thirteen knots,
than in fifty-two hours at sixteen knots, though the distance
travelled is the same, viz. eight hundred and thirty-two
miles.   It is the *pace* that burns the fuel.   As the sailor said,
who failed to walk two miles in half-an-hour—"It's the
pace that bothered me; I knew I could do the distance all
right enough."

Anyway, we are here, and, what is more, the weather is delightful, and the bright warm sun is working miracles among the invalids. The city, sprinkled over the lofty hills that rise abruptly from the very margin of the river, looks daintily clean and bright, as if, for this particular occasion, they had done it over with that stuff for "beautifying everything." Like Rome, Lisbon, we are told, is seated upon seven hills. I did not count them, but she seemed all hills to me; perhaps the seven are one on top of another. But, unlike the city of the Cæsars, she can be seen all the way up the hills, from the fine broad river that runs beside her.

From the river to the hill-tops, and from east to west for a sweep of fully four miles, the entire city is compassed by a single glance, and the eye is *stricken* with admiration. "What a happy thought it was of Nature's," as some observant boy said long ago, "to make all the big rivers flow beside the principal cities." Lisbon has a grand shop-window, but without her broad water thoroughfare to exhibit the contents, she would not have taken the third prize for situation in the beauty show among European cities, where Constantinople and Naples took first and second.

Local historians trace the foundation of Lisbon to Abraham, and even fix the date at the year B.C. 3259. Others claim Ulysses as its founder, and from him derive the name Olyssipo, corrupted into Lisboa. From its original possessors, the Turduli, it passed successively through the hands of the Phœnicians and Carthagenians, coming eventually under the sway of all-conquering Rome, and so remaining till A.D. 409.

Julius Cæsar is said to have conferred upon it the name Felicitas Julia, together with the privileges of a municipium or corporate town with particular laws. He seems also to have conferred upon it a sort of monopoly in the production of earthquakes, for Felicitas Julia has certainly obtained a large share of whatever market there may be for those productions. The "output," so to say, has however been enormously in excess of the demand, on many occasions, ranging over the period from 1069 to 1722.

But the period of its greatest activity was reached in 1755. On the 1st of November of that year, the entire city above-ground was almost completely overturned, to make room for an "output" unprecedented in the annals of mining enter-prise. This led to a crisis in the trade; those of the inhabi-tants who were not interested in these mining operations, being much put-out themselves, left the city in a body, thoroughly disgusted, as well they might be. Some adjourned to the marble quay, now the Praça do Commercio; others to the shipping in the river; while others, again, betook them-selves to the banks of the Tagus—all to consider what further measures they should adopt. The fatal concession of Julius Cæsar, however, was soon seen to extend to all these places, for it appears to have embraced not only the site of the city, but the entire bed of the Tagus.

The whirlpool.

The river was soon a scene of blasting opera-tions, fully as destructive as those on shore. Along the river banks, where thousands had congre-gated, the water, rising in enormous waves, engulfed them every one. The marble quay, with the multitudes sheltering there, sunk with them all, and not a body was seen to rise from out that dread abyss. Meanwhile, scores of vessels lying in the river, packed from end to end with fugitives, were one after another sucked down by the whirlpool, and never a waif of the ships, or of their burden, rose up to mark the spot. It has been estimated higher, I believe, but it is certain that, at the very least, sixty thousand persons were swept away to instant death, and two millions sterling lost.

England and Spain sent plentifully of money and aid of every kind, but Lisbon, the Felicitas Julia, had practically disappeared, and it was seriously contemplated to transfer the seat of government to Rio Janeiro.

After breakfast, and while waiting for the launch for shore, I amused myself watching the lighters come along-side with the coal. They all seemed to be manned by Irishmen; indeed, one might have been in Dublin Bay, so typically Irish were their faces. They were all Portuguese, but they are said to be descendants of some of the men of Wellington's "Irish Brigade" in the Peninsular War. Their employer,

Senhor Dom *Murphy.*

the owner of the lighters, reminded me of "Tiger Tim," "tallest of boys or shortest of men, etc.," except that, I'm sure, he did not stand "in his stockings four-feet-ten," nor four-feet-six either. All which notwithstanding, he was the most conspicuous amongst his men, as he stood in the bows of one of the boats, issuing his orders, without noise, but with lightning speed of lip and hand. Never, in my life, have I seen anything like it. He really seemed to be translating all he said into the deaf and dumb language. Ritchie tells me he has known this man for nearly twenty years, in

which time he has possessed himself of boat after boat, and
scraped together quite a little fortune.   He is a thorough
man of business, and seems as merry as he is wise.

At 11 a.m. I prepared to go ashore with several other

" Hooky fingers."

passengers, but remembering Mr. Ritchie's
caution to shut and fasten my port, as
the coaling men at all stations have what
he called " hooky fingers," I went below
and made that safe.   When I returned
to the spar-deck I found the launch had
started, but I caught her up in a boat.   On our way we
passed a number of graceful craft with lateen sails.   I don't
know whether it is the skill of the men or the build of the
smacks, but they fetch along in grand style.

Ashore, I found two friends from our mess—one a Mr.
French, bound for the drainage improvement company in
Rio ; the other a Mr. Dane, an engineer *en route* for
Pernambuco, who spoke Portuguese and Spanish perfectly,
and was, both here and elsewhere, a very kind guide and
interpreter.   We wended our way, first up the hillside and
through the main streets, and then penetrated into the poorer
parts of the city.

The mean temperature of Lisbon is in autumn 62°, winter
52½°, summer 71°.   The most pleasant time, therefore, is from
January to March.   In April, the heat makes sight-seeing a
little tiring, and travellers, with time to spare, escape to
Cintra or Busaco.

There being few leading thoroughfares, a stranger finds it
easier to lose than to find his way.   The lengthy names of
the streets, too, are a difficulty.   You need a good memory
to recollect your address if you happen to live, for instance, in
Travessa da Porta do Carro do Hospital Real de Saõ José ;

and if you say it over every ten minutes while you are out, so as to fix it, you find yourself asking your way, at night, to "Apothecaries' Hospital, South Chelsea."

The house-numbering, too, is puzzling, running into hundreds in no time. The reason is, that it is not house-numbering at all; you find that they number doors inside the houses, and even the windows in some places. The door of the dwelling of the "*Sage femme*," I heard, used to be distinguished by a white cross, but none such did I see, and no White Cross Street at Lisbon could I find.

Bull-fights are held at the Circo dos Touros, every Thursday and Sunday. They are amusing enough, it is said, and quite free from the revolting cruelties practised in Spain—neither men, horses, nor bulls, being in any danger.

A noticeable thing, in a Catholic city like Lisbon, is the absence of priests in the streets. This is more apparent than real; they are *there*, but it is their habit (happy phrase) to dress as laymen. In the Chapel of St. Vincente Cathedral, Basilica de Santa Maria, destroyed by earthquake in 1344, are relics of the saint, brought from the cape named after him. The legend says, they had been watched over there, by two ravens which were brought to Lisbon with them. (We have all seen carrion crows on guard like this over remains of all sorts, and very clean they pick them.) Anyway, two ravens are still quartered in the cloisters, and two things, meant for ravens, are quartered also

"Ha-di-doo?"

in the city arms, where they are represented roosting on the
stem and stern of a ship.

On the top of a high hill stands the church of Nossa
Senhora do Monte (1243). It contains the usual original
holy manger; also the chair of the first Bishop of Lisbon,
in which it is considered lucky for mothers *in posse*, who
succeed in climbing so far up the hill, to seat themselves.
From outside this church, one of the grandest views is to
be had of the city and the river.

Another, and more interesting church, is that called Igreja
da Graça, which contains a wondrous collection of wax
models of diseased limbs cured by patron saints (quite a
little Chamber of Horrors) ; also, many paintings commemo-
rating saintly intervention on sea and land. Crude as these
pictures are, they at least show gratitude, a quality not to
be despised, even if it be "prospective." The wax arms
and legs are horribly natural, and only fit, in some cases,
for an anatomical museum. I counted upwards of a hundred
of these limbs in all, exhibiting every kind and stage of
hideous disease. For certain physiological reasons, it is to
be hoped that mothers *in posse* are not admitted to these
" *ex voto* " collections, as they are termed.

The pictures—whose style is suggestive of a common
origin—illustrate life-saving in all its branches. Here, a
saint appears to be bringing the shaving-water to a man,
bedridden for twenty years, and he is getting up. In another,
while the deck of a ship is burning at sea, the crew are
kneeling to the saint, who is seated, out of the way of the
flames, on the cross-trees. At first I missed the point of this,
but a companion picture, containing the sequel, explained it.
This represents the ship capsized. The fire is out, of course,
and the grateful crew are at prayers on the bottom, while

the saint is seen coming on a rescuing boat, holding out his hat—I beg pardon, his halo—apparently about to make "the usual collection."

One of our party ascertained the address, hard by, of the artist who does these things, and we went to see his stock-in-trade. He had many works of art on hand, descriptive of saintly aid afloat and ashore; he also painted to order. In the ready-made or bespoke trade, he was equally at home. It was a very warm day, and we were very thirsty, and this may, in some measure, explain the drift of the following transaction.

An American of our party, addressing the artist, said, and another translated for him, "What ud yew charge to paint a picture representing my friend here dying for a drink, and me, got up like a saint, bringing him a foaming tankard of champagne and seltzer? No; I mean it straight," he went on, seeing us smile. "Of course, I don't expect you to paint our portraits. You can leave two holes for our photos." At this moment, he sighted a picture on the shop wall, of a man lying back in his chair starving, and a saint bringing a loaf and mug. "That one'll dew me," he said. "How much?" "Seven milreis" (14s.), said the artist. "Very well; just cut out the faces and paint in a bottle instead of the loaf, and I'll look in for it in a couple of hours." And he did; and when I saw it on board, with the photos and a bottle with "Mumm" on it, the effect was most comical. Both men had round fat faces, and to see one as the starving man and the other as saint, was too deliciously incongruous.

On our way from here to the market, we passed a woman cooking chestnuts in a terra-cotta funnel, over a fireplace of the same kind, and fanning the charcoal with a rush

D

brush.   These poor women wear earrings as big as the
palm of your hand, of the purest gold, and costing ten milreis
(20s.).   Others I saw selling Laranja (oranges) along the
streets, wore a pad round the waist, as thick as a horse collar,
to rest their hands on while balancing their baskets on their
heads.   In dress they are something like the German Vier-

laendirenen, and they look both healthy
and happy, as they tramp along and call
their wares.   They eat them too—the
larders for their own apples or what-not
being the rims of their round, black, felt
hats.

There is a peculiar breed of large cats of
a slate colour in Lisbon, numbers of which
start out from every nook and corner of
the poorer parts and feed timidly on the
garbage always to be found there.   The

"Laranja!"   smells in these places are atrocious, and
the dwellings squalid and out of repair.

In a leading street, we passed a very old man leading a
dozen turkeys, leashed to his stick, and, further on, we saw,
for the first time, oxen drawing waggons.   The driver has a
goad in his stick, which I saw one use most brutally,
thrusting it up the animals' nostrils.

The next thing we noted was a funeral, where all were
smoking—riders, drivers, and all; and, closely following it, a
one-horse golden carriage, in shape something like our hansom
—a bridal affair.   What with the maternity-chair I had just
noted at the church of " Our Lady on the Hill " (which
reminds one of the old nursery rhyme, that goes on to say,
" and if she's not gone, she's living there still "), and now this
wedding and funeral, I have seen something of the births,

deaths, and marriages of Lisbon. I once heard a man call them the "imports, exports, and transports" of the city.

Lisbon is supplied with water by an aqueduct erected in the reign of Don João V. (1729–1748). It traverses a distance of some six miles across the valley of Alcántara, on arches little short of three hundred feet high. Long ago, one Diogo Alves discovered certain undeveloped resources in this lofty situation and set about utilizing them. His plan consisted in conveying travellers, at fees varying with their means, from the top of the aqueduct to the valley below, by force of gravitation. The descent was accomplished with safety, but owing, it is said, to the sudden stop at the

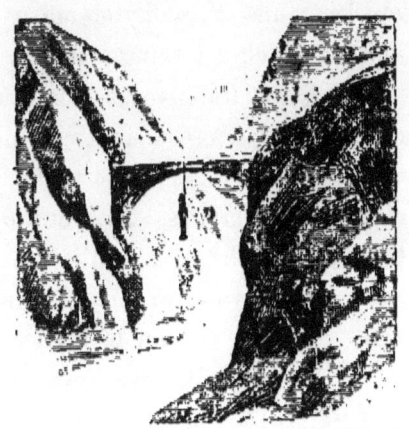

Diogo Alves – A promising career abridged.

bottom, his method was attended with so many fatalities, that at last the authorities interfered. By way of experiment, they tested his system on himself, using a hempen stay to limit his fall. But it had just the same effect, and, like many another inventor, Diogo Alves paid for his discovery with his life.

The market for fruit, vegetables, plants, seeds, fish, poultry, the Praça da Figueira, is worth a visit, perhaps, to see the peasant costumes, etc. No, not to see the "et cætera," certainly. It is cleared and cleansed by 2 p.m. every day, and right well it needs it, I should say. My "etc." just now, included a practice which was new to me then, but with which my after voyage, among Portuguese emigrants, made me unpleasantly familiar. The peasants seemed to be for ever hunting for that which Dr. Johnson once coarsely said women always will talk of—"what runs in their heads." You'd see them hunting one another, like this, all over the densely packed market, only breaking off from time to time to serve a customer, when, of course, they handled the provisions freely. To an Englishman this is unspeakably revolting, and it was by no means compensated to me by the market, which is a thing *to have seen*, perhaps, but not to *see*.

Before the waterworks were built, Lisbon was dependent on her fountains (Chafarizes), which are still very numerous, as also are the water-carriers who are to be seen near them in characteristic groups. That in the Rua Boavista is said to be beneficial for the sight, and is hence called "Bica dos Olhos."

At this shrine, we found our old friend Pog filling a

Aquarius.

couple of bottles with the miraculous water. But we gave him the slip as soon as we decently could, for he was too eccentric. Earlier in the day, just after landing, some of the *Clyde* people saw him walking so nervously, on account of the earthquake of 1755, that the operation looked more like a fat boy feeling his way on thin ice, and whenever he came to a crack in the roadway, he would sound it suspiciously with his stick and fill it up with mud, as a sort of "stitch in time," I suppose.

About one o'clock we made our way to the handsome new railway station, Da Avenida, *en route* for Cintra Palace. Very noticeable here are the two lofty arches forming the entrances to the booking-office. Each is built on the exact lines of the horseshoe. I don't remember having before seen this device used as an arch, and it did not please me. The greatest width of an arch, to be used as a thoroughfare, should surely be at the bottom—which, in the horseshoe, is the narrowest part. Wherever you go in Lisbon you encounter hills, and at this station you take your ticket some fifty feet below the platform. When I was there, they were finishing a hydraulic lift which will connect the two, and save you the climb we had up the zigzag road.

Catching the 1.30 train for Cintra, we were soon whisking along in a comfortable saloon carriage of American build, through the two-mile tunnel that clears you of the city. After another seven miles, you emerge into really very pretty country, through which your route lies for about an hour, the entire distance being some seventeen miles. The aqueduct is seen to great advantage on the way, particularly where it crosses the valley. We had all noticed this point from the *Clyde*, as also the numerous windmills that dot the way. These, with their moving sails, seemed now to start out at us at every few hundred yards, and their revolving, together with our onward motion, made them seem to be running up to the train.

Seven miles from the start, we came to Bemfica, prettily embowered among orange groves, gardens, and orchards. Cintra, a town of some importance, lies on the edge of a granite serra, whose highest point is 1865 feet above the sea level. In approaching it, one traverses long avenues of silver poplar, bay, and willow of huge growth, which, together with oak, elm, and box, hide the road in almost subterranean shade. Cintra is entered at the foot of the hill, which is crowned with pointed and craggy eminences, in singular contrast to the woods that hide its base.

The Royal Palace, situated in the centre of the town, was built about the year 1500. The gardens, in which it stands,

are very lovely. Under the shade of ancient chestnut trees,
and within sound of babbling fountains, rustic seats enable
you to rest, cooled by a breeze that at certain seasons must
be laden with the scent of orange and lemon. These solitary
scents and sounds, amid the stillness, are very soothing,
while the eye, with great tranquillity, rests on the verdure

"Delicioso!"

everywhere luxuriant.   On the
winding road up the hill, ivy-clad
cork trees and giant stone-pines
canopy the way. At the top stands
the palace, once the Alhambra of
the Moorish kings, and, ever since
Lisbon was made the seat of Christian government, the favourite royal
residence. What with its fountains,
terraces, gardens, arabesque win-
dows, slender shafts, reservoirs, and towers, Cintra Palace
is a singular medley of Moorish and Christian architecture.

The first noticeable place on entering, is the Sala das
Pegas, the ceiling of which has magpies painted all over it,
and each bird carries in his beak a scroll bearing the motto
" *Por bem* " (for good). The story goes, that Don João I. was
caught by his Queen kissing a maid-of-honour. Fully equal
to the occasion, the monarch merely remarked, " *E' por bem
minha senhora*," which is said to have quite satisfied the
queen. Well, it was *good*—very good, I dare say ; but, how
a husband saying so should appease a wife—especially an
English wife, for this queen was our Philippa of Lancaster
—I must say puzzled me a *little*, till our guide explained
that used in this connection the words meant " Platonic, my
lady ; " since then, it has puzzled me a *good deal more.*

From certain historical characteristics of Philippa, I

venture to furnish a version of the story, more in keeping
with her habitual warmth of temperament and readiness
of resource.

"POR BEM."

When Don Juan was seen,
By Philippa his queen,
To kiss a fair maid that was near,
He exclaimed, " By my name,
Lip or hand is the same ;
The salute was *Platonic*, my dear ! "

" Oh, I see ! " said the queen,—
As she stepp'd in between,
And dealt each a good box on the ears—
" Now we all understand,
That by lip or by hand,
Our salutes are ' *Platonic*,' my dears ! "

Next we came to the Hall of Shields, on the dome-shaped

A glimpse of Cintra.

roof of which are painted, in two concentric circles, the arms
of the Portuguese nobility, each shield being pendant from
a stag's head. The highest genealogical honour known to a
Portuguese, is for his "*brazão*" to figure in this Sala. Our
showman next took us to the chapel, and the miserable
room in which Don Alfonso VI. was confined. The brick

floor is entirely worn away, on one side, by the ceaseless pacings to and fro of the unhappy captive. It was indeed a "*salle des pas perdus*," as they used to call the waiting-room at the Tuileries. The salon is also shown, where Don Sebastido held his last audience before sailing on his disastrous African expedition, and where the crown is said to have fallen from his head. If Pog had been with us, he would have been rolling his eagle eyes round the apartment, hoping to spot a stray jewel or two.

The views from the sides of the palace are most extensive, and the scenery is in many ways unrivalled. It is flat, and fails to please some, I know; but it is such an immense panorama. The eye can wander afield for twenty miles out there, over the olive, orange, and lemon groves, over the shore and the water beyond it, out to where sea and cloud meet and mingle, and become lost in what looks like a range of mountains.

Far away to the right, lies the convent of Mafra, built on the model of the Escurial, a quadrangular building of immense size, measuring, I believe, over two hundred and fifty yards each way. In the centre of this pile stands the church, behind the choir of which are situated three hundred cells. Beyond Mafra some distance, are the ever-famous heights or lines of Torres Vedras, so skilfully chosen, fortified, and defended by Wellington.

We had made the ascent on donkeys, the road being very steep; and having found *that* very enjoyable, we fully expected a like pleasure going down. But "facilis descensus," etc., does not apply here. The donkeys' saddles are of Mexican build, so thick that one sits quite a foot above the back of the animals, whose skin, be it ever remembered, is *loose*. The road is arched so as to drain it, very steep, and runs in the form of a huge corkscrew. Now, just imagine the feelings of a man who has not been on a donkey since his boyhood, sitting astride *this* saddle and being taken down *this* road at a canter! The animal, for some reason, prefers the gutter at the outside edge, where it is rough and only protected by a dwarf parapet, so you have a view, all the time, of the several hundred feet drop there is for you, if you should come off. Indeed, you can't help seeing it, for you are actually over the gulf, at an angle of forty-five degrees to a vertical line passing through your donkey. What

" Facilis descensus " (?)

a pity there is not a tangible line of that sort, to hold on by. Perhaps, though, the leverage might only lead to your taking the donkey over with you. When we got to the bottom, the others wanted to ride on; but, though not a member of the S.P.C.A., *my* feelings would not allow me to tax *my* donkey further.

If you have time, as we had, there is a good English hotel where you can dine well and put up for the night. In the morning, it is worth a walk or ride of some three miles to see Quinta de Monserrate.

October 27th.—These gardens are said to be unique in Europe—probably in the world—in variety and beauty of vegetation. Plants, from all parts, flourish in the open air. Tree-ferns, of immense size, recall the scenery of the warmer parts of New Zealand. Palms of the Indian Ocean attain full stature and produce fruit, while, hard by and thriving equally well, are flowering trees and shrubs of South America and Australia. The house is not shown; but, to the grounds admission is never refused, and they are one of the interesting sights of Portugal.

An hour further, will take you to another sight worth

seeing—the Cork Convent, so called because the cells are lined with cork. They are about five feet square, and one of them, a mere hole, is pointed out as the cell of the famous hermit Honorius, who died, aged 95, in 1596. In front of his cave, is the inscription—

" Hic Honorius vitam finivit,
Et ideo cum Deo in cœlis revivit."

The hermit Honorius.

In the outlying parts of Lisbon, some few peasants still carry the long, iron-tipped pole which in well-trained hands, it is said, often proved itself a match for the sword in the Peninsular Wars. On one occasion, it is recorded that a mere handful of peasants, so armed, dismounted a large body of French cavalry.

How lovely the country here about must be in summer-time! The oak, the wild olive, the huge cork tree with ferns

nestling in the hollows of its broad trunk; orange and lemon groves, mingling with water-melon and Indian corn, gladden the eye, while the air is laden with the scent of jasmine. The vines, too, lend another charm, creeping at will

" It saves your nose a lot coming through the hedge."

along the simple trellis-work with exquisite grace, untrimmed and perfectly free.

They told me that during the grape season, sticks are fastened to the dogs' collars, to prevent their getting through the hedges and stealing the grapes, of which they are passionately fond. Some dogs, however, seem able to dodge the difficulty—indeed, find the stick of great assistance.

The vine-growers along the shore opposite to Lisbon, used to have a wholesale way of protecting their grapes. They captured their thievish dogs and shipped them to the capital, and this, I heard, accounted for the number of hungry mongrels that used to infest Lisbon during the summer months.

As to our recent difficulty with Portugal over the African question, the new Consul told me when we were anchoring that the acting-Consul, who came on board to meet him, brought the news that things were quieting down in this respect. But, though we were not molested, we found the English were still most cordially disliked. No tradesman dare announce "English spoken," as formerly. Not being prepared, however, to sacrifice business to patriotism, the cunning have hit upon a compromise, and now everywhere you see the legend, "*American spoken*"!

Having seen as much of the place as we cared to, we went on board in the afternoon, though we were not leaving till eight or nine o'clock. And I'm glad we did, for it enabled me to see the embarking of the emigrants and the lighting up of the city—two things which ought not to be missed.

It is no easy matter to ship 576 emigrants safely. They come off in all sorts of boats and barges, and laden with every kind of luggage, furniture, kitchen-utensils, beds, and babies. Here begin the worries of the ship's doctor. So far, Dr. Blandford had had little to do; but from Lisbon to Rio, whither these emigrants were bound, his hands would never be empty. During the whole time they were embarking, he had to watch them closely, as, one by one, they passed him at the gangway.

It is a matter of serious importance to all on board, whether the doctor does this duty well or scamps it. The health of the whole ship depends upon this primary precaution. For disease spreads, of course, readily in crowded places, and isolation is more difficult on board than on shore.

Passeio D. Pedro D'Alcántara, Lisbon.

Besides, though there is a hospital and a well-fitted ship's dispensary, many things (such as fresh milk in a typhoid case) are not at times obtainable, and so an epidemic is less easy to check. The only way, then, is for the doctor rigidly to refuse any one in whom his practised eye detects the faintest signs of infection.

It is not for me to criticise a medical man; but Dr. Blandford did this work, I thought, very thoroughly and with untiring pains. As we often found, he could be mirth

itself at proper times, and show all an Irishman's appreciation of fun in others; but when on duty, all that is laid
aside, and he is the ship's doctor and nothing else.

There were not many emigrants rejected; but, in one case,
a child with a suspicious eruption was sent back, and this
refusal involved her mother also and another child. We
were all harrowed by the sight of these three unfortunates,
huddled together in the police-boat alongside, in very

" Rejected ! "

rough water, tossing about for three hours or more : pictures
of abject misery. Many on board sent them contributions.
One gave all his Portuguese money, another five shillings, a
third ten shillings, and so on. But nothing seemed to break
the spell of their desolation; no, not even the sight of the
food we sent them. It was not food they wanted.

The incident recalls an experience, of early days, that led
me to perpetrate the following verses :—

"BREAD CAST UPON THE WATERS."

In student days, before my fledge,
My nest lay in the mural hedge
O'erlooking Gray's Inn Lane.

I roosted on the topmost bough,
So steps were many, you'll allow,
   From out to home again.

I used to break my fast at eight,
And many a morning could not wait
   Till I had made the tea.
And oh, how toothsome! oh, how sweet!
That roll of yesterday would eat.
   A banquet 'twas to me.

One morn, a hungrier lad than I
Knocked at my door, and, with a sigh,
   Poured forth his sad appeal.
"Here, take this roll," I said; "'twill stay
Your pangs. 'Tis all I have to-day.
   I know how faint you feel."

But how I missed that little roll,
Those only know who give the whole
   Of such a scanty store.
This was at eight, and not till ten
The punctual-calling baker's men
   Would come with any more.

By hunger stung, I flew down stairs,
Two at a time, full forty pairs,
   And out into " the Lane,"
Where—oh, how my inside was riven!—
The roll I from my need had given,
   Lay soaking in the rain!

     *   *   *   *

That night, when I came home to sup,
There it was *still*. I picked it up
   And laid it at my door,
Hoping some dog all bone and skin—
Some poor out-pensioner of the Inn—
   Might find and prize it more.

Next morn, that roll of yesterday
At last *had* fed a castaway,
   Who stayed to lick my hand.
I took him in, and there and then,
That he was partner of my den
   Soon made him understan l.

Friends ever from that day were we,
And true as steel was "Jack" to me;
   We lived for one another.
Ten years he nestled by my side,
And when at last he drooped and died,
   I felt I'd lost—a brother.

Thus, "bread upon the waters cast,"
Before a single day had passed,
   Taught me a lesson plain;
So plain that now I dare to say
If that poor lad asked bread to-day,
   I'd do the same again.

Sympathy affects different men in different ways. A certain Alderman, after hearing a piteous tale, rang the bell, and in tears exclaimed to the powdered footman who answered it, "This man's misery is breaking my heart. Poor fellow! For Heaven's sake—*show him out!*"

The Captain would, I think, have passed the mother and her two children, but the Doctor was wisely inflexible. We could all, the Captain included, see *how* wisely, within a very few days.

The emigrants were a very grubby set, unkempt, sallow, and badly nourished, and their costumes a quaint medley of all colours and shapes. Here is a rather good female specimen of incongruity, I think, and there were fifty more just as glaring. Hair caught up in an old-gold silk handkerchief— the favourite colours for these things are old-gold, canary, terra-cotta, and gamboge—black pork-pie hat with green bow, cardinal figured jacket, and "Reckitt's blue" skirt. With this lady, was a gentleman in a scarlet coat, but I afterwards found this was *inside* out, a common way of preserving the black side for Sundays and saints' days.

Their comforts are well provided for in every way; there are separate lavatories, baths, and offices for the sexes, and separate cabins for the women, fitted respectively with fourteen, twenty-four, and twenty-six bunks, on the main deck. The men are on the lower deck, where each has a separate berth. Three meals a day are served to all—at 7.30 a.m. beef and rice, half-pint of "*vino tinto*" (red wine), beef and maccaroni, fish and rice (two or three times a week), stewed beef and potatoes. At 12.30 p.m., soup, cheese, beans, green vegetables, potatoes twice a week, and half-a-pint of wine. At five o'clock, tea and bread and butter, and cheese twice a week.

All the emigrants were Portuguese, hailing from Douro-e-Minho, Transmontes, on the northern frontier, bordering on Galicia. They are a very frugal, thrifty people, making their own wine, although it costs next to nothing to buy. Their plan is to sell one out of every three bottles, and keep the two for their own consumption.

At dinner, we found the tables fitted with the ominous

"fiddles," as the wooden rims are termed that prevent plates, dishes, bottles, etc., rolling off with the tossing of the vessel. We were expecting bad weather, it seemed. Already, in fact, the ship was lurching considerably.

Just as we finished the meal, a new steward sent every one into fits of laughter, by starting off with a pile of plates and dishes *down* the slope, as the ship rolled, without, as experi-

A collision at sea.

enced hands do, throwing his body back to correct the pitch. When he had once got started, there was no stopping him, and he ended by dashing into another steward, who was similarly loaded at the other side of the saloon, but wisely biding his time to move. Neither got hurt, except, perhaps, just enough to make their mutual recriminations very animated, and a quarrel between two men loaded with china is a very funny spectacle.

The sight of Lisbon, illuminated, was one not to be missed. It looked like a thousand Crystal Palaces blown into atoms along the Surrey hills.

> The city hung with diamonds all ablaze,
> In terraces of scintillating rays;
> From the blue river to the bluer sky,
> Is twinkling music to my spondee * eye.

---

* I had the word "listening" here, but a friend—a poet by profession—reading the advance proof, wired me: "Last word but one spondee;" so, of course, I altered it, though—I must say—to my ear "spondee" inadequately describes the then *tip-toe* condition of my eye. However, poetry before everything. Readers will please take their choice. All who prefer "spondee," kindly signify the same in the usual way, and so decide the point for the next edition.—C. C. A.

CHAPTER II.

LISBON TO ST. VINCENT.

As we pass rapidly down the river, the lights become fewer and fainter, and the water rougher and rougher, and as we cross the bar, about ten o'clock, we find ourselves in for a gale.

Having here to shift my berth, and being very tired after the moving in addition to my shore fatigues, I shortly after turned in, to turn out (or rather to be turned out), very unceremoniously, four hours later.

About 2 a.m. the ship's course was so suddenly altered, that, in one second, she seemed to swing through 50° or 60°. This had the effect of pitching everything right and left. All over the ship, one heard things crashing and smashing

*Un*stable companions.

in the wildest confusion. Every single thing in my new quarters fell in one chaotic heap in the centre of the cabin, amongst them —literally so — myself and my " stable - companion," a Brazilian coffee-planter from the berth on the other side.

It is rather trying to be introduced, thus abruptly and without ceremony, to an utter stranger and foreigner, in pitch darkness, among a lot of loose luggage, in the middle of the night, on your hands and knees—especially when you have no common language between you to explain things. Well we used *uncommon* language; at least, I did, and I should say in such cases Brazilians do, from what I know of them. The worst was, there was no standing, and even sitting or lying was risky, amidst the wild stampede of the iron boxes, trunks, bags, boots, hats, and sticks.

However, all troubles have an end, and, after a while, I found the button and turned on the electric light. By its bright aid, the Planter and I, in silence, captured and restored to their lairs the wild denizens of the regions of the under-bunk, and then, for want of better means of communication, we shook hands, smiled, got into bed, and turned out the light.

But I could not sleep after this shake-up, so presently went on deck, where I was a little consoled to hear there was good reason for the change of course. It appears it was to avoid a collision with a ship in a threatening position on our starboard bow. My collision with the Planter was preferable to that, anyhow. The ship was rolling heavily, and the sea sweeping her decks, every now and again, from end to end, and as standing on the deck was difficult, I stretched myself, for a while, in the lower saloon, where I was soon after joined by Pog, who evidently did not recognize me.

The fact is, while in Lisbon I had removed a month's growth of beard and whiskers, and this, coupled with the night attire, disguised me. " That roll fetched you up, too ? " I said. " Well, rather ! " said he, and with that we fell-to and chatted.

Here, I should explain that to each berth there is a little parapet which, if screwed up, prevents your falling out.

Thinking this was intended to widen the bunk, poor Pog had let it down, laid on it, and so came out, as I did.   "Yes, sir," he said in his thoughtful way, "the wonder to me is, that any remained in their berths in such an earthquake.   You want grappling-irons on your night-shirt to keep in bed such weather."

Ideal sketch of Pog's pyjamas.

He then proceeded to tell me of himself.   He had injured his head in a railway accident, and was now going to visit his son in Argentina.   His eye, too, troubled him, he said — the one the Spanish lady lifted him up by, with her thumb.   But he had found some water in Lisbon, two large bottles of which he had brought away (we saw him), possessing almost miraculous powers.   There was no one, he said, at the fountain to. give directions about the water: but he intended trying "*a teaspoonful daily, fasting.*"   Well, I should have used it as a lotion *myself;* but I said nothing. "Do you find your head better for your visit to Europe?" I asked.   "Oh yes," he said.   "When I came over last time, in 1884, you would not credit how nervous I was. Now, nothing affects me—Bay of Biscay—Lisbon earthquakes—nothing.   But this is an awful night, isn't it?" Here he slipped on to the floor, but pulled himself up and tried to smile, and took a nerve-strengthener from his flask.

"Did you notice, sir," he went on, "a man, a little under your height, with a beard, Inverness cape, and slouch hat, as we were nearing the bay?   Now, *there's* a timid man, if you like.   He intended going to Buenos Aires; at least, so he told me."   Then, warming with his subject, he went on : "But he'd had enough of it, and got off at Lisbon.   He

smiled, and tried to put a good face on it, sir; but before we reached the Bay he had to give it up. It may be natural timidity; but my idea is, that man is a murderer fleeing from justice, and if I was sure of it, sir, I would *shoot him down* with my own hand, as I would " — a pause for a suitable simile — " as I would a sack of coals."
I ventured to remark, that I thought I had seen the

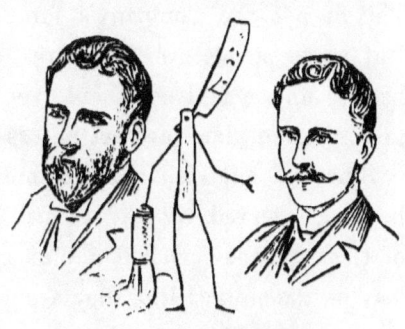

SENHOR DOM RAZOR, *loq.:*—
"In a beard you | "Now you're clean
pride yourself." | beside yourself."

man he described, come aboard before we left Lisbon. "Not the man I mean," he insisted. "I think it is the same person," I said, "and, if so, he is on the ship, and I will find him for you to-morrow." With that, we parted for the night; he remarking that he had hoped he'd seen the last of that "timid man," and I chuckling, as I saw unfolding before me a melodrama in which I was to double the leading parts.

October 28th.—After breakfast, we got up a shilling sweepstake on the fifteen hours' "run" to noon, and then held an auction of the tickets, some favourite numbers fetching as much as twenty shillings. At noon the Captain's notice showed us to be in lat. 36° 2′ N., long. 12° 1′ W., and the distance run from Lisbon 216 miles.

At 12.30 p.m., I went to see food distributed to the emigrants. It was served out in tins, into which young and old, men and women alike, dived their hands and filched what they could, so it looked to me. They behaved more like wild beasts—clawing, pushing, clamouring. Ten hands were at one time in the dish, fighting for the larger bits of meat, which they tore up with their fingers and gnawed like wolves. This is not the Company's fault; everything is provided. But these people are the poorest of the poor; they know no better; and would not thank you for knives and forks and tables—even plates are not necessaries to them.

Since we left Lisbon, the common red wine of the country has been served, *ad lib.*, to us free of charge. And each of these people has had a pint of the same daily. After leaving the ship at Rio, they are going on in coasting vessels to the coffee plantations at Santos, where there is plenty of work for them. They are a contented, jovial race, and when not feeding, they group themselves in cliques or families, dancing, playing the old-fashioned accordion and guitar, and singing their national songs. Their favourite dance consists of two couples, each couple taking it in turns to step to the centre and clap hands high in the air, while at the same time the four people are moving in a continuous circle. They look very picturesque, too, in these groupings, despite

their tatters and the curious mixtures of colours. We called them "the three R's," the "ragged rainbow regiment."

They gamble, too. Around the Bo'sun's locker, forward, there is always an excited crowd playing the favourite game of "Ronda." Properly, they ought to remain aft, and it is the best place for them. They are

Emigrants playing " Ronda."

very dirty, filthy indeed, and it is best for passengers to be to windward of them. A few used the lavatories—some

even to excess—but the majority did not wash the voyage
through, I'm convinced, and all seemed to indulge in the
sickening practice I noticed in Lisbon market—only more
so. Over and over again I have seen a lover (!) *bag five
or six brace to his own gun* (as one might say), in a patch
of his lady's head no bigger than the palm of your hand.
My friend, Mr. Ollendorff, has with him an instantaneous
photographic apparatus. By its means he got some good
little bits on board in the Bay, and afterwards on shore at
Lisbon, and is now taking an emigrant toilet scene.

The wind has lulled a good deal, but it is still, by the log,
" fresh wind and heavy sea on starboard quarter." Chatting
with a friend, about Pog and the " criminal escaped from
justice," we hit on a plan. He, being near my height, was to
go to my cabin, slip on my Inverness and hat, and go to the
second-class part, while I led Pog to a spot half-way towards
it on the lower deck. Then, the " acting suspect" was to
pass across the gangway in the light, return to my cabin, and
disrobe. It answered perfectly, and so convinced Pog, that,
from that moment, his one idea has been the capture of this
man. Such jokes may not be of a very high order; but
aboard almost anything tickles you into laughter, because
all the conditions are favourable to health and happiness.

After dinner, I had a chat with a young fair-haired Saxon,
standing 6 ft. 4½ in. in his socks, and broad in proportion,
and weighing, he told me, fifteen stone. After many rough
experiences in California and elsewhere, he is going to try
for some more refined employment in Argentina. Hitherto
a stay of two or three months in England is all he has
been able to stand; by that time, the nomadic fever has
always culminated in his taking his blankets and starting
for America, as he called it, " on the tramp." There, so

long as any money remained, he would loaf, and, when that
was gone, work for his daily food. He had had a college
education, and was, as I afterwards found, first cousin to
a peer. His brothers were in the army, and I'll venture to
say no one of them is better fitted naturally for that profession than he.

On reaching California, he told me, the first man he met
and knew was an old schoolfellow, who proposed that they
should start, in partnership, what is called a " hash-slinger "
—a shop, where meat is boiled in a cauldron hung on a tripod
in the middle of a shed. The stuff is served in a pannikin
with bread, to the customers seated round on the ground.
They opened, and the business must have thriven, for at
the end of fourteen days, Mr. Long told me, he sold his
share for sixty dollars, and started once more on tramp.

He has had many experiences, but they have not been
wasted on him ; the hard life has sobered him, and here
he is now—having acquired some Spanish, and really
good shorthand and type-writing—about to begin life again,
at twenty-five, in far South America. It is a worthy effort,
if somewhat late in the making, and I heartily wish him
good luck in it; but English clerks, with far better quali-
fications, are at a great discount. The German, living on
a crust, can afford to work for a mere song, has usually
four or five languages at his command, and in Argentina,
as everywhere else, he cuts us out.

October 29th.—A young fellow, engaged in the telegraph
department at St. Vincent, says the two coal companies
there supply 400,000 tons annually to the ships coaling at
that station. The English on the island number about a
hundred; there is no church for them, but we are very considerately taking them a clergyman who will hold service, I

hear, in the cable buildings. The two very intellectual, re-
fined-looking women, who saw him aboard at Southampton,
were his sisters, I guess.

He has a sort of stammer or stutter in his walk, if one
may so say. In the smoothest weather, he seems to be allowing for a lurch at every step, but never in the right direction.
In appearance, he is a tall, plump, ruddy-faced Rufus, and,
being fond of the leather ball, will be an acquisition to the
Island, where every one ranks according to his cricket ability.

Noon.—The notice is up—" Lat. 31° 12′ N., long. 16° 17′ W.
Run, 360 miles." Just now the clergyman and a tall Yankee,
I can see, are having a bout on doctrinal matters. What a
contrast they make, sitting on adjoining deck-chairs! The
clergyman is speaking fast, greatly excited, and leaning
towards the other, but he restrains himself somewhat by
clasping one hand firmly
in the other, leaving all
action to his head and
face. The attitude of the
American is that of abso-
lute *dolce far niente ;*
head back, legs out,
eleven-inch feet resting
on their heels (like the
hands of a clock at ten
minutes to two), one hand

A contrast.

thrust into his waistcoat, while the other, poised on its
elbow, balances a large cigar, at which he gazes, and from
which he every now and then seems figuratively, as well as
literally, to draw *inspiration.*

The conversation I cannot hear, but, judging from a remark
or two of the Yankee's yesterday, I should say the most the

clergyman can expect is a draw or a "stale mate." "Well,"
he was saying, "in theology I call myself *a total abstainer.*
I never employed a priest in my life, and wouldn't. As an
infant, I was of course baptized according to custom, but
even that was involuntary on my part, and it never *took*
when the time came. I was married by civil process, which
has lasted me quite as well as the clerical method, and
when I *send in my checks* I'm going to have my remains
cremated. What do I think of Christianity? Well, I've
read, one time and another, very near the entire *prospectus,*
and from all I can figure out, I've come to the same conclusion as another of my countrymen, that the *promoters of
that concern were a very smart syndicate.*"

There's a whale spouting (the first I have seen), but the
clergyman is far too busy to look, and, to his opponent, the
thing is nothing new. While I am looking, I hear the
Yankee say (apropos, I suppose, of the other's mission to
St. Vincent), "If there's only a hundred whites, I should
think you ought to *pull them through.*"

But there goes the dressing-bell for dinner, a ceremonial
where all differences are sunk, a shrine where all may sacrifice in sweet communion.

In the evening, there is music in the saloon. Mr. Manley,
a young Englishman bound for the Argentine to acquire a
knowledge of business, sings, with good effect, the tuneful
though hackneyed ballad, "White Wings." Before going to
Balliol College, he had a year in Germany and another
in Spain; besides which, he has very good French. With
four languages, an Oxford education, and the good introduc-
tions he carries with him, he should begin hopefully. A
lady bound for Rio also rendered many simple ballads
brightly and with taste. Sir Vivian Bland sang, to his own

accompaniment, the pretty old air, " Oft in the stilly night," and, being encored, followed it with " Believe me if all those," etc., Moore's sweetest melody, as I happened to say at the time. " Whose melody did you say ? " said a passenger, listening with me outside the music-saloon. " Moore's," said I. " Ah," he replied quickly, " clever feller that More—so's Burgess *at the other end.*"

10 p.m.—The sea is lumpy, as indeed it has been ever since we left Lisbon. We are passing Las Palmas, one of the Canaries ; the light, flashing every fifteen seconds, is on our port bow as I go to bed below.

October 30th.—Up at 6.30 a.m. My sea-water bath felt quite warm ; the sun is bright, and so hot that the awning has to be spread over the promenade-deck. Ever since we started, this deck has been lined from end to end with chairs of every shape and make, but up to now many have been empty. This morning, although the sea is still roughish, everybody seems to be taking the air, and they are all full. Not only so, but the children, of whom there are, I should think, fully fifty, are making merry in all directions ; and how cheering their presence is. It is a complete nursery scene. They must be having " a high old time " (as Americans say), for everybody pets them, plays with them, nurses them, carries them about, and lays himself out for their delectation.

Jack and Jill.

Since breakfast, Sir Vivian, who is on his way to Rio, has been telling me some of his experiences in the Bulgarian and Servian war. They interested me greatly, and I wish I could record them, but I can't. Some delicate dishes will not bear *réchauffé* treatment. When he is at

home, he takes a great interest in the County Council, of
which he is a member, and I should say a very earnest,
hard-working one.

One of his favourite pastimes is ballooning, and the
last descent he made, bade fair to be his last indeed. The
balloon was over the Crystal Palace, when suddenly a seam
gave way, and the gas rushed out so fast that—though
they lightened the car of everything, even to their mathe-
matical instruments—the loop carried away a chimney-pot,
and the first thing their grapnel caught was a drawing-
room window in the middle of Norwood. His companion,
who had made upwards of three hundred ascents, despaired
of saving the balloon, but happily it and they escaped
without hurt. On this occasion Sir Vivian had left the
County Council to make the ascent, and had contemplated
a long run, but its abrupt conclusion left him free to return
to the meeting, which he found still sitting. Doubtless
many a member during his absence had risen, made a short
motion, and resumed his seat—and so had he.

An Irish balloonist once remarked in my hearing, "We
speak of the number of a man's *ascents*, as if that gave the
measure of his skill. It would be more to the point, I
think, to speak of his *descents*, for those are the real tests."
" I thought the one involved the other," modestly remarked
one of the company. " Then you thought wrong, sor," re-
joined the other. " The balloon makes the ascent for you,
but you must arrange the descent and make it for yourself,
for if you leave it to the balloon, all the saints in the
calendar won't save you. As a matter of fact, I knew a
man, who, as they call it, 'made' *two* ascents and only
one descent, for, when four miles high, the balloon was struck
by lightning, and it and all in it were swept away into

space, where to this day, in all human probability, it is revolving in impalpable dust around the 'oarth.'"

One thing in particular I learnt from Sir Vivian, the perfect equilibrium of the balloon. In an ordinary way the dropping of a mere pinch of sand is sufficient to instantly arrest its descent. It has the same effect as the touching of the rope in a hydraulic lift.

Noon.—Lat. 26° 8′ N., long. 19° 53′ W. Run, 360 miles.

3 p.m.—On the starboard bows, we have just sighted a vessel, the first since we left Lisbon. We have exchanged salutes, and she proves to be a Hamburg steamer.

" You are requested not to cross the line!"

5 p.m.—A three-master on our port bow is passing us full sail, or rather we are meeting and passing her.

9 p.m.—The deck-chairs and their occupants are very picturesque, but the legs of both get in your way, and sadly spoil your after-dinner constitutional. What with these and inconsiderate couples who will take arms, exercise (except in bad French) is very much restricted; the line ought really to be drawn somewhere. I should like it to be a chalk line, beyond which all deck-chairs trespassing should be impounded and, like stray cattle on a common, only released on payment of a fine.

Sir Vivian has been showing me a pretty experiment

with claret and water. First, you get two glasses, and fill
one with wine and the other with water. Then, placing
a card on the latter and inverting it on the former, if
you gently withdraw the card, the water, being the heavier,
will be seen sinking in a fine stream through the wine and
a claret fountain rising through the water.

He also told me how, on another occasion, when ballooning,
by getting outside the car, holding on by the netting, and
pointing a camera at the car and towards the earth, he
managed to get a view of the car and its occupants, and part
of Denmark Hill lying 4000 feet below.

My acquaintance bound for St. Vincent says, when he first
went there only a few years ago, the island depended for its
water on the supplies brought in ships from other islands
in the Cape Verde group. Salt water is still used for
washing purposes, although a fair supply of fresh is brought
by pipes from springs far inland. It speaks badly for this
water, however, that every one, whether coming first to
St. Vincent or returning to it after a holiday, undergoes a
sentence of fourteen days' diarrhœa.

October 31*st.*—Noon. Lat. 20° 52′ N., long. 23° 11′ W.
Run, 366 miles. Weather delightful. What with the grand
air, regular meals, plenty of rest (either on deck-chairs or
below), early hours for rising and retiring, frequent gentle
exercise, genial society, and (I cannot help thinking) the
beneficial action of the salt-laden air upon the skin, my
nerves are getting braced up noticeably, and I sleep well.

After breakfast, Mr. Ollendorff took some capital photographs of emigrant groups, and of our own friends, and
managed to hit off a flight of flying-fish. In what misery
those wretched fish would live, if they only knew what we
know! They have fins as well as wings, and have pretty full

occupation for both, as their lives are incessantly threatened by the bonito and albicora, day and night. But the worst and swiftest enemy of this unhappy creature, is the dolphin.

It appears that, owing to the heat of the sun, the wings of the flying-fish will not support its body more than two hundred yards. Having flown so far, it is obliged to descend and wet them again before it can resume its flight. The moment, therefore, that it takes to the wing, the dolphin, who is chasing it and

" After you, I'll be first."

knows full well of this failing, darts forward under water in the same direction as his prey above it, and is generally at the spot where it returns to wet itself.

2.30 p.m.—We have just met an American schooner yacht, heavily laden with penguin or whale, and looking very travel-stained. These vessels are often out whaling for eight or nine months at a stretch, in the Antarctic seas.

The Venezuelan fleet.

5 p.m.—We are passing a flock of "Mother Carey's chickens," harbingers, as sailors say, of bad weather. The

Chief Officer, Mr. Constantine, to whom I am indebted for many kindnesses and much information, has just been amusing us with the story of the old steamer *Conway*, of this line. She was bought by the Venezuelan government for service as a man-of-war, with the stipulation that two of the Royal Mail officers should accompany her and remain three months, in which time they were to teach the natives navigation! This they did, and left. No sooner were they gone, than their pupils, thinking themselves now qualified naval experts, got up steam and put to sea; but they had not been gone three days before they lost their reckoning. By a stroke of luck, they managed to grope their way back to their starting-place, where, in a huge funk, they ran the ship ashore; "and there," said the Chief Officer, concluding, "she lieth unto this day." " Here endeth the first lesson," said Pog, who was listening.

8 p.m.—A flying-fish has just come splashing on to the spar-deck. It is about the size and shape of a herring. Just behind the gills are two mottled wings, measuring from tip to tip, when extended, exactly twelve inches, and two fins midway between these and its tail. Hearing that they were very frequent visitors on board, I threw the creature over-board while still alive. It gleamed for a moment as it touched the water, like a lighted cigar, and, the next, was lost in the darkness. (As a fact, only two others came on board during the trip—one of them *to me*, two days later.)

We expect to fetch St. Vincent at daybreak to-morrow.

November 1st.—3 a.m. Glorious moonlight. We have had it every night. As we were approaching St. Vincent and it was very hot in the cabin, I went on deck and lay down in a deck-chair to watch for the first glimpse of the St. Antonio light. In hitching my chair round, to get a better view, I

broke the leg, and down I went on the back of my head. In
a moment I seemed to see, not only the
St. Antonio, but the Porto Grande light,
and others too numerous to count. Find-
ing that playing at look-out man was
not my forte, I have returned to my
cabin, where my thermometer stands at
78° by the way, and we are but eight
days out—only six days steaming.

" Any remarks you
may have to make
should be addressed
to the chair."

5 a.m.—We have sighted St. Vincent—first the St. Antonio,
and then the Bird Island light. The outline of one of the
hills bears a resemblance to the profile of Napoleon I., while
another is called "Washington's Head."

5.50 a.m.—We are passing the *Himalaya* troopship lying
in the bay, homeward bound with the "Inniskillings" on
board.

6 a.m.—Anchored. The Verde Islands, of which St.
Vincent is the best known because of its convenient harbour
for coaling, were discovered in 1446. They are used by the
Portuguese government as penal settlements, and the
punishment is said to be much dreaded. The natives are
ignorant, and their religion is a mixture of Catholicism and
heathen worship imported by slaves brought from Africa,
the coast of which, at Cape Verde (whence these islands take
their name), is but two hundred miles from St. Vincent.

Near the sea the temperature in summer ranges between
80° and 90°. On some of the islands, occasionally, rain has
not fallen for three years. The climate is not considered
unhealthy, but a nasty kind of bilious attack, locally called
"*levadias*," is epidemic here in the month of May. Famine
raged all over the islands from 1831 to 1834, during which
time thirty thousand people are said to have died.

F

The principal exports are salt, nuts, hides, coffee, maize, sugar, cocoanuts, dates, and bananas. Among the imports

must be reckoned quails and turtles, which in large numbers work their passages from the African coast to lay their eggs on these sandy shores.

St. Vincent may be said to be absolutely treeless, owing to the fury of the north-east winds. Grass even is so rare, that cricket, the staple amusement of

Real turtle and mock turtle.

the English community, has to be played on cocoanut-matting pegged down over the required area.

But happily St. Antonio (or more correctly St. Antao), only eight miles off, is fertile and able to supply its less fortunate neighbours with grain and fruit. One of its mountains reaches a height of seven thousand feet. During a visitation of cholera in the summer of 1856 fully half of the people of this island either died or left it. It boasts a mountain three thousand feet high, and the neighbouring island of Fogo one of like altitude, in full work as an active volcano. The population of Brava, the most southerly of the group, ekes out a living by victualling whalers.

Porto Grande, the harbour of St. Vincent, hemmed in on all sides by small islands whose mountains, moss-covered in patches, average four hundred or five hundred feet in height, affords grand shelter for vessels. In the centre and facing the entrance to the harbour, stands Bird Island, a tiny thing, in shape like an inverted peg-top, and just capable of holding a lighthouse, which looks like the illuminated peg of the top. On the harbour front of the island

stands the "city" (!) of Mindella, a mere village consisting
of wretched-looking dirty white houses, and stores where
baskets, mats, straw-hats, fans, etc., are sold at reasonable
prices.

The foreign consulates are situated among the bare
rocks, whence their forlorn occupants cheer themselves with
occasional glimpses of the vessels calling here to coal. The
island is a mere burnt-out volcano, a barren desert, cheer-
less in the extreme, with bare craggy pinnacles rising
abruptly out of the golden sands that fringe the rich blue
sea. It is a vision of coral rocks, yellow sands, and quaint
volcanic peaks. In this land-locked, mid-ocean harbour
there is space for full three hundred sail; but the anchorage
is not always secure from squalls which rake the surrounding
valleys. The heat in summer must be terrific, for it is 90°
in the shade now.

Besides cricket, the only amusement seems to be "quarantine," which, but for the other, would be even more indulged
in than it is. The knowledge that every ship quarantined
means to the residents the loss of a cricket-match somewhat
tempers the official scrutiny.

The children, all blacks or half-caste, drive a lucrative
trade in shell-necklaces which they offer at three or four for
sixpence. The houses in the side-streets are squalid dens
and mostly windowless, all but the door being boarded up.
Small-pox, typhoid fever, and cholera are frequent visitors.
This broiling day, we saw a boy in an overcoat, and learnt
from his father that he had just recovered from small-pox.
There were many disfigured by this disease, principally
among the coloured inhabitants, who form nine-tenths of the
population.

The sentries were all blacks, I noticed, and the government officials and the labourers—male and female—employed in landing timber, half-caste. The timber-men arranged the

planks on the heads of the women, who, one at each end of the load, went off up the shore with it at a trot. This struck me as a curious division of labour, but as the ladies concerned looked happy and satis-fied, laughing and singing as they

The land where woman's rights have supplanted man's.

went, and the men seemed happy in conferring so much happiness on others, I suppose it must be right.

Everybody, man, woman, and child, composing the nonde-script crowd of the "submerged tenth" that greets each newly arrived vessel, has the same way of addressing the visitor—"Gee me penny." If you throw one to the half-naked little savages on land, they scramble and fight like fiends for it; and if you pitch one into the water, a dozen bronze statues are after it, and capture it long before it touches the bottom.

This diving is the sight of the place. Even before the *Clyde* had anchored, whole boats full of really beautiful specimens of boys and men ("God's image cut in ebony," as the divine Fuller—or rather Fuller the divine—once happily described the negro) were alongside, clamouring for money to be thrown from the vessel. For every silver piece there would be half-a-dozen competitors, and if you were willing to promise them a florin, there were always two or three ready to dive completely under the ship and up on the far side. This I saw done several times.

Some of these people were absolutely in their "birthday suits," and none had more than a rag round their loins. They all seemed to be in perfect condition, with not an ounce of superfluous flesh, and when coming out of the water their skins looked superb and glistened like the skin of the seal. On our way to shore many followed our rowing-boat, and kept pace with it too. Their hand-over-hand swimming is not so graceful as our side-stroke, but they forge along through rough water far faster than we should. The truth is, constant practice has

Diving, at St. Vincent.

made them simply amphibious—land or water is precisely the same to them. Their diving was the most graceful and noiseless I have ever witnessed.

The building in which those engaged on the telegraph cable (twenty-five in number) work and reside, is spacious and fitted with all the comforts of a club. Their costume is a kind of semi-uniform of some white material and a distinguishing cap. They made a party of us very welcome, and refreshed us most hospitably. Cricket matches with in-coming vessels are all planned beforehand by cable. One with the *Himalaya* was fixed for the following day, Sunday. The odds were slightly in favour of the islanders on account of their familiarity with the cocoanut-matting, sort of cricket-on-the-hearthrug arrangement. Their welcome of the new clergyman appeared to be very cordial; so warm indeed, that I could not help thinking religious zeal would not account for all of it, and hearing them afterwards speak of him as their "new wicket-keeper" explained much. I wonder how he liked his first service at 11 a.m. the following day (Sunday), and whether, like Peter, he "stood up and was bowled," as an irreverent riddle hath it.

This cricket-mania has a curious effect upon its votaries. Everything becomes tinged with it. All thoughts find expression more or less through the medium of its phraseology. The weather is good or bad, *for cricket;* the incoming vessel is not fast or slow, well or ill appointed—she is classed according to her *cricket.* Mention a name known to a St. Vincent man, and he won't say, "What a nice, or clever, or amiable person that is!" but comes at once to business with "He's a grand field," or is "Always good for forty or fifty runs." They have brought the thing to such a science, indeed, that a pretty, accomplished, married woman, distinguished "in her own right," so to speak, ranks below one not so gifted who is wife to a good bowler or wicket-keeper. In fact, they are not called Mrs. Brown or Mrs. Jones, but Mrs. "Slip," or Mrs. "Longleg."

Even the island doctor, familiarly known as Dr. "Bat," became so infected with cricket that he could never get the game out of his head. A certain merry member of our party said he consulted this practitioner once, not knowing of his peculiarity. "Dr. 'Bat,'" he said, "came, straight from a match, in his flannels, and shouldering his bat. When he

The consultation.

entered my room, after a hasty glance round to see where he could put his men, I suppose—for I found afterwards he was captain of the team —he held his bat between his legs and gently lowered himself till he sat on it. Then, taking a good look at me, he said, 'Well, and what's your average?' Thinking he meant my age (for

I am no cricketer), I said, ' Fifty-two,' at which he seemed
pleased, and remarked, ' If that is so, I think you ought to
be able to carry your bat out.' I said I thought I could do
that any time. ' Don't be too sure,' said he: and then he
went on, something like this :—

" You're a bit *off colour*. Too many *duck's eggs* lately,
eh ? They upset some people—but, lor', they're *nothing*.
In future be content with *one at a time*, and if you can *keep*
'*em down*, you ought to be *good for a century !* "

But as this anecdote was related after we had been re-
galed by the cable-graphists, I retail it with some hesitation,
and for two reasons. First, because the narrator was, I think,
too merry to be exact ; and secondly, because, if accurate, I
don't like telling tales out of school of our kind hosts at
St. Vincent.

CHAPTER III.

ST. VINCENT TO PERNAMBUCO.

November 1st.—2 p.m.   We are leaving.   As the bower
anchor comes up the ship
swings round, and we dip
our flag to the *Himalaya*.

The *Himalaya*.

2.30 p.m.—The steamer
Gulf of Suez, from Valparaiso, is on our port side.
She belongs to what is
known as the Gulf Line.
Starting from Greenock
they call at Glasgow, and
go thence direct to Valparaiso, returning by the
same route.

3 p.m.—I have been trying to get my thin flannels, the
heat being very great—the temperature in my cabin 86°.
But they were packed for me in a bag fastened by a puzzle
lock, which has well deserved its name. This lock was a
new idea on the part of my people, and one has to be careful
not to forget the word used. " Choose a short word," I said,
" and don't fail to tell me what it is." But in the hurry
of leaving I only got the " key " as the train left Waterloo.
" Don't forget ' Mouse-trap,'" said the packer of the bag,
" something " (I couldn't make out what) " and letters."

"The letters," I supposed, had reference to my writing from certain points. Well, if I spent a minute, I spent three hours yesterday spelling "mouse-trap" in every imaginable way to that incorruptible-Robespierre-of-a-lock, till I got to think there was no such word. I interviewed all sorts and conditions of men, women, and children as to the spelling—all in vain.

This morning, first thing, I was at it again with the same endearing expressions; and once more I wooed it this afternoon, but it remained inexorable. At last a little girl of six has solved the riddle—for a riddle it was. In a moment the whole idea came to mind, "don't forget mouse-trap in three letters," i.e. cat! Oh, what a watch-dog that "cat" has been! However, five minutes after, the cat was literally "out of the bag," and so were my flannels.

7 p.m.—At dinner we had fresh oranges and bananas from St. Vincent—the former ripe though green; but I prefer the St. Michael's. The bananas were not so very much richer in flavour than those we get in England, but their warm juices seemed still circulating, and their hue was dazzlingly golden, which made all the difference.

8 p.m.—All deck-chairs are stowed away for dancing by the electric light, to the violin of the butcher and the banjo of one of the quarter-masters. Not too much band, but just band enough. Some Spanish ladies bound for Buenos Aires danced very prettily and with marvellous spirit. They had, of course, never met their partners before, but, for all that, they danced as though they had been united from birth like the "Siamese Twins."

Splendidly matched, too, were a Scotch gentleman and his charming young wife. But to my thinking the most graceful, refined, and accomplished woman at this, as indeed in all she did, was the wife of an engineer bearing an unmistakably Welsh name, who was returning to Monte Video.

Many more would have danced, I think, if some responsible person (the Captain, preferably) had started a quadrille to bring the people together. The Captain's presence is a sort of guarantee of propriety. But one must not expect too much from any man. Captain Spooner has the name of being an excellent seaman, and one ought to be satisfied, and more than satisfied, with that.

" The rhythm of unresting feet."

10 p.m.—I " turned-in " to the strains of the dual band and soon fell asleep beneath the ballroom, to the rhythm of unresting feet.

November 2nd (Sunday).—About 2 a.m., I was awakened by a peculiar fluttering of something cold and wet under my knees, as I lay on my back with my feet drawn up. At first I thought it was a dream, but on turning up the light, what was my astonishment to find a live and very lively flying-fish capering about all over the bunk, which was the top one on the far side from the port at which it must have entered. The light woke both my cabin-companions, who were almost as astounded as I was.

10 a.m.—The news has spread through the ship, and many and various are the explanations about the flying-fish. Among them is the theory that the two Brazilians, one an old man, the other an invalid, put the thing there to frighten *me*. But the prize solution is that I took it to bed with me

to frighten *them*. Well, the man who can believe that any one out of Hanwell and going about loose will put a cold, wet, live flying-fish under his legs at 2 a.m. to frighten two other fellows, total strangers to him, will believe anything. However, every one to his choice. Meanwhile, as the incident seemed to be doubted, I this morning got my friend Mr. Dane to copy in Portuguese a certificate, which I wrote in English, and I have now the signatures and addresses of the corroborators affixed to the record, signed, sealed, and delivered, of the facts as I state them.

Armed with this *conviction*, as I thought it, I waited on the unbelievers, feeling sure of a good haul of converts. The deuce is in it, I said, but now they must yield. But he *must* have been in it, for they didn't budge. First, they treated it as a forgery, and when driven from that ground by the signatories themselves, they finally decided I had hypnotized my witnesses. Hypnotism, the modern euphemism for witch-

"Thou com'st in such a questionable shape."

craft! Heaven help me! if this had happened a hundred years ago, I and my flying-fish would have been grilled alive.

Even Pog saw the absurdity of dubbing me "practical joker" and "hypnotist" too, and contented himself with asking some reasonable questions as to the distance of the bunk from the port, the size of the fish relative to the opening through which he was stated to have come, etc., all of which I answered. After shutting his eyes for a moment to obtain mental abstraction, he said slowly, "Fish, twelve inches; port, sixteen inches; ship going sixteen knots, allow-

ing for windage, etc. Hum! Well, if you'll do the same
thing to-night under test conditions, I for one will withdraw
my unfavourable comments." "And what are they?" I
asked, with some asperity (for Pog, left to himself, would,
I believe, have credited my story if I'd produced a boot-jack
as the flying-fish). "Why, sir, I was saying to these gentlemen, that you and the two Brazilians were either moonstruck through the 'opening of the *port*,' or drunk *from a
like cause.*"

But for the pun, I should have challenged that man.
As it was, instead of sword or pistol I called to my aid
two *old saws* and reasoned thus :—"' A man that will make a
pun will pick a pocket.' 'Sooner or later the thief goes to
jail.' *I will not kill him; I will leave him to his fate!*"
Besides, this being Sunday, officers and men were parading
on deck preliminary to service in the dining-saloon, and no
duels are allowed on Sunday on board the *Clyde*; no, nor
games of any kind, not even chess, in public.

Mr. Ritchie told me of a certain captain who, having
forbidden " bull " on Sunday, was caught playing chess in
his cabin. On this apparent inconsistency being pointed
out, and permission being again requested, he replied, " Yes,
that's reasonable; you may play ' bull,' I think,"—and then
added, as they were hurrying off for the apparatus—" er—in
your own cabins, of course."

But it is 10.20 a.m., and the roll is being called, as
officers and men muster in line along the port side of the
promenade-deck. At 10.30 we all go below—I notice the
temperature is 80° in the saloon. At the upper left-hand
corner of the table stands the Captain, with his book on
a cushion covered with the Union Jack, and on his right
the Chief Officer. First there is the opening hymn, and

then follows the ordinary church service (minus the Litany) which is read by the Captain; the lessons falling to the share of my friend, Mr. Constantine, the Chief Officer. The hymn I shall never forget, the men seemed so to revel in it. It was "Onward, Christian soldiers," to the tune known as "St. Alban." What immense voices the crew had! What chest notes! And how they swung along with that peculiar fo'cas'le chant of theirs!

"St. Alban."

A musical friend described their singing of "Onward, Christian soldiers" in these touching words :—"The final syllable of the first line is slurred to a note high up, and then in a vague 'arpeggio' down to an indefinite bass note, as it were feeling after the 'tonic;' and the end of the second line is similarly embellished with a suggestion of the 'dominant.'" My knowledge of this subject is limited to occasional performances on the triangle and jew's harp, but I should think you could get my friend's prescription made up at any respectable chemist's; anyhow, there are the ingredients, and nothing short of trying it for yourself will ever convey any idea of its droll effect. The organist, too, added to the humour of the thing; for, I suppose from a desire to in some measure hide the peculiar fo'cas'le grace-note at the end of each line, he introduced an end chord to accompany it. The whole production was unique and delicious beyond description.

My place was next to Pog, whose singing was the thinnest thing I ever heard come out of a man of his dimensions—as out of proportion as the elephant's shrill trumpet to his unwieldy body. He had the voice of a girl of ten—not a day more—and as he held his head up, his double chin vibrated like the throat of a crowing cock.

When service was over—it occupied only about forty minutes—and we were preparing to go, the Yankee, who had come, as he said, "out of compliment to the Captain," caught sight of a blue bookmark hanging from the Captain's book, with certain large white letters on it: "I thought the Captain's initials were *J.D.S.*," he whispered to us. "Misprint," said Pog under his breath and without moving a muscle. This explanation seemed quite to settle the Yankee, and I must admit it fairly settled me.

Noon.—Lat. 11° 45′ N., long. 26° 59′ W. Run, 330 miles, *i.e.* for twenty-two hours only, as we left St. Vincent at 2 p.m. yesterday.

3.30 p.m.—I have been trying to chat with the Purser, an Irishman and a rattling good fellow, but he was casting his books, and, though I tried every subject I could think of, nothing seemed to interest him. Yet sometimes he is such a nice fellow! My smartest flashes seemed not to move him this afternoon. Every now and then he would look up, his pen would stop at some figure, and slowly and sadly he would mutter "*one—thirty-nine.*" Presently he would say, with what I took for a smile, "*three—forty-seven,*" and so on. This occurred many times, and at last, just as I was starting a dissertation on the applicability of the *binomial theorem* and the *differential calculus* to the ordinary purposes of the counting-house—as I thought, a most apposite theme —he said, "*four—twenty-five,*" so loudly that I thought he must mean it was within five minutes of afternoon tea-time. So, thanking him for the warning, I left.

His clock, an American, which I noticed had the days of the month around the face, and a pointer to denote each

day as it comes—a useful reminder at sea, where you lack
the help of the daily paper—stood at a quarter to four as I
quitted his office; but I felt that he knew best. However,
on inquiry, I found tea would not be served for three-quarters
of an hour. So I suppose he made a mistake in calculating
the longitude. Mem. Never try to compute differences of
time while casting, or you may, like the Purser, deprive
yourself of three-quarters of an hour's interesting and
instructive conversation.

4.30 p.m.—A large sailing vessel on the starboard bow.
She has signalled with her pennant flown from the mizzen-
mast, and we have replied, hoisting our name indicated by
three flags—yellow at top, red white and blue in the middle,
and at bottom a white pennant with a red circle in the centre.
She has hoisted four flags to spell hers, but the distance
prevents our reading them. She is thought to be an
American, laden with timber for Rio.

5 p.m.—So far we have had neither boat nor fire drill,
and as a consequence certain thoughts have been troubling
me in connection with our
emigrants. Many and many
a time, strolling on deck
on a hot night, have I
looked down into the little
Portuguese town astern, in
the very bowels of the ship,
and never, I think, without
my thoughts wandering
away in mid-ocean medita-
tions of the following
kind:—Was it forty boxes

Portuguese emigrants on board
the *Clyde*.

of matches—I won't be positive, but I believe so—that the

Captain took from these thoughtless people, our first day
out from Lisbon ?   And if so, can one feel sure that all were
captured; ay, or half ?   And these Portuguese are for ever
smoking cigarettes, and pitching the matches away while
still alight.   The utter carelessness of these people !

Besides, we know that the unimaginative, those who can't
foresee a danger, are often the most shiftless when it stares
them in the face.   Suppose at this instant smoke and flame
were to issue from that hold, what would be the wisest thing
to do ?   Not, surely, to ring that firebell and arouse, together
with the crew, five hundred panic-stricken people to impede
their efforts.   Yet how could one collect the crew *alone ?*

The truth is, everybody, passengers and emigrants alike,
need to be made familiar with the appliances for life-saving,
and we ought not to leave all to chance at the eleventh
hour.   Fire is bad, and so is shipwreck; but is not the
terror these disasters create a factor also to be reckoned
with ?   It is hardly too much to say that fear is the *most*
potent element of the three, for its presence baffles and
paralyzes efforts which otherwise would avert a catastrophe.

" Fear nothing but fear," some one has said.   It is the
arch-enemy of peace, afloat and ashore.   With fear, as with
everything else, I am persuaded, prevention is better than
cure.   Accustom all on board to the use of fire-hose and the
boats when no danger threatens, and thus will you train
them to meet it under the best conditions if and when it
comes.   That Irishman was not so far out when he said of
his pair of new boots, " I must wear these a few times or
I shan't be able to get them on."

7 p.m.—A North German Lloyd steamer from Buenos
Aires, on our starboard bow, has been signalling us.   We
ran up our flag, but for some reason didn't " break it," as

the sailors say, *i.c.* shake it out. She is on her way to
St. Vincent, homeward bound.

We are approaching the Doldrums, where the refreshing
breeze we have been enjoying all day will leave us. This is
the region where sailing vessels roll listlessly at times for
weeks together; but our engines will drive us through in
quick time. After that, we *should* feel the comfort of the
south-east trades, on whose favouring breezes all vessels
rely, when bound for the Cape of Good Hope. At this
moment we are over two thousand five hundred miles from
home, and two days off the " line."

7.30 p.m.—It has turned cooler, and the wind is rising.
A Mother Carey's chicken has been blown on board. The
Quarter-master says it is raining hard behind us; but we
are out of reach of that storm. He says, " When the breeze
comes before the rain, you may get under easy sail again;
but when the rain comes before the breeze, you may shorten
sail as soon as you please." This is a sailing-ship proverb,
of course, but it shows that our prospects are good.

8 p.m.—It is raining heavily; but coming *after* the
breeze, all is well. Had a long talk with my dinner *vis-à-vis*,
Mr. Courtney, who, after seven years of sheep-farming in
the country " camp," as they call it—west of Buenos Aires
—which did *not* pay, turned his attention to wire-fencing and
well-sinking, which *did*. Whereupon he invested his profits
in a well-wooded estate of nine miles in extent—the twenty
thousand trees upon which will, sooner or later, as the timber-
buyers reach his property, turn him in one pound apiece.
At present, these eventual customers are some six miles
townwards from him; but already the property has been
improved by the Western Railway Company having cut
through it during his absence in England. He says water can

G

always be found at a depth of three feet, and is obtained by
wells peculiar in construction—ten yards long and two or
three wide. The pumping is done by a horse which, ridden
by a boy, draws a rope and lifts the water in a valved box,
whence it flows into a trough.

An ostrich farm of African imported birds was tried near
him, but failed. Starting with one hundred pairs, worth
£100 each, they finished in a couple of years with but eighty
pairs. The plucking, he told me, makes the birds very
tender, and they are consequently very savage at that period,
so that the attendants have to be armed with three-pronged

" Stop 'er! Turn 'er starn ! "

forks. If caught by the
tail, however, the ostrich
can be *steered* at pleasure !
This amused me much, but
the gallantry of the creatures pleased me even
more. At their fiercest
they are docile with women, who can enter their enclosures
with impunity when no man dares do so.

November 3rd.—The only deadly specimen of the tarantula
spider I have ever seen was in the British Museum, and it
was quite a small thing. Mr. Courtney tells me in the
Argentine they reach the size of a five-shilling piece, and
are poisonous. The hand and arm of a man who was bitten
swelled enormously, and his life was only saved by the
frequent and free use of brandy. The drink of the country,
he says, is Canã (pronounced Kannia), a white rum made
from sugar-canes.

11 a.m.—Several schools of porpoises have been disporting
themselves for the last half-hour, rolling and playing quite
close to the ship.

We have just had our first experience of tropical rain— a drenching storm which in a few minutes flooded the deck all over three inches deep.

The news has reached us of a case of measles among the emigrants, scaring all who have children, notably the Scotch lady with her first baby.

Noon.—Lat. 6° 14' N., long. 28° 49' W. Run, 350 miles.

2 p.m.—At lunch the great heat was rendered still greater by closing the ports, to meet the wishes of people who feared the spread of the measles. Camphor and other preventives were in great request. Pog had a piece at which he took surreptitious sniffs under cover of his handkerchief, but as he never pulled out the one without dropping the other, it was a very open secret. On inquiring how the "eye-water"

"Camphor? Not mine, I assure you."

answered, he said he thought very well so far; the eye was certainly better. To my question whether he still took it the same way, he said: "Well, not exactly. I mix it at lunch with my whiskey."

3 p.m.—I've been looking at the emigrants, and thinking how difficult it must be in such a crowd to prevent the measles spreading, and what discomfort it must cause them all. Now I am thinking what annoyance it will be *to us*, too, for it means quarantine sooner or later at some of the ports.

One must have a big bump of philanthropy if, seeing all

the dirty tricks of these people day by day, he gives them all his pity and keeps none for himself. I'm afraid my charity begins at home, and—well, is very domesticated. The keystone of John Stuart Mill's political economy was, "the greatest good to the greatest number." Since his day, some one has added a rider thereto, that the greatest number is "No. 1."

My friend Mr. Ollendorff has just been telling me of some utterly vile Brazilian practices. Mr. Dane agrees, and adds "they are the refuse of Portugal." Brazil has long been and is still, he says, not only the receptacle for the poor, but also the "far country" of the "prodigal" sons of Portugal; with this difference, that no fatted calf awaits his return, be he rich or poor. He is considered contaminated, and should he bring home a Brazilian wife, she would not be received, no, not if she was armoured with six-inch plates of eighteen-carat gold.* Well, things might have gone otherwise if the original "prodigal son" had brought home *a daughter-in-law.* We don't know.

Pog hearing us discuss this, and being nothing if not critical, has just pointed out an error in the parable which the new version has not rectified. He thought that, instead of "fain would he have filled his belly with the husks that the swine did eat," the last part should read, "husks *similar* to those the swine did eat." "I may be hypercritical," he said, "but of course the son didn't want to eat the *identical* husks that the swine ate!"

---

* This, I have reason to believe, is greatly exaggerated. A good authority tells me that the true-born Brazilian holds the Portuguese in undisguised contempt. The reader who is given to "putting two and two together" will observe that the one statement in this case cancels the other, like adding *minus* two to *plus* two. Well, that only shows that two and two do *not* invariably make four. Doesn't it?—C. A. A.

There is generally tit-for-tat in life. "Great fleas have little fleas upon their backs to bite 'em, and little fleas have lesser fleas, and so *ad infinitum.*" Just as the Portuguese treats the Brazilian, so is he in turn treated by the Spaniard. And it is on ship-board one sees these racial distinctions to perfection. The Brazilian is, as it were, the "country cousin" of the Portuguese, who in like manner is deemed utterly "bad form" by the Spaniard. And these gradations are rigidly observed on board, where the three nationalities are for ever meeting and mingling, but never mix.

8 p.m.—To-night the Spanish Argentines, young and old

Nursery rhymes.

have been singing patriotic songs, and now they are clapping their hands to some seemingly well-known and humorous nursery rhymes, the children's merry voices predominating; and although most of the tunes are common to both countries, not a Portuguese has lifted his voice to join in them. They and the Brazilians, in separate cliques and coteries, stood

aloof, moody and embarrassed, to the evident delight of the
dashing Spaniards, who are as showy, self-asserting, vivacious,
and passionate as the others are quiet, retiring, inert, and
lethargic.

In dress, too, the one is lavish and likes colour, wears
hats with graceful curves about the face, and toys and
gesticulates with his gossamer cigarette, much as his lady
with her fan. The other heaves his chest and draws his
full-flavoured cigar stolidly through to the bitter end, as he
sits for ever doubled up on his deck-chair, with his head
encased in a plain black-silk smoking-cap, the ugliest design
that ever entered a head or that ever a head entered.

The difference in temperament between the Argentine and
the Brazilian is traceable, no doubt, to the difference in
the climates, which a passenger, resident in Buenos Aires,
compared respectively to Heaven and Hades. Our Yankee
passenger to the Argentine, who holds Rio to be peerless
among cities, and whose friends are numerous there, on
hearing this said, "Well, sir, if you ask me, I only echo an
American sentiment when I say ' Heaven for climate, Hades
for company.' " Apropos, I may mention that Pernambuco,
which we are now approaching, is literally—according to
some authorities—" Gate of Hell."

The heat in the Brazils soon induces, even in Europeans,
listless, lazy habits, and they would become no better than
the natives, but for the trips they make home every few
years to brace themselves up. Whereas an Argentine, with a
climate resembling ours, is in temperament also more or less
English. A resident in Rio tells me that, during the hottest
weather, the trams, which by reason of the draught are
ordinarily the coolest places—the very paradises of these
burning regions—are mere gridiron tortures. The current

of air as it meets your face, flays and blisters it frightfully.
You might as well take a chair in front of a blast-furnace.
The only way for business men is to begin early, and, finishing between two and three, take the train right away to
their cool residences in the hills behind the city.

November 4th.—7 a.m. Wanting a shave badly, and
having brought with me a "Star" razor, a small blade, so
shielded that you can't cut yourself, which I bought on the
recommendation of Oliver Wendell Holmes in the last of his
many good gifts to the world, "Our Hundred Days in
Europe," I set to work and scraped myself well-nigh raw
but without removing my beard. While thus torturing
myself, in came one of my Brazilian cabin-companions, who,
seeing my misery, got out one exactly like mine, which he
stropped and lent me. It did the work in no time; what's
more, the deed was painless, and I certainly never had an
easier or a more effective shave in my life. How well has
it been said that "one 'Star' differeth from another 'Star,'"
etc. ! I could only thank this good man by signs, but I think
he understood that I was grateful.

8 a.m.—My sleep must have been sound, for I felt nothing
of a stiff gale that sprang on us in the night, catching many
of our ports open and drenching the berths near them.

11 a.m.—Have just had an interesting half-hour with the
Chief Officer, Mr. Constantine. After discussing the ship
and her belongings, we got on latitudes. Having read Dr.
Bell's entertaining account of his voyage up the Nile, in
which he speaks of seeing the "Southern Cross," either at
Luxor or at Assouan, I amused myself trying, with the
Chief Officer's tables and kind assistance, to find the highest
northern latitude at which that constellation is visible. We
found it would be 1° above the horizon in latitude 26° N.,

which is about the latitude of Assouan; also that it would
be visible in these latitudes to-morrow about 5 a.m.

On many occasions I have been indebted to Mr. Constantine
for courtesies and information of all kinds, always accorded
me with the utmost willingness and good humour, despite an
ignorance on my part of things nautical which even I can
now recall as simply appalling.

The sea is of the most heavenly blue, the weather glorious,
the fierceness of the sun's heat being tempered by a delicious

Seeing the equator.   " It's just like
the photo of it in the map."

breeze.   But although we
are within five hours of the
equator, one cannot take even
this as a criterion of one's
ability to stand tropical heat,
for it will be hotter, I hear,
15° south of the line.

Noon.—Lat. 0° 52′ N., long.
30° 46′ W.   Run, 344 miles.
Pernambuco, 592 miles.

4 p.m.—It was fortunate I
had to take this higher-priced
cabin.   The other to Lisbon
did very well in the cool
weather, but in this intense
heat my cabin, well forward
on the starboard bows, where
one gets the fullest benefit of the breeze the vessel makes,
is far preferable.

We are crossing the line at this very moment (while eight
bells is sounding), as nearly as can be ascertained.   The old
practices of tarring, etc., that long obtained on sailing vessels,
and were welcome reliefs, no doubt, to the tedium of the Dol-

drums, find no place in these twenty-knot steamers. Harmless little tricks alone survive, the puny descendants of those giant jokes. One may get an unlooked-for splash of water, another an "apple-pie bed," and so on, but nothing more. Even the little sell of tying a hair across a telescope, that led a young lady once to think she had "seen the equator," claims no victims in these school-board days, so no one cares to try it.

Another relic of the sailing ship now extinct as the Dodo —is shark-catching. This is a fair sample of the sort of juvenile questions I used to bother the long-suffering Chief Officer with. True, we are not bored to death as formerly were those becalmed on a sailing ship; but is that any reason why we should not see how a shark is caught? It never seemed to occur to my belated mind that you might almost as well count on your legs to catch up a fast train, as expect a shark to catch up a bait going twenty miles' an hour through the water. When a steamer captures a shark it is in port, not at sea. At Pernambuco, for instance, we may see some.

9 p.m.—Nothing can exceed the liquid glory of the ship's path through the sea to-night. Standing over the screw in the darkness, the seething waters appear ablaze with phosphorescent light; huge masses, like jelly-fish on fire, as big as pumpkins, are hurling through the boiling waters. For a good mile behind we leave a trail of molten gold. Without question, this is the grandest sight I have yet witnessed.

I turned in at 10 p.m. so as to be ready for my early appointment with "Mr. Cross."

November 5th.—10 a.m.—I was up at 4 a.m. to see the Southern Cross. As usual, the look-out man, whose busi-

ness is with ships, rocks, and other terrestrial objects, knew
next to nothing of the heavenly bodies. " What name did
you say, sir?" " Southern Cross!"   " Oh, that there's him,
lookee, off the weather bow; he ain't much, is he? Why,
he ain't a patch on the *Bear*.   I call him a 'umbuggin'
thing."   I counted the stars, noted their position, and sure
enough they did form a cross, but larger than I had expected
to find it. Still, I gazed with interest, if not with rapture.

Presently something came to my aid. A friend who had
seen it when coming to England, told me that, seen from
his berth on the far side from the port, the Cross just filled
that opening. This settled it, for on going below I found
the look-out man's Cross would not test my friend's bear,
or rather bear my friend's test. It was the Chief Officer's
watch, I knew, so off I went to the bridge. " No," said he,
" that's called the *False Cross*, but it is the guide to the
True Cross.   There he lies, much lower down, leaning at
an angle of about 15° out of the perpendicular, and with his
chief star on the horizon." Fig. 1 gives the relative positions
and comparative magnitude of the stars, and Fig. 2 a rough
idea of the constellation's appearance in the sky : the points
of light much enlarged, of course.

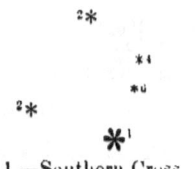

Fig. 1.—Southern Cross.
The figures indicate the accepted
magnitudes of the stars.

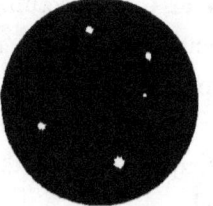

Fig. 2.—Southern Cross.

Alas ! how often have man's best efforts resulted in error,
like this little crusade of mine ! " What a text for a sermon !"
said Pog, when I told him of my mistake. " Oh, wanderer !

Wouldst thou find the one true Cross? Seek guidance from the Chief above; ask not another ignorant as thyself. And from the *false* Cross, on which thine eye is fixed, He shall point thee to the *true*, and show thee how to tell it at a glance for evermore. He knows them all, and sees them all as thou canst never see them from thy finite plane." Yes, I'm sure Pog was made for the Church.

And now I will be candid. As a cross, or even as a constellation, it disappointed me. Perhaps I expected too much in return for my early rising. I know I used to think the blackberries small at 4 a.m. that pleased me well enough in the afternoon. The truth is, as the Chief Officer put it, it owes its distinction not to its beauty, but simply to its situation. Its one bright star, "Alpha Crucis," is the nearest to the South Pole, and so does pole-star duty in all nautical calculations.

But, however one may decry its pretensions, one meets it everywhere in the south, in the Brazilian, Argentine, and Oriental republics, figuring in coins, flags, and devices of all sorts. Perhaps of them all, the prettiest setting of it is to be met with in the really beautiful and only recently minted twenty-reis piece (or half-penny), of the New Brazilian Republic, where it is given the place of honour within a small central circle. In the centre of a circle on the obverse side of the coin is its value "20 reis," and around this the thrifty legend, " VINTEM POUPADO, VINTEM GANHO "—our well-known proverb, " A penny saved is a penny gained."

Twenty-reis piece.

HERE AND THERE.

No wealth will buy a single ray
To light our foggy days,
Yet *here*, if you a ha'penny pay,
They'll give you twenty *reis*.

All must agree with the look-out man, that in a literal sense the Cross "ain't a patch on the *Bear*." It was never intended to be; they are much too far apart. But even figuratively, as he of course used the expression, I am inclined to think with him.

Orion, which was a perfect blaze of splendour directly over our masthead while I was playing at cross-purposes with the true Crux and the false, was incomparably grander. Indeed, what with Sirius like a moon, the moon herself well-nigh as bright as the sun, and Orion fairly dazzling to look upon, all seen through this pellucid air and backed by these blue southern skies, I thought the heavens glorious beyond anything to be seen in northern latitudes, and was amply repaid for my early rising, if not exactly in the way I had expected.

I have been watching Sirius, and trying to grasp some idea of what his distance must be for his light to take sixteen years to reach us. This way of putting it always brings home to me the practical infinity of a hundred billions of miles better than the figures. A string of noughts, with most of us, counts for nothing.

A hundred billions! How many of us realize what one billion means? That no man can count it up. That if Adam had got through a hundred a minute, worked all day and night and lived till now, he would not have reached a billion or anything like it. And how many a minute could he count, say of such numbers as 199,999,999?

A change has come over the eastern sky. Ten minutes ago the blue horizon faded into grey, and I beheld the first faint rose tints warm the grey to pale amethyst, and, growing richer here and there, deepen and redden into tongues of flame. The far-away soft white clouds are now suffused as

from a distant conflagration, while those along the sea-line
blush crimson as they open wide their gates. Now come the
heralds resplendent and of every hue, and as they pass and
sweep to right and left and troop beside the empty throne,
up from his couch of royal blue, in silent majesty, rises the
King of Day.

Water, at all times a beautiful object, is, I think, at sunrise
at its best :

> " Through every swift vicissitude
> Of changeful time, unchanged it has stood,"

and at every daybreak seems newly created, the sun as it
were personifying the " Spirit of God moving on the face of
the waters."

10 a.m.—We are passing on the north side of the island of
Fernando de Norhona, a convict settlement of Brazil; a
desolate spot about three hundred miles from Pernambuco.
Such formerly was the pestilential character of this island,
that ships would go out of their way to avoid passing it to
leeward. The most noticeable feature is a mountain
resembling a lighthouse, which I hear can be seen forty-five
miles away. In the valleys everywhere were to be seen
palm and cocoanut trees, sheltered by the hills, which
looked to be about five hundred feet high. In the centre,
under the shadow of a hillside, lay the few houses we could
discern—but our glasses failed to show us any of the
inhabitants. At the western extremity we could see,
without a glass, what must be an immense natural tunnel,
passing so straight through a hill that the light at the far
side opening was visible to us on board.

Noon.—Lat. 4° 16' S., long. 32° 40' W. Run, 328 miles.

5 p.m.—We have been enjoying ourselves once more at
Pog's expense. He seems to have been seized with a craze

that the "murderer" we've got on board escaped at St. Vincent, so we have been making the ghost walk again, by the aid of my coat and hat and the friend who—ought one to say resembled me ?—no, resembles *what I was*.

This time Pog and I together watched, and I had the greatest difficulty in preventing his capturing my friend and "double" *in flagrante delicto*, that is to say, in my coat and hat. And when we spoke calmly and with indifference —as, being in the secret, it was easy to do—he fairly went for us. "Well, gentlemen," he said severely, "I am astounded at your conduct ! Here is a man about whom the Captain, the Doctor, and the Purser know nothing—for I have elicited so much from them all; a man who, after two days among us as a *saloon passenger*, suddenly disappears at

Lisbon, to reappear a day after among the *second-class passengers*— where he has no berth, mind, for that too I have ascertained. Detectives are on board watching this stowaway, we are told ; they don't arrest him ; why don't *we ?* Are we to wait till he scuttles the ship, or at best walks ashore to-morrow at Pernambuco ? We have no treaty, you know, with the Brazils ; to-morrow, therefore, it will be too late."

" Why don't *we ?* "

This speech just gave my "double" time to return my coat and hat and join us. Whereupon we all solemnly made a tour of inspection through the second-class quarters, headed by the redoubtable Pog, whose pluck, I must admit, moulted no feather during our search for the "timid murderer."

9 p.m.—Wanting a game of chess with Mr. Ritchie, and seeing Pog, who hates the game, looking sad at the prospect, I promised in our joint names, Mr. Ritchie assenting, that the winner should pledge himself to catch the stowaway.

The bait took so well, that Pog has watched the game throughout with intense interest. As the end approached, however, and a draw was seen to be probable, there was no holding him. He declared a draw would be ridiculous, and offered to take either game himself. But as this would certainly have resulted in a win for Mr. Ritchie, Pog being an indifferent player, and in *his* having to capture Pog's *bête noire*, the offer was declined with thanks.

" —— but *not* enjoying it."

I have just left Pog drinking his grog in the smoking-room, the scene of our fray, but, as he pathetically said, "not enjoying it by reason of the crass stupidity of mankind."

November 6th.—5.55 a.m. They are letting go the anchor; we are at Pernambuco. The view is charming as we enter the passage close by the fort built on the rocks, the wood-clad hills rising gradually one above another to the horizon.

The ancient name of the entire place was Olinda, and one of the suburbs—away to the right some three miles—still bears that name. Of this outlying part only a few lofty buildings, rearing their heads above the trees, are visible from the ship; all the rest of Olinda, though built like Lisbon on the hill-sides, is embowered among palms and orange-groves.

9 a.m.—Some churches in Pernambuco are prominent objects from the ship. The one with a St. Paul's-like dome must be very large. That building, of sentry-box pattern, with the half-ball on the top shining like burnished gold, is, I'm told, the Admiralty.

Foam is beating against an immense coral-reef, called the Recife, lying between us and the land. This reef extends for nearly four hundred miles parallel to and at a distance of a quarter of a mile from the shore.

The bum-boats are coming alongside the *Clyde*. The steamer *Imperador* (*Emperor*, rather an anachronism to-day in Brazil), a paddle-boat (screws are no use in this rough sea), is bringing a lighter full of freight, and our emigrants are laying in supplies:—sixpence for three pine-apples: melons twopence each : oranges ten a penny.

Our friend, Mr. Dane, leaves us here after doing yeoman's service as linguist, guide, and general good fellow among us. We shall miss him sorely.

A party of thirteen of us is going ashore at four shillings apiece, for both there and back, twenty-six milreis (fifty-two shillings) for the boat-load. Not bad pay for three miles, *i.e.* a mile-and-a-half each way.

A frigate-pelican is soaring majestically at a prodigious height, watching the shoals of fish about the surf. He stoops like the hawk and seldom misses a good haul.

10 a.m.—Ashore. The thermometer is 90°. Their average is 85°. On our way we passed many rough sailing boats, called *Jangadas*, or *Catamarans*, made of four logs of cork palm riveted together. They form a wedge-shaped craft, capable of carrying three or four persons, standing or squatting on little stools. A single plank forms the keel, and a rough mast and lateen sail complete the little vessel.

Miles from land, in seas that sweep them from stem to stern, do these little ships carry their sturdy crews a-fishing. Their speed is great, and, though wet and windy, they are secure.

We also noticed, showing above the water near us, the dorsal fin of a large shark, who, if he had only known it, could have helped himself to a meal off any of the catamarans. Pernambuco produces the finest pine-apples and

Hut in Olinda, Pernambuco.

sharks in the world. At present, I have only tasted the former, which I found superb; they are said to be superior, both in size and flavour, to those of the West Indies. Some weigh as much as fourteen or fifteen pounds: they have even reached twenty or twenty-two pounds each.

The first settlement here was made in 1530, by a Captain Duarte Cochlo, who received this grant, as a reward for long service in India, from the King of Portugal. Pernambuco—by

some translated " gate of hell ; " by others, " an opening through
a stone reef"—is the modern and business city, and has not
the pretensions to beauty Olinda has and always has had ; for
the name is derived from *O que linda,* " Oh, how beautiful ! "
an exclamation of Duarte when landing with his wife and
children.   For thirty years, under his guidance, it prospered
wonderfully, and the control then passed to his son George,
who was elected " *Commandante* " (Commander) at the
instance of the Jesuits.

This energetic man in five years reduced to subjection
all the surrounding country for one hundred and fifty miles
from Olinda.   But presently the tide turned, and in 1630
Pernambuco was captured by the Dutch fleet of fifty sail, after
a vigorous defence conducted by one Vieira, a youth of but
seventeen years.   Horrible were the atrocities of the victors,
who held the place for a quarter of a century, when it was
recovered by Baweto, viceroy to the King of Portugal, under
whose sovereignty it remained till the declaration of inde-
pendence.

The business part of the city lies on a flat between the
two rivers Beberibe and Capibaribe and the sea, giving it
something of a Venetian look.   Like the Gaul of Cæsar's
Commentaries, "all" Pernambuco "is divided into three parts"
—a peninsula, a continent, and an island.   (1) On the sea
front is the Recife, the commercial quarter, near the port,
with   narrow streets and old houses ; (2) San Antonio,
beyond the two rivers, containing the government-house,
theatre, prison, churches, and railway station ; (3) Boa Vista,
the newest part, extending to Olinda, and full of pretty
houses and gardens.

The Recife and San Antonio quarters are spoiled for want
of some plan in building.   Every one has done just as he

liked. The streets are dirty; the houses, some high, some low, some white, some stained with dirt; and if you see a balcony, it is gloomy and grated like a jail. The litter from the beasts of burden and the refuse from the houses is all allowed to choke up the roads, which are paved as unevenly as they well could be.

For the first time in my life, I saw a butcher's shop full of meat on the first floor of a house; the lower part being the place of slaughter, apparently.

In Boa Vista the buildings are splendid; so also in Olinda, where stand the ruins of the Jesuit College, once a

Olinda (Pernambuco), with the Recife in the distance.

famous seat of learning. The story of the expulsion of the monks of early days is still related with bated breath by the faithful of these parts. How, without warning of any kind, they were seized and shipped wholesale like cattle to "*far* Bahia" (one day's journey by the Clyde), and landed there to shift for themselves. Well, poor fellows, they have not had to shift much, for they took such deep root, and throve so fast that, at the present time, they are represented by a cathedral and a matter of sixty-five churches!

Noon.—Having strayed from Mr. Dane and the others, and wishing to post some letters, I was puzzling to find the office, when a native, speaking very good English, came up, touched his hat, took me to the office, arranged for me about stamps, post-cards, etc., that I needed, and then, with a smile and another salute, went off without letting me even finish my thanks. Much as I have heard and seen to the discredit of the Brazilian, all admit he is a most hospitable being. My benefactor would, I am afraid, stand a long time in Cheapside looking for St. Martin's-le-Grand, before any Englishman would come to his aid.

On the front as you land, is a grove of Algarrobo trees,—planted only twelve years ago, and now forming a dense shade, beneath which, on iron seats around the trees, sit, lounge, or lie, men of all classes, from the sugar-king to the idle nigger. Two good restaurants face you as you land, the Tours and the Café de l'Europe, and, beside them, shops

"Fatima."

where curiosities of all sorts are to be had, from brooches to mummied humming-birds. Opposite these sat the fattest negress I have yet seen, with, as her stock-in-trade, a crate full of parrots of rainbow hues. In some of the back streets, boys and girls of nine and ten years revelled in absolute nakedness, and among them were such villainous faces that "no one would, I'm sure," said Mr. Dane, "be willing to take their naked word."

Trams, drawn by mules three abreast, run in all directions, the chief attraction being the Madeline Gardens. We went for two or three short trips across the rivers I have mentioned, towards Olinda, and so on.

Everywhere one heard them trading in lottery tickets.

Shops sold them wholesale, retail, and by auction, and men and boys buying them for eight hundred reis (1s. 8d.) hawked them through the streets at a milreis (2s.). As this was their sole living, it shows what traffic there must be in lotteries. One ragged old man, with a solitary parrot for sale, smoked a cigar with a golden band, and had grown the long right-hand thumb-nail that here is a mark of gentility, as are long nails generally in China.

The one thing no one need be told to notice here is *sugar*.

Bullock-cart, Pernambuco.

The place reeks with it in every form. You smell it everywhere, see it all round you, and presently you slip on some of it and sit down on a lot more. Niggers carry sugar in black bags on their heads, protected against it and the sun by three hats one on top of the other. Other niggers drive a sort of Alderney oxen, in springless carts laden with sugar, while the native Brazilian, mounted on the high Mexican saddle, rides a horse or mule with panniers full of sugar.

For an hour or so the smell sickens you, but after that you get acclimatised to what is perhaps best described as a "sick-room odour," and conquer your first impulse to return to the ship, if you had to swim there through the sharks.

It is a busy scene. Fat negresses, with baskets of sweets and fruits on their heads, waddle along barefooted and bare-breasted, sweltering in the sun. Merchants hurry

to and fro, perspiring in tall hats, black coats, and gloves, and carrying the slenderest of umbrellas, and the while skipping from stone to stone among the boulders in the roads, to escape the drain-puddles thick and black with sugar.

For all this, what with the palms that meet the eye on every open space, and the black faces around, one begins to realize the change from England to the tropics. One would do so more, perhaps, if one came straight to Pernambuco from Southampton,

The Piccadilly of Pernambuco.

but Lisbon and St. Vincent graduate the transition and lessen the contrast between the home scenery and this.

Wanting a memento, I bought a simple cigarette-holder which I saw, from a glance I took, had a photograph of a note in it. "A Brazilian note is just the very thing in a Pernambuco souvenir," said I to myself. Showing it to Mr. Dane afterwards, I was much disgusted to hear him read out slowly, as he peeped at the photograph, " Hundert Gulden." Oh, these enterprising Germans !

4 p.m.—Gun-fire from the Clyde announces the hoisting of the "blue-peter," the signal for sailing; so, bidding a hearty farewell to Mr. Dane, we go aboard.

5.10 p.m.—We have been delayed by the coffee cargo, but now the anchor is up and we are off to Bahia.

CHAPTER IV.

November 6th.—8 p.m. A little joke occurred this morning, which is the talk of the ship to-night.

There are two saloon passengers on board, fast friends and travelling together, who, admiring one and the same lady, have, I take it by tacit contract, arranged to share her society equally. One of them used to get his face very close to the lady's sometimes, but it is only fair to say that he wore glasses and was evidently very near-sighted.

Every day we had seen them mounting this enjoyable guard with military regularity, neither clashing with the other. To-day both were " off duty," and going ashore with us, the lady remaining on board. There was a heavy swell on, and the boat toppled rather wildly as she lay beside the gangway to receive us. Presently, just as the last of us got into her, and the word was passed to cast her off, up sprang one of the "partners"—frightened, as we all thought— flourishing his umbrella to catch the gangway-stay, glasses astride his nose, tumbling all over the place as if on hot bricks. Partly jump-ing, partly hauling, and

" The girl I left behind me !"

still more by the aid of the ever-present quarter-master, he scrambled back, and at length we saw him arrive, in a heap devoid of all human shape, in the surf at the foot of the ladder.

By this time we were some yards on our way, and commenting in loud choruses of " Oho ! " and groans, on what we thought his faint-heartedness, when we noticed that there was one man among us perfectly silent, who, for some reason, evidently took another view of the matter—his " partner." One by one we began to see the real explanation, and as we did so a roar of laughter rose high in the morning air from every throat. No, let me be exact; again there was one silent among us—his " partner."

His faithless rival's act was not, I believe, premeditated, but all the same it strongly reminds one of the fox who, tired of certain nuisances about his body (and having heard, it may be, that a drowning *man* will catch at a straw), took to the river with a straw held just above the water in his mouth. Then, as soon as all the " nuisances " had climbed to the straw for safety, he gently let it drift and swam back again to uninterrupted peace.

9 p.m.—The ship's coffee after dinner seemed very English, owing to my having had on shore some of the finest I have ever tasted out of Vienna. Others, and good judges too, go further, and say it is the best in the world. It has been an enjoyable, but rather tiring day, and I am turning-in at 9.30 p.m.

November 7th.—5 a.m. What a strange sensation it is to be waked at sea by cock-crow ! It surprises you, much as a bosun's whistle would if heard in your bedroom at home. It gives you a sort of amphibious feeling, and you need to wake quite up before you get the " hang of the thing," as Americans say. There must be many chanticleers on board, for I've heard three or four different calls—question and answer, a sort of *vivá voce* examination. This is the first I've heard of them. I fancy they are English birds, but have only just acquired their sea-legs—an expression not so strange as it sounds, for you can't expect a cock to crow if he can't stand. The crow consists, I believe, of one long syllable, followed by three short, and a final of any length according to taste; not by any means an easy thing to do before a critical world. I very much doubt whether Sims Reeves could give, say, "Sound an alarm" with due effect, tied up in a small crate with Edward Lloyd and twenty other vocalists, tossing about in the Bay of Biscay. He might sing " I-in, the-er, Ba-ay-O-of-Bis-Cay-O " after a fashion, for the line sounds as if it had been composed in a rocking-chair.

10 a.m.—At breakfast we heard of a death that had taken place on board at 5 a.m., the very time those cocks were crowing. The crow—the entire bird of that name I mean—is, as we all know, looked upon as a creature of ill-omen with its ominous croak, its life of rapine, and its deeds of blood. But, of the cock as a messenger of death, I have never read. Yet Pog says it scores just the same: "whether it's a carrion crow or a clarion crow, a crow's a crow." My opinion is that some distinction should be made, or, sooner or later, we shall each receive these premonitory warnings.

However that may be, the poor fellow who was dining with us all, last night, lies already in his rough ship-made coffin, covered with the Union Jack. He looked a hale, hearty man, but unfortunately that does not exempt from apoplexy, which was the assigned cause of his death. He will not be buried at sea, for this evening we reach Bahia.

Noon.—Bahia distant 77 miles. Lat. 12° 18′ S., long. 37° 39′ W. Run, 311 miles.

Worse news has reached me—worse, in that it affects us all. Small-pox has broken out on board; there are three cases already. This may simply ruin my trip, for at Buenos Aires they quarantine you for three weeks sometimes, and even more. Well, in that event I shall at least have the unique experience of going to Buenos Aires and back, without seeing it. We must hope for the best.

Talking with a resident in Monte Video, I learnt how some of the huge fortunes were made in the South American Republics. In order to encourage improvements in property, the government offers to lend owners of land as much as 50 per cent. of its value, as estimated by the government assessor. Here comes in the opportunity for fraud. The owner of property worth (let us say) £10,000 gets this assessor to value it at half-a-million. Upon the strength of this the Government advances £250,000, and when the two swindlers have divided the spoil, the owner transfers the property to a man of straw who, for a few pounds, agrees to stand the racket of legal proceedings to recover the sum obtained by fraud. A simple method this of making money, and one in which a small capital goes a long way; for, as shown by the case cited, a man can clear £115,000 on a single transaction, and then, wiping his hands of all further responsibility in the matter, bide his time and stand ready to repeat the plan as occasion serves.

3 p.m.—We have been coasting and in view of land all the way from Pernambuco. This is the region for catamarans: we have seen fully thirty since this morning, and exquisitely graceful things they look, sailing literally *through* the water.

Counting the revolutions of the propeller by the beats under my foot just now, I found they were sixty-two to the minute: this gives a speed of sixteen knots, or about eighteen-and-a-half miles per hour. At this rate we should reach Bahia before six o'clock. The weather is perfect, and the beauty of the sea, dressed in the bluest of blues, is greatly enhanced by the white caps the waves were wearing, thanks to a strong wind on the port-bow.

4.30 p.m.—We are abreast of the lighthouse on the Cape San Antonio, where we turn to enter Bahia by a passage seven miles wide. Beside this lighthouse, are visible the red boilers of an American vessel, the *Reliance*, which ran ashore last Christmas—another victim to that festive season. It is blowing a gale as we round the point, with the island of Itaparica on our left. The *Thames*, twin-sister to our *Clyde*, is lying in the bay; also an English man-of-war, the *Basilisk*, bound for Rio.

4.40 p.m.—We have anchored. Steam launches trimmed with numberless flags are alongside, full of welcoming friends. Also a heavy, tub-like steamer, named, I should think satirically, *Relampago* ("Lightning"). This bay is said to fascinate every one who has not seen Rio. Speaking for myself, I can say it nearly exhausted my small stock of complimentary phrases.

From the sea, the sight impressed me as much as Lisbon, with the added charm of the bay; and what a bay! There are so many beauties on all sides of it.

My *fauteuil* at the Panorama.

Large as it is—and it is one of the largest and safest bays in the world—one seems to see it all so well from shipboard, and with such comfort.

The rapidity with which the scenery is presented to you has a panoramic charm that never allows the eye to become weary. It flows on as a dream through the brain. Elsewhere the eye must seek its food ; here it is fed mechanically and without conscious effort.

The city occupies the northern slope of the bay, the shores of which are resplendent with tropical vegetation. In form the bay is a semi-oval, and on fully three-fourths of its shores the land, rising to great heights, is covered with houses of dazzling white, yellow, and blue, set off by clusters of stately palms, with here and there the towers of a church to break the line. At one point is one of these churches— I suppose it must be the Cathedral—with four or five spires, recalling Cologne.

The bay of All Saints, before us, stretches away to the south for thirty miles, backed by the deep blue hills, while around us the flags of all nations, fluttering from a hundred masts, lend still another charm to the scene.

The sea has been rapidly changing in colour from deep blue to emerald green. The air is wafted warm and scent-laden from the shores, redolent of pine-apple and orange. One's eyes are ravished by the wealth of tropical vegetation of all shades of green.

7 p.m.—While we were dining, a band came on board playing the Brazilian funeral march, and bore away to shore our dead passenger, who was a man of position here. But the usual compliment of half-masting the flag was dispensed with, to avoid alarm both here and ashore. Everything has to give way to considerations of quarantine, it seems. This is not perhaps surprising when one reflects how much depends on a vessel getting "pratique," *i.e.* a clean bill of health. As a rule it is in the doctor's hands. He meets

the port doctor who boards the ship, and on his tact at that meeting hangs the ship's fate.

Dr. Blandford always 'succeeds'. Irishmen seem gifted with an affability which takes with people all the world over. They are soft-voiced and soft-mannered, strong and yet with a pliant elasticity and bearing that masks their strength. No wonder, then, that, for this duty (other things, of course, being equal), the Company gives the preference to doctors hailing from our sister, the Emerald Isle.

A similar shrewdness, I think, marks their selection of their chief engineers, two-thirds of whom are long-headed, steady Scotchmen; while the captain is usually chosen from among the jolly tars of old England. For all these preferences it would be hard to give precise reasons, and indeed invidious, but every one will detect, I think, a certain fitness in the filling of the respective posts from the three sources at the Company's disposal.

We have just seen five emigrants, suffering from small-pox, taken off the ship to hospital; and now the latest news is that we have typhoid fever on board.

7 p.m.—We have come ashore, landing at the old town. It was worth coming, if only to see the *Clyde* ablaze from stem to stern with tier above tier of electric lights. She lay like a crystal palace which, from the almost insensible motion of our boat, seemed to float from us into the darkness, dimmer and dimmer, till all we could see was her dark outline in a sort of " milky way." We passed many catamarans, with three pretty lateen sails, flitting over the broad bay. One very nearly ran us down while we were sailing, and we had to row as well in order to clear her.

The charm of the town, when viewed from the *Clyde*, is on landing suddenly dispelled, for the streets are foul, and the

smells abominable. It is one of the most unhealthy places
in Brazil, and was in 1850 the nucleus of a yellow-fever
epidemic that spread like wildfire up and down the coast.

If one had time, it would pay to walk to Victoria, the
English quarter overlooking the entrance to the bay, where
—from the Jardim Botanico—is a matchless view, taking in
at a sweep city, bay, and ocean. Instead, we strolled through
the market, which is here rich in fruits. The black women,
too, who sell them, are worth seeing, being among the largest
specimens of the human race, male or female. They delight
in costumes of orange and red, wear large white turbans, and

earrings as much as three inches
in diameter, and sit at trays
spread with melons, pumpkins,
oranges, bananas, mangoes, and
great bunches of flowers gorgeous
in tint but feeble in perfume.

The "navel oranges," as they
are called, with a peculiar small
excrescence at one end, are
without a pip to swear by or at
—large, thick-skinned, and juicy.
A large trade is also done in
feather-flowers, which are better
and cheaper here than at Rio;
also in parrots, marmosets, and
monkeys. One little monkey
completely won my heart by his

" Yours affectionately."

gentleness. Taking my hand in both his and burying his
face in it, he stroked and caressed the back with both his
hands in the most endearing way. If I had been homeward-
bound I should have been tempted to bring him.

A few negroes with Cadeiras, or palanquins, still offer to carry you up the steep zigzag hills that lead from the old to the new town. If you go that way you will pass most of the grand churches, and the cathedral, constructed of marble brought from Europe, where officiates the Archbishop, who is Primate of Brazil. We preferred the more rapid lift, which raised us at once two hundred and thirty feet up from the old to the new town.

A weirdly curious thing is this elevator, lifted by chains as big as a ship's cable. But though it has been running

Elevator from the old to the new town, Bahia.

ten years without accident, no Englishman feels safe in it—human life is held so cheap in these countries.

Having paid your 100 reis (2½*d.*), you enter a gloomy chamber reeking with castor-oil, under which is an awful well for the chain. At the dismal clang of a bell, up you go in a creaking cage, the rattling chain playing a dirge in the semi-darkness. Presently you pass a grating through which you get a glimpse of the town below; another with a wider range; a third embracing views of the harbour and shipping; a fourth extending your field to the limits of the bay; and then you land on the terrace of the upper town, overlooking everything from a height four times that of a London house.

It is a fine sight by day; but at night, when the lights sparkle like fire-flies in the houses on the hill-sides, and on the shipping in the dark bay, the effect is magnificent. Away from the dirt and smells of the old town, one finds up here another city altogether—bright, clean, and filled with fine houses and buildings of some pretensions. The churches have tawdry exteriors, and are allowed to drop sadly out of repair, but within they are resplendent with jewels and decorations.

Thence we took a tram to the Hôtel Paris—here pronounced Pa-reece—where we secured quarters for the night. The negro carrying our bags, having no boots, was not permitted on the tram, and so had to walk. After dinner, to see the city quickly, we trammed again completely through and round it. The treatment of the mules drawing the trams was sickening; two men lashed them the entire way. At the slopes they were taken off and, with only a lad at the brake, we dashed down the incline at a fearful speed, caring for nothing at the cross-roads. We very nearly cut in pieces two negresses and their male escorts, who, according to custom, were walking behind the ladies. This rear-guard arrangement appears to be the fashion with all classes alike in the Brazils.

The scores of streets we passed all presented the same sight: niggers at every window in twos and threes. By the aid of the faint light in the back rooms, one could see their outline in the wretched, dark, dirty, scullery-like front apartment. Everywhere the black heads peeped from these gloomy windows in such absolute silence that it quite depressed one. Of clothes there didn't appear to be a suit among a dozen of them. The town is badly lighted, and a settled desolation appears to brood over the place.

Bahia nevertheless holds second rank in Brazil. It dates from 1549, when Thome da Sousa, a gallant Portuguese soldier, founded the city as "San Salvador," giving the magnificent bay the name of "Bahia de Todos-os-Santos." In 1763 the seat of government was removed to Rio, but Bahia still remained the ecclesiastical capital. The trade in

Campo Grande, Bahia.

all kinds of precious stones is very considerable, in diamonds especially, the prices going by leaps and bounds from £50 for a two-carat stone to £500 for one of six carats. The Estrella do Sul, or "Southern Star," in the Paris Exhibition of 1856, rivalled the Koh-i-nur, or "Mountain of Light," in our Exhibition of 1851. The ex-Emperor is said to have had one of 1680 carats—valued at five-and-a-half millions sterling—as a handy nest-egg in case of deposition.

The first foundations of Bahia may still be traced near

I

the present chapel of Ayuda, and in the old Jesuit church
may be seen the tomb of Father John Martin, superior of
the Jesuit order in Brazil, with the inscription "Non Anglus
sed Angelus."

Bahia's export trade includes indiarubber, rosewood,
cedar, vegetable-ivory, cloves, cinnamon, and coffee. Its
business in cigars is enormous, and my visit increased it by
a box which judges pronounced excellent. The forests are
rich in game, and the river banks swarm with reptiles.

Trees grow to a prodigious size. It is related somewhere
that a cedar tree, brought down by a flood, sufficed to build
a church, and there was enough left then to construct a
house.

In historical associations Bahia surpasses any other part
of Brazil. It was in front of this city that the Dutch
Admiral Adrian Patryd, rather than surrender to the
Spaniards, folded himself in the flag of his country, exclaiming "The ocean is the fittest grave for a Dutch Admiral,"
and leapt into the waters of the bay. The sequel is not
related, but I fear the worst, for the bay is deep, and Dutch
Admirals were as a rule fat and scant of breath. Moreover,
to be rolled up in a flag would sadly hamper the best
swimmer. No—I'm afraid we must give him up, especially
as neither Pog nor I have seen anything among the flotsam
or jetsam at all answering to his description.

The water looks very inviting this morning. I should
like to jump in myself; but mine would be an undress
rehearsal, and without the properties, consisting of one
Spanish fleet, one Dutch galleon, one Dutch Admiral's
uniform, and one Dutch flag.

November 8th.—9 a.m. The "blue-peter" is flying from
the *Clyde* as we come off from the shore.

10.58 a.m.—As we leave this lovely bay I am wondering in what way Rio will manage to eclipse it. It seems an impossible task; but all the world says she does, and what all the world says must, of course, be true.

CHAPTER V

November 8th.—Noon.   One would-be passenger has been left behind, luggage and all.   His boat reached the ship as

the gangway was being hauled up.   For a moment he stood in doubt what to do, then reseating himself, he lighted a cigar, pointed the boatman towards the shore with the match, and

Philosophy.

turned his back upon us.   There he goes smoking ashore, cool as a cucumber and stoically content.

Two or three of the "Ritchie Club," as the gatherers in his festive cabin are called, made up their minds to finish off Pog's ubiquitous myth, "the alleged murderer;" for he was to Pog like King Charles's head to Mr. Dick—there was no keeping him out of the conversation.   Accordingly, with finger on lip and many side-glances, they broke the news gently to him that the poor wretch had committed suicide, and his body had been sent ashore.

"There," said Pog, in a confidential whisper, "I *know* it; I *said* so, directly I heard of the death and that he was supposed to be a *Brazilian*. 'You may call him what you like,' I said, 'but I know who it is.'"   Then with some softness

he added, " I always said those brutes of detectives would
drive the poor fellow to self-slaughter. There's something
very detestable, sir, don't you think, about the calling of a
detective ? "

The weather is good, the sea fairly calm, and, thanks to
a few clouds and a capful of wind, the heat, always great as
you near Rio, is very bearable.

1 p.m.—I lunched off Bahia oranges, and bananas golden
as wheat and superb in flavour, and then went to see the
Doctor, who is laid up with bad sore throat. He looks very
ill, and has his throat enveloped in many thicknesses of
cotton wool. A Dr. Fallowes, bound for Buenos Aires, is
acting for him. The Captain is similarly affected, I hear.
Taken with the ugly rumours of typhoid and the actual
small-pox, these symptoms are not cheering.

7 p.m.—The Captain was not at dinner, and the Chief
Officer is in charge, I am told. I have been playing chess in
Mr. Ritchie's cabin, which has been my Club every night.
What luck to have such a friend on my first ocean voyage!
The Purser is another real good fellow, with a fund of
anecdote, and a vein of Irish humour that is truly refreshing.
So is the Second Officer—a kind-hearted, typical British
sailor.

Of the Chief Officer and the Doctor I have already
spoken more than once. All these were most kind. I was
as free of their cabins as of my own, and many a happy
hour and many a good laugh have I enjoyed with first one
and then another of them.

The trip is a grand trip, the ship a grand ship; but
something more was needed for my complete happiness, and
that I found in the companionship of these genuine good
fellows.

10 p.m.—It is deliciously cool on deck, and as it is 88°
in my cabin, I am going to sleep on a deck-bedstead.

November 9th.—Sunday, 5 a.m. They were washing the
decks, so I had to go below. The " Southern Cross " looked
a little more attractive, I thought, this morning. A thing
that it won't repay you to incur discomfort for, will sometimes please you when you see it at your ease, as I did the
" Cross " from my deck-bed. The false one rose at 3 a.m.,
and was followed by the " Crux " at 4 a.m.

11 a.m.—What with thirty-two children and three
kittens, one never need be dull. The deck in the morning
during this glorious weather is like a nursery, and strewed
with dolls and toys of all sorts. And what a nursery a ship
is, and how radiant the little ones look in the bright sun and
pure air ! It is a pretty, peaceful scene, yet its very happiness calls up other thoughts. One cannot glance from this
picture of unmixed enjoyment over the bulwarks to the deep
sea rolling beside, without sometimes feeling how small a
thing the ship is on that wide waste of waters. The giant
is slumbering now while the little ones play in safety by his
side. But he is a giant still. What if he should wake in
anger ! One could read these thoughts, or something like
them, in many a mother's face, while her voice was all
ripples of laughter and her hands were full of toys.

A cry of " Whale ! " has just sent the toys rolling, and
children and parents rushing to the ship's side. It turns
out to be something more—a fight between a sword-fish, a
whale, and a thresher-shark. They are only about a mile off,
and lashing the sea into foam in fine style. There is a
perfect cloud of it, fully fifty feet high, and we can see the
whale every now and then rearing his huge form out of the
water, and spouting spray in enormous fountains. A second

whale, much nearer, is blowing in the usual quiet way, evidently unmolested. The other sight is the interesting

one to us all, for it is a life-and-death battle. Not a triangular duel, each for himself, but two to one— the whale, as Pog says, " being in the minority."

His most deadly foe is the sword-fish, whose plan is to attack him with his thirty-six-inch sword from

His last gasp.

beneath, plunging it into him repeatedly, while the thresher, leaping into the air, falls upon the whale's back, and so helps to drive home the deadly weapon. I give this version as I heard it on board; but I know the confederacy of the whale's two opponents is denied. The ground for the denial, however—that the formation of the thresher's teeth precludes his *eating* the whale—seems to be weak. The sword-fish does not *eat* him either; he lives on small fish. Perhaps he is a true sportsman, and hunts and kills him as we do the fox, for the mere fun of the thing; and if so, I see no reason why the thresher should not join him in the same true British spirit of sport.

Noon.—Lat. 19° 10′ S., long. 30° 9′ W. Run, 373 miles.

There being no service to-day on account of the Captain's illness, I have been gathering from one source and another bits of general information about Brazil. In extent and power it ranks in the New World second only to the United States. In South America it has no rival in size, population, property, and order—the stability of the social relations being surpassed by the great Northern Republic alone, which has the lion's share in North, as Brazil has in South America.

Except Alaska, the Union has no arctic nor tropical state, but lies entirely within the temperate zone. It has, however, sharp contrasts of temperature—heat in Florida and cold in Missouri and the Great Lakes, while Brazil is almost entirely between the tropic of Capricorn and the Equator, a small portion only reaching southwards into the temperate zone. These conditions have greatly influenced both

On the Serra near Petropolis, Rio de Janeiro.

Republics, accounting for differences in social phenomena and natural and intellectual development.

Brazil occupies three-sevenths of South America, one-fifth of the entire continent, and one-fifteenth of the land-surface of the world. The rivers teem with fish, turtles, and alligators, and poisonous snakes innumerable swarm along their banks. While writing the last sentence, I shouted it to Pog, who was at an adjoining table. "If that's the case," said he, "I shan't trouble 'Rio the beautiful' much. The

presence of snakes would render Paradise itself a howling
desert to me. I should remember the snakes when every
other charm had faded from my mind." Then, breaking into
quotation, he went on, "You know what Moore says of
Eden—

> ' Long, long be my heart with such memories filled,
> Like the vase in which roses have once been distilled;
> You may break, you may shatter, the vase if you will,
> But the *trail of the serpent is over it* still.'"

"Thanks," I said, "I'll insert that quotation. It's very
neat, though a trifle diluted."

Brazil is the home of the parrot, the macaw, and the
humming-bird, and others unsurpassed in beauty by any
birds in the world. Its chief fruits are the pine-apple,
banana, orange, mango, and melon; and its production of
maize, wheat, rice, coffee, sugar, tobacco, and cotton is
immense. Half the coffee of the world is grown in the
Brazils.

The population is mainly composed of the descendants
of Portuguese, Negroes, and Germans. The true Brazilian
of to-day (he of Portuguese descent) is small, slight, and
sallow or dark. Though weaker and less thrifty, he retains
some of the shrewdness of his ancestors. In morals he is
below the Argentine; but he loves learning, and his children
respect their parents.

The rearing of negro children is a difficult process. In
spite of the mistress's great care, three-fourths die in the
weaning.

Among the negroes, legalized or consecrated marriages
are the exception. Africans object to being tied *for life*, it
seems, whether to wife or to master. Over a million of
slaves have bought their freedom and got it in "black and

white," and many more could do so if they did not drink their earnings instead.   Like the Malay, the negro is subject

to fits of murder-mania, when he will "run-a-muck" and kill anything in his way. Many masters fall thus by their slaves' hands; but not enough of them, by a long way, to balance the death-roll of the slaves killed by their masters.

The slaves have one peculiar method of revenge — they poison themselves *en masse* out

" Black and white."

of spite.   One master, much beloved by his slaves, saw them poisoning themselves by the dozen day by day, and tried

every means to stop it, but in vain. By the emancipation law of 1871 all slaves born thereafter were declared free; but in order to avoid the dangers that might arise from suddenly freeing an entire population, it was made a condition that they should serve their masters as apprentices for twenty-one years. Next year, therefore, all those born in 1871 will be absolutely free — themselves and their children.

3 p.m.—As I go on deck, another

Brazil, 1892.

whale is spouting leisurely, and I hear we have passed

through a perfect school of these merry monsters. The sea for miles round us is the colour of clay. At first we thought it was due to some volcanic action in the bed of the sea; next it was attributed to a sand-storm off the land. At last Mr. Graham, an engineer returning to Buenos Aires—a man of world-wide experience, and withal a charming companion —put us all right. It is caused, it seems, by the drifting of huge quantities of a weed, known as whales' food, which is commonly to be found in their neighbourhood—or shall we rather say *they* in *its* neighbourhood?—for I suppose they follow the food, and not *vice versâ*. Now I know what it is, I can distinctly smell the weed, which recalls the odour of Worthing beach.

A pretty little girl, who has been down with bronchitis all the way, was so alarmingly ill to-day—no doubt owing to the great increase of heat in the cabin—that the acting-doctor said she must there and then be moved into a more airy place. Knowing that a certain wealthy potentate on board had just the thing wanted, I asked him if the little sufferer might be moved to his spacious cabin for an hour or so. His reply was that his wife sometimes had a bad throat and would feel nervous. But, I urged, bronchitis is not infectious. "No, I know," he said, "but my wife would be nervous."

Strange how people differ. While we were talking, a kind-hearted lady was acting; and when I left the "potentate," it was to see the little girl breathing with much lessened effort in the cabin of this good Samaritan.

9 p.m.—All well, we shall anchor off world-famed Rio to-morrow afternoon. I can hardly realize it.

November 10th.—6 a.m. Opening the port, I found we were passing a prominent point of land, so I got up and had

my bath, which to my surprise felt quite chilly.   On inquiry
I learnt that the place takes its name from its comparative
coldness—Cabo Frio ("Cold Cape").   Here formerly stood
a lighthouse eight hundred feet high, and constantly hidden
in the clouds.   The sun has caught the clouds on a hill-
top, while its sides remain in darkness—a lovely sight.

7 a.m.—Have just seen my first albatross.   We are
coasting, and in sight of land, which presents a rather
monotonous line of yellow sand with an undulating back-

The " Sugar Loaf," Rio de Janeiro.

ground almost as regular.   Tiny islands here and there
nestling in the bays brighten the scene, and as " eight bells "
sounds, I notice the deck is full of people.   We are bounding
along over the bluest water I ever saw.   Every one is busy
with glasses, and the talk is on all sides of the glorious
weather and of " Rio the beautiful."

10 a.m.—The famous Sugar-Loaf Mountain, nine hundred
and ten feet high, is in sight, and all eyes are bent in that
direction, when suddenly we plunge into a shoal of dolphins,
twenty or thirty of which seem to leap up and dart at the

vessel. They cause quite a commotion in the water for a good five hundred yards round the ship. A whale-bird passing at the time seems to be watching them.

As we near Rio Harbour the first thing our glasses reveal to us is a vision of palms close to the water's edge, waving over the sea-swept rocks. Presently we reach the Sugar Loaf and glide between two islands—which barely lift clear of the sea their wealth of palm, cactus, and verdant shrubs—and find ourselves at the entrance of the bay, with on the right the fort of Santa Cruz, and on the left fort Saõ Juan and the Sugar Loaf.

Having entered, and looking to the left, there follow in succession:—Viuva Mount, with a battery on the terrace in front; the Ville Gaignon Fort; Ilha das Cobras; and Ilha Fiscale (or Custom-House Island). Meanwhile on our right we have passed:—Boa Viagem Fort on the mount and island of that name; Gravata Fort on the mainland; and the village of Saõ Domingos on the point in the district called Nitherohi.

Further in and lying over our port bows is Botofogo, studded with snow-white villas, which, standing in their verdant gardens, sparkle in the sunlight like diamonds in emerald settings. But what can one say of the bay that now opens before us, which has been the subject of poetic panegyric ever since its discovery?

Stretching inland from the sea for sixteen miles, with a varying width of from two to seven miles, it encloses an anchorage of fifty square miles, and has a coast-line of sixty miles round. Such a sheet of water would be beautiful anywhere; but framed as this is by the varied colouring and exquisitely graceful undulations of the surrounding mountains, it is the very gate of paradise. Nowhere else

surely is there at once a coast so bold, a cluster of mountains so picturesque, such a maze of inlets and outlets, and
such a burst of all-pervading vegetation. It is well said
that the traveller, who has rounded the world, returns to
Rio with as much delight as though it was his first tropical
experience, and never fails to find there some fresh charm.

10.50 a.m.—The Chief Officer has brought us in beautifully,
the Captain being still too ill for duty. We have anchored
in the bay close to the old Dutch Fort. To our left stands
the mountain Corcovado (literally " Hunch-back," and so

A glimpse of Petropolis.

called on account of its shape), that keeps sentry over the
city, towering aloft more than two thousand three hundred
feet. On one side is a sheer descent of seventeen hundred
feet, and on this side, at the summit, one can see the shelter
whence the finest view of Rio and the bay rewards those
who make the ascent. Tijuca, a still loftier mountain, over
three thousand feet high, is seen some twelve miles further
in, on the same side. Away over the indent of the bay lie
forest-clad hills, and overtopping these, thirty or forty miles
beyond and visible faintly only through the mists, rise the
fantastic pinnacles of the Organ Mountains (resembling a

colossal range of organs), rearing their crests seven or eight thousand feet above the level of the sea.

In the loveliest part of these mountains, and at an elevation of two thousand five hundred feet, bowered and shaded by trees of luxuriant foliage, is situated the flourishing town of Petropolis. Here is one of the palaces of the ex-Emperor, and around it in all directions are the palatial residences and gardens of the—I was going to say, ex-merchant princes of Rio. "Ex," in the sense that while still engaged in the city in the morning, they leave it in the early hours of the afternoon for this enchanting retreat.

The city, as seen from the ship, is little more than a chessboard, but the environs, Botofogo Bay, Larangerias, and the heights of Tijuca and Corcovado, are said to rival the loveliest spots in either hemisphere. Looking across the great expanse of water towards the Organ Mountains, one sees how the perspective narrowing of it must have led its founders to think it a *river*, and so to name it "Rio." "Janeiro" needs no explanation; it is simply Portuguese for January, the month in which this bay of matchless beauty was discovered. The aborigines wisely evaded such niceties of geographical definition, and simply called it *Nitherohi*, or "hidden water."

Noon.—A large party of us is going on shore in a splendid launch, which has just come for our friend Mr. Ringer, of whom I have spoken, Tijuca being our ultimate destination for the night. The sea is calm to-day, but it can be angry. Just outside the entrance lies an island formerly used as a prison, which during a gale was flooded so completely, that the prisoners were all drowned in their cells.

One lands at Rio in its most unsightly, malodorous, yet interesting quarter—the market-place: in the very middle of it, among noisy boatmen, yellow, brown, black, and extra-

double jet, and in the midst of oceans of fruit and seas of
filth.   Well worth noticing are the Africans here, magnificent specimens of men, splendidly developed and clas-
sically modelled in limb and muscle.   Passing through the
market and among marvellously clean negresses, whose dress
consists of simply an exquisitely white chemise and cap, one
comes suddenly on the main thoroughfare.

The Imperial Chapel, Rua Primeiro de Março.

The Rua Direita, or as it is now called officially, Rua
Primeiro de Março (1st of March), is the principal business
street, and wide and pleasant.   It runs from the gate of the
palace to the Convent of Saõ Bento, and contains the
Exchange, Post Office, Custom-House, the Imperial Chapel,
and many churches.

Rio, if she cannot equal Bahia in the number of her
churches, at least comes in a good second with a record of

fifty-two. They are all built in the "Jesuit" style, and are striking on account of their sites, size, and the barbaric magnificence of their decorations. Two especially call for mention—La Cadellaria, majestic with its lofty towers, and La Gloria, crowning a beautiful eminence in the bay.

The streets are mostly narrow and mean. Even the fashionable Rua do Ouvidor, running at right angles out of the Primeiro de Março, and lined on both sides with handsome shops, is a mere alley scarcely wider than our Holywell Street, Strand, W.C.

On the road to Tijuca the surrounding country is extremely romantic, and the vegetation luxuriant and graceful. Conspicuous everywhere are the palms and the silky green leaf-blades of the banana tree. Of the primeval forest that once covered these mountains but a small part remains, and that little has been preserved from wanton destruction by rigid

The small cascade, Tijuca.

legal enactment. But the famous Tijuca Falls, formed by a stream rising on the highest crest of the cliffs, flow on for ever unaffected by time or change.

From Tijuca one obtains an excellent view of the entrance of the bay, with the huge figure named the "Stone Man," formed by the grotesque hills collectively—the Gavia* giving

* A rugged mountain near the entrance to the harbour, in appearance totally unlike any of its conical neighbours.

the face in profile, and the Sugar Loaf doing duty as the feet. From these hills is chiefly derived the splendid supply of water that feeds the fountains in the streets and public squares of Rio, by means of the grand aqueduct which here crosses the valley, seven hundred and forty feet wide and ninety feet deep.

Some of our party drove the twelve miles, while others took the rail which lands you near the summit, whence by carriages or donkeys you make your way to the Hôtel Villa Moreau, better known as White's Hotel—English and very

Hôtel Villa Moreau, Tijuca.

comfortable—where you should book your bed (if you have not already secured it by telephone from Rio, which is the only safe way), and go out while dinner is preparing, and see the sun set.

Far away at your feet lies the city, and beyond it the vessels rest sleepily on the peaceful waves awaiting a flood of glory in the golden sunset. It is coming. Long tongues of flame sweep through the valley and are broken into rippling

streams of liquid colour across the bay, gilding here a mast
and there a spar : now brightening the gloomy recesses of
some far hillside—now crowning with a blood-red nimbus
its palm-covered summit.

At length he sheds his farewell glories and sinks behind
the hill, behind the waste of rolling waters, into the fairy
depths, where all around lie the myriad-tinted fleeces from
which are woven the ribbon of the rainbow. In these
parts there is no twilight, and as the sun sinks, therefore,
Rio breaks into illumination, and the sparkling lights, which
appear more numerous than in England because nearer
together in a given space, render night beautiful indeed.

November 11*th.*—10 a.m. It is 111° in the shade, and not
the day to attempt Corcovado, whose head, moreover, is
wreathed in clouds. I must reserve that treat for my return
journey. So we make for the city *en route* for the Botanical
Gardens at Botofogo. One is told to drive out there to see
the beauties of Rio; but really, go where you will—clear of
the city—the whole road inland or along the coast is one
unbroken garden.

The streets do not impress one favourably. They are so
narrow, indeed, that it is with difficulty
one keeps the pavement. The main street,
Rua Direita, is the only exception: its
breadth is most ample. Here, on the extra
space, all the shoeblacks and newspaper-
sellers do congregate, driving, I'm told, a
very paying business; for Rio people are
notoriously free—too free, indeed, in their
payments for trifles. Boot-cleaning, for in-

Grin and bear it.

stance, costs you a hundred reis (2½*d.*). Laden negroes crowd
up and down the narrow avenues, always on the trot and in

full song, mostly grinning from ear to ear as though determined
to display every one of the dazzling white teeth they possess.

These narrow passages must be very bad in times of
epidemics, which are not infrequent here. Yellow fever has
its periods of revival, in spite of all the city-improvement
schemes devised or in progress. It is said to find most of its
victims among the ill-fed Italians. Next come the Germans,
then the French, and lastly the English, whose " good food
and good brandy " are said to save them. Perhaps the good
food, in *spite* of the brandy ; I don't know. Bad as are the
streets, one meets little oases every now and then in most
unlikely places, affording the grateful shade of the palm and
the banana. And as one approaches the suburbs, flowers
superbly rich in colour toss their profuse branches over the
paths. These suburbs are indeed natural gardens crowded
with beautiful examples of tropical flora in unmatched
luxuriance. As one makes one's way through Botofogo, one
is struck with the magnificence of the houses and gardens
close down by the shore. This is the choice end of Rio.
From their windows the residents look out upon one of the
most picturesque little bays imaginable—a bay within *the* bay.

Further along, one gets a glimpse of the aqueduct-arches
peeping out from among a wealth of palm trees, and soon
after come in sight some palms of immense height, upon
which most people bestow so much praise that little is
left for *the* famous " Avenue of Palms " just round the
corner not five minutes further. In the nature of things
the one detracts from the other. It has much the anti-
climax effect that would result from a man eight feet high
asking you, at a show, to step inside and see a giant eight
feet two inches. So in this case, I found the snack spoil my
appetite for the banquet.

The situation of the gardens is a grand one. I should think unique. Lying in a recess of the mountains at the foot of Corcovado, which soars majestically above it into the clouds, it is screened in all directions from the winds which are at times boisterous at Rio. It is in all respects the most tropical of positions, and an ideal one for a garden.

But here, as everywhere in these torrid regions, what one misses is the presence of human beings to enliven the scenery. The natives never seem to use the lovely things. The well-dressed classes, some of whom in England would grace a beautiful promenade like this, and even the working classes, who lend life and movement to our gardens at Kew, are conspicuously absent here. In a country where everything will grow anywhere, none will go an hour's journey like this to see a mere collection of the common objects of the street.

Who would go from Oxford Street to the Oval to see a thousand policemen gathered and arranged in various taking attitudes? Pug, to whom I had addressed this, as I thought, unanswerable bit of argument by "reductio ad, etc.," promptly replied, "The cooks!"—an interruption to my train of reasoning which now, as then, I pass over in silence.

But indifference is not the only or most potent cause of their absenteeism. They have a mortal dread of the sun, and no wonder, when yellow fever is always busy among them, and few years pass without thousands being carried off by this fatal disease.

The only places to see the ladies of Rio are under their verandahs by day, and in their carriages in the cool of evening. The botanical gardens were absolutely without one human being besides our own party, and to me they looked dead-alive and spiritless. The Avenue of Palms,

straight as masts, and fully two hundred feet high, looked
very symmetrical, and formed such a perfect line, that
standing twenty yards behind the end one, it hid the entire
row of seventy odd.*   But the tufts on their summits were
thin and gave no shade, and did not meet even so as to form
a canopy.   No; I was not impressed.   That snack outside
spoilt me, I know.   Still, these stems are taller than the

Avenue of Palms, Botanical Gardens, Rio de Janeiro.

others, so "Palmam qui meruit ferat," if he *will*.   But these
bear very little palm.

The other trees and shrubs were not remarkable; one had
seen them all at Kew, where, of course, they are curious.   A
crocodile is a curiosity in the "Zoo," but not, I dare swear,
on the banks of the Amazon.   There was a huge bamboo

* The exact number in the two rows is one hundred and fifty-three, I find,
which is odd in every sense for a double row.   Necessitating an odd half-tree
on each side, as Pog would say.—C. C. A.

jungle, the stems reaching a height of some twenty feet; and a cascade with five or six falls tumbles down the hillside, but the small body of water makes it utterly tame. The butterflies surprised me most. They were as big as sparrows, and with the wings extended measured as much as nine or ten inches from tip to tip. A green lizard, a good eighteen inches long, with a head fully six inches thick, looking and moving like a small alligator, crept out of the jungle, and at a touch of my stick plunged back again with an angry flourish of his armoured and aggressive-looking tail. Pog and I took this flourish as a hint to go, and, being hungry, we obeyed it.

On leaving the gardens we made once more for the city, where, at the "Maison Moderne," we dined and tasted, among many other things, a dish of mixed snails and oysters, which I tried hard to enjoy, but in vain. While at dinner, what I took to be a mouse ran under my chair, and towards a hole in the wall. On stopping it with my foot, I found it was a huge cockroach, three inches long, and an inch wide. All things grow apace here.

The drainage of Rio is simply a scandal to a civilized people. The refuse of the market, which is supposed to be taken in barges to a neighbouring island and there burnt, is, as I saw myself, carried out about a mile from shore and heaved into the sea. Not knowing this yesterday, I took my usual bath, and the smell was so offensive that I had to use fresh hot water and soap and brush freely before I could rid myself of the pungent and filthy odour.

No one sleeps in Rio itself if he can in any way avoid it, and rather than do so I am returning to the ship. The heat is intense, though it is only Spring here.

8.30 p.m.—I have just reached the *Clyde* and am jotting

down some verses that have been burdening my soul all
day.   Here they are—

FROM TIJUCA PEAK.

One morn in foggy Albion's Isle,
I woke up with a sickly smile,
    From out a troubled dream.
Oh, would that—leaving fogs behind—
'Twere mine, said I, to sail and find
    (Or better still to steam)
The lands where milk and honey flow:
It must be like a fall of snow
    Composed of clotted cream.

Not that the clotted cream seemed good—
I could not touch the simplest food,
    The sight would turn me sick.
My eyes were weary, nerves unstrung,
A nutmeg-grater was my tongue,
    My pulse a feeble tick.
With care oppressed, of hope bereft,
I really had not even left
    One solitary kick.

Thus would I toss about all day
From side to side, then faint away,
    And could not lie, sit, stand.
The doctors bade me, for health's sake,
A voyage of discovery make,
    To some "untrodden strand."
And, as the Strand in W.C.
Is not, well, quite unknown to me,
    I other regions scanned.

They could not mean the Emerald Isle,
For that's been trod a longish while,
    By poor down-trodden Pat.
Nor yet, I think, far Afric's strand,
Where fountains roll down golden sand:
    For all the world knows that.
No, nor our good old Plymouth strand,
Where bold Armada's fate was planned.
    What *were* they driving at?

The more I thought, the more I dreamed,
The clearer to my mind it seemed
    Things pointed to the West.

And as I further threshed it out,
Beyond all possible shadow of doubt,
    Brazil " panned out " the best.
Sou'-west, said I, I'll steer my way,
And try, as pioneer, to lay
    This spirit of unrest.

Discovery is the cure for me,
The doctors say : that means the sea;
    So I must find a ship.
Thus, to the Royal Mail I hied,
And boldly booked aboard the *Clyde*,
    To take an eight-weeks' trip :
And, in due course, I reached a place
Whence, climbing up a mountain's face,
    I perched upon the tip.

And there below lay all I sought :
The fairyland my dreams had wrought.
    Here was a slice of luck !
Not all in vain discoverers roam,
Who bring such conquering colours home,
    Out-streaming from the truck !
Rio Janeiro's name and mine
Shall linked in history's pages shine.
    Hurrah ! for British pluck !

Perhaps you think this far too strong :
Read on and I will prove you wrong,
    If you'll attention pay.
Permit me, sir, by argument,
To try and put you on the scent
    Of what I want to say.
If Livingstone had had no name,
When enterprising Stanley came,
    Would he have found *him* —pray ?

America, I've heard them say,
Was by Columbus found one day,
    But that I rather doubt :
He *with a name*, the place *with none*,
I think the odds are ten to one,
    'Twas t'other way about.
All the world over 'tis the same ;
Until a place has got a name,
    How can you find it out ?

Wherefore, I think, 'tis fair to say—
And let the past say what it may—
    That I;—(volente deo),
Whatever others may have done,
That I;—(perhaps not I alone,
    Yet ipsius facto meo),
While others may have found the *Bay*
Without a name, that I can say,
    I have discovered " Rio."

To me it seems extremely clear,
That those who first came spying here,
    Could not know what to seek.
Here come some toilers up the slope,
I'll cheer them with a little hope,
    As they approach the peak.
" Rio Janeiro! friends," I cry,
To which they smilingly reply,
    " Thanks, we've been here a week."

    *   *   *   *   *

'Tis ever thus the door is shut !
I'll just make one more effort, but—
    It must be done by stealth.
I'll fly to golden Argentine,
And to the Plate of silver sheen,
    And find (electro) wealth !
    *   *   *   *   *
Ah, no ! I'll leave all that to you :
There's but one thing for me to do,
    That is, *discover health.*

" How shall I set about the task ? "
Ah, how indeed! myself I ask :
    I've only got her name.
I knew her once, and knew her well,
And how I lost her cannot tell :
    She went just as she came.
But when I find her you shall know,
How, when, and where you ought to go,
    If you would do the same.

CHAPTER VI

November 12th.—10.20 a.m. The anchor is up, and we are leaving Rio and threading our way through the groups of tiny bright green islands that dot the channel in all directions, under the shadow of Corcovado towering superbly over all the minor mountains. Presently we pass the Sugar Loaf and round the point, again meeting the welcome breeze we had as we entered. This time the *Clyde* faces it, and cutting through it makes for the open sea.

The emigrants went ashore at Rio, and so did a large number of passengers. The ship seems quite deserted, and the dining-saloon at lunch looked very bare. At dinner we shall compress ourselves into a smaller space, and leave some tables vacant. We look a very unsociable set at present, *three, two,* and even *one* only at some tables.

Noon.—Although we must be thirty miles away, the smell I got last night of the market, an utterly indescribable stench, still lingers with me. It is almost painful to think of this Eden lying in a bay so fair and yet so utterly polluted. Would it not be possible to drain the city by cutting a channel from the foot of Corcovado through the lagoon that lies to the left of the Botofogo road?

3 p.m.—The Captain has just made his reappearance, with his throat in layers of cotton-wool like the Doctor, who is

still invalided. It is only inflammation of the tonsils, but the depression it causes, which is a well-recognized feature of the disease, is great. Both of them look wretchedly ill.

4.30 p.m.—We have just met the *Cleopatra* (Captain Musgrave) from Monte Video—an English man-of-war, on her way to Rio, where she is to meet the *Basilisk*, from Bahia. They are sent by our Government to salute the flag of the Republic on the 16th inst., the first anniversary of its birthday, and so to recognize the change of government.

6 p.m.—As the dinner-bell rings, the sky becomes suddenly overcast, and a native of these parts, with whom I am talking, predicts bad weather. These appearances are well-known indications of the cyclone known as the "Pampero." Heavy rain is falling, another ominous sign, as we go below. I may have the luck to encounter some real Monte Videan experiences.

8 p.m.—The weather-threats continue, and Mr. Graham

The cyclone.

most opportunely relates one of his experiences of a cyclone in the Japan seas, in a brig of but eight hundred tons. They lost their rudder and the greater portion of their deck, and three out of a crew of six were disabled by a wave that hurled them the length of the ship. They were at first reported as washed overboard, but were afterwards found in the stern-sheets badly injured. During the four days the gale lasted all fires were out, and passengers and crew, living on biscuits,

worked in relays night and day, bailing the ship, whose boats
went under and filled at every lurch. The captain had
twenty-three hours' duty at one spell, lashed to the bridge,
and had at the same time to deal with a mutinous mate who
refused to set a sail the captain ordered, insisting on
running under bare poles. In twenty-four hours the ship
drifted seventy-two miles.

Midnight.—All signs of a Pampero have passed away.
The sky is clear, but it is blowing half-a-gale, and our small
cargo of oranges has broken from its boxes and lies strewed
over the hold.

1 a.m.—The ship is rolling heavily, and smashes and
crashes are frequent. I remain on deck on the chance of
seeing a bit of weather. The "Southern Cross" lies just
above the horizon, over the port bow, inverted, or rather the
diamond has risen from the oblique to a little above the
horizontal.

November 13*th.*—After breakfast the Yankee, who had I
suppose begun to get liverish, and wanted to be at his journey's
end, addressing us generally said, "I should like to know
what amount of coal is saved by laying this 'bumboat' to
every night at 10 p.m. Well, putting her at half-speed, anyhow. If they'd only kept her at full steam last night, she
wouldn't have had time to go jumping and fooling around so
much." Others have made a similar mistake. The throbbing
noise that ceases so suddenly at 10 p.m. is caused by the
refrigerator, which is stopped between 10 p.m. and 6 a.m.,
not to disturb the night's rest.

This Yankee's rattling style of comment on the ship,
reminded me of another American, who left us at Rio, whose
way of expressing himself was similarly free and florid. His
great delight was to get hold of the Chief Engineer, who is a

passionate admirer of the big ship, and to draw comparisons
between the Royal Mail and the New Zealand Companies, of
course in favour of the latter.   On such occasions he would
allude to the *Clyde* as "this nine-knot coal-barge."   "As to
enterprise, it is a thing unknown on the Mail line.   Why,
the N. Z." (as he called the other company) "would secure
a thousand tons of cargo while the Mail was getting fifty
tons."   One night, in Mr. Ritchie's cabin, this American was
in a particularly unscrupulous humour, and seemed determined to spare no local colour to illustrate his reasons for
preferring the "N. Z." to the "R. M."—not at all with a
view to convincing us or because he believed what he said
himself, but simply to "rile" friend Ritchie.

"Well, I'll just give you an instance of what I'm driving
at," he began.   "A smart young captain of one of the N. Z.
steamers I was on, while we were lying off Pernambuco
waiting for boats to take our cargo inside the Recife, got
disgusted at the crawling style of those parts.   At last, after
waiting twenty minutes, he made up his mind to leap the
reef.   Well, sir, he just sent his engineer below, mounted the
bridge, waited till a wave of more than ordinary height was
fifty yards astern, and then signalling 'full steam ahead'
he rode his ship on the top of that wave, danced her over the
reef, and so took his cargo to market."   "And what height
was that wave?" asked our patient Chief Engineer with well-
assumed simplicity.   "Well," said the unblushing humbug,
closing his eyes as if to recall the exact figures, "I remember
the height was much discussed at the time, but no one fixed
her crest at less than a hundred and seventy feet from our
taffrail.   One put it as high as a hundred and eighty feet,
but that I think," said the candid narrator, "*a shade too
generous;*" adding with delicious coolness as he relit and

puffed at his cigar, "*There's no good in exaggeration.*" In
which sentiment, considering the amusement this man's
yarns afforded us, I am not sure that I quite acquiesce.

11 a.m.—At Rio, the whole of this spacious cabin, nine
feet by seven feet, became mine. It is quite a little territory. And now that I can keep the port open as I please, it
is never too hot, and I fairly revel in it, reading or writing
here in preference to in the saloons.

It is a lovely day, the heat far more bearable, and the
breeze grand. In the night, indeed, the draught so blew
my sheet about that I had to close the port, and partly
close the door. The ship is light, too, and rolls much; my
boxes rambled all over the cabin in the night.

Noon.—Lat. 27° 48' S., long. 46° 51' W. Run, 343 miles.

12.40 p.m.—One of the ship's kittens has been causing
roars of laughter among the children. She was toying gently
with the leg of a deck-chair, when a huge wave so tilted the
ship that it caused the chair to (seemingly) rush at her in
a most threatening way. Though scared and retreating,
she humped up her back, puffed out her tail, and was trying
to sidle out of the conflict, when in doing so she backed
into a second chair. Mistaking this for a second foe, she
spat a double broadside of oaths, by which she hoped to rake
both their decks, and taking a flying lopsided leap in the
air, finally alighted on the top of her first assailant. The
next moment (how soon one becomes calm amid life's
heaviest shocks), she was busy catching a butterfly or something under her left arm.

2 p.m.—At lunch it occurred to me that this was my birthday—six thousand miles from home! As I always like to
know where I am on important occasions, I put the question
to the Chief Engineer. "A little below Santos," he said,

" and as nearly as possible off Rio Grande do Sul (the grand river of the South), in lat. 28° S., long. 47' W." Multiplying these figures by seventy (approximately the miles in a degree) one gets about five thousand three hundred as the distance from Greenwich as the crow flies (or would fly if you could convert him into an aquatic bird). The difference of seven hundred miles represents windings and digressions to avoid shoals, collisions, etc., I presume.

8 p.m.—At dinner, after the sparkling wine, in celebration of my advent into this world of care, had produced the usual toasts and speeches, I heard a funny story illustrating the Doctor's powers of mimicry. One night when Mr. Ritchie was reading in his cabin

deeply absorbed, with his head between his hands, the Doctor passed, imitating the Captain's voice and way of addressing him : — " Ah, Ritchie, ah!" Again and again he passed, seven or eight times, on each occasion

"Ah, Ritchie, ah!"

giving the same disturbing call. At last friend Ritchie could bear the thing no longer, and the next time the interruption came, without moving from his. book, he growled out beneath his teeth, "Gi' out! Shove your head in your mouth." Alas! This time *it was the Captain*. Tableau!

November 14*th.*—It has been getting cooler and cooler. To-day it is cold, and I have had to change to warmer clothes. The temperature is but 52°. There is quite a little gale on from the south-west. Only two ladies showed up at breakfast, and these both left early. The ship is pitching continuously and violently for the first time. She was greatly lightened by the cargo we left at Rio, and disproportionately, for we are drawing twenty-four feet aft, and but sixteen feet forward. One of the Brazilians left a bottle in my cabin purporting to contain a French cure for sea-sickness. It has acted like a charm on one lady who was wofully bad.

Despite the weather, they are arranging a concert to-night on a grand scale in aid of a charity, but I don't see how the performers are to rehearse while they are all lying down in their cabins, and the piano is up in the saloon.

11 a.m.—My *vis-à-vis*, Mr. Courtney, has just given me, from his own experience, a good description of a Pampero, a storm very common in the Argentine Campos, and indeed all over the Plate district. It takes its name from the Pampas over which, after gathering in the Andes to the south-west, it sweeps with terrific fury, venting itself on the countries bordering on the Plate and the shipping in that mighty river, and carrying, according to its strength, mayhap a favouring breeze or swift destruction to vessels far out on the ocean we are now toiling over.

The first warning of the Pampero is the drifting of the white electrical clouds from the north to their southern *rendezvous*, their volume increasing all day till about 4 p.m., when, looking southward, you will see them piled up range above range like the very Andes themselves, and massed as it were in battle-array awaiting only the word to charge. No, not the word; their signal is more solemn than word, bugle-call, or wild war-cry. It is a dead calm—the air stagnant, and laden with a heat as of molten lead—the mere act of breathing a labour and a toil. The skin is parched, the body bowed, and life itself a heavy load to

L

bear. The stillness is complete, intense; every living sound is hushed, even the song of the myriads of insects in the baked grass. It is an awful silence, steeping the spirit of man in dread forebodings.

But look, now at last there is a movement in the southern sky; all is ready for the grand cannonade. The foremost range of cloud-mountains, advancing from end to end of the horizon in majestic convolutions, gently stirs the air, which anon ripples into a grateful breeze, the herald of the coming storm. On and on, faster and faster, roll the mighty masses, while stronger and ever stronger grows the breeze till it becomes a gale.

The Pampas-grass is bending level with the earth. The sky totters under its stupendous burden, looming black and lurid in the fast-fading daylight, only a glimmer of which is still unintercepted by the on-rushing avalanche of cloud. It is a moment of supreme grandeur. Every living thing cowers earthward and seeks the nearest shelter—in the grass, behind the trees; the sheep to leeward of some stump or other, the rider beneath his horse—or, should there be time, the horse lies prone on the grass, his master beneath the saddle hastily ungirthed.

And now, close your eyes and ears, for all the powers of heaven and earth are giving way and rushing in the wild frenzy of their new-found freedom. The heavens seem suddenly to fall between the sun and earth. The loss of light is sudden and awful, and almost complete darkness follows at once from the myriads of birds driven before the on-rushing gale. The thunder is crashing, roaring, bursting, and multiplied in echoes ten-thousandfold. The rain-torrent descends in a cataract illimitable. The hail (the stones each a handful in size) brings death to the unsheltered cattle, and even tears a pathway through houses roofed with zinc.

The tempest-driven gossamers, each with its freight of tiny insect life, torn everywhere from their hold upon the trees and shrubs, or caught in their airy wanderings across the Pampas, are swept and gathered in ever-increasing clouds, filling the hurricane leagues-deep with creatures swarming in their silken cocoons, till the blast is laden with their glutinous and gauzy nests. A hundred miles away at sea the rigging of many a ship will be sparkling with these web-like nests, borne, it may be, on a gentle-tempered zephyr which left the Cordilleras a wild and raging Pampero.

Caught once in a cyclone of this kind out in camp, Mr. Courtney and one of his men had a narrow escape, for in the small space of twenty yards that separated their hiding-places, the lightning, flashing like a thousand balls of fire, consumed every blade of grass and every living creature. They were terror-stricken, and each thought the other dead till he found breath to answer to his name.

Thinking this bit of description rather " good copy," I read it over to Pog just to see him writhe. Bless you, his withers were unwrung; the only remark he made was, that " *timid people ought not to go out in such weather without umbrellas.*" The laugh with which I received this sagacious comment offended him, I suppose; for, shifting his ground, he tried his hand at more dissective criticism. And here I must confess he scored better. Repeating my concluding words : " each thought the other dead till he found breath to answer to his name," he fixed his eyes on me and said, " Now, sir, if each man answered to his name, who was it called it ? " " The other fellow, of course," said I promptly. ' Then, sir," retorted Pog triumphantly, with a judicial shove of two books near him to indicate the two men, "if *this* fellow heard the *other* calling his name, how came he to think the other dead?"

Thus cornered, my only chance lay in the tactics of the cuttle-fish, which baffles its pursuer by enveloping itself in an inky fog. "Sir," said I, touching each book in turn, "you appear to have overlooked the fact that *this fellow was the other fellow.*" "What!" screeched Pog, visibly swelling with excitement. "Calm yourself, my dear sir," said I, "while I prove it to you. There were two fellows, were there not?" Here I placed Pog's two books just as he had done. [" Well, sir!"] "That's one fellow over there." [" Well, sir!"] "Then *this* fellow," said I, with a flourish of the nearest book, "must be the *other* fellow!"

He uttered not a word, and I left him with his glassy eye peering into space. Thus did this fine old-crusted and sempiternal joke, wherewith Noah may have beguiled the tedium of his Arkic voyage, survive to beguile the modern Pog.

"CAPTAIN CUTTLE."

Once a shark, of the genus called Pog,
Had a cuttle-fish cornered, for prog,
When, behold from a chink,
The fish squirted some ink,
And then scooted away in the fog.

Noon.—Lat. 32° 42′ S., long. 51° 7′ W.　Run, 368 miles.

3 p.m.—A passenger who joined us at Rio tells me not to fail, on my return, to pause at Santos, and run up to Saō Paolo—the Paris of the Brazils. It has, he says, a glorious climate, and is Alpine both in air and situation.

8 p.m.—The ship is performing a sort of perpetual horn-

pipe, like a cork on the top of a fountain; but as the announce-
ment of the concert had not been withdrawn, all who could
do so walked or crawled to the music saloon. The audience
represented all shades of opinion on maritime locomotion,
from the man who could stand with the aid of a taffrail,
to him who could only lie down by holding on to the floor ;
from the lady who, determining to be present, had stretched
herself in the saloon early in the day, to the poor sufferer
who, more dead than alive, contrived to stand by getting a
sailor to lash her to a pillar.

To this grotesque gathering presently came the manager
of the concert. I say " came," but that word hardly conveys
a true idea of the manner of his arrival. Paralytics I know,
and drunkards I know (by sight), but this man's entrance—
he was perfectly sober—can only be described as a strong
mixture of the two. All day long had the poor man, paper
and pencil in hand, been cruising about this floating earthquake, interviewing invalids (himself little removed from
one) for particulars of the music, songs, etc., for the concert.

One minute you'd catch sight of him, arm round a stay,
face to face with another man holding on to the bulwarks,
and trying to make a note on the paper, which would
suddenly jump up and poke the pencil in his eye. The
next time he would be grappling with a saloon chair, while
conversing with an invalid through the half-open cabin door,
which would dash at his features and fell him to the floor.
A little later, you would see him and a possible performer
he was overhauling on the deck, brought together in such
a way as to make them ever after, one would expect, bosom
enemies.

Well, this concert-agent-in-advance having by a series
of athletic exercises reached the piano, his remains thus

addressed the audience :—"Ladies and gentlemen" (sits on the
music-stool), " I regret to inform you that circumstances over
which " (head strikes the piano) " she has no control, deprive
us of the pleasure of hearing Miss ——'s song. The Doctor
tells me also that, Miss —— and her father having this
morning fallen down the companion-ladder (in the order
mentioned), the young lady has felt rather below par and
must be excused." (Clutches at music on the piano.) " Miss
——, who was to have sung ' Lay me in my little bed,'
finds she has now no excuse for the song, as she has not yet
got up. Mr. —— is present, and prepared to play the violin
if any gentleman will kindly hold it for him, as he requires
one hand to steady himself. Miss ——, who was to have
played a harp solo, has had an accident with the instrument ;
something wrong with the ' C ' led her to run over the
strings, and she unhappily fell through them." (Grabs at a
friend's hair.) " The gentlemen down for recitations are all
in attendance, but the noise caused by the wind renders
reciting difficult, so the Captain has lent his speaking-
trumpet, by the aid of which we hope to be able to hear
them." (Does an involuntary hornpipe.) He then produced
the trumpet, at sight of which, while weak women fainted
and strong men shed tears, an impetuous scramble was made
on all sides for the doors. Here there stood two men with
plates, and pointing to them the manager said, as he tried to
wrestle with the music-stool, " *The collection will now be
made !* "

And so ended the charity concert, which I hear was
pecuniarily a big success. As to the enjoyment, I never in
my life witnessed more perfect unanimity. I saw several
people on the other side of the saloon so overcome with
emotion that they rushed over to and embraced those on

our side as if death alone would part them. There is nothing like a *movement* of this kind to bring people together.

November 15th.—5.30 a.m. "Munty, Viddy," as our ex-naval Quarter-master calls it, is but five hours ahead. On the starboard side land is quite close: it is the Ilha dos Lobos, "The Island of Seals," near Moldonado. The sea, always green as one approaches the land, is here a brilliant emerald. It is a dangerous bit of navigation. Hereabouts is a shoal, known as the "English-bank," with but two fathoms of water over it, and yet there is no lighthouse. There *was* formerly,

but it was shifted to the main-land, because the owner of the seal-fisheries, where they captured from twelve thousand to fifteen thousand annually, complained that the light frightened away the seals. For the ship's course to be good, the land-light has now to dip behind the island, which lies low, and—as the obscuration

" Light astern ! "

is but momentary—very careful watching is needed. The *Clyde* has the island on her right, but if she had it on her left, and she were to try to pass between it and the mainland, she would be lost.

The cold is intense. In the night, besides my blankets, I had heaped upon the bed my railway-rug and Inverness. This morning I have my thickest clothes, mackintosh, and winter gloves all on, and still am not warm. Scarcely any one took his tub, I find. Mine was only made bearable by adding a lot of hot water.

9. a.m.—We are off the Ilha dos Flores, "The Island of Flowers" (as they euphemistically call the wretched quaran-

tine station here), and within sight of Monte Video. This roadstead is utterly unprotected, and one of the most dangerous in the world. A proper port would long ago have brought a stream of commerce, that would by this time have made of this beautiful city a second Singapore.

10 a.m.—We are abreast of the city, whose long straight streets rising from the sea, cut the buildings into symmetrical blocks. Standing on a promontory, open to the bay on one side and to the broad Atlantic on the other, its streets are constantly cooled by the fresh sea-breezes that sweep them from end to end. On the front is the Cerro, or mount, that gave the city its name; it is five hundred and five feet high, and visible twelve miles out at sea. On the summit is a lighthouse whose revolving light can be seen more than double that distance. It occupies the middle of an old Spanish fort, which has frequently been used as a prison for political offenders. The sides of the hills are very steep, and render the place so difficult of access that during the nine years' war, from 1842 to 1851, it was never once taken.

The bay, which is only about a mile wide at the entrance, expands inwards into the form of a horseshoe, with anchorage for five hundred vessels, but the draught rarely exceeds fifteen feet.

10.30 a.m.—We are at anchor, and have hoisted the yellow flag, as all vessels are required to do until they have obtained "pratique." The quarantine doctors have visited us and, hearing of the death on board, have gone ashore for instructions. This has an ugly look. Here and at Buenos Aires these almighty doctors have the character of being very exacting, and at times capricious. On one occasion, an in-coming vessel was visited by the inspecting doctor while the Captain was dressing, who, not to delay his visitor, ran out to meet him as he was, coat in hand. Before he could get it on or utter a word, the doctor was at him. "You seem in a hurry, sir; I will give you four days' quarantine to finish your dressing." What's more, he kept his word.

Surely there is some way of stopping this sort of thing. How would reprisals answer? For instance, for us to pass as usual all passengers landing in England except Argentines and Uruguayans, who, every soul of them, should be subjected to "fourteen days off the 'Mother Bank.'" I fancy something of that kind would have a good effect.

Our passengers are busy already, five or six of them fishing to kill time till our fate is settled. They are killing fish, too. I saw them land a lot of fine Corbinas, very good eating, and some catfish from two to three pounds apiece.

11.15 a.m.—Launches are coming alongside—there are seven now, and more are on their way, all flying the yellow flag, and full of friends to greet our passengers. But between us and them there is a great gulf fixed, to be bridged by salutation only from ship to ship. None are allowed to board, unless they are prepared to remain should we be quarantined. But they have sent us quantities of lovely flowers. A handsome brunette and her good-looking husband are rocking violently in a launch at my feet, and emphatically waving hands to friends aboard. She has a *lovely smile, full of white teeth*, and is dressed quite in London style. Her husband is in a light dust-coat and low-crowned white hat, the lady in a silk dress of claret shot with salmon, over a pink skirt. Surmises are endless as to quarantine, but nothing is yet known. Patience!

The roads are full of shipping. Over our bows is a French Messageries Maritimes steamer, and behind us a Pacific vessel, bound for Valparaiso. The latter is the *Aconcagua*,

Mr. Graham tells me, 3200 tons, and was in Port Philip when he was there in 1877, at which time she was the largest vessel that had entered Melbourne. She and the *Lusitania* were the rival boats of those days. Now, I suppose, there are vessels running there as big as both these rivals put together. Even the *Clyde* looks double her size.

Mr. Petty, the thirty-seven-years' pilot of these parts, and by far the best-known man in them, has just come on board. He is a rough-looking man, but a very genius at his business, I hear. He has a standing salary from the Royal Mail Company of £1000 a year, and is said to be worth £30,000 at least.

Noon.—The order has come—quarantine for twenty-four hours, "for observation," as it is termed. Only those for Monte Video will be landed at Flores, twelve miles back, to which we are now returning. The discipline is very galling. To be landed in a rough sea at a lazaretto; there to be lodged in barracks, fourteen beds in a room; to be guarded by sentinels with loaded rifles; to have one's luggage fumigated by disinfecting steam which spoils all silks and leather;—all this, I say, makes up a fair amount of discomfort. But it must be remembered that only twenty years ago imported yellow fever turned Monte Video into a mere city of the dead. And seeing that we *have* had a death on board, although *we* know there was nothing infectious about it, we must make some allowance for scepticism in those who have the news at second-hand.

1 p.m.—"By the mark five," cries the Quarter-master, sounding as we approach Flores, and sharp comes the word from the bridge—"Let her go!" We anchor off the lazaretto, and half-a-mile from shore, as the lunch-bell rings.

While the poor folks, who for their sins are to be interned

in this hole, are getting their last snack of decent food, the
ship's boats and steam-pinnace are being got ready to land
them, for no help comes from the shore people. Mr. Courtney
says on his first journey he had fourteen days' quarantine here.

3 p.m.—Our steam-launch, after swinging in the air over
our starboard side, and kicking up a row as if gasping and
coughing from its own smoke while steam was being got
up, has just towed two boat-loads
of passengers to Flores, and returned for two more. It is about
as desolate an "island of flowers"
as you could find. Not a tree or
shrub upon the whole half-mile of
it. Nothing but some white-
washed sheds with tiled roofs, and
a white-washed lighthouse with a
red cap and weather-cock. These
at one end : then come a hospital

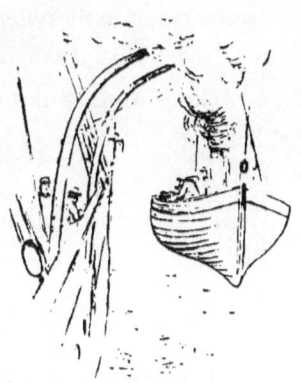

"A chip of the old block."

in the middle, and a cemetery at the other end. No wonder
the charges are inclusive ; *there are no extras,*—nothing but
a shed, a hospital, a grave. The order is charmingly suggestive of the natural stages of life, and here there is not
much choice amongst the three. You can use any you may
require, or indeed all of them, if it so minds you.

From the ship we can see the smoke of the fumigating-
house, creating literally a purgatorial fog through which I can
discern our poor imprisoned people wandering about listless
and wretched. The order is only for twenty-four hours, it is
true, but caprice may make anything of it up to fourteen days
—or even a month—and they don't give you "the *option* of
a fine." Indeed, the sentence always *includes* a fine of two
and a half dollars (roughly 12s. 6d.) per day per head.

5 p.m.—At last we wave our final farewells to the captives at Flores, and steam back to Monte Video, where for the second time we cast anchor at 6.5 p.m., for the night.

A basket of pears has just come aboard. They look superb, and remind me that I have heard of pears here during the season weighing as much as ten pounds the dozen. The cargo of oranges and bananas is being discharged into lighters which will remain in quarantine; the oranges are transferred by bucket-loads poured down an air-shaft funnel. The bananas, in bunches of a hundred, are thrown from hand to hand by a chain of eight men reaching from one hold to the other.

While shipping and stowing our boats just now, I saw one of our black sailors nearly lost through the slacking of

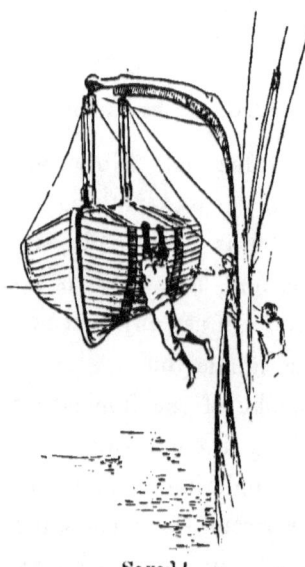

Saved !

the tackle. He leapt for his life, poor fellow, luckily caught the swinging boat, and hung on by his finger-tips till his comrades rescued him. The manning of this boat was accomplished, I hear, in four minutes. The shipping of it occupied twenty minutes by my watch.

It interested me rather to see how the davits, from which the boat hung, were worked. The boat is suspended over the side from two upright long-handled hooks, so arranged on pivots that the handle-ends are, by means of a hand-screw, forced outwards from the ship; the hooked ends move inwards till the boat hangs over the deck.

7.30 p.m.—Mr. Ritchie and I, leaving dinner before the rest, were just in time to see the sun set. A blood-red western sky irradiated with orange, flooded Monte Video (facing it) with pale rose, softening the angles of the streets, toning down the stiffness of the blocks of buildings that cover the hill-sides from the country to the sea, and paving the broad thoroughfares with gold. No twilight here to effect a gradual transformation—all is sudden and full of surprises. We had been looking perhaps five minutes, and in that time the sun had sunk behind the sea. On looking again at the city, the rose tint has faded away, and out flash the stars and with them the lights on shore a score at a time—here, there, and everywhere—till it seems as though the diamond dust in the blue vault above us, that illumines the ocean and the shipping, is falling in a silver summer shower upon the city.

8 p.m.—Pog, who leaves us to-morrow—going straight to Corrientes, five days' journey from Buenos Aires—has been spinning us his last yarn.

It appears that in the Jubilee year, after a week's festivities in his native town, a watch was found in the cricket-ground. The news soon spread, and brought no less than three claimants for it—whom we will call respectively A, B, and C. The first two were strangers to the town, and C a resident. Unfortunately, though none had seen the watch, all three were in some way able to describe it as "a silver hunter," and none of them could do more.

Strange to say, each claimant had lost it on a different day, and as the watch when found was *going*, there seemed little doubt that it belonged to C, the man who said he lost it the night before it was found. But to A and B this was not conclusive, for each asserted that *his* watch would often stop when put down, and begin going again when taken up.

" It was at this point," said Pog, " that the finder, being in a fix, asked my advice. All the men were in my hall; would I interview them? Not seeing my way to be of any use, I protested, refused, begged, entreated. Then, all on a sudden, a thought struck me, and I said, ' Lay the watch on the table, show the men in one at a time, and I will hear what they have to say.' It should here be explained that on the table there was nothing but a silver hunting-watch and an open penknife, and that I arranged to put my questions from a chair half-turned towards the fireplace, where, as I sat apparently reading, a sloping mirror over the mantelpiece enabled me to see the reflection of the table and any one standing there.

" Presently in came A. ' You say that the watch is yours, sir ? ' I began. ' Be so good as to tell me by what marks you know it.' ' Those,' said he, pointing with the penknife to some marks in the inside of the watch, ' are my initials.' I looked and saw they were. The watch was given him, he told me, by his uncle, when he returned from the Crimea. ' You may go,' I said. Next came B, and, strange to say, he also was able to show me a distinctive mark. The watch was given him by his mother, a deeply religious woman, in her last illness, and there, yes, *there* was the very cross, the sacred emblem with which she had marked it. Then came C, who at the merest glance said decidedly that the watch was not his; that *his* had no initials and no cross. Yet all had thought this man was the true owner. ' Well,' said I, ' then it rests between A and B ; please call them in again.' They came, and when all three stood before me, I spoke thus: ' Gentlemen, it is quite clear to me, that the

watch that has been found does not belong' (turning to
A and B) 'to you or to you, and as C says it is not his,
why, I'm going to keep it myself, and with that I began to
fasten the 'silver hunter' of the cricket-field on to my chain.
'Stay, sir,' said C; 'may I look once more?' 'By all
means,' said I, handing it to him; when instantly he
exclaimed, 'But *that is* my watch!' and pulling a key out of
his pocket he showed us all how it exactly fitted the watch.
'Take it, sir,' I said, 'for I can trust your bare word for it.
The watch I showed you all *at first*, the one C said was not
his, and in which two of you have so kindly scratched certain
initials and a cross, *was my watch;* and, believe me, I shall
always treasure it the more for the hieroglyphics in memory
of A's uncle, and the pretty device placed there by B's
mother.

"And with that," said Pog (finishing his whiskey), "I bowed
out A and B and smoked a cigar with C and the finder.
There's the very watch," said he,
showing us the scratched initials
and the cross. "It is a treasure,
and too good to wear at sea, but
my other is in hospital with a
dislocated hand. Some of you
may have heard the story. You
perceive it is a cripple. During
the voyage I broke off the other
hand and lost it in my pocket, but
a scientific friend, knowing the
magnetic power of the dynamos
below——" He had got so far

"Solomon Pog, Esquire!"

with this oft-repeated tale, when the contrast—·I suppose
it was—of his cuteness just exemplified, and his childlike

simplicity in the matter of the dynamos, which of course had been the talk of the *Clyde*, so tickled us that we all burst out into one long ringing guffaw. "And now, gentlemen," said Pog, snapping the watch and returning it to his pocket, and not the least bit disconcerted by our rude reception of his intended anecdote, "good night!" And he was off before we had time to reflect, or I believe some of us would have carried the dear old boy to his cabin, so pleased were we with the yarn and its telling.

"Boys," said the Yankee, who was among the audience, "raise your glasses with me to the health of Solomon Pog, Esquire." And we did.

November 16*th* (*Sunday*).—7 a.m. We left Monte Video, I hear, at 2 a.m. I got up at 6 a.m., since when I have had a long chat with Mr. Petty, the pilot, who lives at Colonia, or "Little Town," thirty miles up the River Plate. As he speaks from a long experience, I thought his views worth noting.

He holds that trade-unions have utterly ruined Englishmen. When only a youngster and working as a stevedore, he made up his mind to do whatever fell in his way. "Others," said he, " might fight and abuse the Captain for giving them an extra watch—not I. Nothing ever came amiss to me. Your English sailors everywhere, now, look for extra pay for the least bit of extra work. Trades-unionism has made them mere machines. So much fuel produces so much work, and no more. All enterprise is gone. While every other race out here thrives, the Englishman is a failure, and none will employ him. I have a man (a Spaniard) at home, who has been with me for years, and is worth at least £2000. He cleans my boots, tends my horse, and does anything I tell him. If I send him a wire to meet me, he is up at 4 a.m. and has to drive thirty miles, and when he has taken me home he's good for twelve hours' work, if I want it of him. Why, while a German, or a man indeed of almost any other nationality, will save out of a small screw, the Englishman must be a member of half-a-dozen clubs and is for ever in debt."

A Union advocate would probably reply to Mr. Petty's views when a *stevedore*, that for one stevedore that would become a capitalist on his plan, the Union could show ten or a dozen, and that as to his *present* point of view, a capitalist is not likely to approve of labour uniting to thin his profits. But whatever the "pro's and con's" of this question may be, whether trade-unionism is good or evil, or like most men and things a mixture of both, and whether being either, neither, or both, it has aught to do with producing the shiftless Englishman of Mr. Petty's experience, is a small matter beside the undeniable fact, whatever its cause, that the average Englishman is not in favour in the Republics of South America.

"On the word of an Englishman!"

A friend tells me that in Argentina every drunken man is said to be an Englishman, and when an Englishman dies, drink is always recorded as the cause. Indeed *borracho* (drunkard) is the opprobrious name bestowed on Englishmen indiscriminately, varied only by the term *gringo* (dog, greenhorn, or fool), equally offensive to the man if not to his moral character. They have a pretty proverb illustrating their contempt for us :—"An Englishman and a dog go on the sunny side of

M

the street."   As a set-off against this, it is cheering to find
in the Brazils that the strongest asseveration a man can use
is the phrase, "On the word of an Englishman."

As an Englishman—*borracho*, *gringo*, or whatever else it
pleases the Argentine to term me—I should like to ask him
where he and his benighted country would be now but for
the money that we *borrachos*, *gringos*, or what-not have
found him.

I know he has a pretty busy life, investing John Bull's
money in cigarettes, champagne, button-hole bouquets, and
general self-adornment, and I wouldn't hurry him for the
world.   But when he can for a brief moment "unstring the
bow," I should like an answer.

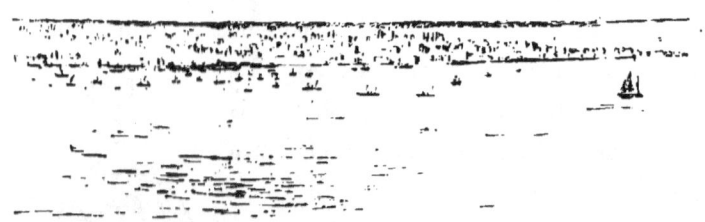

Monte Video, from the mast-head of the *Clyde*.

CHAPTER VII.

November 16th (Sunday).—9.48 a.m. We are anchored fourteen miles off Buenos Aires in the river Plate, that being
the nearest approach to shore our draught will permit us to
make. At Monte Video this mighty river is sixty miles
wide, and at Point Piedras, on the south side of its mouth,
the water is nearly fresh. Here at Buenos Aires, which is
a hundred and twenty miles up the river from Monte Video,
it is still thirty-five miles wide. The rivers composing the
estuary called Rio de La Plata ("the silver stream") are the
Uruguay and the Paraná. The former, rising in Brazil and
dividing the southern portion of that country and the
Republic of the Banda Oriental from the Argentine Provinces of Corrientes and Entre Rios, is nine hundred miles
long. The rivers Paraguay and Paraná meet at Corrientes,
and there unite to form the greater Paraná.

Geologically the two shores of the river Plate differ greatly,
the soil on the Buenos Aires side being alluvial, and producing not a stone as large as a marble, while that on the
Monte Video side possesses an abundance of granite.

Noon.—The launch has come to take us and our luggage
ashore.

Till quite lately, a good part of the landing was effected
by means of high-wheeled waggons; now, an Agent of the

Villa Longa Company (authorized by the Government) comes
on board and takes charge of your luggage at a cost of from
2½*d*. to 1*s*. per article according to size, and the tenders take
it and you to the door of the Custom-House.

1 p.m.—The launch is dashing along through a lumpy sea.
We have already passed no less than eight wrecks, with the
masts showing above the water, but no buoys to mark them.
A fat, puffy little frigate, named *Terror del Mundo*, is on
our port side. Then come more wrecks to starboard—more
—more. Two canoes are in full flight up the river. More
masts peep out of the water. Two dredgers are hard at work.
The new part of the town is now visible to the right, and
presently we pass a cemetery on a hill.

In 1881, twenty thousand people died in Buenos Aires
alone of yellow fever, and were buried there a hundred at a
time, gum-trees being planted on the spot as disinfectants.

A breakwater is just in sight, with shipping lying thickly
off the point of it; then come huge emigrant-sheds, beneath
tall factory chimneys, and the dock and Custom-House.

2 p.m.—We draw up beside the famous *Stirling Castle*,
s.s., now re-christened the *Sud America*, just arrived from
Naples, her smaller draught allowing of her coming right
into the docks. She it was, I think, that made the fastest
run on record, twenty-one days, from Naples to Sydney
Heads. While waiting to pass our luggage, Mr. Ollendorff
and I went over her, but she looked dull, sombre, and dirty,
after the dainty *Clyde*.

6 p.m.—Pog has passed his things and taken his farewell
of us *en route* to Corrientes. I shall miss him terribly on
the home voyage. What with his good humour, his comic
face, and his quaint style, he was, and liked to be called,
" the ship's comedian."

La Boca, Buenos Aires. Arrival of s.s. *Sud America*, late *Stirling Castle*. *Page 164.*

7 p.m.—It has taken us just five hours to pass our luggage. Many got *all but one box* four hours ago, but that last box, perhaps, was at the bottom of the second or third tender-load, and so made all that difference to them.

A party of four or five of us is bound for the Hôtel l'Universelle in the Calle St. Martin; Mr. Ollendorff kindly takes me to dinner at his Club, "The Residents and Strangers" in the Calle Victoria, and also makes me "transeunte," *i.e.* free of it, during my stay of ten days.

In recording a few impressions of Buenos Aires and the surrounding places of interest, it will I think be better to drop the diary form, and to present them so far as I am able, in the form of a continuous narrative embracing the whole of the short period of my visit. Afloat, the mention of incidents *in the round of the clock* may help others, as it did me, to realize the length of the voyage. But ashore, there is no such need. I propose therefore to treat the subject as a whole.

By way of introduction it will be only necessary for me to say that the Argentine Republic, of which Buenos Aires is the chief city, has a population exceeding four millions, of whom one million are Italians. It occupies a territory triangular in form, some two thousand miles in length and about one thousand at its greatest breadth. It is divided into fifteen provinces, each of which manages its own internal affairs. Its army is a medley of Indians, half-breeds, and negroes, most of whom are married, and, comical to say, are accompanied on the march by their wives and children.

One's first impressions of Buenos Aires itself, the land of "good winds" (and pet-named by its inhabitants "The Pearl of South America"), are far from pleasing. The houses near the docks, or "Boca" (Mouth), built in the dull Creole style, are heavy and sad looking: but things improve as one approaches the more central parts of the city. In form Buenos Aires is very like Monte Video ; that is to say, it is built in "Quadras," or squares, so that viewed from a balloon it would look like a huge chess-board. It lies true to the points of the compass, N. S. E. W., which they say is a mistake, as the streets are all more or less deprived of the cooling effects of the prevailing winds, which do *not* blow from those quarters.

Two sets of streets cross one another at right angles one hundred and fifty yards apart, and the houses are numbered up to one hundred only, the numbers being given to doors, windows, anything to exactly exhaust the hundred. By this plan the location of a house is easily determined : No. 2020, for example, would be in the twenty-first block, and so on. As a few of the principal thoroughfares are as much as three miles long, some such system is indispensable, more especially as flys are hired at half-a-dollar per twenty squares.

The old houses are of one floor only, and are arranged in two or three "Patios," or courtyards, into which the various rooms open. The new residences are built on the "Altos," or upper floors plan. But they have also a Patio, visible from the outside through the gate, in which are plants of all kinds—palms, ferns, small olives, etc.—and generally a fountain which gives them a delightfully cool appearance. The whole is screened from the sun and rain by a huge awning. Rents are huge also—about three times as high as in England.

Modern improvements are seen on all sides. The old way of calling attention when visiting a house, for instance, was to clap the hands and cry "Ave, Maria !" now they hail

Maria, or whatever the servant's name may be, with the electric bell.

The streets are lighted by brackets from the walls, thus freeing the thoroughfares from lamp-posts. The lamps give a good light, but the streets are dull compared with ours, the reason being that the intense heat causes people when at home to sit in the dark, and the streets suffer in brightness accordingly.

Plaza Victoria, Buenos Aires.

Founded by Spaniards, Buenos Aires had for a time all the characteristics of a port in the south of Spain, but as settlers came—British, French, German, Italian, Portuguese, Brazilian, and Uruguayan, etc.—each brought his own notion of architecture, till its buildings, like its half-million of people, have become a hotch-potch.

The first thing that strikes the stranger is that nobody

seems to walk, but he ceases to wonder at this when he sees
how plentiful horses are. All flys have two, and well-horsed
trams will take him anywhere for about twopence. Indeed,
any one seen walking outside the town is known at once for
a *gringo*, *i.e.* (at its mildest) a greenhorn, or fresh arrival
from Europe.

The next point I noticed in my drive through the city
to my hotel, was the extraordinary number of squares,
or " Plazas." Ten or twelve years ago, Mr. Ollendorff told
me, these were mere barren patches, evil-smelling rubbish-
heaps, where the *gauchos* stabled themselves and their
ox-drawn waggons. To-day they are adorned with trees,
flowers, and fountains, and form one of the sights of the
place. The principal of them is the Plaza Victoria, occupy-
ing eight acres, and bordered by double rows of palm trees.
In the centre is a fountain and the monument commemo-
rating the 25th May, 1810, when Argentina threw off the
yoke of Spain.

On one side of the Plaza is Government House, called
Casa Rosada, from the pink stone of which it is built. Here
the late President of ill-repute, Dr. Celman, gave balls
and banquets rivalling in splendour the entertainments of
European courts, till the revolution of 1890 caused him to
retire, on a fortune of very many millions sterling, to Rosario
de Santa Fé, where, strange to say, he is allowed to remain
unmolested and in possession of his stolen hoards.

Facing this is the Bolsa, or Exchange, where every twenty-
four hours the value is declared of the fluctuating paper-
dollar. In 1825 the Argentine dollar was worth 4s. 2d., but
the nationalizing of the Buenos Aires Bank made it the tool
of the government, who caused it to issue paper beyond its
capital, and the dollar began its downward course. For

although the law declared paper a legal tender for which specie could not be demanded, the bank's credit so suffered that by 1828 the dollar had become worth no more than a shilling. It made a spurt after the war with Brazil, and got recognized as worth 2s., but it could not "stay," and was soon offering itself for sixpence, then fourpence, then threepence, and eventually became literally a *tuppenny-ha'penny* affair. During the time of my visit, at the end of 1890, it fluctuated between 1s. 2d. and 1s. 5d.

On a third side of the square stands the Cathedral, built something in the form of the London Royal Exchange, topped by a small dome and dwarf spire at one end. It

The Cathedral.

contains the remains of General Saint Martin, who, after liberating Argentina from the Spanish yoke, was expelled in 1850 and allowed to die in exile in France. Thirty years later, in 1880, the tide of popular opinion turned in his favour, and his body was brought home and interred with great pomp. Four statues guard the grave, personifying Agriculture, Industry, Justice, and Liberty—Industry being represented (somewhat incongruously in a sacred edifice) by a hammer and saw.

The fourth side of the square is unfinished, and still retains very distinct traces of its ugly Spanish origin.

The finest church in Buenos Aires is the church of the Recoleta (Remembrance), of pure Roman architecture and Italian marble beautifully carved. It is the property of Señor Don Carlos Cuerrero, a wealthy citizen, and was built —at a cost of £50,000—in memory of a beloved daughter who was murdered by her lover in 1878. She is buried beneath the altar, and a stained-glass window, brought from Florence, illustrates the chief incidents of her life.

The principal street, Calle Florida, is looked upon by the Argentine as the El Dorado of the world; it is his ideal promenade. The trams that used to run down it have been diverted, and the street has been paved with wood, and has become to him more precious than is Regent Street to London, the Boulevard des Italiens to Paris, Unter den Linden to Berlin, or Fifth-Avenue to New York. He fairly revels in enthusiasm about this fourteen-foot road with its two-foot pavement, and takes the stranger there as the first thing he ought to see. In this, and the adjacent Cangallo, Piedad, and Saint Martin streets, are situated nearly all the business houses. A local guide-book speaks of Florida in the following pathetic terms. The description (I give it verbatim) is, I should say, from the pen of a naturalized German, judging from the style.

" Such a spectacle cannot be witnessed anywhere else in the wide world. All that is young and beautiful is here. Young gentlemen loll about on the narrow pavements, got up in the latest style, rosebud in perfectly-fitting frock-coat, feet squeezed into patent leather boots, with thin cane in gloved hand waiting for the Beauties to pass. And the Beauties pass in bevies, in light silks cut to show the contour of their figures, and with elastic step they flash glances from their naughty eyes to their admirers, from whose lips delighted exclamations of insipid compliments and not seldom insolent importunities proceed—some of which, in Europe, would be considered as serious insults. They are distractingly beautiful, and carry themselves with a rare grace and native-born 'Chic'; they know their loveliness and like to hear it from 'others' of the male gender. If the compliment paid is not too provoking, the complimented fair one or the complimented fair one's mother, or sister, or aunt, will turn round and with a be-witching gravity reply with a '*graçias, caballero*' (not 'good gracious!' but 'thank you, sir':) A foreigner hearing and seeing such for the first time, generally stands still, open-mouthed, no doubt fancying himself in a modern Sodom. But these coquetries are

" Graçias, caballero!"

not to be looked upon as want of virtue. The beautiful, elegant, and coquettish young ladies with their brilliant-glancing eyes, and who use their fans with such 'chic,' are not worse than others who blush at the least bold word."

Among the principal places of interest must be mentioned the Recoleta Catholic cemetery,—accessible by the Palermo tram—where, as the same guide reminds us, "nothing is to be seen outside, because the creative genius of Torquato de Alvear (an ex-mayor) has put a high wall all round the graveyard." Here I came upon the oldest grave, the resting-place of an Englishman who—as my guide quaintly said—" had the *pleasure* of being the first person buried there."

At the circumference of this wall are the graves of the poorer classes, and in the centre the family vaults or mausoleums of the wealthy, mostly of marble and with domed roofs. On looking through the iron gratings abutting on the intersecting paths, the coffins may be seen laid in rows on shelves round three sides of the vault. All are decorated with flowers and wreaths of *immortelles*, and on certain of them vast sums must have been expended, for they are veritable temples or chapels, and their decorations very chaste and effective.

The epitaph on one grave tells of an awful tragedy. It reads : " Don Francisco Alvarez, Asesinado por sus Amigos, 1828 "—" Assassinated by his friends." Having lost their money to him, it seems, they lured him to a lonely spot and wiped out their debts in his blood. It is something to the credit of Argentina, at that time a rather lawless country, that despite great influence they were executed.

In another part lie, in one common grave, the victims of the tyranny of President Rosas. Don Manuel Rosas, the blood-and-iron president, who ruled from 1830 to 1852, was what is known as a *gaucho* (gowcho), that is, a descendant of the aristocratic Spanish Dons who in early days consorted with Indian women : for the Grandees and Hidalgos, who ruled these Spanish colonies, did not hesitate to seek the society of the Pocahontases of the Guarani race.

In character, I am told, the *gaucho* is at once indolent and active, dividing his time between racing the hurricane on his tireless *broncho* (horse), and holding high revel with his mistresses and his chums.

In his native wilds he will not steal nor do a mean act, but when he becomes a resident he will rob a blindman. He eats beef roasted on a spit, without salt or bread, and drinks *yerba mate*—Paraguayan tea—which he sucks through a tube. He yields obedience to no law, is polite and cruel in the same breath, and equally dexterous in playing on the soft mandolin or slitting a throat. When sober he is peaceful; when drunk, a howling, savage, remorseless fiend. He is brave as a lion, nimble as a cat, has great powers of endurance, is a loyal friend and an implacable foe. With all these qualities, it is not surprising that the *gaucho* has exercised a powerful influence on Argentina, retarding civilization until immigration had infused new blood in excess of the old.

A *gaucho*.

Don Manuel Rosas, then, was a *gaucho*, and the son of a wealthy Spaniard who held a kind of patriarchal sway over the Peons that tended his flocks and herds. As the son grew up, the father had to yield place to his stronger will, and young Rosas became a sort of *gaucho* leader, in which character during the war of 1829 he commanded a regiment against the Indians. From this powerful position of chief of the *gauchos*, the step was easily made to the presidency

of the Republic, in which capacity this self-appointed
dictator remained the head of an absolute despotism for the
greater part of a quarter of a century—in defiance of the
laws and the constitution.

Inheriting from his father the arrogance and superstition
of the Spaniard, and from his mother the craft and cruelty
of the Guarani Indian, and supported by the loyalty of
his *gauchos*, of whom all the people of the towns stood in
fear, he ruled the country, with his inflexible *will* for its
only law and *death* for its only penalty.   Crafty as a fox,
bold as a lion, trusting none but his daughter Mannileta,
he played the tyrant from Paraguay to the Straits of
Magellan, till blood flowed like water.   He killed alike
friend and enemy, and no man could go to his bed in safety
from his *masorqueros* (secret assassins).   He made blood-
shed his trade, and stayed his hand only when the nation,
tortured into subjection, lay quivering at his feet.   He had
his oldest friend, who had been a second father to him,

murdered in cold blood.   No tie of family
or friendship was of any avail, nor did
obscurity secure any from his daggers.

Perverting even hospitality into a
weapon, he invited two Caciques Indians
to a palaver and treacherously hanged
them.   At another time, posing as champion of the Church, he executed a young

The palaver.

English lady and the priest who had seduced her.

From first to last his victims numbered five thousand eight
hundred and eighty-four.   Four were poisoned, three thousand seven hundred and sixty-five died by the sword, one
thousand three hundred and ninety-three were shot, and
seven hundred and twenty-two assassinated.

The money issued during his tyranny bears testimony to his egregious vanity and arrogance, for it bore, in addition to his portrait, the inscription "Eternal Rosas." For all that, as luck would have it, this "Goliath" was made to bite the dust one day, in the year 1852, by a "David" in the modest person of General Urquiza : and once again—

> The giant "Might"
> Was overthrown,
> By stripling "Right,"
> With sling and stone.

It is not pleasant to read that this reptile speedily found asylum, and a warm welcome in England.

The domes and towers of the Recoleta, as seen over the wall as you pass onward by tram to Palermo, are very striking, having quite an oriental appearance. By the way, these trams are worth a moment's notice. No mules here, horses being far cheaper. A mule will fetch £20, whereas you can buy a horse for 30*s.*, a decent one for £5, a good one for £10. Notice, too, how the hills are negotiated. Without stopping the tram, a boy smoking a cigar on an odd horse with lassoo round the Mexican saddle, gallops up, throws his rope which is hooked on to the side of the tram, and off he goes dexterously paying out the line till it becomes taut, and up we go to the top, where he is cast off. The tram-driver clears his way with a horn, on which he plays quite a little tune by fingering the end like a picco pipe.

A tram auxiliary.

The tone is something between a Punch squeak and a Swiss pipe.

There is one excellent arrangement about the trams here; they run out by one route and home by another, so that a single line suffices, and the traffic is also better dispersed throughout the city. In fact, a second line of rails would consume the entire width of the widest streets here, and the others would not hold two rows at all.

A quarter of an hour from the Recoleta the tram, after passing through the really fine Avenida Alvear, lighted throughout by electricity and containing some of the best examples of large family residences the city possesses, stops at Palermo, where is a grand Corso fully sixty feet wide, under the name of Avenida Sarmiento, which stretches from the high-road to the river in one unbroken line for over a mile. It is a thoroughfare of which any capital in the world might feel proud. The footpath on both sides is shaded the entire way by overarching palms, and is bisected by the Rosario and the Northern railways, between which lies what formerly was the palace of the tyrant, President Rosas. This building, once the scene of monstrous orgies rivalling in debauchery the worst Roman Saturnalia, is now used as the Argentine military college.

Here begins the park called "3 de Febrero," thickly planted with semi-tropical plants, poplars, and paradise-trees, and brightened by artificial lakes and rivers crossed by rustic bridges. It is also the site of the Zoological Gardens, which are here free as the park itself, and thronged with visitors on Sundays and holidays, when a military band adds to the enjoyment of an exquisitely beautiful promenade. The sight here in the cool of the evening, when all the wealth and beauty of Buenos Aires flutter out like butterflies

The Corso, Palermo, Buenos Aires.

Page 176.

from their noonday shelter to this breezy park, is truly magnificent.

The paths are lined with well-dressed pedestrians, and handsome park-phaetons, American trotting-cars, or chaises with little awnings, sweep along the broad Corso beneath the electric light. It is a crowd of all nations, gathered from every corner of the globe, arrayed in every colour of the rainbow and possessing every type and tint of face from Calmuck to classic Greek, from black to blonde.

The night I saw it, the park, Corso, and river were all bathed in moonlight, and the effect of the young moon, with

Belgrano, Buenos Aires.

Jupiter close by her as a satellite, was charming and brilliant beyond anything of the kind to be seen in Europe.

The fire-flies here are superb. I captured a few—some blue, others brown—the largest measuring as much as six inches across the wing.

Besides Palermo, the chief suburbs are Belgrano (the English quarter), a little further on by the same tram, Flores, Caballito, Almagro, Lomas, etc., abounding with picturesque "Quintas" (or country seats) owned for the most part by British and North American families.

Coming back to the city, the Plaza General Lavalle, also

called Plaza del Parque, claims attention as being not only
a fine square, but one of the scenes of conflict during the
revolution of July, 1890.   Here the insurgents struck their
first blow by seizing the guns and ammunition stored in
the Arsenal; and from here the attacks of the government
troops, stationed three squares away in the Plaza Libertad,
were repulsed.

Another enormous square is the Plaza Once de Septembre,
where stands the terminus of the great Great Western Railway, the centre of all transactions in the produce of the
country—wool, hides, wheat, maize, etc.   The terminus of the
Great Southern Railway, said to be the finest building of its
kind in the country, is situated in a vast square decorated
with artificial grottos, the Plaza Constitucion.

The chief clubs are the " Residents and Strangers," and the
" Cosmos "—the latter a gambling resort, and patronized
mostly by the fast young men about town.

There is a well-supported and prosperous rowing club,
that has its head-quarters at Tigre, a most fashionable resort
about an hour by rail up the river.   The annual regatta
here is held in high esteem, and is said to rival Henley in
the brilliancy of the company it attracts.

Cricket, football, lawn-tennis, polo, swimming, sailing,
horse-racing, each has its representative club, and some—
such as "The Hurlingham "—count their members by the
hundred.

But apart from these luxurious provisions for the comfort
of the well-to-do, it is cheering to notice some philanthropic
undertakings.   Foremost among them are the public institutions, founded by the English-speaking community, viz.
the British Hospital, a large well-built edifice standing in
its own grounds, and the Victoria Convalescent Home.

This brief sketch would be incomplete without some allusion to English journalism. "The fourth estate" seems to be ably represented by the *Standard* and the *Buenos Aires Herald*, both of which publish a weekly edition destined for Europe, and the *Southern Cross*, the organ of the Irish Catholic residents.

One of the first and most noteworthy places I visited was the Plaza General Lavalle, the scene of the revolution of but sixteen weeks earlier. But I had scarcely left the Hôtel l'Universelle before my friendly guide found me something interesting. This was a milkman on horseback, with skin panniers, in which the milk was actually churned by the jolting of the horse. These milkmen bring their supplies from great distances in the country, and teach their horses the peculiar jolting walk, a sort of half-trot, in fact, so as to churn the milk as they go. It is no uncommon

The *lechero* (milkman).

thing for a man, short of butter, to give what he has and to say he will call with the rest after another round or two of the square. Thus, the milk in Buenos Aires is what we should call skimmed milk. If you want it richer, they will bring the cows and milk them at your doors, which is a striking commentary on the confidence one Argentine reposes in another.

A little further on, my friend drew my attention to another and more scientifically interesting object. In the same street, Calle Saint Martin, is a clockmaker's shop in which a curious incident occurred. In 1861, a place called Mendoza, the terminus of the railway towards the Andes, and eight hundred miles from Buenos Aires, was visited by an earthquake. Before the news of this calamity, involving the death of fifteen thousand people, had time to reach the city, the proprietor of this shop had made the discovery that every one of his clocks differed twelve seconds from his chronometers. The tidings of the disaster brought the probable explanation, for not only had the earthquake

Plaza Lavalle.

occurred at the exact time of the clockmaker's discovery, but *the shock had lasted precisely twelve seconds*, no doubt retarding the pendulums for that period.

Arrived at the Plaza General Lavalle, we found it almost in the condition the revolution had left it, scarred in all directions with shot, shell, and bullet. On the day of the outbreak, this square was guarded by a regiment of artillery, which presently joined the citizen-forces, already numbering about two thousand. Krupp guns were then stationed at each corner of the square, and as regiment after regiment deserted the colours, they assembled in the centre of the

square, which thenceforth became the head-quarters of the
revolutionary party. The national troops, drawn up in
the adjoining square, Plaza Libertad, attacked this position
in the morning of the following day, but were repulsed with
a loss of five hundred men. The entrenched rebels lost
three hundred, and hundreds of mere spectators were killed
on housetops and balconies. By 10 a.m. a flag of truce went
up for burial of the dead, who numbered over a thousand.
It makes one smile to hear that at this crisis, an undertaker,
instructed by General Lavalle, who commanded the national
forces, to provide a large
number of coffins, declined
to do so *except on cash
terms.* Some generals
would have strung him
up over his own door (not
a bad signboard for an
undertaker's) and helped
themselves to his stock
in trade. But this revolu-

A street scene during the revolution.

tion seems to have been characterized by a politeness which
is quite refreshing to chronicle. Or perhaps one ought
rather to say the tactics were somewhat of the playground
variety.

In the café at the corner of the square, they showed us
bullets by the score, and several shot and shell, all of which
had been picked up in and about the house. With my penknife I extracted a bullet from a blank wall hard by, and I
have brought it—the bullet, not the blank wall—away as
a memento.

The greatest sufferers in this outbreak appear to have been
the police. The Argentine laws are excellent, being an

embodiment of the best of all countries.   It is their adminis-
tration that is defective.   The police, whose pay is always
in arrear, are driven to any and every means of earning their
bread.   Their natural perquisites, of course, are bribes; but
all people will not bribe.   It is difficult to bring yourself,
for instance, to pay a constable not to " run you in " when
you slip down in the street.   But you had better do so,
because *he* would overlook the offence for a dollar, whereas
if you leave it to the commissary, it will cost you forty
times as much.   A man of distinction in the city, told me
he had to pay $40 for slipping on a piece of orange-peel.
The charge preferred was " drunkenness," of course, and no
protest was of any avail, for there are no magistrates, and
the commissary's decision is final.   In this country, if you
ask the commissary what you're *charged with*, he invariably
replies—mechanically—" $40."

Another told me he was taken before one of these gentry,
and fined $20 for being found with a gold watch-key hanging
to his woolly coat.   After paying the fine, the constable was
allowed to go home with my informant, to hear if there

Argentine police.

was any truth in his statement that the
key was his wife's.   But would you believe it?—when this was proved to the
satisfaction, or rather dissatisfaction of
the constable, who had been entrusted by
the commissary with the fine, he coolly
returned $15 only, saying he hoped he
might retain *his* $5, as he was a poor man.

It may be imagined, from these instances of their conduct,
in what contempt the police force is held.   Hated alike by
both sides engaged in the revolution, they were put in the
forefront and made, as it were, a buffer between the two

Plaza Libertad, Buenos Aires. The 3 a.m. gun—the signal for revolution—was to have been fired from the tower of this church.

forces. One present and under arms told me that if there was nothing else in sight, rather than be idle he shot a policeman, and he saw a man quietly kneel down, take aim, and knock over *three* one after another.

If you want to pass the time,
  Shoot a p'liceman !
A proper skittish time,
  Shoot a p'liceman !
Every member of the force
Must be cotched and slain, of course ;
If you want to pass the time,
  Shoot a p'liceman !

The death-roll of the police shows the share they had in the fighting. Five hundred killed out of six hundred !

These figures and those already given make an ugly butcher's bill; but were it not for this grim aspect of the rebellion, the account I had of it from an eye-witness would be truly comic. I cannot resist giving it verbatim, just as I noted it down. The story seems almost incredible, but my informant, a man of good position and repute, told it me in the presence of three others, who like himself had seen the whole affair, and they corroborated him.

"Disaffection existed in the army as far back as 1874, when three or four officers out in the pampas planned a revolt. It came to nothing, however, on that occasion, either from lack of funds or of pluck. But the spark of revolt smouldered on until July last, when, all being supposed to be ready, the outburst came. The orders given were that at 3 a.m. on the 26th of July, a small cannon was to be fired from the tower of the church overlooking the Plaza Libertad, as the signal for a general rising. At this signal one body of citizens, already selected for the duty, were to seize the President, Dr. Miguel Juarez Celman ; a second detachment was to arrest the Vice-President, Dr. Carlos Pellegrini; and a third were to secure General Lavalle, the Minister of War. This done, balloons were to rise from the rebel head-quarters, as a signal to the fleet in the river (the *Maipù*, the *Vallarino*, and the corvette *Patagonia*, which had agreed to join the revolutionary party) to open fire on the government buildings.

"Well, all these orders were carried out *except four*. First, the squad who had to take the President, deemed him such a contemptible scoundrel that they would not

"No go!"

waste their time on him. Secondly, Pellegrini remained unmolested because the *thirty men* detailed to seize him could not get rid of the *one policeman* on guard at his house, and who ought to have gone off duty earlier. Thirdly, the Minister of War escaped because his intended capturers did not hear the 3 a.m. gun, though they listened with their hands to their ears till 5 a.m. And no wonder, for it was afterwards discovered that the officer who was to have fired the signal-gun had *forgotten to do so*. And fourthly and finally, the fleet looked on through its glasses in silence, because the men who were to have given the balloon signal *had forgotten to get any balloons*. A day or two later, however, the fleet attempted to retrieve its laurels by opening fire on the city *during an armistice*, having this time (for variety) mistaken their comrades' signals.

"The end of this four days' shooting (which I have heard some Argentines dare to compare to the American Civil War) was worthy of the tactical skill displayed on both sides during hostilities. The government agreed to the

President being superseded (the one thing the rebels had fought for), and to all rebel officers retaining their rank, *provided the government were acknowledged victorious.*

"The fact is, the entire reconciliation seems to have been based on a pack of falsehoods. The people had won all along the line, they held all the arms and ammunition in the city—depositories were found crammed with them at the close of the struggle—and they could have dictated what terms they pleased to the effete government. But from first to last, from the time when those entrusted with the signals forgot(?) them, to the time when the rebels were advised to surrender, the whole transaction was a fraud. Is it credible," asked my informant, concluding, "that a *victorious* government would retain the services of mutinous and disaffected officers, restore them unpunished to their former position, and leave them free to hatch (as doubtless they are now hatching) another revolt?" To this, I take it, there can be but one answer.

There was not one morning during my stay in Buenos Aires, when our breakfast was not disturbed by the newspaper-touts in the street shouting, as they ran, rumours of a fresh revolution. And little wonder, with gold one day at 280 per cent., and the next rising to 350 per cent.

May I be allowed to say what this means? It means that my English sovereign will to-day just suffice to buy an article marked S14 in a tradesman's shop, and that if I defer my purchase till to-morrow, he will have to give me S3½ change out of it. The day before I left my hotel, gold was at 350 per cent.; the following day it had fallen to 280 per cent. The drop came thus. On the Tuesday morning, not only was the price on the Stock Exchange 350 per cent., but even higher offers were being made, when some heavy loser by the increasing value, rushed in and

expunged all the day's transactions from the slate. Knives and revolvers were drawn and freely used, and another revolution was only averted by the prompt action of the military, who cleared the place

The metal exchange.   "Lead is moving."   and made a demonstration in the Plaza Victoria in front of the Bolsa.

The following day, there being no quotations, the money-changers throughout the city, heartily sick of the immense price they had been paying for gold, formed a "corner," and refused to give more than 280 per cent. of paper for £100 in gold; that is to say, refused to give more than $14 to the sovereign. The effect to me was this. If I had paid my hotel bill of $70 on the Tuesday, I should have received out of my English £5 note £1 change (each sovereign being worth $17½, four of them would have sufficed); whereas, paying my bill on the Wednesday, when but $14 were obtainable for each sovereign, my £5 note was only just enough to meet it. Multiply this by one hundred, and see what it means. It is briefly this—that if you had yesterday £500 a year in the funds, to-day you are worth but £400 a year! Why, such a country must be a very hot-bed of revolution.

But I must not dwell on these questions; they are a little out of place in a narrative of this kind. My only excuse for referring to them at all here is that they interested me— not unnaturally, I think, seeing how they touched my

pocket—and I want to give any who may follow me something of everything that in any way coloured my experiences.

Calling at the London and Brazilian Bank one morning
to get some change, I met, and recognized by a strong
family likeness, the son of a very old friend in London.
This young fellow, of about twenty-three, had just come
out to the bank at a salary of £250 a year in gold. This,
with the exchange at 350 per cent., means that he can take
his 250 sovereigns to one of his own cashiers and turn them
there and then into £875 in paper.

I don't mean to say everything—board, lodging, clothing,
etc.—remains, as in the case I cited just now, unaltered, while
gold is careering up and down the scale. Prices are adjusted,
and many shops mark all their goods m,n (thus $10.50 m,n
means $10.50 money national). But for all that, while gold
rises, other things do not rise *in the same proportion*, and it
is safe to say that you get thirty shillings' worth for your
sovereign.

The news, just received, of the failure of Messrs. Baring
Bros., is responsible for the enormous rise in the value
of gold. They must have found it very hard indeed to
collect some of the rates they relied on here as interest on
their money. If a man thinks his water-rate too high, he
refuses payment, and if necessary
kicks the collector, whose only
remedy lies in a slow legal process,
for the law forbids the cutting-off
of the water supply. An Italian
on board said a good thing that fits
here:—"The credit of a man of
your own colour may be *nearly*

Expectations. | Expectorations.

good enough for you to trust him: you can't say as much

of any other man. A Spaniard will lift his cap for a loan and spit a receipt for the money."

The contrast between the Spaniard and the Portuguese is very marked. The Spaniard is—as I have noticed on board, but one sees it more strongly marked here—turbulent and rash. He is said, too, to be given to dangerous experiments, rushing from bigoted royalty to the extreme of rebellion; from tyranny to anarchy. The Portuguese, while fully as vain-glorious, is more practical, cool, and cautious.

The qualities which distinguished the two peoples in the Peninsula still influence their colonies and settlements. The Spaniard seeks to model his new State on the pattern of the French democracy and American federalism; but Portugal, under English influence, acquired such conservative tastes, that when the House of Braganza fled from Lisbon, not only was it welcomed at Rio, but Brazil became the Sovereign State and Portugal the dependency, until absolute separation was effected by compromise.

Brazil has lately *drifted* into a Republic, I know; but I do not think that proves much. It was not *fought for*, and the general feeling in the Rio is that the Emperor, dethroned without a blow, could be as easily restored. At no time in their history have the Brazilians shown a keen desire for Republican institutions, and it is noticeable that they took but very slight interest in the Argentine and Paraguayan wars. They appear to have joined without any selfish motive, and retired on the first opportunity.

Their morality is higher, and they are far more trustworthy than the Argentines, whose probity is tempted and corrupted in every way, till one marvels, not that so many are dishonest, but that any man remains honest. The paper currency, with its ever-fluctuating value, saps the very conscience of the nation, and opens the door to every species of fraud. Some of us find it difficult to go straight in England, where the shilling is always worth twelve pence. Just imagine what things would be like if a shilling counted (at different times) for anything between 3½d. and 6d.

Let me give an instance of the effect of this uncertainty as to the value of paper, upon one class only. The railways, of course, safe-guard themselves by fixing their fares in gold, and the market-price is wired every day all over Argentina to the ticket-issuers, who should charge passengers accordingly. But the *passengers* have no such information. They have simply to pay what they are told, and so are at the mercy of the railway officials, who—educated up to thieving in such ways, as a livelihood—one may be sure fully utilize the opportunity.

Even waiters at restaurants drive a dirty little trade in the exchange business. At one place I frequented, my waiter one day treated my sovereign as worth $14, and when I showed him the quotation $14.80, said, "Yes, that is this morning's: we don't act on that till to-morrow;" while another time it was: "Yes, that yesterday's, but here is to-day's"—just according to how it suits the pocket.

Ready for the Britisher.

The country is a grand country, the laws grand laws: but the one has no rulers and the others no administrators.

Moreover the paper-currency is about the most scientific form of *infection currency* that could be devised. I have seen the paper used for all sorts of purposes. If a man soiled his hand in a train-car, his bunch of paper money

was used as a matter of course to wipe it on. Yet these
foul rags are the legal tender of the country, and rich
and poor alike handle and smooth them into shape for
payment.

It was enough to make one's gorge rise sometimes to see
this unrecognizable filth caressed by a tiny gloved hand, and
then to reflect through what slums it may have come, and
what pestilential microbes it may harbour. And this, in a
country where everybody perspires so freely that the paper
is always moist. Oh, Mr. Goschen, ponder on these things
before you poison people's pockets with polluted pieces of
paper! Or, if we must have them, then call them all in
once a year, before the " dog days," and have them cremated.

During my stay we had the wind constantly from the
North, making it hot (108° in the shade), moist, and relax-
ing, so that even natives suffered from headache, and said
that although only late Spring, the heat was as great as
in Summer. The native remedies for this kind of headache
are curious: one is an Acacia leaf moistened by the tongue
and stuck on the temples. Here is another: the inside
surface of a split broad-bean is scraped by the teeth,
moistened by the tongue, and each half is then applied to
the temples. Negro women are often seen ornamented with
these white patches : even young Argentines of position are
not proof against the innocent superstition.

Indeed, they are proof against very little of anything. The
climate is favourable to pretty nearly every form of frivolity,
and the men seem fully as pleasure-seeking and dressy as the
women. A London swell would be deemed insufficiently
adorned in Buenos Aires. Here you must have a figured
white waistcoat, a flower always in your coat, and, even in
business, your boots must be patent-leather, or, if common

calf, they must be burnished like steel. To this end three or four boot-blacking shops in every block do a brisk trade, and there, seated on a high chair, the young Argentine may be seen twice or thrice every day being glorified at the small charge of five centavos (just under a penny).

For my sins, it fell to my lot once during my stay to see a native dandy dress himself. I will not mention the circumstances lest he should recognize them, for the description is, as photographers say, "wholly untouched." His toilet occupied just seventy minutes.

In a beautifully fitted dressing-case was every kind of luxury the Burlington itself could produce. In front of this altar his manicure and pedicure devotions occupied fifteen minutes. Then came his scented tub, in which, quite undisturbed by my presence, he disported himself for fifteen minutes more with his sponge like an adult "won't-be-happy-till-he-gets-it." Next came the important selection of a shirt (two being passed over as faulty), and of a waistcoat (there were four of different patterns in white twill), then necktie, trousers, patent-leather shoes, each requiring careful discrimination. When these had been laid ready on the sofa, came the washing of face and hands and the re-trimming of nails. Then hairwashing with some stuff that formed a lather. Time, fifty minutes. After this I witnessed the brushing and parting of the hair, the latter a most delicate and difficult operation, during which perfect silence was maintained. Next followed a thorough "spring cleaning" of the teeth with some Parisian charm, which of course was all right enough. Time, one hour. The next eight minutes were devoted to getting into the clothes, and the final two minutes to scenting a handkerchief on both sides while it lay on a pillow, and (this the last touch of all) spray-

ing hair, face, and neck with scent from a regular hair-dresser's
india-rubber double-balled spray-producer.

Early as it is in the year, the mosquito (from *mosca*, a fly—
mosquito, a little fly, in Spanish) is on the war-path, and for
a little fly he is very fly indeed. He is not always little,
though, for I have seen him an inch long. He hides himself
in a crack in the wall while you are undressing, and you
may search everywhere, you will find him nowhere ; yet
the moment your light is out he is everywhere, and you are
nowhere. That's just the difference.

As to curtains, they're very like burglar-proof safes : with
patience they can be easily picked. The way to use them is
first to make sure that no little nuisance is inside already.
Next you must get a fan. Then, lift the curtain edge six
inches, blow out the light, whisk your fan, dive under on your
stomach, and draw in your legs. If you do these five things
within one and a half seconds, you may hope to be safe for
the night. I never could do them under 1·8 seconds, so the

mosquito always won. Once I
partly did it in 1·5, all but the
legs ; I forgot them till too late,
and two mosquitoes had settled on
and marked them for their own.
But most times, being unused to
leap-frog in the dark, my dive
would land me plump into the
curtain, making a slit big enough
to admit every animal in the ark,

Achilles in his tent. His
vulnerable point.

let alone a mosquito ; and, as a rule, these efforts ended in
my going to roost rolled up in the curtain.

Lying like this the other night, I heard one approach with
his trombone, clearly bent on serenading me. At first, with

becoming modesty, he seated himself on my uncovered knee, and seemed about to begin the overture. No, he was only tuning up, I found. But what does he want that angler's stool for? Confound it! There goes the spike into my leg. Augh! I could stand it no longer; with one fell swoop of my brawny arm, I knocked him and his little trombone and stool into the middle of the room.

Nothing daunted, and only pausing long enough to collect his scattered kit, the troubadour returned, so to say, " beneath my casement " (the trombone a little flat, I thought, from collision with the table-leg), and was sticking in his stool as before. Augh! I bore it while he cleaned his spectacles, and then, just as he put them astride of his nose, I sent him bag and baggage flying through space away among my clothes on the sofa. Some time now elapsed, the interval being doubtless occupied by the mending of the spectacles with postage stamp, and straightening the trombone with the leg of the stool. But no time was wasted, for well under five minutes the band was on its legs again.

Now, at close quarters, even a sound trombone is an infliction to me. Judge then of my feelings in this case, where a short-winded performer was endeavouring to extract melody from an instrument battered, cracked, and bulged, by swift contact with half the bedroom furniture.

Pity for his youth and inexperience weighed with me for a moment, but only for a moment, and then, summoning all my strength, I brought my Nasmyth-hammer fist crashing down on his entire stock-in-trade; and utterly callous as to the massacre, fell calmly asleep among the ruins, murmuring his epitaph as I fell, *Requiescat in pacibus*—let him rest in *pieces*.

Asking a friend what was good for mosquitoes, I got the

reply, "Why, *you* are, or they wouldn't eat you, my dear fellow."

The garçon, who attends to my room, has a capital plan for getting rid of them. He knows of some stuff, to be had for a dollar, that will so "make to smell" my bedroom that no mosquito will remain in it for ten seconds. "Burn this," he says, "for four days." "But I leave here in four days from to-day," I explain. "Mon dieu! then," says he, "ve must begin at vonce." Nothing would do but I must give him the dollar; but I have got him to begin on the room of Mr. Courtney, who is not leaving till Thursday—five days hence. Thus have I secured my friend at least twelve hours' peaceful occupation. It gives me sincere pleasure to do Courtney this good turn, as I broke his stick the other day, pointing out a cockroach with it to a friend. It was altogether too slender a thing for pointing out Argentine cockroaches.

Say what you will, there is a brotherly bond amongst us English, that links our lives and interests, wander where we may the world over.

Sauntering through the Mercado Centrale (Central market) one very hot day, and while lunching off some fruit there, I noticed a tall well-built man of slim figure, in a tightly buttoned frock-coat, tall silk hat, and trousers, all in good condition except that the trousers were muddy and kicked into rags, and, being too long, were gathered in folds or shreds above a pair of boots burst in every direction; his age was perhaps thirty-five years. Meet him *coming up* your club stairs, and, from his refined carriage, you would take him for a barrister or M.P. for the pocket-borough of his family. (He reminded me of Col. Hughes-Hallett, ex-M.P.) Meet him *coming down*, and you would want to know why the hall-porter admitted such a tramp.

He passed me to get to some filthy rotten fruit displayed
in heaps on a large basket—black, moist bananas, pinky-
grey strawberries, and mildewed oranges—all nearly hidden
under black masses of flies, who were having dessert, after
dining on the putrid meat at the next butcher's stall. He
paused, turned the garbage over in his mind and with his
finger, and bought the lot for ten cents (about 1½d.), had it
put up in a newspaper, and carried off his parcel in front of
him by the lower end, as if it had been a bouquet.

What did he intend doing with that refuse? I tried to hope
it was for his rabbits (though I felt it would have killed them)
—but his boots and trousers at the
ankle forbade that consolation. I
followed him, hoping to get him to
accept a trifle, though he had a proud
look that didn't promise me much
success. Alas! he vanished, where to
or how I could not tell. Confound
it! I grumbled to myself in self-pity,
he has utterly spoiled my dinner.
With this and similar comments, I had
wandered through the market, and
was turning to leave it, when I came
plump upon him again. "Sir!" said
I quickly, pulling out my cigar-case,
"will you allow me to offer you a
cigar?" "Thanks!" he said, with a
look of surprise, and took one. We

Came to the last.

chatted about the price of gold and the rumours of revolution, and I soon found he was an educated Englishman;
and then I made bold and asked him straight out if he
would dine with me. "Thanks—no," he said; "I must go

now, for I have an appointment." And then, lifting his
hat, added, as he moved briskly off: "Besides, I *have* dined.
Good day!" And he was gone. But oh, worse than all,
his *parcel* was gone too, for he had nothing in his hand,
I saw, as he moved away. He had dined! An Englishman and starving! worse—existing on that which must soon
bring awful suffering before death comes with the welcome
warrant of release.

> While in my cup of Life I meet
> Bitter proportioned to the sweet,
> As husks are to the grains of wheat,
> I'll take the mixture with complete
>   Consent.

> Grant me one smile for every tear—
> That life be not too painful here—
> That friendship dear, be not too dear—
> I am—though I may not appear—
>   Content.

Yes, he had utterly spoiled my dinner—ay, and not only
my dinner, but, as a consequence, my night's rest also.

The heat, too, was intense that night, but I am afraid I
could have borne the one stoically, the other patiently on
board ship, or indeed anywhere but at the Hôtel l'Universelle,
which is the centre of a universe of clocks. I don't say
they will wake you if your eyelids have got a good grip, but
if from any cause you should wake, woe betide you! I
wouldn't give a cigar-end for your chance. There's no
getting away; and what can you do? "How many fingers
do I hold up?" is a game that I admit has been known to
brighten the twenty-eight days' enforced seclusion which,
under the name of honeymoon, is the punishment for the
offence called matrimony. (Well, it's just half bigamy, so it
ought to carry a stiff sentence.) But there's all the difference between playing a game in daylight and trying it in

the dark. How is a man to guess how many fingers he holds up in the middle of the night? It's ridiculous.

But to return to the clocks. Within earshot of this hotel there are—well, I hesitate to fix the number, because I differed with myself several times in the night on that point. I offered to strike an average, but this was rejected on the ground that there were *strikes* enough already. Well, we'll call it fifteen—it's under the mark, but near enough. Now (and this is where the fly gets into the pomatum) my theory is, that these clocks are timed so as not to interrupt one another. At any rate this is what happens. No. 1 strikes the hour; just sixty seconds afterwards No. 2 does the same, and so on. It is evident that one minute after the fifteenth clock strikes the hour, No. 1 will chime the quarter! And thus runs the world away.

Now, I acknowledge that by this handy little plan a man can, after a fashion, tell the time to a minute the night through, wake when he may. But then, look what a tissue of falsehoods it is. Will any one tell me that fraud of this kind—perpetrated no doubt in the interests of the Church, and therefore *pious fraud*—is not a discredit to any country? How does it (forgive the vile word) *strike* you?

If this thing is done by way of advertising the churches, it succeeded with me, for the following day, I suppose having got church-clock on the brain, I mechanically entered the church at the corner of the Calle Reconquista. The congregation was composed entirely of women. Barring the priests and the two half-choirs of boys with cracked voices, I was the only representative of the inferior sex present.

The priest who preached was the smallest, quickest, jerkiest man I ever saw. He shot up into the golden pulpit like a jack-in-the-box. Then up he jerked a golden cross, and down he bobbed and down bobbed the ladies. Then down went the cross and up came the priest and everybody else. They did this, it seemed to me, a dozen times, and were just about doing it again, when I said to myself, " This kind of thing is catching," and made a shot for the door. I was only just in time, for when I went to put on my hat, my head went up into it with a jerk enough to knock it off—showing that I too had been *ducking.*

In fact, ten minutes after, on joining my friends at dinner, they all remarked that my gait was that of a man with one leg shorter than the other. It grieves me to say that they received my plea, that I caught the trick in church, with undisguised scepticism. Thus ever are our best actions misjudged by a cold censorious world.

A bad night's rest seems to awake all one's faculties to their highest pitch of sensitiveness. To-day the smell of some lemon-squash I had, nearly choked me. The odour was a sort of mysterious something between tar and tobacco. One can only call it a tropical smell. It meets you on this voyage first at the Verde Islands—perhaps faintly even at Lisbon—and stands by you throughout your wanderings in tropical cities.

My sad experience with the clocks the night before sent me to bed last night at 9.30 p.m. It was as well, for I had just scored five and a half hours' sleep, when one of the cocks they keep in the hotel, I suppose to wake the servants, not being gifted with the necessary discrimination, woke me as well. At first I thought it was a mistake, but no—he repeated his demand so often that, finding him determined, I got up. The servants, I am ashamed to say, did not. This cock, I am sure, was English, like those we had on board. There was a bumptiousness, an insolence about the

challenge that showed his John Bull origin. But in England
he would not have waked me for another four hours. It's
conceit, that's what's the matter with him. He has heard
that there are English in the hotel, and so wants to display
his knowledge of the difference of time by allowing for the
58° west longitude. Now, patriotism is all very well, but I
think it is carried too far when it is used as a lever to get
me up at 3 a.m., because forsooth it is 7 a.m. in England.
Thank goodness! that last crow of his seems to have killed
the beast. It was clearly his destiny to die this morning,
but from the perfect joyousness of that last expiring effort
he could not, I should say, have thought his end so near.
Perhaps he had his fortune told in England, and they warned
him that he would die at 7 a.m., so he felt safe at three
o'clock. Ha! ha! Hoist with his own petard—the Fates
ran up his blue-peter at 7 a.m. *Greenwich time.* Well, I
don't wonder at the Fates having their clocks synchronized
from Greenwich. I should do the same if I had to run a big
concern like theirs. When you've got to despatch your
clients at the rate of one every second, there is no time for
logarithms. Still, that four hours' short weight was rather
rough on the rooster, who, I dare say, had several appoint-
ments to keep before 7 a.m. Argentine time. It is a sad
thought that the stable-heap, the pinnacle from which he
flung his last loud challenge to a listening world—worse luck,
I was one of them—is now his silent mausoleum. Let us here
in America whistle his funeral march, " Yankee-Doodle-Doo!"

Five of us from the *Clyde* are staying at this hotel. We
sleep and take early coffee here, getting all other meals at
the Café Filip opposite, where the cooking is excellent, and
the wild strawberries (*fraises*) a dish I shall ever remember.
We had them twice every day during my stay. Many of

the delicacies used in private houses are prepared at the convents by nuns, who are most skilful in their production. One article of dessert is very peculiar to European notions ; it resembles hard-boiled eggs, but the egg-shells are really only the moulds, in which the white turns out to be *blanc-mange*, and the yolk quince-jelly. Only give the proprietor of the Café Filip a little notice, and he will turn you out * as nice a little dinner as Buenos Aires can give you.

All the cooking in this city, it should be said, is done with paraffin stoves—no Argentine houses have ordinary fire stoves of any kind in the living rooms. The climate is supposed to be such as to render fires unnecessary. Pure fiction ! Men have told me they have known the cold here to be as trying as our bitterest English weather.

There is, however, no blinking the fact that the air here owes much of its exquisite purity and transparency to the absence of smoke. The effects produced by the getting rid of this one nuisance are truly wonderful, and one is constantly thinking what might not even London be made, if all the houses were by law fitted with smoke-consuming stoves. The marvellous beauty and unsullied grandeur of these evening skies make even the dull narrow streets of Buenos Aires delightfully soft and rich in colour. The city seems bathed in perfectly bewitching limelight effects which try in turn all the colours of the spectrum. The dingiest old crock of a town would be glorified by such treatment, and Buenos Aires is not, on the whole, dingy. Its squares—and there are eleven of them—are superb, but its streets are too narrow to do much with. All that is possible in the way of titivating, the sun does for them, dressing them in his choicest robes—and fine feathers do make fine birds, after a fashion.

* Don't pause at the word " out," or you may misunderstand me.—C. C. A.

Just now, however, the heat, which is phenomenal for the time of year, won't let you enjoy the city. There has been no rain for three months, a fact one's nose attests—and even London drains go all wrong when not well flushed. A city like Buenos Aires wants heavy rain once a week to keep it sweet. In the camps, up country, the cattle are suffering and dying by thousands. One noticeable feature in times of drought is the increase of insect noises. Wherever you light on a plot of grass, there is a positive shrieking and whistling as of myriads of crickets, and the frogs seem to have the full organ on. A bull-frog, as they call it, the other night in a hollow tree made a noise like a woodpecker.

The present heat must be exceptional, because the natives speak more of it to me than I to them. This might be taken for pure sympathy with *me*, a stranger here, were it not for their boiled-lobster look, and the mopping and fanning that goes on all day everywhere. Going with my kind friend Mr. Horace Wood to the London and River Plate Bank one afternoon, I found most of the officials were in black alpaca or thin yellow silk coats, and wore lawn handkerchiefs loosely round the neck.

There was only one man who had a high collar, and he had a good two and a half inches of it. Moreover, he was dressed in a tightly buttoned frock-coat of our winter texture, and had cuffs fully two inches and a half below the sleeves. *He* didn't seem to know it was warm. He was a broad-shouldered chap of about thirty years

"It's a bit milder to-day."

of age, six feet high, plump, florid, and good-looking; a

description which will not fail to find him for any one who wants to know how to keep cool with the thermometer at 110° in the shade.

One of the pleasantest trips of Courtney, Manley, and myself, was from the Central railway station to Tigre, about thirty miles up the river. The place stands in much the same relation to Buenos Aires that Kingston does to London, and is covered with handsome villas and larger residences, belonging to wealthy citizens, most of whom have businesses in the city. The train takes you through a country cultivated much after the manner of the *Pampas* camps further afield,

A *Rancho* on the Pampas.

and dotted at intervals with *Ranchos* of mud or wood : only here and there do you find a brick house.

On the way, I counted the skeletons of eight horses. There is no burial; as the horse falls so he lies, and the flies and vultures clean his carcase in ten days.

On the river at Tigre were a couple of large torpedo-boats, a number of yachts, steam-launches evidently well cared for and prettily fitted, and small boats without end. The whole country round was a garden of flowers and shrubs of every kind. Wild roses in luxuriance made bright the hedges, and honeysuckle of an immense size wreathed itself into bowers and climbed the trees in all directions.

The place possesses a magnificent hotel (almost up to the form of our "Star and Garter"), where we had afternoon tea, the only really good tea we had tasted since leaving England, for ship's tea is never up to much. In the hotel were several English people, and one tall, slim gentleman, with a fine grey beard, was there in yachting costume, just as I have seen him any time these twenty years at Henley-on-Thames.

In the cool of the evening we took the little tram that runs from the hotel to the station. Never shall I forget that ride. It gave me what was really, though I have mentioned them before, my first introduction to one of the sights of the country—the fire-flies. They swarmed out in myriads, lighting up the fields round about us for two or three hundred yards.

The country was closely covered with noble Quintas, or country-seats, the grounds being laid out in perfectly English style. On the tram with us was an English nurse and party of laughing English children, who got down at one of the best of these charming estates. It was a treat to hear their merry voices, and the lovely country seemed even more lovely for their bright presence. Altogether it was to me one of the most enchanting experiences I have ever known—here or anywhere else.

It is almost impossible for any one, in the midst of all these flowers, to realize that it is mid-winter in England, the season of snowballing and skating. Anyhow, I was fairly fooled by the Tigre river-scenery and the summer skies. It was 7 p.m., and the sun still lit up the hotel and the long reach of river. "Yes," I said to Courtney, "it is *very* lovely, but it is *not* the Thames. Just picture yourself at this moment away on an island, say above Great Marlow. It is sunset, and the tender English twilight will, for another half-hour, allow our eyes to rest on yonder fringe of willows where our boat is lying, and on that little bay where those fair girls in boating-dress are making the light air breezy with their rippling laughter, to the soft bass vocal accompaniment of their bronzed be-flannelled companions. A little flash from the midst of the merry group, and up curls the blue smoke from the fragrant weed which, next to woman, is man's best friend."

Thus far Courtney had borne with me, but here he shook his head. So did Manley, but for different reasons. Courtney, I think—I say I think—wanted to debate the question of precedence, preferring to place them in reverse order—viz. tobacco and woman. Manley was on quite another tack. With a face

Caution!
" Mind the longitude ! "

wreathed in smiles, he "ventured to remind" me that my picture hardly hit-off the Thames "*at the end of November, and 11 p.m.—allowing for the difference of longitude.*" Confound the longitude ! It is always getting between my legs and tripping me up as his sword does the new Lord Mayor.

There are two places of interest in the near neighbourhood of Buenos Aires, both of which should be visited—Rosario de Santa Fé and La Plata.

Next to the capital, the most important place in Argentina is Rosario, a town of fifty thousand inhabitants, and the port of the province of Santa Fé, situated at the western elbow of a bend in the Paraná, and a hundred and ninety-five miles north of the capital. Some day, when the network of railways in contemplation shall have been completed, they say Rosario will entirely eclipse Buenos Aires, and monopólize all the

Rosario de Santa Fé in the Argentine Republic (from the river Paraná).

trade of the interior. At present, with all the elements of civilized life, Government, Foreign Consuls, Hotels, Clubs, and Churches, the place is utterly devoid of beauty of any kind. The caravans of bullock waggons from north, west, and south, whose picturesqueness formerly gave to the place a certain primitive prettiness, have disappeared before the locomotive, and so deprived it of the one charm it possessed. A prey to dust and wind, there is an east-end look about it that renders it an unpleasant place of residence ; and though a general interest and one's through-ticket tempts one to *go*, there is nothing to induce one to *stop*. One, or at most two days of it, in the glare and choking dust, among fleas, mangy dogs, and locusts, is as much as one can stand.

There are two large Protestant churches, and one Catholic church. The shops and private houses, too, are fine buildings and of most enduring structure, a quality which they are said to owe to the mortar, which, made from pure river sand, is the finest in the world, and the lime, which, prepared from Córdova marble, is as hard as Roman cement. The Hôtel Central, built in Moorish style, is finer than any hotel in Buenos Aires, and the charges are reasonable. You can live there for 10*s.* a day, inclusive of good native wine.

Rosario, in the past, has been the home of political plots, and a dozen revolutions have been hatched there within two or.three years. But in recent times, increase of commerce has brought plenty, and, as usual, peace has followed in its train.

La Plata, the new provincial capital of Argentina, and a city of some sixty thousand inhabitants, lies thirty miles to the south of Buenos Aires, at the harbour of Ensenada, and is connected by twenty-six miles of railway with Ferrari on the Great Southern Railway. The story of its birth and

P

growth—it was born only seven years ago—reads like a fable.

Owing to the development of outside cities, their populations had so increased that at length a point was reached, when they exceeded the population of Buenos Aires itself. At this crisis it was found that an "outside" man, named Roca, was aspiring to the Presidency of the Republic. Whereupon the Portenas, as the people of Buenos Aires are called, began to feel jealous of the ambition of their country-cousins. So, to appease them, Roca boldly proposed that a new city should be built at government expense. The bait was taken. And as there was no time to lay out a state, application was made to the United States, and five hundred ready-made

THIS ELIGIBLE LAND TO BE LET FOR BUILDING PURPOSES

houses were shipped like toys, and put up with the rapidity of a country fair. A spot was chosen in the Pampas; all the revolutionary leaders were allowed to share in the speculation; war was averted; and so a brand-new city sprang up like mushrooms in a night, at a cost of nearly half-a-million sterling to the Government. It is already lighted throughout by electricity, and a most flourishing place — indeed, one of the

"Please send me one detached villa for corner of projected main Avenue."—John Jones, Pampas, La Plata.

sights of Argentina. It is much frequented by Portenas, who are as proud of this last member of their family as we are of our first member, Adam; and, strange to say, each *was born an adult.*

Argentina is a wonderful country, and destined for great things, and in visiting it, an Englishman cannot help feeling

Chalet Gobierno, La Plata, in the Argentine Republic.

disgusted with the disgraceful capitulation in 1807, which robbed us of an Australia distant less than seven thousand miles, or three weeks' journey from our shores. Its markets exchange produce with nearly every country in the world, the United States alone neglecting to profit by its great resources of production and powers of consumption. It is almost incredible that a pushing people like the Yankees should leave such a field undeveloped, and not have even direct communication with it. But, of course, it is all the better for us.

Something of its importance may be gathered from the following crude statistics. A mail arrives from, and another leaves for, Europe nearly every day; twenty-three lines of steamships connect it with the European markets, and from forty to sixty vessels sail to and from it every month. In Buenos Aires harbour—or what does duty for one—are dozens of steamships and scores of sailing-vessels flying every flag but that of the United States.

The Republic imports manufactured merchandise to the value of twenty million sterling every year, one-third coming from England, a fifth from France, and a fifth from Germany. The Pampas, which correspond to the northern prairies, feed a hundred million sheep (more than any other country in the world), yielding for exportation alone two hundred million pounds of wool. The Argentines not only grow wheat enough for themselves, but export nine million bushels annually; while their post-office in 1889 handled no less than twenty-five million packages.

Everybody who is anybody keeps a carriage, and anybody who does not want to be nobody rides horseback. You can buy a pair of the best horses for £30, and saddle-horses equal to any in the world for from £5 to £8.

Being a diffident man, I have deferred making any allusion to the appearance of the ladies of Buenos Aires. On most subjects I find no difficulty in offering some sort of an opinion, but on this particular question I feel great delicacy, for, while silence might be construed into want of appreciation of their many charms, words are apt to betray one on such a theme. One either says too much or not enough. Shutting my eyes, then, and making a plunge *in medias res*, I should say, that they have at any rate one of the characteristics of the Viennese, viz. most exquisite complexions. In a cosmopolitan population, such as that composing Argentina, one of course meets with all types and shades; and, as may be supposed, the mixed marriages which occur among those of the many different nationalities still further multiply the varieties of form and feature. Argentina is one of the human conservatories of the world, where may be seen every variety of species in every variety

Thirty-one last birthday.

of condition of intermixture. Perhaps the most striking charms of the Portenas are the ardent beauty of their eyes and the profusion and fineness of their hair, unsullied by oil or cosmetics of any kind. The inactive life they lead is, however, unhappily destructive of litheness of figure, and so we find the contour apt to become a little too pronounced after twenty-five to please the English eye, and after thirty to please any eye at all, unless indeed it be that of the "King of the Cannibal Islands."

CHAPTER VIII.

BUENOS AIRES TO RIO DE JANEIRO.

November 26th.—1 p.m. We have had a Pampero, which has left the air much cooler, but the sea very rough. As the tender starts with us for the ship, we meet cargo returning from her which it was impossible to embark on account of the heavy sea. It is very boisterous, certainly.

2 p.m.—Once more on board the good ship *Clyde*, Mr. Horace Wood and Mr. Courtney kindly coming to see the last of me. We all dined together, and then the bell sounded for strangers to leave the ship. As they and other friends, many of them ladies, went on board the tender, a most disgraceful scene took place.

It appears that a large number of men, whose foul and filthy language proclaimed them quite unfit to be allowed on board any ship, were resenting the foresight of the Captain and Chief Officer, who had refused to admit them. It was, indeed, Billingsgate let loose, beyond anything I had ever heard or seen. They had come to see their friends off, and the only thing that could be said for them was, that they had paid $6 fare by tender in the hope, no doubt, of being allowed to go aboard as our friends did. Nothing, however, could justify their vile behaviour; and it was with many fears for our friends' safety that we saw them going ashore in such company. As the tender drew off from us a free fight began, and I saw knives brandished by two or three people. The others, however, appeared to overpower these ruffians, and I hope all went well. But it was a disgusting sight.

8 p.m.—The anchor's weighed. The Chief Officer tells me that last trip they took fifty navvies on board, and on that occasion permitted their friends to accompany them. These guests got so hopelessly drunk, that it was with the greatest difficulty they were got back to the tender; indeed, some had to be lowered by ropes. So it was decided this time not to receive them at all. Perhaps it would have been better had this been made known to them while on shore. It must be annoying to pay $6—the same as saloon passengers —and then to be refused permission to board the ship with their friends, while saloon passengers were passing on *their* friends freely. Nor did it improve matters to let this tender full of disappointed people lie alongside during our dinner; for, of course, on the return of the favoured guests, the others found vent for their feelings and proclaimed their wrongs after their peculiar manner.

9 p.m.—Mr. Lloyd, a Welshman long settled in Buenos Aires, and now crossing to Monte Video on business, gave us, in Mr. Ritchie's cabin, a few samples of Argentine *cuteness*. One of the largest silk-importers in Buenos Aires was lately caught passing huge consignments of silk (which pays heavy duty) as soda-water (which pays none). He was fined, but had been so many years at the fraud that he could afford to laugh at the trifling punishment. Another gentleman who had the building of certain government offices, and so was allowed cement for them duty-free, used to import it largely in excess of his requirements therefor, *and sell the stuff*. Selling it under the trade price, however, as of course

he could afford to do, brought the rest of the trade upon
him, and so led to his discovery.

Our Welsh friend spoke tenderly of Llangollen, where his
heart was evidently fixed. He had left the old home five-
and-twenty long years, but still spoke of
a dear *girl* who had stayed there all that
time waiting for him. Poor young thing!
One of the "maids of Llangollen," I ventured to say. His answer recalled Charles
Lamb at the Scotch dinner, where Burns'
son was expected. "I wish it had been
his *father*," said Lamb. Whereupon, in

Waiting.
" He cometh not,
she said."

chorus, they solemnly told him that *that* would be impossible,
for the father had been "dead many years." Mr. Lloyd, in
almost the same words, replied to my remark, "My dear sir,
the maids of Llangollen are all dead long ago." (By which he
meant the *historical* maids, no doubt.) "Wha—a—a—t?"
shouted one sturdy member of the party. "Bust my canvas!
You don't mean to say you've waited five-and-twenty years
to wed a widder!"

November 27th.—4.40 a.m. We have anchored in the
roads off Monte Video. The *Wordsworth*, "Lamport and
Holt" line, is here; she is due with the mails to-day at
Buenos Aires. The *Cleopatra*, of our navy, is also here,
returned from the visit which, as we came out, we met her
on her way to pay the Brazilians at Rio, in recognition of
the new Republic. Her commander, Captain Musgrave, I
hear, won the chief prize of $50,000 in the lottery here last
year—dollars of the Banda Oriental, worth nearly 4s., not
Argentine trash. Any way, they said, the prize was worth
£8000 sterling.

After breakfast I went ashore for a five hours' ramble.

The city is built in blocks just as Buenos Aires, but it is altogether lighter and brighter. Much of this is no doubt due to the slope it stands on, which shows you more of the houses and streets from the sea. Of Buenos Aires you see absolutely nothing from the water, the place is so flat. But

The Prado, Monte Video.

in Monte Video the streets are very broad; most of the main thoroughfares are from forty to sixty feet wide, and the houses of pale blue, pale brown, or dazzling white, give the city an air of newness that is very pleasant. One sees none of the gloomy windows of Argentina; here the Venetian blinds are all light in colour, and the bright effect in the street of even such a trifle as this is very noticeable.

I said just now the city looked new. It is not new, however, for it was founded as long ago as the 1st of May, 1717, by the Governor of Buenos Aires, Don Mauricio Zavala, who succeeded in expelling the Portuguese settlers. Till 1726 it was only a military port, but in that year it was peopled by families brought from the Canary Islands, who were provided gratuitously with sheep and cattle. From 1778, when it was declared a free port, its commerce rose so rapidly that in fourteen years it became the greatest port in South America, with a trade of more than seven million dollars. The old town consists of one hundred and twenty-four and the new of two hundred and ninety-three *manzanas*, or blocks, each covering about two acres. Its water supply is pumped from Santa Lucia (a distance of thirty-three miles),

Plaza Matrix, Monte Video.

the second largest pumping main in the world. The water-pipes extend one hundred and fifty miles.

Of the old fort, San José, which used to stand at Rompe Olsa near the Custom-House, little now remains. From this point formerly ran in opposite directions the *Bovedas* or casemated arches, till, having encircled the old town, they met again at the old market, where Boulevard 18 de Julio now commences. Some traces of these fortifications are still visible near Mr. Jackson's *barraca*. They were constructed by two thousand Indians, who are said to have been engaged seven years on the work. So strongly did these Indians build, that in 1807 the place sustained nine days' cannonading before a breach was made.

The Bolsa, or Exchange, considered one of the finest buildings in South America, is a copy of that in Bordeaux. Its hall is decorated with the flags of all nations, *in fresco*. The Cabildo (or Town Hall), in Plaza Constitucion, serves for law-courts, senate-house, and prison. The Matrix, now the Cathedral, on the opposite side of the same square, contains, in its left aisle, the tomb of General Flores, murdered in 1868.

One of the handsomest buildings in the new town is the Church of the Immaculate Conception, built in 1858 by the milkmen, market-gardeners, etc., and commonly called the Church of the Bascos. The Boulevard 18 de Julio, said to be incomparably the finest street in South America, terminates at the English cemetery. It is undoubtedly a magnificent thoroughfare, and greatly in favour with the residents, but I am told the most fashionable quarter is in the suburb Paso Molino.

According to a local guide-book, the most remarkable monuments are those to the victims of Quinteros, and to the

heroes of Paysandú. I am ashamed to say the only heroes
of Paysandú I can recall, are the proprietors of the huge
establishment whence come those luscious tongues, in which

" Heroes of
Paysandú."

the fat and lean are so sweetly blended as
to form, if one may so say, a "confusion of
tongues." By the way, those heroes (hero and
heroine) are at this moment passengers with
us on board the *Clyde*, returning to Scotland.
They go to and fro every year, I hear, with their bright
little girl, to look after their enormous business.

A pretty ride is to be had by train from Plaza Inde-
pendencia (every half-hour) to Union Village, five miles out
north of the city, whence is obtained a view overlooking the
coast in the direction of Pando. After passing windmills
innumerable, and many strikingly pretty rustic damsels, you
come to the Bull-ring at the end of the village. Long ago
abolished in the Argentine, the sports of the Circo dos Touros
have flourished here. But its days are numbered, for a law
was passed last year abolishing them throughout the Republic
Oriental. A mile further north is the English racecourse,
where meetings are held twice a year.

Another good excursion is by train from Calle 25 de Mayo
to the Aguada. Alighting here and ascending the Hill of
Bella Vista, a fine view is obtained of the city and bay.
This quarter is also a favourite one, as evidenced by the
beautiful country houses, plantations, and gardens that line
the road.

The *Banda Oriental*, or *Eastern Strip*, was once a part of
Argentina, which was then known as the Banda Occidental.
Uruguay is the old Indian name and the legal one, but the
people are known as "Orientals." The Republic has a
population of five hundred thousand, and an area of seven

thousand square leagues, or about the same as England. The soil, however, is said to be so productive, that it would support fifty times its present population. Any grain or fruit will 'grow—coffee, corn, bananas, pine-apples, wheat, sugar, potatoes, apples, and oranges. Food prices are remarkably low: beef and mutton 2½*d.* a pound, partridges 5*d.* each, chickens and ducks 7½*d.* The Pampas support eleven million sheep and seven million cattle. At the same time they manage to produce five million bushels of grain, and to feed seven hundred thousand horses. But while food is cheap, rents are high; it is hardly too much to say that they are four times as high as in England.

A Mr. Evans, one of the principal residents in Monte Video, and a millionaire, began life in the Oriental by nearly losing it in a wreck, from which all he saved besides himself was a ship's boat. In this boat he earned his bread as a longshoreman, carrying passengers to and fro between the harbour and the ships. He has now the finest private park (Prado) in the River Plate country, and in the basin of an immense bronze fountain in the centre of the park, still floats, as his most honoured guest and pensioner, the boat that saved his life and shared his fortunes.

He and she.

The tram lines here are single, as in Buenos Aires, but, unlike them, they go and return by the same route, causing continual stops. The time wasted in this way alone, the

city through, must cost the citizens thousands of pounds in
the year.

The waggons are of the very roughest make, springless, and,
like brewers' drays, buttressed in three places at the side ;
they are usually drawn by oxen three abreast.   Here, as in
Buenos Aires, horses draw the trams, which take you five
miles for four centavos (2*d*.).   Mules are reserved for working the rough carts in vogue here, which are built like large
crates on wheels.

The butchers' shops I noticed had over them some rather
well-drawn sketches of a goat, a pig, and a bullock in
triangular form, signifying the three kinds of flesh sold
there.

Here, as in Buenos Aires, milk is sold by men on horseback, unless (which is common) the cows are brought and
milked at your door.   But butter is made by placing the
milk in leather bags, which, fastened to the end of a lassoo
hitched on to the pommel of a saddle, are rattled over the
stony roads as the horseman gallops into the city.   Thus the
rider tows his milk to market, and churns the butter as he
goes.

My first purchase gave me quite a surprise.   I had just
come from the Bolsa, where gold was 140½ per cent., *i.e.* 40½
premium only, which should have reminded me of the
enormous difference between the value of the dollar here and
in Buenos Aires.   But it didn't !   I took a fancy to a little
paper figure of a Spanish dancing-girl, and hearing it was but
80 cents, bought it, and not until after I had left the shop
some moments did I realize that this paper trifle, for which
I thought I was paying dearly at 9*d*. or 10*d*., had actually
cost 3*s*. !   Both here and in Buenos Aires, anything artistic
is sure to have been imported and paid duty, and is therefore

expensive. To find anything representative of the industry of the place was most difficult; they import from all parts, but make next to nothing themselves. European goods fetch enormous prices, being in high favour; but except the few things used in horse-capture and breaking-in on the Pampas, I know of few articles suitable to bring away as souvenirs.

Mr. Turner, a resident here, who travelled with us and was my kind friend going out, came off to-day to bring us

Monte Video.

his good wishes on our homeward voyage. We shall miss him and his bright little girls going back.

My observations with regard to the women of Argentine apply to the Uruguayans also. Their beauty lies in complexion, and not in form. The texture of skin here is even finer than in Buenos Aires, a fact attributable, I feel convinced, to the greater purity of the water. Ladies everywhere little know how much of their beauty they owe to this element. Have you ever noticed, my dear lady, how soft your skin has become when staying at certain places; and has it ever occurred to you that *the water* was your real benefactor?

Some day, perhaps, I will tell you how to obtain just that very water at all times, in your own house, so simply, cheaply, and effectually, that you will open your eyes with wonder that such a necessary has been so long disregarded.

4.10 p.m.—The anchor is up. Farewell, Monte Video ! I can hardly believe it is but twelve days since I saw you first and last. The excitement of Buenos Aires life made one's nerves so keenly sensitive that one felt, as it were, on tiptoe all the time. In such an alert condition, every throb of life is felt and notes itself deeply in the memory, and the sum of all these impressions produces an exaggerated estimate of the time they occupy. We judge time by events, and if any particular hour has as much thrust into it as we usually experience in two hours, the impression is that two hours have passed.

Here we are, once more rushing back to Flores, but happily not to stop. The city and shipping along the white shore for many miles look very pretty in the bright sun. Going to and coming from the shore to-day the sea was tipsily rough, our boat rolling and pitching and shipping sea after sea. Yet here, only a few hours later, we are gliding along on an unruffled surface.

I have just extended a new deck-chair, or bedstead, I bought in Buenos Aires, a most luxurious thing. It would have been nice to have had it on the way out, but in our then crowded state it would have been smashed to a certainty. Everybody helped himself to chairs, books, field-glasses, anything, without asking—ay, and broke and lost them too for you. Now we are quite a small party; so far, indeed, I have had the whole of my cabin to myself again. My seat is, of course, as before, at Mr. Ritchie's side, and I am perfectly happy.

My health has greatly improved, and my appearance has undergone such a change, they tell me, that I am constantly cautioned not to expect to be recognized at home. Several have offered me certificates of identity, at varying charges, but I have not come to terms with any one yet.

We left Buenos Aires with about sixty saloon, thirty second-class, and one hundred and ninety steerage passengers, in all two hundred and eighty, as against eight hundred and thirty going out. At Monte Video we added slightly to the saloonists, of whom we have now seventy, I think.

7 p.m.—At dinner there were three nice fellows at our table, and the ice was soon broken under the influence of champagne, which usually circulates pretty freely during the first days of a voyage. I am to be lucky again, it seems.

Some reason can always be found sufficient to justify what the Australian diggers used to term "a shout." It's a man's birthday, or his mother's, or a friend's, or a friend's aunt's: or we are leaving Europe, or sighting America, or quitting Argentina, or bound for England. The mention of England was a good card at any time. But, for the first day or two

" Bricks and their mortar."

no excuse is needed; all drink sparkling wine as being the best kind of mortar for making a composite body out of human bricks.

And I must admit it answered admirably, for we soon began to feel interested in one another—to my mind, a condition necessary to the enjoyment of travel of every kind, more especially on ship-board. The ship is a forcing-house for character, bringing out whatever is in a man of good or evil, so that in three weeks you shall see him through and through, inside out, and upside down (for the motion of the vessel produces both these results), and know him more thoroughly than in three years on shore.

And so it must often happen, I think, that after the three weeks' voyage out, there will be some people in whose company you would rather not journey home again. The pleasure with which I found myself at my old friend Mr. Ritchie's table once more is to me, therefore, the sincerest testimony to his uniform affability and good nature.

But this reminds me that the reader, who may be presumed to have, as it were, voyaged out in *my* company, may not care to return with *me*. I cannot but feel that, touching as we shall touch at the same ports on the home run, my subject must lack that freshness, without which interest is with difficulty sustained. Moreover, in describing the ports as I went out, I have deprived myself of that element of interest on the way home.

Then, too, I have counted on the leisure of my return trip for expanding my notes, and I feel, therefore, that my second part must and will share the fate of all second parts, even of such treasures as " Robinson Crusoe," or Bunyan's " Pilgrim's Progress," and suffer from comparison with its elder brother. They said Sheridan was deterred from writing a second play by fear of the author of the "School for Scandal." And in my humble way I feel that though my voyage out is not likely to prove very entertaining reading, my return bids fair to be even less so.

I merely mention this so that when the reader shall have come to the same conclusion, I shall at all events have the little satisfaction that every one feels more or less, of saying " I told you so."

I heard of a nail-maker once who, having made a bad nail, promptly cursed the *man who should use it.* When asked why, he replied, " To be even with him; for whoever uses that nail," said he, " is sure to curse *the man who made it."* With this argument before me, I will only say, the reader of this " home-coming " *has my strongest sympathies.*

At one time I had hoped to have been able to make a little variation in my homeward route, for, on the notice-board at my Club in Buenos Aires, the *Clyde* was announced to touch at Santos. Had it done so, I should certainly have gone ashore there, run up to San Paulo, and then on by rail to rejoin the ship at Rio. But unfortunately, my inquiry at the Company's office had only the effect of making them send and correct the notice-board. The *Clyde* never touches at Santos.

The Falls of Itamarati, Serra de Estrella, near San Paulo.

Of course you could get there from Buenos Aires, or Monte Video, in a coasting vessel, starting three or four days ahead of the *Clyde,* and rejoin her at Rio; and, from all I can hear, this would be worth doing, for San Paulo is a sight that ought not to be missed by any one coming within near range of it.

9.30 p.m.—As I lie in my berth, the Southern Cross,

still inverted, fills the field of sky seen through my port-
light, exactly as my friend described it, every star falling
within that area.   It seems clearer and brighter, and shows
to better effect in my dark cabin and cut off from the
surrounding stars, than I have yet seen it.   Its isolation is
the secret of its success to-night, I think.   " Fair as a star,
when only one is shining in the sky," as Wordsworth sings.

10.30 p.m.—The sea is rising.   There is a long and heavy
swell on "full abeam," i.e. on our broadside, and the *Clyde*
is light, and tumbling about very much.

November 28.—7 a.m.   This has been one of our roughest
nights.   Short of coming out of my bunk, as on our first
night out from Lisbon, I have performed every conceivable
acrobatic feat.   My bed-clothes came off several times
through the vessel rolling me about, and the getting out
and in were as difficult as getting into a boat alongside in
a gale of wind.   You had to wait and time your jump in
or out, and even then you would usually land with either
your head or your shin against something harder than itself,
which, as the reader doubtless is thinking, is more remarkable in the case of the shin than in that of the head.   Fore-
seeing which process of ratiocination, it will be observed that
I have been careful to say " *your* head," and " *your* shin."

Noon.—Lat. 32° 34' S., long. 51° 11' W.   Run, 306 miles.

1 p.m.—My cabin steward, a man named Vine, who had
been most attentive going out and was still looking after me,
has come with the news that the lunch bell has gone.   My
watch is only 12.35, so we have already picked up nearly
half-an-hour.   He is right; they had just finished as I
joined them in the saloon.   Note—" *In Vino veritas.*"

My *vis-à-vis* at breakfast, Mr. Mervin, a bright merry
young Irishman returning from Buenos Aires, tells me we

were on the very brink of revolution last Monday when they sponged the Bolsa slate. He saw ammunition served out to the troops under arms in the Plaza Victoria — an amusing spectacle for the police, I should say, seeing that however little damage the combatants do one another, the Vigilantes (as they are called) are sure of the warm attentions of *both*. Well, it only shows — all theories of bad pay to the contrary notwithstanding — what a very good berth a policeman in Argen‐ tina must have. For surely the pickings and perquisites must be large, that would tempt a man to stand as a target for *both* sides, in

A "marked man." Suggested uniform for the Argentine police.

a competition where a "magpie," or an "outer," scores as much (or means as much to him) as a "bull's-eye."

3 p.m.—It is very rough, and an elderly English lady has been in a great state of agitation all the morning, asking all sorts of questions about the life-saving appliances, and why *separate boats were not reserved for ladies*. In all her trouble, she has shown consideration for those engaged in working the ship, by putting her questions to the passengers only. "You know," she said to me, "I am never nervous, because I always make it a point to learn exactly *what to do*. In a train I ride first-class, not because of the company, but because the carriages are well padded, and I choose one near the guard's van, because most collisions occur in front. A full carriage is preferable to an empty one, for two reasons: —there is not so much space to be flung about in, and you

may be warned of an approaching accident by others before you would discover it yourself. And forewarned is forearmed."

This lady was returning with her husband from Valparaiso to England, and to avoid the long and boisterous voyage round the Horn, they had come across the Cordilleras on mule-back and thence by rail from Mendoza. Several young German officers had come by the same route, and were going through by the *Clyde* to Antwerp, and so on to Berlin.

What a palace such a ship is as compared with the very finest vessels of the General Steam Navigation Company! Last year I and another were three days battling with not more than half-a-gale from Hamburg to London, and so bad was it that we got off at Harwich and came to town by rail. The real discomfort to me, I remember, was not so much the violent motion of the vessel as the all-pervading smell of one hundred and eighty ponies we were carrying. It hung about me for days after. On the *Clyde* there is nothing of that sort, and as to the half-gale, she would make very short work of that. She runs from Southampton to Antwerp in sixteen hours, if I am not mistaken; and only look at the difference of comfort on board!

8 p.m.—The Captain is unlucky in getting the greatest nuisances at his table. The end seat on his right has acquired the name of "Drunkards' Corner." For some time a Brazilian, on our voyage out, sat there in an almost chronic state of intoxication, behaving himself, after the manner of his kind when in that condition, like a wild animal. In the end he had to be shifted to the second-class quarters (a step which the occupants resented fully as much as he did), where he was in charge of an attendant night and day. This inebriate's explanation of his conduct was, that not drink but grief was the matter with him, brought on by heavy losses—

the said *losses* being somewhat of a negative character, it seems. His complaint was that he had inherited only *two-thirds* of a large property of which he had expected the *whole*.

In this very seat now daily sits another passenger who conducts himself like a baboon. After drinking and sleeping alternately the day through, he comes to the table dazed and unkempt as if he had been used as a duster to wipe out a hay-cart. As soon as he can sit down (no easy task), he at once opens the ball with a large bottle of champagne, and talks louder and louder as he swills it down, sops his bread in his soup, picks his fish with his fingers, dangles slices of meat over his mouth and eats away up to his hand, and finishes up by devouring a dish of salad from between his elbows, consuming it (as a horse would hay) bit by bit as it hangs in a bunch from his mouth, and all the while with eyes fast shut. Such a sight is utterly disgusting to decent people, but I do not know how it is to be prevented without adopting very extreme measures.

To-night we shall pass Santos, to the coffee plantations of which, it may be remembered, the emigrants were bound on our way out. It lies about three hundred miles on this (the south) side of Rio, and ranks in point of its exports as the second port of the Brazils. It is a dirty, damp, unwholesome place, and would call for no mention here did it not afford a key to one of the most beautiful spots in the whole Republic.

San Paulo—which has been called the Paris of the Brazils—offers to those who have time and opportunity, a charming diversion which can be taken on this route either going or returning. From Santos there is a tram which takes you some four miles along the Bay, to a delightful spot from which to view it; but *the* sight of course is San Paulo.

An English railway, forty miles long and built about twenty years ago, takes you from Santos over the coast range of mountains, the Serra do Mar. For a distance of five miles a cable-road runs over the mountains in four inclined planes, the ascending being balanced by the descending train. The extreme height of the ridge is two thousand five hundred feet, and the greatest railway gradient is one in ten, the train being worked by a powerful engine at the top of each incline. The views from the top are superb, I understand, extending over valleys full of magnificent trees of brilliant foliage, and away over the mountains where peak rises above peak from the sea to San Paulo.

Here grows in profusion the shrub known as the Mandioc, whose large roots when scraped to a pulp, pressed, baked, washed, and dried, become the tapioca of commerce.

San Paulo, a city of fifty thousand inhabitants, lies upon a great plain bounded by low hills which everywhere form its horizon. It is a great coffee-growing country, yielding two and sometimes three harvests a year. It has the healthiest climate in the Brazils, and is remarkable for the beauty of its scenery, and the opulence of its residents, whose houses— though but one story high—are both comfortably built and luxuriously fitted.

The railway journey to Rio, a distance of three hundred and ten miles, occupies by express train about thirteen hours. There are no less than fifteen tunnels, and the climbing of the Serra is effected by two engines, one at either end of the train. The scenery is said to be indescribably grand, including as one of its chief beauties a view of Itatiaia, the highest mountain in the Brazils, rising nine thousand feet above the level of the sea.

29th November.—8 a.m. The rattling of the cable in the

Railway, Santos to San Paulo, Brazil.

tube down which it passes to the hold, disturbed my rest sadly in the night. At last the officer on the bridge, to whom I complained, had it wedged and all was well. But this was 4 a.m. Punctually at 7 o'clock the ever-prompt Vine, as usual, brought my Van Houten's cocoa, which Mr. Blinkhorn, the chief steward—to whom I am indebted for many favours —procured me at Monte Video. Of course, I was sound asleep, and had to be waked up. Boiling in castor-oil is too gentle a torture for the man who calls me when I am asleep in the morning after a sleepless night! Vine literally kills me with these kind attentions. He breaks his way into the cabin like a fireman who is determined to save my life or die in the attempt. He is so atrociously thorough. Well might Talleyrand condemn zeal. No doubt he once had a punctual man to wake him. Vine was a man who would actually come and tell you it was *not* time to get up yet. Ye gods, just think of it! Cocoa, boots, bath, breakfast-bell, any mortal excuse was good enough. One would think I was suffering from belladonna poisoning, and Vine had instructions to keep me awake. If this should meet the eye of any one so afflicted, I can strongly recommend Vine when he leaves me. Apply to my executors, *after the funeral.*

Noon.—Lat. 27° 33′ S., long. 47° 00′ W. Run, 373 miles.

12.45 p.m.—The bell has just sounded for fire-stations and boat-drill. As all the waiters are mustered with the sea-men, and lunch is at one o'clock, there is but a quarter of an hour.

Heroes rehearsing.

2 p.m.—It proved far more than enough, however, for both performances. And we were saved! It was almost painful to see some of the heroes of this gallant band, within ten

minutes of their daring exploit, handing round potatoes in the saloon as if nothing had happened; and then to reflect, had the ship been on fire or on a rock, where we should have been now but for the coolness of those with the buckets, and the daring of those in the boats !

4 p.m.—The weather has been perfect to-day. With bright sun and cool breeze we have been bowling along at a uniform sixteen knots, *i.e.* over eighteen miles an hour, 18·24 miles exactly. A Brazilian frigate, very trim and pretty, passed us within five hundred yards, the only object we have seen since we left land. But one never feels dull at sea, eyes and ears are so busy on board.

We brought away one hundred and ninety steerage passengers from Buenos Aires, nearly all Portuguese—home-comers—and differing greatly from the out-goers we took to Rio. They have clearly thriven, and are going home with enough saved for their simple needs, perhaps £1500—£500 for a bit of land and £1000 to stock it—but *all their own, and in their native country.* They all seem happy and well-clothed, but still faithful to the flaring colours of their race, and to its dirt in their persons and their habits. They hate water with greater intensity than the Frenchman hates it.

One day going out, when a baseless rumour got about that owing to a hitch in the bath-room there was no water, it was real sport to see the alacrity with which all the dirty Portuguese, to a man, rushed for their sponges and flocked to the baths, hoping to score " good form " before the water-supply returned. But to see their faces when they found all was as usual ! And the deference with which every one was for giving way to every one else, who wouldn't, of course, *hear* of such self-sacrifice !

A friend said the only parallel to their surprise was that

of some fellows he knew tiger-hunting, who rushed with lighted faggots to a cave to prevent the tiger taking refuge in it, and—*found him already there!* One could only say that their going pace was put hopelessly in the shade by their returning record.

8. p.m.—Mr. Ritchie has been telling me a funny thing about a former third engineer, when he (Ritchie) was second. Seeing him loafing about, Mr. Ritchie asked if he had done a certain job he had set him to do some time before. "I'm going to do it when I go down," said "Third." "You're going to do it *now*," said Ritchie, "and then you're going to tell me why you didn't do it when I told you." Five minutes later, hearing a frightful noise, as if the engine-piston had got free and was pounding into the works, Ritchie went below, and found the delinquent facing the boiler, on which was chalked in outline a figure with a peaked cap which there was no mis-taking. By the aid of a ten-pound sledge-hammer, he was evidently serving the sketch as he would like to have served its original. Not a bit abashed, the youth swung round, sledge still in hand, and apologizing for his delay in fulfilling instructions, voluntarily explained that now he was only

"cracking a nut." "Then give me the kernel," said Mr. Ritchie, "for that nut" (pointing to the sketch) "is clearly mine." "We were capital friends ever after," added the Chief Engineer.

The returning emigrants have been doing a native dance. Two men, one with

The Monedas.

castanets, faced each other and performed ten figures with

differing steps to the music, or rather the time given by a third man on an old tambourine. Both dancers were fagged out at the finish, yet each had retained the stump of a cigarette between his lips all through. The dance is called the *Monedas*, or money-dance.

The tippling passenger has just been amusing some of us. Stepping off a thick mat, the two inches of descent seemed to startle and send him plunging forward as if he had had a deep fall. He pulled himself together, and seemed to argue that, bad as the fall was, he must not let it frighten and conquer him. So bracing himself for an effort, he cautiously returned to the mat, faced round, and *lifting* his foot (for a *downward* step, mind you) a full yard high, advanced, strode triumphantly over the precipice, and awarded himself first *and* second prizes at the bar—both " cock-tails."

Apropos, I have just heard of a comical experience that the man on my left at meals had last night. Being very thirsty from having had too many " drinks," he called the cabin steward and, unable to speak English, tried to make him understand by signs that he wanted some lemon-squash. At first a biscuit (!) was brought, but on his imitating the motion of squeezing the lemon, the steward felt that with such clear pantomime there could be no uncertainty about his wants, and so brought him a glass of *milk*, which, hopeless of getting anything else, the poor sufferer drank. Dumb motions are at times misleading.

This reminds me of a little story a great man once told me relating to his nursery days, a story that has always seemed to me less humorous than pathetic. " One morning," he said, " while my sister and I were watching from our window a knife-grinder at work on his double-pedalled machine opposite

our house, my father, who was near-sighted and had nearly
lost his hearing, seeing us interested, came and stood between
us with his hands on our shoulders. Presently the knife-
grinder, having finished his job, got off his seat and was
preparing to go away, when my father, who had evidently
mistaken the side view of the man and of his pedal movements for a musician playing a harmonium (or seraphine, as
it would then have been called), gave the nurse a few pence,
saying, 'Ask him to play the children one more tune.'
Booby-like, I remember the thing so tickled me that *I*
laughed, but only one little laugh, for my sister's sad, pitying
look stopped me at once. Quick as lightning, with that
happy intuition which nature has bestowed upon the gentler
sex, my sister snatched the money from nurse's hand,

ran across to the knife-
grinder, and taking him
into her confidence, by the
aid of the pence she got
him to stop and sharpen
one more knife! This
he did, remounting his
machine and slowly and
solemnly pedalling as be-
fore. Then dismounting
once more, the fellow,
with a true appreciation
of *his* part in the little
drama, touched his hat to

" *Dear, kind* Papa."

my father in itinerant musician style, and went his way.
With like dramatic instinct too, I remember," said my
informant, " my little sister clapped her hands, and I, from
mere mimicry, did the same. In memory I can see her

now, as she stroked father's hand upon her shoulder and
kissed him many times (while the man sharpened that
last knife), and many times too he must have read, upon
her lips and in her eyes, her oft-repeated, ' *Dear*, *kind*
Papa !' "

In the Organ Mountains, Rio de Janeiro.   (From a painting by
Walter W. Buckley.)

Botofogo Bay, Rio de Janeiro. Residence of the artist Walter W. Buckley. (From a painting by himself.)

November 30th (Sunday).—9.30 a.m. We breakfasted in sight of the famous Sugar-Loaf Mountain, at the entrance to Rio Harbour, and we are now in full view of Corcovado. There has been a nasty smell near my cabin lately, as of sour milk. The Quarter-master has just explained that it is some *Carne Serra*, dried flesh, as the Brazilians call it, or in sailor parlance, "jerked beef," sewed up in sacks, which we are landing at Rio, I'm glad to find.

10.30 a.m.—For the last half-hour we have been waiting for pratique, and having now got it, we are moving again and going up to our old anchorage. A Brazilian coaster has just hauled down her "blue-peter," and put out to sea. The fort on our right has dipped its flag.

11 a.m.—We are at anchor, and I am going on shore at noon to " do " Corcovado.

1 p.m.—Ashore. It being Sunday, and all the money-changers in Rio closed, I went to lunch at the Hôtel Globo, where they knew me, and would take my English money. There I met two English fellows, who most kindly put me in the way of tramming it to the Mountain Railway. They also kept me company in the tram nearly all the way. From them I heard that an armed attack had been made the night before on the office of the *Tribuna* newpaper, which is in sympathy with the dethroned Emperor. It seems to be my

luck to get into hot places in every sense. This disturbance looks like a bad business, to judge from the way all are talking about it and wondering how it will end. The excitement is intense and widespread.

4.30 p.m.—After a charming tram drive through the favourite suburb of Botofogo, I have reached Corcovado and am waiting for the five o'clock train up the mountain. I am

Paneiras Railway, Corcovado.

the sole representative here of the *Clyde*, though there are eleven other people going.

6.30 p.m.—We have been to the top and seen the sun shed his farewell glories upon Rio and the Bay.

The railway is of somewhat peculiar construction. Between the wheel-rails is a barred eight-inch ratchet, into which a cogged wheel, beneath the engine, fits. In this way a grip is got sufficient to *push* the train up the steep incline, the engine being behind. The road is circuitous, making a two-mile journey of the distance, which, measured as height, is but two thousand four hundred feet. Some six hundred feet from the bottom you cross the first bridge, a red, slender-looking iron thing, bridging a chasm of six hundred feet. Shortly after you pass over a second and smaller one, and arrive at a landing-place called Paneiras, where there is a very good though small hotel, kept by a rather morose Frenchman.

Your first glimpse of the city is obtained just before reaching the first of these bridges, and thence to Paneiras the

" An awful corner." *

little railway cuts its way through sandstone rocks which in places overhang it rather too suggestively. Winding through these and the dense tropical forest of gum-trees, palm, acacias, india-rubber trees, cactus, etc., the view is entirely obscured, but a lovely bit of the bay comes in sight as you reach Paneiras, where you change trains. Till lately, this was the terminus, and the rest had to be done on foot. Now you enter a second train which takes you to the summit.

In this top piece lies the only sensation that at all tests one's nerves. At a certain point— which point I unhappily knew only too well, having looked up at it from the deck of the

* This sketch was accidentally taken from the *negative* of the photograph. To get the proper aspect hold it in front of a looking-glass, or view it as a transparency through page 248.—C. C. A.

Clyde—the line traverses the very edge of a precipice seventeen hundred feet sheer down. Passing this point, if you have nerve to enjoy it, you get a delightful view of Botofogo and the Botanical Gardens, conspicuous in which is the Avenue of Palms, dwarfed into nothingness by our great height, but exquisitely symmetrical. The line then makes a sharp turn from this precipice towards the summit, and in doing so gives you an ever-increasing prospect over its side. It is a very trying experience, especially for those who, having seen this awful cliff from the sea, know what it is they are thus climbing higher and higher over. You cannot help thinking what eternal smash a little crack or flaw in the machinery would produce at and above this awful corner.

But if you feel this going up, what of the downward trip? Yes, what indeed! Well, I confess it did make me hold my breath. There is no use in mincing matters, for the life of me I could not enjoy the divinely grand view here *coming down*. The same sort of thing on Vesuvius did not touch me compared with this. For me, it was impossible to breathe at all till we had passed this utterly horrible spot. We actually came down that gradient of one in five at five or six miles an hour! Perhaps it was safest so, and the speed was certainly merciful as putting me quickly out of my misery. Going up you *knew* of the danger, but this way you had to *face* it. The other passengers had never seen the precipice, you could tell that from their behaviour, and their ignorance was bliss to them. How I wished, for the sake of my enjoyment of that splendid view, that I had not. But I *had*, and of course gave myself the full benefit of the knowledge at the critical moment. Ugh! I shall never forget the sensation down my back and legs.

At the top is a huge structure (it looked like a pill-box

from the ship) big enough to shelter five hundred people, a
sort of iron canopy with open sides, where refreshments can
be had. They charged me eight hundred reis (1s. 8d.) for
some ginger-ale and a nip of cognac for the railway-guard.
Here I waited to see the sun go down behind the lofty sister-
mountain Tijuca, glorifying all the lesser mountain peaks
for fifty miles round. Then suddenly, for there is no twilight
here, the city sprang at once into its spangled nightdress,
the lights starting out all over the immense expanse of

Paneiras Hotel, Corcovado, Rio.

houses as if a fireworks display, worked by electricity, had
been planned for my particular delectation. The sight was
magically grand; yet, of the eleven people who had come
up with me, not one remained to see it.

When we got back to Paneiras, I found there was not a
bed to be had, so, utterly disconsolate (for I had longed to
see the sun rise from the mountain, and to wander in the
forests on its sides in the early morning), I took my seat in
the last descending train. Luckily this did not start for
ten minutes, during which time I became more and more

discontented at the prospect of no sunrise and no orchid-hunting. At last I could bear it no longer, and just as the whistle went I sprang out of the train and let it go without me. The proprietor of the hotel, seeing this, again assured me that there was not a bed vacant. " Then I'll sleep on a chair, or in that little railway carriage," I said. At this juncture the railway engineer spoke a word for me, and, one way or another, it came about that they let me have a room—bright, clean, and if not large, large enough.

At dinner I found myself seated with one other visitor, with whom I spent the rest of the evening most enjoyably. He was an Englishman—Colonel Alexandre—staying permanently at the hotel, and he had with him some of his own sherry, which he kindly shared with me. The Colonel, who has retired after thirty-nine years' service in the Royal Artillery, came to Rio to advise the ex-Emperor on its fortifications. He was fully up in the political situation, and gave me many interesting comments thereon.

Last night's attack on the *Tribuna* was, he told me, brought about by military officers disguised as civilians, who, resenting some of the articles in that journal, determined to smash and ruin it. The article which was the immediate cause of the *Tribuna* outrage, contained an attack upon the newly made President who was the Emperor's right hand. Reminding him that he owed all he is and has to the Emperor, it proceeded to inquire whether it gave him no qualms of conscience to reflect with what base ingratitude he had requited his benefactor, by becoming the moving spirit in his enforced abdication. In brief, it was a homily on " Et tu, Brute ! " In the assault, swords were drawn, shots fired, two people wounded, and hundreds more frightened almost out of their lives. The cry of *Fecha*, " Shut up shop,"

Rio de Janeiro from the roads.

soon spread and grew into one of *Revolucão!* and the stampede in the streets was becoming alarming, when troops made their appearance and by degrees quieted things down.

The ex-Emperor seems to have been a very feeble man for such an exalted position. He received everybody un-announced. Court ceremony there was none. You could walk into the palace as into a public office, and, as like as not, you would find yourself asking the Emperor himself the way to the Imperial presence. He drove about in the shabbiest of carriages—a mere fly, indeed—and used to get hustled and pushed about through going to railway stations unattended.

There must be something in the old copy-book text about " familiarity " and " contempt," after all. An Emperor may be quite of the common or garden variety, if only he will live in a hothouse and not show himself. He remains dear to the people till he makes himself cheap, which seems really to have been the greatest fault of the dethroned Brazilian. There is a demand for gooseberry-juice labelled " Champagne," but how much champagne could you sell honestly labelled " Gooseberry " ?

My friend the Colonel thinks a permanent Republic is out of the question here, where the population is of such mixed nationalities that there can never be a community or identity of interests. As in Argentina there are a million Italians, so in Brazil there is a huge German population. The Colonel gave me an illustration. Say a Brazilian, sent as Governor to a state wholly or nearly German, makes rules which he deems wise, but which do not meet with approval there. The local papers " Guy " him and say he is a fool ; he appeals to the central authority for support ; he fails to get it, and retires. This is constantly happening.

Leaving my congenial companion, after a parting cigar on the terrace overlooking the bay, I turned in for my short night's rest at 11 p.m.

December 1st.—At 3.30 a.m. I was on the move again, and out at four o'clock in the dark, wending my solitary way once more to the summit. No sound but the hissing whistle of swarms of frogs and an occasional salutation from a goat far away up in the black recesses of the mountain, no light (for the moon lay lost in a bed of cloud) but the glimmer of the fitful fire-fly. During the previous evening these fire-flies had lighted up the shrubs on the heights near the hotel, till, what with the stars above, these gipsy lights around, the spangled city, and the lights of the ships riding in the Bay, one felt in a new world altogether. It was as if the lamp of Aladdin had transported us, the sea, the city, and the everlasting hills, somewhere up into the region of the " Milky Way."

It is now 4.30 a.m., and I have climbed to the topmost point of Corcovado, through the clouds.

Last night, as the sun set, I stood here while broad belts of flame, in token of his parting benediction, shot out between Tijuca and the neighbouring mountain. The rosy panorama I then beheld to seaward lies colourless before me now, the dim outline only sketched by the great world painter, ready for colouring when he comes this morning. There it lies on his gigantic easel. The Master is coming, and before him, sweeping up the mountain sides and through its rifts, blundering and huddling along and jolting each other, the masses of black cloud, through which I struggled a few minutes ago, are whitening like silver fleece.

Glancing over my right shoulder to the south, my view stretches over an open sea. Turning slowly towards the left,

Corcovado and the Sugar-Loaf, in the Bay of Rio de Janeiro. (From a painting by Walter W. Buckley.)

it first passes four or five islands. Then comes a further glimpse of sea and I am looking to the front due east, where on the broad ocean's calm surface lies darkly just one little ship. Slightly further to the left of this is the far-famed Sugar-Loaf Mountain, the entrance to the bay, and the mountains on the many islands and mainland. Still further to the left is the bay, and between me and it lies the whole of Rio, while, forming the extreme background in the same direction, stand the dark blue Organ Mountains. Thus one has a panorama filling three-quarters of a circle. Should

Mouth of Rio Bay, from Santa Thereza Hill, Rio de Janeiro.

I wish to complete the circle, a slight turn brings into view the rugged range of mountains rolling far away behind me to westward, with at its northern end Tijuca, the sister-peak to this, rearing her head three thousand two hundred feet above the sea.

4.50 a.m.—The east is still merely grey, pale blue in places, and with just two dashes of rose. Out to the north the Organ Mountains are clothed in a hue of *lapis lazuli*, the snowy clouds below their summit showing up the blue superbly. At my feet is Rio, a harmony in all shades of green, the toy houses looking like models in pink card, and

s

the ships in the bay reminding one of specimen beetles on grey card—the masts mere pins to hold them in position. The islands, great and small, that dot the surface from my extreme left to right, seem mere sand-patches left dry by the receding tide.

Straight before me to the eastward, a moment ago, a vessel full sail was but a black speck. She is on fire now, and through my glass every spar and bit of canvas is as burnished gold. Yet, but a little to the left of her, the islands and distant mainland are still of uncertain outline, and patches of grey cloud here and there are lingering and unwilling to go—patches so small, many of them, that they

The Gloria Church, Rio de Janeiro.

might well have been caused by some half-dozen guns saluting the new flag. Ah, there they go, helter-skelter, hurtling over the hills.

It is ten minutes after five, and the sun himself has come at last; but the red is fading out of the eastern sky, which has become a pale yellow, softening to dove-colour. The little vessel is dark again, having moved out of the path of the sun's rays which form, as it were, a huge ship's wake of shimmering rose from the horizon to my feet.

To the left, a group of velvety islands of a deep plum-bloom tint sit in a row on a cushion of rose, while far

away to the right, what I know to be four or five islands of
considerable size, lie like large grey limpets on a bed of
slate. The sun seems to have passed from the clouds, out
of which he emerged to show himself for a few moments
only, and has entered an immense, dense cloud-bank between
here and the sea. He will not appear again, I fear, and it
is six o'clock and I am cold; so I say adieu to him—no, *au
revoir*, for I hope to see him many and many a time on the
homeward voyage.

On my way down I gathered some lovely ferns, and lost
my way wandering from the railway track, but soon found
it again by following the
channel of a mountain tor-
rent where water was rushing in fanciful cascades
among the moss-clad rocks.
After a good breakfast, I
started for a couple of hours'
orchid-hunting through the
mazes of the forest down
the mountain side behind
the hotel. Twelve were
all I could find in the time
I had, and in all my life
I never felt hotter nor did
harder work. Gustav, the
hotel waiter, procured me

Orchid-hunting.

a box and some mould for my ferns and orchids, and also
a handkerchief to cover them; indeed, he was a capital
fellow.

In the train all went well; but the tram-officials made a
great to-do about my parcels, no luggage of any kind being

allowed on the passenger trams. However, by dint of per-
severance, and a most fortunate ignorance of Portuguese,
I got through to Rio with all my little belongings.

After making a few purchases in Rio, and lunching at
the Hôtel Globo, I made my way on board the *Clyde* about
three o'clock, and at 3.50 p.m. we sailed away, and sad to say
for the last time, from Rio Janeiro—the most lovely spot
I have ever visited in my life.

As an impartial observer, however, it behoves me to record
not only what I *see* but what I *hear.* Of the disadvantages
of Rio as a place of permanent residence I have said something on my way out. Since then the indictment has been
amplified in many ways. Perhaps I may be excused for
introducing here some verses embodying the opinions of
a resident. They were addressed to—that is to—hem! an
infatuated visitor. It is not well to identify one's self in
these matters.

PRO'S AND *CON'S.*

'Twere bliss, you think, to live and die
    In such a lovely vale.
If you'd been here as long as I,
    You'd tell a different tale!

It *is* an exquisite delight
    To come and see the views.
But live here, and you'll find it, quite
    Another pair of shoes!

Our streams and woods have rosy paths,
    And bowers the woodbine makes;
The streams are alligator baths,
    The woods preserves for snakes!

The mountains piercing azure skies,
    The wealth of flowery dells:
All these, of course, you'll memorize—
    But what about the smells?

With every tint in flower, and bird,
    And tree, to charm thine eyes,
The scents and songs most smelt and heard
    Come from the nigger styes!

What though metallic plumage glare,
    And gaudy flowers gleam:
The rose no perfume lends the air,
    The parrots only scream!

This " Eden " spread from sea to sea,
    And climbing to the skies,
The salle à manger seems to be
    For all created flies!

And when the sun breeds pestilence,
    The fly, where'er he feeds,
Displays a plaguy diligence
    Distributing the seeds!

At home you're all sun-worshippers,
    Because he veils his face.
His mystery your devotion stirs,
    You summer-loving race!

But here on view the whole year round,
    The sun's the god of evil:
His very name a deadly sound:
    We hate him—like the devil!

Go home!   And when in sunless days
    You wish that you were back
Where Phœbus lavishes his rays—
    Remember " Yellow Jack ! "

For me ; when I can homeward stump
    And quit the place, I will.
I'd rather far be Aldgate pump
    *Than Emperor * of Brazil !*

8 p.m.—Acting on the advice of my friend Mr. Mervin,
I have clipped off every particle of green about the orchids,

---

* A slight anachronism. He
    Must mean the " *President.*"
    The " *Emperor* " is an absentee,
    And not *a resident.*—C. C. A.

and stowed the roots in ashes, and the steward having kindly procured me a champagne-box for my ferns, they are doing well under a fresh-water tap which drips day and night. While I have been on shore, Mr. Ritchie has most kindly attended to my "Star" razor, which now bids fair to shave well. Everybody—but he more especially—is so thoughtful in these little things, which after all go to make up the thing which we call "happiness."

December 2nd.—7 a.m. While attending to my ferns just now, out came two spiders from a small orchid I had set in the mould with the plants; the creatures measured about three-quarters of an inch long and half an inch wide. On showing them to some Argentines, they at once declared them to be tarantulas. This has set me thinking what risks I have been running through sheer thoughtlessness. In the forest yesterday morning, I remember noticing what I thought was a black slug partly out of a hole in the rotten trunk of a tree. The quickness with which it disappeared into the hole when I touched it, struck me at the time, but only now, on talking it over with others, have I been able to realize that, likely enough, it was a poisonous snake.

In a butterfly trip like this, flitting from spot to spot—from England to Spain, Portugal and Brazil, all within a few days, one does not, cannot grasp the full effect of the transitions. It is next to impossible, for instance, to go thus quickly to Rio and appreciate, while there, that one is in the Brazils and not in Europe. Yet there are plenty of novel features that should act as constant reminders. It must be that the general interest is so roused as to be out of focus for detail. Just as one will often remember dreamland events, without being able to recall the scenery in which they occurred. Speaking for myself, although my notes fill two hundred pages and a great part of them include descriptions of scenery to aid my memory, while I can recall every incident of the entire voyage out and home, the localities with which they should be associated in my mind have faded, and are with difficulty furbished up in a fashion by the help of sketches, notes, and photographs. This being the case, it has come upon me since I left Rio, almost with the force of a blow, that in my orchid and fern-hunting in the Brazils, the very nest and hotbed of the reptile world, it was very foolish of me to put my hands freely as I did into all sorts of holes and crannies. Yet never once did the thought cross my mind while there and doing it.

Noon.—Lat. 20° 44′ S., long. 39° 43′ W. Run, 264 miles.

It has been raining hard all the morning, so I took the opportunity of playing a celebrated chess player, a Mr. Eissengarthen—whose great forte is blindfold chess, five or six games at a time—a level game. To my joy I was able, after a hard struggle, to force a draw. My opponent kindly invited me to have another and decisive game, but I am quite satisfied that I should not improve upon my present position, so am resolved to rest on my hard-earned laurels.

3 p.m.—A curious story was told me by a passenger this afternoon, of a man he travelled with to America, who used to take opium pills. A second passenger, he said, having a dog on board, whose howling kept his master awake, bethought him of these pills, and not seeing the other fellow about, ventured to take two from his cabin without asking. These he gave to the quarter-master to quiet the dog with. Next day, on casually mentioning what he had done, the owner of the pills got livid and frantic, rushed off to the dog, and muttering something scarcely intelligible about "danger,"

"fatal," and so on, administered an emetic to the poor dog, but without apparently any satisfactory result.

Thus baffled, he began bidding for the animal, £5, £10, £20, £30, £40, and in the end gave £50 for him—the master judging, as the price rose, that there must be a sufficient reason for it. At the next port, the master's destination, it was arranged that he might take the dog's silver collar, and so he did, leaving in the last boat before the ship sailed on her way.

The bell had rung, the gangway was hoisted, and the screw

had made some half-dozen revolutions, when the dog was seen to take a flying leap over the ship's side into the sea, where, fighting his way, he soon reached his master's boat and was lifted into it. A narrow escape for the poor fellow, who, had he remained, was destined to undergo a surgical operation in quest of two diamonds worth £500

A " returned empty."

apiece, which his purchaser was smuggling in the opium pills!

But the funniest part of the story is yet to be told. The quarter-master, when questioned, admitted having forgotten altogether to give the dog the pills, and was presently prevailed upon for a gratuity to produce them. Whereupon it turned out that they had been taken from a box of genuine pills, and those containing the diamonds had not been touched. There is only one more fact to add, namely, that the authorities on shore got wind of the story, *arrested the smuggler, and confiscated his diamonds !*

To which I have but this to say,
That fifty pounds is a lot to pay,
For an *empty* dog that runs away.

9.p.m.—Talking just now with an Englishman long resident in Argentina, he kindly corrected my pronunciation of that word. The "g" is like the German "ch"—Archentina, therefore, is the correct sound. Mr. Scott, a passenger who joined us at Rio, hearing this little lesson, said it reminded him of the policeman of whom a Frenchman inquired his way to "Karing Cross." Drawing himself up to his full height and looking down his nose at "Froggy," the man-in-blue delivered himself thus: "It ain't 'Karing Cross;' the diphthong 'ch' is not hard as in 'cab,' 'cucumber,' 'cork,' but soft, as in 'sherry,' 'sugar,' 'shirt.'"

A vessel passed us while talking, and we all remarked a curious effect of her lights. While the red port-light seemed where the ship was, the white masthead-light looked to be three or four miles further off. It was really impossible to believe that both lights were on the same vessel. Another has since passed us presenting the same peculiarity. Slowly as we are going, fourteen knots only, each ship was in sight but just ten minutes.

Strange to say, our slowing down is due to our having been *delayed* an hour and a half over our time yesterday at Rio. If we had cleared by 4 p.m. we should be going full steam, and should reach Bahia by 5 p.m. to-morrow; but leaving as we did at 5.50 p.m. we cannot fetch there till too late for business purposes. So we have made up our minds to go slowly and enter Bahia at daylight on Thursday.

December 3rd.—7.30 a.m. Have just seen my first whale at close quarters; I could have hit it with an orange. He was one of the club-headed species, built like a river chub, and as he rose for air, he blew a cloud of white spray such as one sees round a fountain on a fine summer's day. Three or four times did he give us this sight quite near to the ship.

Several of us in pyjamas and dressing-gowns were watching him from the deck, whither we had strolled as usual after our baths. Ladies are not expected on deck till after 8 a.m., and if they come they should be prepared to tolerate this trifling amount of *déshabille* in a man's attire. On this occasion a lady audibly commented and withdrew, though for the life of me I cannot see what indelicacy there is in shirt and trousers and a dressing-robe. Linen suits are the chief wear in the Brazils —silk and linen, silk, silk and flannel, and flannel. To debar a man so attired, and who has just tubbed and had his coffee and cracknel, from the natural sequitur of a blow on deck, would be cruel. And I'm sure no lady would wish to be cruel to the inferior sex, unless indeed she belongs to the *fin-de-siècle* female guild, which has just discovered that man is woman's "under-study;" in other words, that "the proper study for mankind is"—woman. From such there is no quarter. It is war to the fruit-knife with them (they are mostly vegetarians), and, against man, as their natural enemy, they have drawn the bodkin and flung away the case.

The shocker.

Noon.—Lat. 15° 53' S., long. 38° 26' W. Run, 308 miles. Bahia 175 miles off.

3 p.m.—There has been so much to do writing up my notes and keeping an eye on current events, that I have

omitted to record my final leave-taking of Rio. The city was in a great state of commotion, and there was a military parade in force along the Rua Direita, the main thoroughfare in which is the Hôtel Globo, where I lunched. While there, I met Colonel Alexandre, who was coming aboard to take a farewell of our Minister at Rio, who was going with us to England. When I got on board, I found, to my great joy, Sir Vivian Bland also there, and had the pleasure of bringing this gentleman and the Colonel together, whereby I claim to have provided each with a very entertaining companion.

Sir Vivian had come to take leave of the old ship homeward-bound, having himself to remain some time longer in Rio. I strongly urged him not on any account to sleep in the city, which is a fever den, and recommended the hotel at Panciras, where the Colonel has been staying for some months. The rooms are small but very clean and cool, the food is excellent, the forest hard-by is full of choice ferns, and orchids are to be found in plenty. If ever I had to stay in Rio, I should make Panciras my head-quarters, that is to say, where I should lay my head at night. By rail and tram you reach the centre of the city in seventy minutes.

Candidates for the Plaza " Victoria Cross."

8 p.m.—An Argentine has just told me an amusing incident of the Revolution. On July

29th, when the fighting and bombardment were at their
height and shells bursting in all directions in the Plaza
Victoria, an Englishman and his wife were seen quietly
sauntering across the Plaza, about as much concerned as if
the troops there were merely on parade. At the door of the
Congress Hall they stopped, and each turned a big opera-
glass upon the squadron and watched the shelling. Then
sauntering back across the square where shells were falling,
to Government House, they advanced towards the President,
who with many others was seated there, and each shook

.The Harbour, Bahia.

hands with him. The gentlemen all raised their hats and
were too polite to allow a muscle of their faces to indicate
their amusement at this *sang-froid*. But when the eccentric
couple were out of earshot, one of the deputies exclaimed. in
Spanish, " Good God! What a race! No wonder half the
world belongs to them."

This all sounds very neat, and I am sorry to spoil a good
thing; but really when one hears of shells falling thick and
fast in the Plaza Victoria, one must call a halt. They never
fell *thick* or *fast*, and the sighting for Government House,

which the squadron wanted to hit, was so atrociously bad
that it and the square around it were about the safest places
in the city. Again, this "bombardment," it should be
remembered, occurred during the armistice, and was of course
speedily silenced. And yet again, when the other fleets saw
the wild firing, fearful of being hit themselves, they laid
their heads together and sent an ultimatum to the Argentine,
that if he didn't cease firing the combined English, French,
and American fleets would open fire on *him*. All which
goes to show that the shelling must have been very brief as
well as wide.

December 4th.—5.20 a.m. I wake with the rattle of the
cable, as we anchor once more in Bahia. One can't go
ashore without first getting something to eat, and by the
time one has tubbed, dressed, and fed, it is seven o'clock.
As the notice is up that we sail again at 10 a.m., it gives at
most a couple of hours on shore.
Still, I am going.

10.30 a.m.—I have had another
look round the interesting old
place, peeped into a church or
two, which are even at that early
hour well filled with black women
dressed in the brightest colours
obtainable. At intervals during
the services, a very peculiar effect
is produced by the firing off of
crackers. It is supposed to indicate a *festa* (feast), but you
hear them constantly. Nearly

Festa at Bahia.

every day is a feast-day here. To the English ear, the
going off of crackers is about the most unimpressive sound

imaginable. And when some sixty churches set to work ringing bells and firing crackers, the effect is positively ludicrous. In Bahia this is for ever going on. You hear it far away on entering the bay, and you never quite lose it for an hour the day through.

It is related of Bahia, that once upon a time a certain Captain anchored in the bay during hazy weather. After carefully listening for an hour or so for the well-known sounds of bells and crackers and hearing none, he gave the word to "weigh anchor," and cleared out, convinced, as he said, that he was *not in Bahia at all.*

CHAPTER X.

December 4th.—11.32 a.m. Our Captain has just given similar orders, and soon we shall not be "in Bahia." We had rather an ugly experience going on shore. A friend and myself had engaged a boat, and were sitting in the stern waiting to start, when ten or a dozen of our Portuguese steerage-passengers sprang unceremoniously in too. Of course our boatman was delighted, for he got a milreis (2s.) from each of us, and we found had bargained to take these Portuguese at half-a-milreis apiece. Their weight, principally aft, brought the gunwales of the boat dangerously near the water, I thought, and when, a minute afterwards, our boatman flung a hawser to a passing tug to take us in tow, I guessed what would happen. The instant the rope was taut, we rushed through the water with a wave six feet deep following in our wake, and if six or eight of us had not rushed forward and eased the boat, we must have swum for our lives—and it is a very sharky spot.

Coming back, we had quite a row to get the men to take us aboard again in time. The Portuguese had not come up at the time fixed, and we determined to go aboard without them. But we had to overpower the men and take the oars ourselves; and then, as luck would have it, after all our trouble the laggards appeared in sight, and for very shame

we had to put back and take them in.   Poor fellows! among
them all there was only one who could write and cipher—
and the way he reckoned up the amount he was to pay the
boatman for eight of them, at five-hundred reis each, was by
*putting five hundred down eight times over, and then adding
up the eight lines!*   My friend and I both saw him solemnly
doing this—and saw too in what respect the feat seemed to
place him with his companions!

The weather was threatening going, and it rained hard
coming back.   Now a perfect deluge is falling—a thorough
tropical storm.   There are two *Catamarans* out in it, with
sails close furled: the men must be drenched through and
through.   There can't be a dry thread on them.

The Chief Steward has kindly brought me off some fresh
mould, and I have just replanted my ferns, which are looking
healthy.   There are about twenty-five in all—only one or
two rare ones.   All the better; the commoner the hardier.
All I want is to get some of them, good, bad, or indifferent,
alive to England, as mementoes of Rio and its giant guardian
Corcovado.

The Doctor has just opened a cage containing the wildest
of wild marmosets, about the size of a rat.   He screamed at
us like a very maniac, and curled his head under his body,
rearing his back and glaring at us horridly.   He looks like
a little old man with grey whiskers, and reminds me exactly
of the fiend in " Rip Van Winkle," who lures Rip to his
fateful sleep on the mountain.   The intervals between the
vicious-looking teeth, the white patch on the forehead, and
the grin full of sin were all there.

4 p.m.—One of our friends has just been telling me how
he was able to give a liberal contribution to a charity fund
on board ship, during one of his many voyages.

Somehow it leaked out that he had a "curiosity" with him on board the ship, which is like a board school—anything will do for a diversion. Men will pay a shilling, or five shillings, to see on board what they would not go to look at if it were shown for nothing on shore. My friend's marvel was an animal which was announced to be going out to the Buenos Aires "Zoo," and certainly a most eccentric freak of nature it purported to be, viz. "half-dog, half-bear."

There was a little poetic licence in this description, but it answered beyond his wildest dreams. Everybody came to see it, and everybody paid a shilling. The thing was a mere hoax, of course; but as the visitors were admitted but one at a time, each saved himself from wearing the fool's cap by handing it on to the next comer. The animal in question was a French poodle, the hinder half of which, being shaved, constituted him, in sound at least, "half-dog, half-bear" (*i.e.* bare). By deftly manipulating the prices of admission according to circumstances, charging more for some and less for others, he actually realized for the charity a sum of five pounds.

"Half dog, half bear."

8 p.m.—There has been a great to-do in the Captain's cabin. One of the emigrants has been robbed of a diamond ring, and his piteous cries mingling with the protestations of a suspected companion, and interspersed with the comments of the maitre d'hôtel, of a gentleman who is acting as interpreter, and of the Captain, make up a very Babel of sound—as some one just said, "there was a sound of *devilry* by night." From all I can hear the net result is that the poor man who has lost his ring, has been cautioned to be more careful in future. From which I gather that our Captain is

T

not a *gaucho*, or at least not a Facendo Quiroga, who was a *gaucho*, and who was called as a pet name the "Tiger of the Plains," of whom there is a story told which, for shrewdness, certainly runs Pog's plan for discovering the real owner of a watch, very close.

It appears Quiroga's soldiers had, amongst them, managed to "find" some article of value "before it was lost," and the matter was accordingly submitted to the chief.

Ordering a sufficient number of twigs to be cut, all of an equal length, Quiroga handed them round to his soldiers, who each took one. They were then told—and *gauchos* are incredibly superstitious, and would believe anything and everything their chief told them—that they were to parade the following day, by which time the twig of the real culprit would have grown an inch, while the other twigs, of course, would not. The following day, at the dread hour, all were paraded. The chief, with stern brow, passed solemnly down the lines in perfect silence. Nothing happened, all seemed over, and one heart in those ranks began to beat again, and to hope that all was well. When suddenly, wheeling round as he reached an elevation from which he always viewed his men in line, he called aloud in a voice of thunder the name of one of his soldiers. "Advance, thief!" he cried, and forth came the poor staggering wretch, whose haggard looks and faltering steps made full confession of his crime before his words. Snatching the twig from the trembling hand, Quiroga cried aloud : "Behold the thief! To death with him!" And as he went to his doom the self-convicted prisoner confessed, that in fear lest the growth of his twig should convict him, he had *shortened it by one inch*.

Ordeal by twig, and doubtless the origin of the expression, "Don't you twig?"

December 5th.—8 a.m. The night has been very hot and oppressive, by reason of the closing of all the ports. There was a head wind, which caused us to ship a little water now and then, and so at 3 a.m. we were all disturbed by the steward coming to screw up the port-lights. Being thus thoroughly waked up, I utilized the opportunity by going on deck for a blow at 4 a.m.

The "Southern Cross" was higher in the sky than I had ever seen it, and by dint of oft-repeated overtures I am positively getting to like the thing. Like the wart on an old friend's nose, time is consecrating it as a tender memory. It is still upside-down—not the nose—no, nor the wart, I mean the "Cross"—and leaning east and west at an angle of forty-five degrees, and has never looked to such advantage. Usually it has been low in the sky, and therefore partially obscured by the clouds that gather along on the southern horizon on most nights. Orion, instead of being over the masthead, is about twenty degrees to the east of that position, and Sirius (more brilliant than I have ever seen him) about forty degrees.

The wind caused by our rushing through the air at eighteen-and-a-half miles an hour, felt quite warm to me, though I was hatless and in nothing but pyjamas; but there was motion in the air, and even that was a treat after the deadly stillness and heat of the cabin. In fact, it had much the same effect as rapid fanning, or the swinging of a punkah in a hot room. The glass in my cabin stood at 86°, and when I brought it up on deck it dropped to 80°, where it remained stationary.

Noon.—Latitude, longitude, and run not announced.

All the way from Bahia we have been coasting within sight of the shore, which looks extremely pretty with its golden strand gleaming like ripe wheat, and bright green hills, and far away behind these the pine-capped mountains. It is, I

believe, in reality, a desolate shore, and the natives are most
inhospitable to any poor fellows wrecked on their coast; but
from this safe point of observation—perhaps ten miles out—
it at any rate possesses all the enchantment that distance
lends to view. Away to the right, and well within view,
lies the last point we touch at on the American coast.

1.5 p.m.—Pernambuco! We have just passed the *Liguria*,
Pacific boat, anchored here, and are at this moment dropping
anchor ourselves.   In less than
five minutes the bumboats are
alongside, with oranges, bananas,
melons, and luscious magnificent
pine-apples.   I am counting on
getting a barrel of pines as presents for my friends at home, and
have commissioned the Chief
Steward to buy them for me on
shore. We stop but four or five
hours, so I shall not land myself.

Bumboats alongside the *Clyde*.

Of live stock they brought
on board monkeys, parrots, and
cages containing from twenty to fifty small birds of all sorts,
with brilliant plumage of every hue. The steerage passengers
haggle from the spar-deck with the bumboat people, and
when a bargain is struck, up come the purchases in a bag,
pulled on board by one string and guided from the boat by
another, the money being sent in the returning bag.

3 p.m.—The after-deck is covered with all the birds and
animals for sale, and this is the last chance for anybody
intending to take a monkey or a parrot. There are cages of
from thirty to forty blue-plumaged tiny birds that fight, and
when they peck, hold on to one another like bull-dogs. They

have no song, but their colouring is grand. None for me,
thank you. I should not mind a parrot if I could attend to
it myself, but you are not permitted to take a parrot into
your cabin, and if you hand him over to the butcher, which
is the only other way, it costs you five shillings for his keep,
and he may die. That is, he may die *by proxy.* There is a
ship's proverb that "the butcher's parrots never die," the
explanation being that if one of his should "shuffle off," his
dead body is put on a living bird's perch, and the live bird
is—well, we'll say *adopted* by the butcher.

4.30 p.m.—The Doctor has most kindly bought two parrots
and given me my pick of them. My choice has fallen on a
little six-months'-old chap with no tail, and only one-and-a-
quarter wings. I never saw such a disgraceful case of clipping;
it is more like amputation of the wing.
But he's a merry little chap, and is
singing and chattering already as I
write on the top of my broad-brimmed
hat. He cost me three milreis (six
shillings), and I call him cheap. (If
the punctilious Pog were here, he'd
say, "No, you don't; you call him 'Che'
only. You might have added the rest
while you were about it." But this is
"too previous," as they say. See
further on.) He would certainly not
be cheap as an article of food (baked

Aspiring to the crown.

parrot is by no means an unsavoury dish), for he would be, I
should say, a mere shrimp when plucked; but he has a note
out of all proportion to his figure.

Some *men* are built that way, with voices utterly belying
their looks. I remember once getting a surprise in that

respect on entering a " 'bus." At the end were an elderly
lady and her daughter, and opposite them a tall, fat, beefy
young curate with perfectly auburn hands, to whom they
were listening with solemn rapt attention. Out of this
mountain of plumpness, a good six feet high and eighteen
stone in weight, there was wafted along the centre aisle of
the " 'bus " a sound so fluty, so dulcet, that no one would
ever dream of its coming out of *him*. It was the proverbial
" Mountain in labour, bringing forth the mouse." He had his
eyes closed, and this is what he said, or rather sang :

"The German nation is a more musical nation than the English nation,
and hence we find that the German piping-bullfinch is a more melodious
songster than the English piping-bullfinch."

The ladies smiled through their tears, and seemed
quite overcome, and I—I got on to the roof for fear of giving
way myself ; there was such tender pathos—such a tear, as
it were, in the voice—that, before I knew where I was, I
found my hand in my pocket instinctively scraping the edge
of a threepenny-bit to see that it was not a fourpenny in
view of the coming collection. It was the exact ideal voice
for a charity sermon.

We have had the funniest afternoon performance with the
parrots and two small marmosets the Doctor is taking home.
The smaller and tamer one, being loose in the cabin, and
seeing the parrots in the adjoining dispensary, tried every
dodge to get to them, climbing over me, time after time, and
looking out for a possible jump to land him near the " *Papa-
gayo* " (Gay Papa), as the Brazilians call the parrot. At
last we let him go, and the mite-of-a-thing capered straight
up to my bird, and, standing on his hind legs, challenged the
good-natured fellow. Polly made room for him, and " gave
him best," as they say ; but all would not do. The little demon

Anchorage of Recife, Pernambuco.

flew up at once and fearlessly snatched her piece of orange, not because he wanted it—oh no—but just out of pure cussedness; for, the moment he got it, off he started right under the parrot's beak (where, if so-minded, the bird could have chopped him in half with one snap), and quietly went to work gnawing the bird's foot; and when the poor sufferer screamed with pain, the little devil screamed too, and, turning upon the second parrot, served her the same. For two hours did this little scamp fight, first one and then the other, and beyond a noisy but harmless protest, neither has cared to do anything to defend itself. The arena of conflict has been crowded to witness the antics and prowess of this little marmoset.

5 p.m.—Mr. Blinkhorn has returned from shore with the news that the *Liguria* and another vessel, coming in ahead of us, have cleared out the entire stock of pine-apples in Pernambuco! Many on board besides myself are bitterly disappointed, and so will many more be at home. The *Orinoko* (Messageries Maritimes) has just steamed out past us; they are dipping to us and we to them. The *Liguria* left while we were at lunch, I hear, but we shall overtake her, Mr. Ritchie says, in twenty-four hours.

5.50 p.m.—We are off again just as we are trooping in to dinner. "Farewell, America!" I hear friend Mervin say. A sure sign that champagne will be called into requisition at dinner. Well, it *is* an event, there's no denying that.

8 p.m.—At dinner the electric light went bang out, for the first time in my experience on the *Clyde*. It has often gone dull for ten seconds or so and then revived, but to-night it went out, simply. Amid shouts of "Chief Engineer!" my good friend Mr. Ritchie hurriedly left the saloon, and we heard him tell the gunner, Bo'sun, third engineer, or somebody to "get up" (I suppose the said somebody was sitting

on the wires) and immediately the light returned, and so did Mr. Ritchie, who was received this time with frantic ejaculations of "Saved, saved!" On shipboard a joke of any kind, a poor seedy thing that you'd be ashamed of in your silliest dream, is welcome. Hence my *vis-à-vis* was able to score well, on the spur of the moment, with this atrocity—(Question) "What goods does it pay best to export?" (Answer) "The Electric light, because whenever it 'goes out' its full value is 'brought home' to you."

Pernambuco, as I have before said, is famous for its sharks. Here is a photograph of the first, or a *bit* of the first caught aboard the *Clyde*. The bonny, bearded face in the centre of the picture belongs to one of the Quartermasters.

The two parrots and one of the marmosets had a little tea-party this afternoon. The Doctor and I had been having afternoon tea in his cabin, and there being some tea left in my cup I handed it to my parrot, whom I have christened "Che" (pronounced Chay), the name in Argentina answering to our "chappie." He at once accepted the gift, cup and all, and standing on the edge—it was a heavy cup—drank, bowing in stately style at each sip. The fiend monkey watched him for a couple of moments, and then, getting insupportably jealous, climbed to the cup-rim too. At this point, the second parrot attempted to join the tea-party, but the moment he put one foot on the cup the monkey bit it, and, standing up on his hind legs, he grinned, yelled, chattered, and gibbered in such a way that he appeared to be slanging the intruder in several languages at once. Finding this eloquent gibberish had no result, he went right and left for both parrots, who, utterly staggered by the suddenness and violence of the assault, fluttered off anywhere out of the little tyrant's way, screeching at the tops of their voices. Whereupon, having

The Clyde's first shark.

a clear field, the little humbug took just one sip, and then, sneezing and sputtering, went straight off after them to bite their feet in that masterly style which he has now made so completely his own. In doing so he tried to leap the Doctor's cup, and fell into the tea, where he would assuredly have been drowned, but for the prompt action of my "Che," who, seeing his struggles, hauled him out by the scruff of the neck, and dropped him into the sugar-basin, to dry. How human these monkeys are! Thus snatched from the very jaws of death, his first thought was of the sugar sticking to his clothes; his next of his rescuer, at whose feet he fell—fell-to, perhaps, I ought to say—with redoubled attention. Of course "Che" didn't understand that all he wanted was to place her foot upon his neck, to indicate his subjection after the manner of his country, and so there was a further row till I stopped it. Parrots are so ignorant.

This little chap's determination to attain whatever he wants, reminds me of Darwin's anecdote about a monkey and kitten. Placed together as stable companions while very young, they fared along very well and were capital friends, till the kitten began to develop her claws. These weapons severely punished the monkey, who had nothing but cunning to match against them. Wit, however, and not for the first time in the world's history, stood the poor victim in place of armament—for one day he was found holding down the kitten, every one of whose claws he had nibbled off. By this simple method was the balance of power once more adjusted in their household. That monkey must surely have heard some one's rude remark, that "A rose without thorns is a woman without nails."

The parrots I have spoken of are each eight or nine inches high, while the body of the little marmoset doesn't

measure three-and-a-half inches all told.   His tiny neck
is no thicker than a lead pencil, and one single peck from
their powerful beaks would have silenced the little imp in
one second, and for ever.

December 6th.—8 a.m.   I got up and went for a stroll on
deck at 3 a.m., and had a fine view of the " Southern Cross,"
and also of the so-called " False Cross."   They stood thus :—

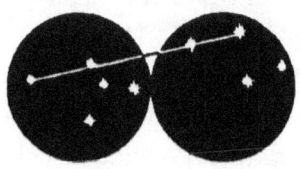

True Cross.   False Cross.

Mariners find the " false " Cross a useful guide to the " true "
one.   A line drawn as I have indicated will act as a pointer
and give the right direction.

Noon.—Lat. 4° 31′ S., long. 32° 45′ W.   Run, 250 miles.
Fernando de Norhona, 45 miles.

The Doctor has just told me that the imp located in the
dispensary, overcome by curiosity, during the night removed
the stopper from the bottle containing tartar emetic, and
indulged in a handful of what he doubtless mistook for
sugar.   The result is, as I have just seen, that he is holding
on to the wires of his cage outside with both hands, and
retching like an inveterate drunkard.   In bringing him to
my cabin to attend to him, the silly little chap got frightened
and leapt off my shoulder over the bannisters down to
the main saloon.   Cat-like he fell on his feet, and seems
none the worse for what, to so tiny a creature, must have
been almost equivalent to a man jumping off a housetop.
I made sure he was dashed to pieces.   Not a bit of it; he
trotted off into the bows, and I, following with my hat in

my hand, cornered him in the fore-hatch. He screamed, writhed, and snapped maliciously, and finally sprang on to my head, where I captured him by popping on my hat. I have returned him to his prison with the larger chap we call the "untameable fiend."

Monkeys are for ever either jumping or climbing. The Doctor's pet, a universal favourite on board, by name "Jacko," succumbed to his climbing propensities. He essayed to ascend the smoke-stack, and was frightfully scalded by a jet of steam. "Ah," said the Doctor reflectively, "I always told him his tricks would get him into hot water some day." Poor Jacko had been the Doctor's faithful ship-companion for two years. He would lie on his back, with legs in the air in imitation of his master, and pretend to read any book or paper he could get, peeping round the edge every now and then the better to hit off the Doctor's style. When the Doctor was shaving, Jacko would come to have his towel on, and then would proceed most solemnly to lather his face and shave himself with a paper-knife, wiping the lather on his thigh, where he had seen the Doctor wipe his on a piece of paper. When the Doctor threw his towel off, Jacko would do the same, but the trouble used to come when the Doctor threw his piece of paper away.

Having no paper on *his* thigh, Jacko used to pull at his fur till he screamed with pain; and when at last he found that the skin and suds would not come off, he'd take the suds in his hand and wipe them over the face of the nearest parrot outside the cook's galley.

Jacko, loq.: "That stout must have had a head on it."

He stole and drank a bottle of stout once, and as a result got an awful drunkard's headache. There he lay, huddled

up in a corner, with his head pressed between his hands
cooing and looking up at every passer-by for pity. It took
him three hours to sleep off the effects of that debauch, and
ever after, if you showed him a bottle of stout, he would
assume that melancholy attitude illustrative of the "dire
effects of drink." Thenceforth, says the Doctor, Jacko became a blue ribbonist; ay, and proudly wore the ribbon,
too, attached to his collar. No more nasty stout for him.
But he would drink *whiskey* like a fish, and unblush-
ingly lie and sleep off the effects, drunk as a fly, with his
blue ribbon fluttering in the breeze. His idea, probably,
was that when you have drunk "till all is blue," you should
loyally hoist your colours.

> He earned the blue ribbon through giving up *stout*,
> And therefore did right to accept it.
> 'Twas a limited promise he made, without doubt,
> But in letter *and spirit* he kept it.

Poor little Jacko, his one delight was the bit of blue
ribbon—the emblem he had unwittingly desecrated—and
when he was so fearfully burnt, and they took the ribbon off
because it hurt his wounds, he cried to have it put on again,
and wore it to the last.

3.30 p.m.—We are just passing the convict island of
Fernando de Norhona. We are over three hundred miles
from Pernambuco, yet here is a *Catamaran* merrily dancing
along as if close at home. Mr. Mervin tells me in India the
Catamaran consists of a " dug-out " (*i.e.* a tree burnt out in
the form of a boat) with one plank at right angles to its
stem, and another to its stern, connected by a third running
parallel to the boat. She carries an enormous sail, and goes
at a great pace, and can never capsize because, being pointed
fore and aft like a boy's tipcat, she can run either way, and

always has this sort of timber outrigged-deck to steady her
to leeward.

4.30 p.m.—We are overhauling the *Liguria* within the
twenty-four hours, as Mr. Ritchie promised we should.
She has been hanging on and trying to race us this three-
quarters-of-an-hour, but we are walking in "hand over
fist," as they say, though she is puffing and blowing and
making every effort to hold on to us.

5.30 p.m.—A five-masted American schooner on our starboard beam. Mr. Ritchie has just put the *Clyde* up to sixty
revolutions per minute so as to shake off the *Liguria*, and

A *Catamaran.*

we are leaving her inch by inch, but quite perceptibly. As
the dinner-bell goes we are showing her a clean pair of heels.

8 p.m.—All dinner-time Mr. Ritchie was smiling and
glancing through the saloon port at the outstripped *Liguria.*
What a sell for the people on board of her! She left Buenos
Aires two days before we did, and four friends of Mervin's
hurried off by her, thinking, of course, she would reach
Southampton before the *Clyde.* Yet I hear it is quite certain
we shall beat her by three days.

December 7th (Sunday).—7 a.m. The night has been so
cool that with the port open I was glad to throw my rug
over me. This is something to remember, for in two hours
we cross the line.

U

9 a.m.—There goes the breakfast-bell, so I am actually stepping out of the Southern into the Northern hemisphere to breakfast.

11 a.m.—The Doctor and I have been having some fun with Clark, Mr. Ritchie's black servant, a capital man and wonderful at "cock-tail" making. Nothing like his brew is obtainable on board. Like all good black servants, Clark is scrupulously particular about the cleanliness of everything he has in charge It is a religion with him, and Ritchie is his deity, and anything of Ritchie's is sacred. I have over and over again caught him talking to the things about the cabin, as he dusted and polished them, as if they were human. Imagine his feelings, then, when the Doctor and I went in and, surveying the cabin, made, *sotto voce*, certain

suggestions for converting it into a temporary menagerie "to relieve the dispensary," as we said. I thought poor Clark would have had a fit. He dared not speak, of course, because we were careful not to address him, but he fairly trembled with apprehension. And when, speaking louder, we decided on having brackets here and there for two parrots and three marmosets, and utilizing the T-square and sword (that sacred weapon) for perches (!), Clark went giddy, and had to crawl out for a drink of

Dumfoundered. water. Poor Clark! It is a shame to tease him in this way, for he is really as simple and trusting as a child; ay, and as tender-hearted, I verily believe.

Noon.—Lat. 0° 51′ N., long. 30° 51′ W. Run, 343 miles.

They had service in the saloon, but I was busy at Sunday school with my parrots and marmosets, which take up a great deal too much of my time.

It is a tax every day, I find, to keep pace with events,
first jotting them down in my note-book, and then elaborating
them; but I am determined to carry out my plan of employing
my leisure on the homeward voyage in doing it, otherwise
it will never be done at all, and I want a record of this
delightful cruise for myself, and perhaps for others—but
" that all depends."

This morning the Doctor was not at breakfast, and on
visiting him I found he had been up the greater part of the
night, attending a steerage passenger who is dying of heart-
disease. The regurgitations to the heart so paralyze it that
he is constantly at the point of death. He is a Portuguese
returning to his home; and although, having made money,
he could afford to travel in a better class, he is "going steerage," as he says, so as to leave more money for his family.

Rather pathetic this forgetfulness of self at such a time.
But the sacrifice has its reward, for his illness has entitled
him to a berth in the hospital, an airy cabin where there are
eight beds—all happily empty—so that really he is better off
than if he had travelled second-class. There is poetic justice
about this poor man's case, so far, that pleases me thoroughly.

3.30 p.m.—At lunch we had Rio prawns, six inches long
and an inch-and-a-half thick, with antennæ (samples of
which I have brought from the table as curiosities) measuring
over twelve inches long. They were delicious eating.

A Mr. Scott, who is returning to England after twenty-
two years in Rio, has just been singing us some solos from
Judas Maccabæus most beautifully. He has a rich, full
baritone, and can use it with great skill and taste, and is
quite up to professional form. He has long been accounted
the best singer in Rio. His stock of yarns, too, is simply
inexhaustible. I hear him at breakfast—he sits at the

Purser's table, next to ours—keeping them constantly supplied, and look or listen when you will, everybody at his table is either laughing or nearly black in the face from trying to restrain himself. This morning I heard him telling of the French Missionary who, "understanding English," addressed a Scotch congregation in the following terms—I spell the words phonetically, just as they reached me: "De tegs is tegen frum de furteth jebder uv de buke uv Jeremie, end dee ninse vairse, 'Ken dee Ediopienne changie eis kin, ou dee lay opard eis sports?'"

8 p.m.—My *vis-à-vis* in the dining-saloon reminds me much of my kind friend who sat in the same seat on the outward voyage—not only possessing many of his characteristics, but actually some of his mannerisms. He has a way of expressing doubt, for instance, that simply reproduces his *alter ego*. The smile on one side of the mouth, the long slow pull at the cigarette, the touch of the ash with the little finger, and the gentle flick at the knee with the same finger to deftly remove the speck that has caught in its fall, are all as eloquent as words, that he is *not quite* of your opinion. So distinctly is this feeling expressed, that I find myself answering the evident objection without waiting for any audible assertion. Both men have this peculiarity in common, both are impetuous, and both are right down good fellows, full of thought for others, but apt to be precipitate and ill-timed even in their kindliest actions. If it should ever fall to the lot of either of these gentlemen to make an offer of marriage to a lady, it is ten to one he will select the inopportune moment when his divinity is bang in the middle of some sweet ballad, the very burden of which had probably been selected—for such devices are not unknown to the sex—to bring her lover to her feet *at the finish*. But would—could any woman accept

a man suing in this abrupt and inconsiderate fashion ? Why, it is as bad as laughing and trying to slope-off in the middle of a man's best story ; neither man nor maiden can afford to be treated so.

Or again, if you happened to say during the day that you must get change for a sovereign, such is the brimming good nature of this sort of man, that should he wake in the night and remember your casual remark, and find that he had twenty shillings or more—bless his kind heart, you'd have it, never fear, if he had to count out the

Premature. "*Mis!* t··r Vavasseur, are you not aware there is another verse? This abrupt—— No, I cannot, will not bear it !"

money in the dark, ay, and if it came to his giving you twenty-five shillings for your gold piece. There and then he would walk the length of the ship or the hotel barefooted to reach you, and *would* reach you too, if it involved breaking open your door with a crowbar. "Here you are, old man," he'd say, "don't bother to wake ;" and, shoving the twenty-five shillings or so under your pillow, he'd leave you to give him the sovereign whenever you thought of it, for he'd never think of it again. That's Courtney, and that's my present *vis-à-vis*. Both real grit, but, like milk, they boil over when

you least expect it. One of them on one occasion—wild
horses shall not drag from me which—brought me a choice
cigar when I was fast asleep one morning at 1 a.m.! and the
other pressed me hard to taste some marvellous brandy, of I
don't know what age, and worth £2 a bottle—before breakfast! Heaven save us from our friends! It reminds me of
the fable of the elephant, who, having accidentally trodden
on and killed a partridge standing near her brood, turned to
her young ones, exclaiming, "Poor little orphans, I will be a
mother to you!" and forthwith *sat down upon them.*

December 8th.—Awoke at 5 a.m. It was quite dark,
and remained so till nearly six o'clock, when the sun rose
languorously from a dark velvety couch and arrayed himself
in splendour. The fleecy speckled clouds hung like ermine
about his shoulders, while for a robe he wore a "sweet girl-
graduate" costume of grey and gold. As boys, we used
to be fond of the puzzling dynamical problem, to wit,
"What would happen if an irresistible force struck an im-
movable object?" When the sun has such a tempting bed

"Arf seas over, yer woshup
—is it to (hic) be (hic)
fine?"

to remain in, and such equally tempting raiment to induce him to rise,
he wisely compromises the matter,
and gets up late. Yesterday morning I saw him rise at four o'clock;
this morning it was 5.40 a.m. before
he threw his coverlet from his bed,
and 5.50 when, having taken his
tub, he lifted his ruddy head over the
side of his bath and began to dress.
Just as I was finishing writing this
in my bunk, from which, through
the port, I could see him well, a small black cloud, one

of a number at his right hand, came and stood before him like a "drunk and incapable" before the magistrate. Was he about to hear the night charges prior to commencing the regular business of the day? At first I thought so, for that little black cloud had a sailor-like roll about him, as if he had not quite slept-off the effects of the evening's diversions. But on second thoughts, I incline to the idea that the episode of the tiny cloud was a mere blind—literally, a blind—to screen him from public gaze whilst he imbibed his matutinal "cocktail," or "S-and-B." Well, I'm sure he need not be ashamed; no one in England would begrudge him a cocktail, or a round dozen of them, if it would only get him up in the morning.

Such a thing as sounding the bell twice on board ship for the same half-hour is of the rarest occurrence, but somehow they managed to oblige me with the experience this morning, for "three bells" was sounded at 5.30 and again ten minutes later. I hope the longitude has had nothing to do with it. It was bad enough to have to shove your watch on every day going out, but it is simply ruination to it to keep putting it back as we have to now. It thoroughly upsets its digestion, and leads to an attack of liver. I declare my watch begins to look quite sallow in the face.

7.30 a.m.—We have just had our first, and I hope last, burial at sea. The poor unselfish Portuguese died in the night. His terrible sufferings are past, and "after life's fitful fever he sleeps well" in his ocean grave. Our good honest tars wound his body in sail-cloth with some fire-rods to weight it, and laid it on a grating near the after-hatch, where they had draped the bulwarks with the Union Jack. The Captain read the funeral service, and at the solemn words "we therefore commit his body to the deep" the order was given to "let go," the end of the grating was lifted and the body glided into the sea—the ship being slowed and turned slightly from her course so as to clear the screw. Mr. Mervin tells me that to this end on such occasions the "P. and O." steamers describe a complete circle.

Noon.—Lat. 6° 18' N., long. 28° 58' W. Run, 348 miles.

The Doctor tells me that in the night an English steerage passenger, foolishly lying near an open hatch, rolled over and fell to the deck below, where, dazed with his fall, he seems to have turned over and actually fallen a second time into the hold! He is bleeding from the mouth, ears, and nose, and only at intervals conscious.

3 p.m.—What a charming passage we are having! The sea is smooth as a lake, and the only wind is the breeze of our own making as we spin along at the rate of eighteen or nineteen miles an hour through the water. The sun is bright and warm, but never too warm, and the flying-fish are flashing about in every direction in shoals. St. Vincent the day after to-morrow, and then good-bye to gossamer costumes and flowers in the button-hole, out will come the overcoats, warm jerseys, and gloves. Our ship was decked—good word "decked" —with flowers for the last time at Pernambuco. My ferns seem to have stood the changes so far bravely; but a sort of orchid I had set among them has faded away, and already I find that three floral vultures in the shape of tiny spiders, no bigger than large ants and with the most brilliant scarlet bodies, are busy with its remains.

Speaking of flowers reminds me of a good story the Doctor was telling the other night of an actress's admirer who sent his fair goddess a bouquet. Wanting to write four appropriate lines, and finding himself stumped after inditing two, he left his friend to add two more while he went behind

the scenes to the lady and cracked a bottle of champagne, a
liquor she loved not wisely but too well. In due course the
bouquet was flung to the dramatic star, the piece came to an
end, and the admirer took up his usual position at the stage-
door to receive the smiles of the adored one, when to his
horror the lady " cut him dead."

Talking the misadventure over after supper, the two
friends, as if by inspiration, both came to the same conclusion, that the lines *must* have had something to do with
the change in the fair one's demeanour. "Yet, why?" said
the first, " I cannot divine ; all I wrote
was—

> ' The violet lives within thine eye,
>   And in thy lip the rose.' "

" Well, it is curious," said the
other, " for all I added was—

"All I added was—"

> ' And when in eye and lip they die,
>   They'll blossom in thy nose.' "

And—would you believe it?—that trifling incident caused
a rupture between the two friends almost as bad as that
between the quondam lovers. So deep was the feeling, that
the writer of the first couplet left his brother author to pay
for the supper. Yet what else could a rhymester write, with
" die " to go with " eye," and " nose " with " rose "? Thus
basely ever, doth one poet treat another !

8 p.m.—This evening I had a talk with the Captain. He
likes the sea for himself now, but disapproves of it for his
children on account of the rough, and in some ways objection-
able, experiences of the early training which all must
undergo. I've often thought I shouldn't mind being a sailor
myself, if I could be gazetted " full captain " right off. But

no holy-stoning the deck for me. It makes your trousers bag
so at the knee.

December 9th.—10 a.m.—The reader may remember that
when at Monte Video I mentioned the exquisite complexions
of the women, which I said they owed mainly to the
marvellous purity of the water there. This morning I was
reminded of another important matter affecting the skin,
viz. soap. On our way out, a Uruguayan gave me a cake
of really wonderful stuff, which I have used ever since with
the result that my skin no longer resents shaving, and feels
like velvet—well, *velveteen*, any way.

The donor, moreover, told me the simple secret of its
preparation, and also a curious story about its inventor, a
Fred somebody. He was a friend of his, and came to
England, a wealthy man on pleasure bent. Unfortunately
his all was invested in Argentine securities, and being
unable, as they fell, to cut his coat according to his cloth,
he came to grief. If I ever give this soap to the world,
Fred's story shall enfold each cake. It will read somewhat
thus :—

URUGUAYAN SOAP.

I heard of one who, Fred by name,
 Indulged in every hobby,
Spent money faster than it came,
 And overran the Bobby.

He drank his fill of Pleasure's cup,
 And gambled night and day,
Till, one fine morn, they sold him up,
 And took his all away.

His head so swam at Fate's demands
 With which he could not cope,
That when he went to wash his hands
 He pocketed the soap.

"What," say you, "will he do with it?"
  Well, Fred was wide awake,
And when you hear you will admit
  His method "takes the cake."

Away he trudged to Regent's Park,
  And stretched him on a seat,
And evening fell, and it grew dark,
  And he'd had nought to eat.

"Come, Uruguayan soap," he cried,
  "Be thou in lieu of food !"
And then a little bit he tried,
  And found it very good.

As round his mouth a froth appeared
  A gentleman came by,
Who looking, stopped, and said he feared
  Our Fred was going to die.

A good Samaritan, and rich
  (As such should be, I say),
He bore Fred to his mansion, which
  Was just across the way.

He had one daughter, only one,
  To leave his fortune to,
And so, the one thing to be done
  Fred did—and so would you.

And thus the happy time went by,
  She nursing him in tears.
And feeling that if Fred should die
  Blank were all after years.

She wiped his lips, removed the soap,
  Restored his vital powers,
And nursed him back to life, love, hope,
  In four and twenty hours.

At length he found a chance to speak,
  And as she bowed her head,
She let him kiss her blushing cheek—
  —And now she's Mrs. Fred.

Doubtful MORAL.

So you, who "rapid" lives have led,
  Need not abandon hope,
If you, like luckless, lucky Fred,
  Use Uruguayan soap.

> If, later, for divorce you yearn,
>   That soap will loose your bands,*
> Suggesting, of the whole concern
>   That you should " wash your hands."

Noon.—Lat. 11° 38' N., long. 27° 4' W. Run, 337 miles.

1 p.m.—Mr. Ritchie says we shall fetch St. Vincent about this time to-morrow. It surprises me rather to find how differently I am behaving at the ports coming home to what I did on the outward voyage. For one thing, there is less time. We did not stop more than three or four hours at Bahia and Pernambuco. But fancy my not even going ashore at the latter place. Well, I suppose the novelty of the thing has worn off in some measure. Besides, I know exactly what I should see, for there is a distinct limit to the distance one can wander inland. Also and principally, the facilities for landing at the Recife are not good. There are plenty of boats, and, for the matter of that, my good friend the Purser, who of course always goes on shore everywhere, would have let me accompany him most willingly.

No, none of these objections quite explain the circumstances. The real truth is, that my notes and their final expansions occupy all my time (I was going to say my *spare* time, and that would not be so very far out either, for I have not only to take notes of the day's incidents but to write up those of the day before—sometimes of many days before), so that one way or another I am pretty constantly at work.

More than once, and more than one person, on our way out thought I was a detective from seeing me so frequently note-book in hand, though one would hardly have thought that was quite the way for a detective to retain his *incognito*. I have before me at this moment, a card of Mr. Graham's that he sent me one day at dinner, on which he jokingly

* You loosen your *wrist*-bands when you wash your hands.—C. C. A.

asks, in allusion to this suspicion, "whether what everybody is saying, is true."

Fancy a detective hauling out his note-book every ten minutes! Though I'm not at all sure, when one comes to think about it, that such conduct would be more absurd than that of his superiors who shoe their police with heavy boots, teach them a measured stride, and train their movements with the exactness of trains, so that a burglar not wanting to catch them, or rather to be caught by them, knows to a nicety where *not* to go.

One is reminded of the song which a rather daring young damsel is supposed to sing—let us hope in confidence—to a friend—

> "There's a path by the river o'ershadowed by trees,
> Where people may walk and may talk at their ease,
> And save by a bird not a sound can be heard,
> So do not come there, if you please, if you please,
>   So do not come there, if you please."

The policeman's conduct is so considerate, that one would hardly be surprised to hear him singing something of this kind confidentially to the merry burglar on his beat—

> "There's a crib near the river, o'ershadowed by
>   trees,
> Where the cracksman can practise his trade at
>   his ease,
> And never a word or a sound can be heard,
>   So do not come there, if you please," etc.

"So do not come there, if you please!"

8 p.m.—We have just met the Pacific s.s. *Portisca*, from St. Vincent, which signalled us with two white, two red, and two green rockets. As she passed us in a full blaze of electric light, I thought her an imposing and beautiful object, and the signals in the darkness were extremely effective.

Yarning has been the order of the evening in Mr. Ritchie's cabin. Our host, expostulating with one yarner who was rather over-drawing the long bow, used the phrase, "One must draw the line somewhere;" without a moment's pause the speaker hit out with, "Line! We crossed that some days ago, my dear sir," and went straight on with his story.

December 10*th*.—8 a.m. I had my parrot in my cabin, and he woke me by climbing from his improvised perch to the open port, where he set up a scream that, coming from him in such a position, nearly slew me on the spot. There was the little wretch, standing on the very brink of a watery grave, and crowing and bobbing with his beak and flapping his wings in an ecstasy of delight as he watched the waves roll by. Vine must have frightened him when he brought my cocoa and slice of bread-and-butter at 7 a.m., I suppose. Any way, presence of mind was, I felt, the only thing to save him. What a marvellous gift is *self-possession!* I remember a fellow once saying how flurried he felt when, a lady entering, he had to offer her his chair. "Ah!" said another who was present, "that's because you are clumsy in your way of offering your chair, that's all. You should lay it on thick and say, 'May I offer you my chair? Do allow me—any chair suits me—indeed I don't care for an easy-chair at all,' and that sort of thing. Pave the way well, you know." "I do," said the other; "that's just the kind of thing I always say—it's when I get up out of the chair that I am done." "Get up!" exclaimed the other. "Oh, if you do *that*, my dear fellow, what can you expect? You must never do *that*. What I suggested must be said *sitting* or *half-sitting*, with the hands on the elbows of the chair. To get *up* and *out* of the chair is fatal—fatal to *self-possession* especially."

But I've left my "Che" far too long on that port. Acting

on this worldly advice, I did not *get up* either ; I simply took
my bread-and-butter (my hands shaking with the severe
discipline I was giving them, so that they tore the slice in
half), and sipped my cocoa with it, and anxiously awaited
events with my heart choking me with its violent throbbing.
In misery I finished my meal, hoping and hoping every
moment that " Che " would be tempted by the bread-and-
butter, of which he is very fond. No—all no use ; there he
bobbed and fluttered just the same. Then a bright thought
struck me, and I went on deck above him to take him in
flank—tied my hat to a string, dropped it over the side, and
flapped it at him. But it was no good; nothing came of it
but screams, " only that and nothing more." Still I perse-
vered, feeling convinced it was the only way. At last, all
on a sudden, the screams ceased. Guessing the cause I flew
below, upsetting myself and everybody else on my way, and
only arresting my wild career as I neared my cabin door.
This I opened most stealthily, and glanced at the port. Not
there ! At one glance I scanned the entire cabin—here,
there, high, low, everywhere. He was nowhere to be seen !
In sorrow I had to accept the only explanation, that when
his voice ceased, my poor " Che " must have taken his death-
plunge ! And now I half blamed myself for going on deck
with the string, for I found Vine had in the interval fetched
away my cup and plate, and it was his entering perhaps that
had lost me my bird. I had got so far in my musings when
" Che's " well-known voice fell upon my grateful ear from his
own little bunk, made out of an old hatbox. At that moment,
too, in came Vine, and I heard all about it. He had come
in, seen " Che's " dangerous position, and quietly replaced
him in his bunk. Presence of mind, it seems, may display
itself actively or passively ; Vine's took the active only,

while mine took both forms. But mine was not what you would call a success, and I was still more ashamed of it when, on examining " Che," I found him *tied safely by a long string to his box.* In my fright I had quite forgotten about the string, which I myself had fastened to him only the day before!

My needless anxiety reminds me of the case of a man who, after dining rather too well at a friend's, had to. cross Hyde Park to get home. Whether the blanc-mange had been made too strong, or he was overpowered by the joint effects of the cigarette and the cool air, we are not told, but he found himself in the dark, holding on to one of the railings that surround and protect the trees. Feeling his way round and round, and finding no opening, he at length came to the conclusion that he was in jail,

" Let me out ! "

and screaming for help there presently came to his aid a constable, whom he attempted to bribe, at first with a shilling only, to set him free. The story goes that, rising to the occasion, the policeman did eventually *let him out* for half-a-crown, and saw him safely home, where he received another. Who shall say now—

> " Stone walls do not a prison make,
>   *Nor iron bars a cage* " ?

11 a.m.—We have just sighted San Antonio and are entering the group of islands (Cape Verde), of which, it will be remembered, St. Vincent is of chief importance.

12.30 p.m.—We are at anchor, and the divers are already busily plying for employment. Everybody on board is throwing his loose silver into the sea for the pleasure of seeing how cleverly it is recovered, long, long before it reaches the bottom. Indeed, the human body sinks so much faster than the coin, that the one catches up the other with great rapidity. You can rarely count as much as ten seconds before the diver's head reappears above the water; and the money is always stowed in his cheek. I timed one chap who, for two shillings, went in on one side of the *Clyde* and came out on the other. He was only twenty-eight seconds.

The *Stuttgardt* (North German Lloyd) is here, and preparing to start. She left Buenos Aires three days before us.

2.30 p.m.—She has just started, and the *Uruguay* is also getting up steam. It is nice being in a vessel like the *Clyde* that can give all these so many points. We shall overhaul them both in the night.

This morning there was a row between the Portuguese steerage passengers and an Englishman of the third-class. (We can only call him "third-class" on board, there being no lower grade, but thirty-third would be nearer his mark on shore.) I heard the former, in the person of a rugged, weather-beaten, grey-bearded mariner-sort-of-chap, debating the case with our Captain, Chief Officer, maitre d'hôtel, etc. The "thirty-third class" scoundrel seems to have assaulted the Portuguese (who are a very long-suffering class) most brutally. In the end the ruffian was "put in irons," as they always call placing a man under restraint aboard ship.

Over and over again have I heard it said by first one officer, then another, that a thousand Portuguese give less trouble than two third-class English passengers. The airs

X

the English of this class give themselves are positively comic in their audacity. The Doctor has just confirmed this remark by an apt illustration our present voyage afforded. He has had great difficulty, he tells me, on this homeward trip with a busybody Englishman of the third-class, who has been constituting himself spokesman and champion of any and everybody's grievances since we started. In the interests of another third-class passenger this morning " Mr. Busybody " presented himself at the Doctor's cabin and, over-reaching all the rest, there before him, insisted that he should come at once and see and prescribe for the sufferer ; and, on the Doctor declining to take cases out of their turn, the meddler reported him to the Captain.

4 p.m.—I used to wonder whence we English inherited our great administrative ability in *other* people's affairs, till I recently came upon an American song entitled, " The English are the Heirs of Kings," which accounts of course for the regal airs we give ourselves. All I can say is, if I'm the heir to a kingdom, I'm deeply grateful to the man who has usurped my exalted position.

A NOBODEE.

The boy that swings upon a gate
And envies no one, small or great,
Why is it that we make him sing,
" Hooray ! I'm happy as a King " ?
A Prince might swing upon a gate,
But not a King, at any rate.
If ever you should tempt a King
To get upon a gate and swing,
'Twould be a very scurvy trick.
His Highness would, of course, be sick :
And then (as biters oft get bit)—
Why, you might have to " swing for it."
Happy, as what ? A King ?—Poor chappie !
They've not made *yet* the King that's happy.

Uneasy to a head's a crown.
No wonder, for you can't lie down.
Why, sleeping in a stove-pipe hat
Is awkward, for you can't lie flat.
But stop; no more upon that head—
I'll get a cup of tea, instead.
One warning word, before I go.
Pray, take things easy here below.
Go get upon Life's gate and swing,
And don't attempt to be a King.
Would you in life and death be free?
Then live and die "a nobodee"!

CHAPTER XI.

ST. VINCENT TO LISBON.

5.50 p.m.—We are weighing anchor, and moving off just as the sun is setting in a flood of gold away behind the mountains that hem in this quiet harbour and most convenient oasis between America and home. The giant head that some call Wellington, others Washington, and others still Napoleon, and that lies face-upwards on the mountain-tops directly behind the lighthouse, is looking its very best, its features radiant with the glow of an amethyst sky. How beautiful even these arid hills look, glorified by the setting sun, as it tones down all their ruggedness and enriches their simple garbs of lichen and sand. No one could fail to be struck with their charm to-night.

But, as I write, the light is fading from the sky, and the hills and valleys and the boundless sea into which we are moving are sinking into shadow which in five minutes will have deepened into the blackest of palls. Then out will spring the stars in their thousands, as though the cloak of heaven had fallen upon the earth, revealing the blue velvet cushion studded with diamonds which is the jewel-casket of the gods.

It is all so magical in these latitudes. Almost theatrical,

St. Vincent, Cape Verde Islands. Cablegraph clerks in foreground. Washington's Head face upwards on the mountains.

for one can hardly believe that these grand transformations
are all unrehearsed.*

8 p.m.—Shipping only a hundred and four tons of coal at
St. Vincent I find took us five hours and-a-half! It is much
cooler; so cool, indeed, that standing on deck before dinner
in my thin tropical flannels was chilly work, and, for the first
time since leaving the old country, I was glad of the hot
soup, and actually enjoyed getting into my black clothes for
the stately meal, because they were thicker and warmer.

Now that I am clothed in and out, however, I find the
breeze on deck delicious, just perfect—neither too hot nor
too cold.

11 p.m.—We have been lying hour after hour on deck,
Mervin and I, thoroughly enjoying the soft evening air and
the calm of the deep blue skies. He has travelled much, and
is most excellent company. To my mind also there is
something very infectious about the hilarity and exuberant
enjoyment of youth. It is so in earnest in everything. To
see Mervin spring out of his chair at the sound of the dinner-
bell almost makes me hungry, and to hear him sparkle and
bubble over with delight at the prospect of seeing old
England again, and at the joys of the coming Christmas
festivities, etc., makes one feel a positive veneration for fog
and indigestion. One man on board, who had been long in
the tropics, said it was delightful to him to think that at
last he was going to a country where "Reckitt" couldn't
advertise his patent colour all over the sky.

December 11th.—8 a.m. As to-morrow will probably be
the end of summer for me this year, I dressed in my flannels
for the last time, and went on deck to meet the sun on what

---

* A friend has reminded me that these effects are not "unrehearsed;"
they have had a "run" of an infinite number of nights.—C. C. A.

may prove his P. P. C. visit. It is well sometimes not to be
the first to recognize any change that one may see pending:
so I dressed lightly and brightly, and pretended not to understand that any serious breach of our hitherto cordial relations
was about to occur between that luminary and myself.
Never go to meet a quarrel.

It may sound strange to the sceptical, but a friend assures
me—and I'm not going to disbelieve a friend because his
experience is not mine—that he has often staved-off a wet
day by putting out ready overnight a light summer suit.

The demonstration
in force.

That's his first plan. The approach
amicable. If the evening continues
lowering he tries a demonstration—(the
safest position, next to being the clerk-
of-the-weather's friend, is to let him see
you are prepared for other events)—
and hangs out of window his mackintosh, goloshes, and umbrella. This
generally has the desired effect, and
all is well again. "The approach
amicable" answered in my case, for old
Sol has been literally beaming all over
his face. He hadn't the heart to be
the first to break up our merry summer
party, while our costume spoke so clearly our hopes of his
" continued countenance and support," as the grocers say.

Noon.—Lat 20° 21′ N., long. 22° 54′ W.   Run, 240 miles.

The weather is grand—bright and cool—and the sea so
smooth that there is hardly any perceptible motion even
here in my cabin where I am writing, quite in the bows,
where the slightest dip or roll is sure to be felt at once. My
parrot is getting very tame, and goes with me everywhere,

standing on the crown of my soft felt hat, whistling to his heart's content. He also permits me to carry him covered up in my coat—the way the organ-grinder carries his monkey —as, out of the cabin, he feels the cold. The Doctor, after getting four bites from his *Papa-gayo*, determined to chloroform the gentleman this morning, and clip his treacherous beak—Mervin and I assisting. There was nothing else to be done if he intended keeping the brute, for he was horribly vicious. Only yesterday he bit my finger to the bone. We gave him the anæsthetic on a towel, gagged him with a pencil, and then clipped a shred off both the upper and lower portions of the beak. "Rounding the Horn"—the Doctor called it. The little fellow remained perfectly drunk, and incapable of standing, till we brought him to with a bottle of salts (ammonia). He bit me the very moment he recovered consciousness, but not in the old deadly fashion.

8 p.m.—Before I forget it I must record some of the humours of last night's dinner, an *impromptu* by Mr. Mervin. We had a private dish of "sturgeons' roes" (caviare) that was a little bit "off colour." "New reading," said the irrepressible jokist; "the *roes* by any other name would smell as sweet." Then some of them proceeded to criticise the *ménu* in most unmerciful fashion. The truth is that, during coaling, the galleys are covered up with canvas, to exclude the black dust that makes its way through every crack and crevice, and so, the cooks having to work in the dark, things are not so good as usual. Allowing themselves full poetical licence, the grumblers relieved their feelings in a way that caused the rest of us almost to rejoice at the annoyance that had produced so much sport. These are some of the audible comments that caught one's ear every now and then. "Soup! Ugh! *consommé au*

charbon!"   "Fish! Bah! Fried eggs and butter with coarse
starboard side of haddock boiled in sea-water!"   "Hunks
of duck with bits of feather-beds still sticking out of them
through the greasy mud they call sauce!"   Then followed
the meat—"Thick slices of porpoise hide!" muttered one.
"Stood in water," said another, "like boots in a shop-
window, to prove they're waterproof;" and so on.   One
fellow, out of pure cussedness, at the end of the meal called
the steward, and without moving a muscle, calmly ordered
"tea, bread-and-butter, and a brace of eggs," as if he had
had no dinner.

December 12th.—8 a.m.   Thinking over last night's grum-
blings at dinner, I have come to the conclusion that if one
would keep well and even-tempered on board ship, one must
not eat all the meals provided.   A heavy meal at nine
o'clock, another at one, and a third—heavier than either—
at six o'clock, are too much for any one limited to the
exercise the ship affords.   And as a result, men become
liverish and fastidious.   Then, too, the complainers are
generally those who do not go ashore, and so are exposed
to all the discomforts of the coaling.   The fine dust settles
on the bulwarks, so that they can't hang over the sides
of the vessel, and falls on their flannels or white costumes.

Well, to a certain extent, it is a drawback to the enjoyment of the cruise *if* you stop on board; but then, those I
am addressing would *not* stop on board, and so would *not*
get liverish for want of exercise, and would *not*, therefore,
complain of the dinners.   So there's an end of the matter.
If they get liverish in spite of going on shore everywhere
and taking a brisk three-mile walk on deck every day, then
there is only one thing to be done.   "Walk more and eat
less," as Abernethy used to advise his patients to do.

The weather is perfect, the increasing cold being so gradual you can hardly perceive it. The sea is absolutely as calm as the most indifferent sailor could wish. I want to know where that cyclone and Pampero are coming in, that the Company almost promised me would be included in my return-ticket. If they don't come off, I shall have to apply for a rebate of a five-pound note or so. A trip of this kind without a Pampero is flat as a honeymoon without a tiff.

Noon.—Lat. 25° 3' N., long. 20° 26' W. Run, 315 miles. Las Palmas, 261½ miles.

The Chief Officer has kindly promised to get me a cage made to take my little "Che" home in. All the poor marmosets are dead, and now it is the parrots' turn. They all begin to die off as soon as you pass Teneriffe, or Las Palmas, at this time of year.

3 p.m.—We have been watching one of the prettiest sights to be noticed over the side of a ship—the rainbows in the spray. Going at the pace we do, the rollers are cut by the bows and thrown into the air some ten or twelve feet high, whence the water falls in fine spray which is blown into still finer particles by the force of the breeze we make. As it falls before you, and the sun shines on it from behind you, the rainbow effects are charming, and one never seems to weary of watching the constant play of colour, and listening to the music of the ever-falling waters.

8 p.m.—Mr. Ritchie has a capital dodge when any one proposes "a gamble"—which is not an uncommon thing—to see who shall pay for liqueurs after dinner. It is called "honest quaker." Say there are five persons—the numbers 1, 2, 3, 4, 5, are written on a card. Then some one starts by writing one of them on the back, unseen by the other persons concerned. Say he puts the figure 5. Now the others have

each to strike out a figure on the face of the card. If anybody strikes out the 5, *he* is the victim; if not, and the others amongst them strike out the 1, 2, 3, and 4, then the starter who placed the 5 on the card's back has to defray whatever the cost may be.

One incident to-day should not escape notice. Two gentlemen on board bought monkeys at Pernambuco. One is in a cage and the other loose. This morning both were brought on deck for sun and air. The loose one is a little lady and suffers much from the cold, so no sooner did she espy the other than she made straight for his warm-looking cage, and sat closely up to it, chattering through the bars as if begging for shelter. Unmaidenly, perhaps, but certainly not unnatural. The poor prisoner, a gentleman, seemed quite touched with this little attention, and replied most plaintively to her petition. "You see how it is," he seemed to say, "I am not my own master; even this den is only mine *to stop in*, not to leave. If *only* I were free!" This quite overcame the lady, and she kissed him through the bars, and he put both his arms out and held her to his heart in true lover style. After a while, the thought occurred to him that perhaps his visitor had not lunched,

"Romeo and Juliet."

and with many squeaky apologies— no doubt eloquent of love for the lady —he drew in his arms and selecting some of his many dainties, fed her through the rails of his cage, cracking nuts, and never eating one himself, but handing every kernel as he got it to his companion.

We watched them for quite twenty minutes in this peaceful *tête-à-tête*, and then the respective owners let them meet in freedom. Ever since, they have remained on the same loving terms, but he having now twined both arms and legs around the shivering little creature, it has devolved on *her* to feed *him*, and this she does.

9 p.m.—The owners have just parted them for the night. It was quite a Romeo and Juliet balcony-scene between them at the last, and they played it with more " go "—no joke intended on the severance—than many actors I have seen. Indeed, this is a drama in real life, for it is death to Juliet to part from the warmth of Romeo—and he and the lady both seem to know it too. If they had been mine I should have left them together. To-morrow we pass Teneriffe, which is the region where parrots and monkeys begin to feel the chills, and they die off like flies. These monkey lovers seemed to know they were approaching their " tomb of the Capulets."

December 13*th.*—6.45 a.m. We are passing Las Palmas as the sun is rising, Teneriffe lying in the morning haze to the eastward. Going on deck, I found we were abreast of the island, which seemed to me to be in two pieces, but I suppose the cleft is really only a deep indent. There were few signs of vegetation up the sides of the mountains; a long range of which runs from end to end of the island. Their crests are clothed with palms, which showed up grandly against the brightening eastern sky, and formed a fretted skyline fringing the peaks and bluffs with a wonderful kind of lace-edging. Here and there a white square stone house on the mountain-side, or peeping over that parapet from the crown of an inner range, looked out to seaward. But, though we passed within a mile of the shore, nothing else was observable, for the town is on the other side of the island.

10 a.m.—It was very cold standing about on deck in one's pyjamas this morning, so I was glad to go down, turn in again,

and drink the cocoa Vine brought me at 7 a.m. Yet now
after breakfast, when the sun has gained a little power, I am
wearing the same clothes as yesterday, flannels, and find
them quite sufficient. My parrot, too, is clearly well content
with the warmth, for he is singing on the top of my hat as I
walk about in the sun. The pretty note he had the first day
disappeared with the cooler weather, and has only to-day
returned in quite its pristine purity. It is the sweetest,
flutiest thing in whistles I have ever heard.

Mr. Ritchie has given me a couple of sapodillas, a sort of
sleepy pear in flavour, and in appearance like a shrivelled
russet apple, and "Che" is eating one on my head. He looks
upon my sombrero as far more his than mine. As I write,
in Ritchie's cabin, I can see the little fellow—in the glass—
standing in the very centre of the top of my head on one
leg, the sapodilla in his other foot—or hand, one ought to call
it, for the parrot uses it more like a hand than a foot. It is
funny to see how he manages to balance himself as the ship
rolls, which she does a little and with great regularity. He's
a clever little chap!

Noon.—Lat. 29° 40′ N., long. 17° 19′ W. Run, 329 miles.

This is a better run than yesterday, and directly the
Captain found what we had done, he asked the Chief
Engineer to put the engines back a bit, or we should be in
Lisbon too soon. Last trip the *Clyde* got home two days
before her time, and though on that occasion the irregularity
was forgiven on the ground that it was her first trip, and so
a trifle of zeal might be excused, the directors gave distinct
instructions that it was not to be repeated.

Among those on board, to whom the sea is but a highway
from home to business or what not, the knowledge that the
ship's speed is being deliberately slackened is doubtless very

galling. To me, on the other hand, the longer she takes the better. I wanted a sea trip, and shall never quarrel with the Company for giving me brimming measure for my money. There are some very wealthy men on board, and two of them have tried to induce the Captain to let her run full pace. Each will give £100 for the extra coal, if that is of any moment; but of course it is not. The Company must keep faith with the public, and run their ships as far as possible to fit in with the times advertised.

8 p.m.—There is the strongest of all inducements to the Captain to get in as early as he dares, for it is just touch-and-go whether he and all the officers and crew will spend Christmas Eve in England or not. As I have said before, the *Clyde* goes on to Antwerp, and if she only reaches Southampton on the 20th, the date she is due there, as she practically takes two days *to and from* and stays three days *in* Antwerp, she will not return to South-ampton before Christmas Day.

This is the all-absorbing topic on board just now with everybody, from the highest to the lowest, and I'm quite satisfied that a

Jack ashore, at Christmas.

good deal will be risked in the way of blame in order to accomplish the universal heart's desire, to gather in the old home and on the old soil, beneath the mistletoe-bough and the red-berried holly, to sing old songs and tell old stories to the crackling of the Yule-tide log, and among the smiles and voices of those who are dear to us.

December 14*th* (*Sunday*)—8 a.m. I can hear the organ going. They were practising last night, and are evidently at it again now, for the full choral service that has been promised. There are eight or ten fine voices on board, and three gentlemen at least who would take high rank anywhere as vocalists, having good and well-cultivated voices. But oh! I can hear we are going to have "Onward, Christian soldiers," our old friend of the voyage out. Now, it's all very well for the choir to get this up and produce it by themselves, but what will the sailors do with it?

I was once at a picnic on the banks of the Thames, where the white cloth and the viands, and the *ensemble* of the ladies' toilets, and the airy costumes of the sturdy boating-men made a very lovely picture. Suddenly a boat with some friends of ours put in close by us, and following it on shore came a huge, wet, shaggy, St. Bernard puppy, who, knowing us all, made straight for our dainty circle. "Fido! Fido!" everybody cried—for all knew and liked the dog—"Come along! Come along! Good boy! Good dog!" and so on. Thinking, I suppose, they all meant what they said, Fido, nothing loth, did "come along;" and, fully believing his hosts wished to make him as happy as themselves, plunged and floundered headlong after the manner of puppy-kind into the well-spread table and among the lobster-salad, jellies, and jam, much of which he carried among the ladies' dresses. "Oh, what an alteration!" as some one sings. In a moment, no word of reproach was strong enough to describe Fido and all his works. It was only by pelting him with every article we could lay our hands on that we could drive him off. Such a wreck as he and we made of it all in ten seconds I have never seen before nor since. It beat all records.

Much the same sort of thing will happen to this prim,

trim, hymn, I suspect, when the jolly tars get, so to say, into
the thick of it. Well, anyhow, I dare not trust myself to be
present at their rendering of it with their favourite fo'cas'le
song. It stands out in my memory as one of the funniest
things I ever heard in my life. Alas, poor ladies and gentlemen of the choir, you know not what is in store for you!

Noon.—Lat. 33° 49′ N., long. 13° 32′ W. Run, 316 miles.

3 p.m.—Somebody, it seems, put the authorities up to the
little difficulty about the hymn, so we sang the same words
to a different tune, and all went well.

" A dream of fair women." " The Angel Choir " and their guardian.

There is a family of seven girls going to England with us.
They are entirely by themselves, I hear, having lost their
mother through yellow fever, that deadly scourge of Rio, where
their father still continues in business. They all sit together
at a table just below me, and are all dressed in white, and
have for this reason, and their love of music, obtained the
name of " The Angel Choir." At the head of their table sits
a very staid young gentleman of perhaps two and twenty,
also, I hear, a native of and resident in Rio, who is in a way
both father and mother to them on board, attentive without

Y

demonstration, and discreet without diffidence. Exerting the gentlest influence with the very best results, he keeps his little flock together far better than many of his elders could ; and somehow contrives to make them happy, I should say, for their table seems always merry without noise. He is familiarly known as " The Guardian Angel."

He seems to manage his little lambs with the ease and tact of the collie dog—one little " wow," and in come the stragglers. If ever he should want a testimonial as to his fitness for conducting a nunnery on new principles, or a boarding-house for young ladies, " with all the comforts of home-life," I know two or three on board who will certify him.

8 p.m.—The wind has been freshening and the sea is running rather high, foreboding queer weather in the Bay. On these occasions it is comical to notice the behaviour of the elderly lady I mentioned once before, who is " never nervous, because always prepared." There is no ostentation about her, but she is evidently determined to be " on the spot," and ready for any emergency. But while wistfully eyeing the officers as they pass her on the deck, she never troubles them with questions. She appears to have no confidence whatever in her husband in regard to the appliances for safety in case of disaster at sea, much preferring the opinions, good, bad, or indifferent, of any one else on board. Perhaps the best and briefest summary of her temperament is the one a friend has just given me, but it is not, I regret to say, any too complimentary—" self-willed and fickle-minded."

The ungallant author of this libellous (though I believe accurate) diagnosis has been telling me of an old lady on one of his voyages, who in bad weather used to take her seat near a certain boat, which she invariably referred to as "my lifeboat." At such times her bulk would be nearly twice that of other days, owing to the number of dresses she would have on, so as "to be prepared," like our friend now on board. With her, however, preparedness had been elevated into a fine art, for she had always in her lap a basket of provisions *and a Bible.* He adds that though at other times a pretty regular attendant at meals, on no other occasions did she ever appear with her Bible. She too, which was much to her credit, never troubled the Captain, as some less nervous ladies do when the clouds gather, except one day when things looked unusually black. On this particular day she had evidently settled in her own mind that they would all have to take to the boats. And what on earth do you think she said to the Captain at this awful crisis? "I would not ask you if it were a mere question of comfort," she said, "but, you know, it acts also as a life preserver;" and then she produced and asked him to inflate for her an *air-cushion!* You will observe that I have used only one note of exclamation there. I'll tell you why: because I want three for my next remark, viz. *and he did!!!* All I can say is, that captain was a gentleman, and all I will add to that statement is, that I know his name and shall ever remember it with respect. For so obliging a man, the name was singularly appropriate: "Captain Grant."

> So here's a health to Captain Grant,
> Not only gállant, but gallánt.

It is only the really great who are brave enough to do these little services. The incident deserves to rank with the well-known toad story of Wellington. The Duke seeing a little boy crying on his return to boarding-school, inquired and found that his grief was caused by having to leave a pet

toad at home. "All right, my little man," said the hero of a
hundred fights, "I'll look after him." This story I have
heard described as apocryphal, and began to think it so
myself until recently, when I came across one of the many
autograph bulletin letters the boy from time to time received.
It ran somewhat thus : " Field-Marshal the Duke of Wellington begs to inform Master —— that his toad is quite well."
Oh, these little things! Some one somewhere, and somehow
I cannot quote, has said that, "to do great things,"

> " Seldom to man is given :
> But little things on little wings.
> Bear little souls to heaven."

As soldiers, many of us have pride enough to keep us from
risking a bullet in the back, and dash enough even to *blow
up* a magazine. But how about blowing up that old lady's
air cushion ?

December 15th.—8 a.m. The weather is bright, but much
colder. I took my usual cold bath, but it will be my last
this year. It cut like knives. It has been a rough night,
too, and the ship rolled and pitched heavily. And once again
the cable rattled and struck such sledge-hammer blows
every now and then, that sleep was perfectly impossible.
At last I sent a Quarter-master to the Second Officer on the
bridge, and in five minutes they had wedged the cable, and
all was silent. It is greatly to the praise of the officers of
this ship, that the moment any complaint is made, the thing
objected to is, if possible, remedied, and with the greatest
willingness. Politeness could be carried no further than it
is on board the *Clyde.* One is reminded of the *complaisant*
Frenchman, who exclaimed, when a lady asked him to do
her a favour: "Madame, if it is *possible*, it *is* done. If it is
impossible, it *shall be* done."

Noon.—Lat. 38° 3′ N., long. 9° 44½′ W. Run, 313 miles. Lisbon, 49 miles.

While writing in my cabin this morning, Mr. Ritchie and the Doctor came to me, and the latter on leaving "reported" a four-masted schooner on our port beam. I went up to see it, and was "sold." Per contra—a little joke has just reached me which was at the Doctor's expense. It appears there were three eggs this morning available for egg-nog, whereupon, with his usual unselfishness, Mr. Ritchie told his black servant, Clark, to put two in the Doctor's and one in his. This Clark did, but his loyalty to his master's *person*, I suppose, rising superior even to

'Twixt love and duty. A compromise.

his master's *orders*, he was detected by Mr. Ritchie the moment afterwards (while the Doctor's back was turned) *transposing the glasses.*

When they had drunk their eggnog, Mr. Ritchie, thinking Clark's trick too good to be lost, told the Doctor of it, and then me. And now my kind friend Dr. Blandford does not like me to ask him, as I have done many times this morning, in season and out of season, which he prefers, "A two-egged schooner, or a four-masted cocktail?"

2 p.m.—Just as we were coming up from lunch, the *Clyde* cut right in among a school of porpoises, and we saw them quite close to the ship. There must have been fully fifty of them, and the way they tumbled about was, I must say, conduct far more suited to the playground than the "school." A friend suggests that perhaps they were in school, and we accidentally disturbed them in their *exercises*. As a faithful historian of the ship's events, I record this remark, but with sorrow.

3 p.m.—We are once more anchoring off the pretty city of Lisbon. I shall not go on shore, as I want every moment now for my notes, if I am to finish them, as I have always planned doing, during the homeward voyage. Besides, we start early in the morning, and an evening on shore would be no use for anything but a theatre, and indoor amusements of any kind I have steadfastly set my face against, as my trip is undertaken purely for purposes of health.

I found my flannels far too cold, and have changed for almost winter clothes. Everybody is in ulsters. The cold has increased greatly during the last twenty-four hours, and the parrots are dying off by dozens. Strange to say, the two monkeys, Romeo and Juliet, stand it well, and will in all probability reach England: and then—well, much depends on the weather there. A friend has just told me that a parrot he brought safely to Southampton, on a former voyage at this season of the year, died as he was taking it from the dock to his hotel.

8 p.m.—There has been no quarantine here, as all expected there would be, and as there is, eight months out of the twelve, for vessels coming from the Brazils. Many therefore have gone ashore, and we are a small party in the dining-saloon. "Touching Europe" was considered an occasion of sufficient importance to justify the introduction of sparkling wines at dinner, and accordingly corks were popping in all directions.

My consumption of champagne is very limited. On shore I never can touch it, without paying far too high a penalty. As Punch says of cold brandy and water, "It is very nice, but there is a to-morrow morning." Here on ship-board I find anything may be indulged in, in moderation. The grand air makes one so fit.

Lisbon from the Tagus.

10 p.m.—This evening poor Mr. Ritchie broke his famous sword (the one that Clark has polished so long and with such maternal care) trying to show us how wonderfully a Toledo blade would bend. As in everything, he was thoroughly philosophical over it. He only smiled and said, just as he does at chess when he loses a piece: "Serves me right for not being more careful." But I fear he felt the

Act I. Act II.

loss. It was a little two-act drama. In the first act he, like the soldier, "leant upon his sword;" and in the second, I'm afraid, though unseen by us, he "wiped away a tear."

December 16th.—8 a.m. We are still in the Tagus. It was so cold in the night, that I was glad of all the covering I could gather upon my bunk. There were none of the pretty nautiluses visible yesterday; they only show up in mild weather. In going these great distances one does get so muddled about the seasons. When we left the Argentine, summer was coming rapidly on. At Pernambuco it is perpetual summer; and here we are at Lisbon in mid-winter. Only six weeks ago there were hundreds of the lovely creatures off the mouth of the Tagus.

10 a.m.—A curious incident has just occurred. Getting interested in a chair a passenger joining us here was bringing on board—he is a very dark man of Portuguese type, and was speaking Portuguese—I got into conversation with him in French, which they all speak more or less. What he took me for I don't know, but I heard him say afterwards to a friend in English, "Where did that man" (meaning me) "come aboard?" To which "that man" replied for himself,

" At Southampton."   And hang me if we didn't find that we
were near neighbours in the North-west of London!

This reminds me of a digital dialogue I once had with a
poor fellow in a deaf and dumb school on the Margate sands.
At the finish of a (to me) laborious effort, I inquired if he
had been born mute. "No," he fingered back. "Were you?"
" I'm not a mute," I slowly spelt out in reply. " No more
am I," said he, aloud.   He was one of the masters.

CHAPTER XII.

December 16*th.*—10 a.m. A lame man, one of our emigrants who is going on to Vigo, has been at the pains of going on shore here, simply to buy and present a candle to his patron saint. Long ago, when the saint first took him in hand and he was on two crutches, the patient promised two candles if he was cured. Having lately, it seems, been enabled to dispense with one crutch, he has very honourably been ashore to pay the saint, *ad valorem*, one candle on account. Now, I call that business.

"*Le jeu ne vaut pas les deux chandelles.*"

11.30 a.m.—We have weighed anchor, and are once more descending the Tagus with only a light wind, so that things look more hopeful for the Bay. We are passing through a perfect fleet of the graceful craft of these parts, skimming swiftly over the water with their immense lateen sails leaning over almost dangerously before the breeze. In one, sits all by himself, as though for the mere enjoyment of the thing, a small one-legged man, dressed in white and wearing a medal on his breast. He saved the lives of five people whose boat capsized here, they tell me, and out of gratitude they presented him with that boat and a commemorative medal. He has never been a soldier, but all the same, he lost his leg by an explosion—in a mine.

This reminds me of a story they were telling last night in the "Ritchie Club." At a certain watering-place lived two boatmen, both Jones by name, though not related. Each sustained a heavy loss about the same period—the one of his wife, and the other of his sailing-boat. Anon comes a district visitor to condole with the widower:

Lady. "I am deeply grieved to hear of your sad loss, Mr. Jones."

Jones. "Ay, mum, she were a loss, were my Poll."

Lady. "You had long been together, I hear—in sunshine and in storm."

Jones. "Ay, mum, we had for many a year."

Lady. "She must have been very dear to you, I'm sure. When did she first show signs of breaking up?"

Jones. "Well, mum, she were always, as you may say, *tight* up to last Monday."

Lady (puzzled). "You don't mean that!"

Jones. "You see, mum, the boys on the beach was always a playing tricks wi' 'er—but on Monday night they must 'a used 'er cruel——"

Lady (shocked). "Dear, dear; how dreadful!"

Jones (continuing). "For on Toosday, I found 'er with the fresh coat I had give 'er all kicked off 'er ribs, 'er stays all cut loose and flyin' about."

Lady (horrified). "Mr. Jones!"

Jones (continuing). "A dozen on 'em must er been a kickin' of 'er for hours——"

Lady (shrinking). "You appal me!"

Jones. "Why, mum, I 'adn't shoved 'er a mile off the

beach afore she behaved that shameful bad, I made up my mind to run 'er in for the night, bale 'er out in the mornin', and then make 'er tight agen."

Lady (bewildered). "But you don't mean to say——"

Jones (interrupting). "I do, mum; and all in a minnit she give jist one shiver, rolled over, and went to kingdom cum——"

Lady. "Well, but you——"

Jones. "Me, mum? I swum ashore."

"Me, mum? I swum ashore!"

Tableau!

I timed the coaling at Lisbon, and found that we managed to ship two hundred tons in five hours-and-a-half, the exact time occupied in receiving one hundred and four tons in St. Vincent. This is a great improvement, but the day is fast coming, I think, when even this will be considered as so much waste expenditure—waste in money and waste in time. The value of petroleum as liquid fuel is daily becoming more and more recognized. It possess many advantages over coal —it is lighter, so more fuel could be carried; it is more cleanly, and so would be less nuisance to passengers and crew; it would give the engineer greater control over his fires; and it could be shipped in the bottom of the vessel, and so act more efficiently as ballast, while leaving available for cargo the upper space now devoted to coal.

3 p.m.—The Chief Officer has had a capital cage made for

" Che "—a champagne box standing on end, with a perforated door working on a hinge, a perch inside, and a handle on top. Throughout the voyage, out and home, Mr. Constantine has been most kind to me, bearing with my landsman's ignorance and inquisitiveness very graciously. It is a real pleasure to have such a man to go to, and to know that you will always be met with a smile as you enter his cabin.

We have slowed down to barely more than twelve knots an hour, so as to consume time, or rather to save coal, as we don't want to reach Vigo before it is light to-morrow morning.

I have been chatting with a young Englishman who, being with a party of Germans and speaking their language always, has hitherto passed for one of their countrymen. He joined us at Rio. In his cabin he showed me a pair of high boots made of the skin of the young alligator, perfectly waterproof, light, and soft, and splendid things for the swamps so common in the Brazils. He tells me that the reptile's tail yields an oil (as much as from twelve to fifteen gallons) which is utilized for lighting purposes in many parts of that country.

8 p.m.—My ferns seem to stand the change of climate, there are no further deaths. The surviving parrots also appear to have become acclimatized. My own little " Che " is particularly sprightly, but when one recalls the great heat of Pernambuco, his native place, it is easy to understand how he must feel the difference of this northern air, mild as it is to-night. I found my ulster too hot on deck just now.

At Lisbon we got two bits of news. One, that gold in Argentina had reached three hundred and twenty-four per cent.; the other, that a " P. and O." vessel had been wrecked off Plymouth.

A funny thing occurred this afternoon. The elderly lady I have twice referred to, was sitting reading in a chair next

to me on deck, when she dropped her paper in her lap and
took off her glasses quite in a little huff. She is strong on
women's rights and wrongs, and generally has something
amusing to say when she speaks on these subjects, which she
was evidently preparing to do now, so I encouraged her to
relieve herself by an interested sort of look. She was only
too willing to explain, for this time she had a *real* grievance,
I could see. It seems she had found it stated in the paper
she had been reading that more women die than men. That
they suffered more she already knew, and had told me often.
That they were more useful and got less thanks for it was
proverbial. But that after all they should *die* more than
men—this was too much, "the last straw," which, as the boy
said, "gave the camel the hump." "Poor wretched women!"
she ejaculated, nervously bustling about in her chair. "Does
it say *how many* more women than men?" I inquired
sympathetically. "I don't think that matters much," she
said, "but the exact figures are :—for every thousand women,
nine hundred and eighty men." "For every thousand
women, nine hundred and eighty men," I repeated to myself.
"Why, at that rate, there would soon be fewer women than
men, and we know the reverse is the case." And then a
thought struck me. "Does it mention any particular age?"
I inquired aloud. "I don't see that that affects the question,"
she replied sulkily. Then glancing at her paper again she
languidly read to me the entire sentence: "The records
of the Registrar-General show that for every thousand
women only nine hundred and eighty men die *at upwards of
ninety years of age.*" "Which I think means," I ventured to
suggest gently, "that more women than men *reach that age.*"
"Thank you," she said severely; "the Registrar-General
is a *man,* and you are a *man,* and I therefore view all

his and *your* information with suspicion, as coming from *a tainted source.*" And, gathering up her traps, the dear old lady flounced off and left me in disgrace.

"A tainted source."

So I am a "tainted source," am I? It has come to that! Well, I've been a good many things in my time, but I didn't think I should live to see myself a "tainted source." Still, I can't wonder at it, considering the hot climates I've been in lately. Why, in Rio even the worm will "turn."

December 17th.—7 a.m. The sun and I are rising together. We must be nearing Vigo. The weather is dull and rather cold, and the ship rolling in lumpy seas and under the old familiar grey sky. We have had a heavy sea on the bows all night, so that she has pitched freely, and here in the fore part we feel that particular motion most. Early this morning I had to turn out and lash "Che's" box to the sideboard in my cabin, or he would have spent his time among my luggage.

7.20 a.m.—We are entering Vigo Bay by the passage on the south-west side of the bleak bare island of Cies, or Bayona.

8.18 a.m.—We are anchoring near Vigo and close to the rocks on which the Pacific Company's s.s. *Valparaiso* was recently lost. The *Clyde* only stops to land passengers. There is no cargo to give or take, and we do not coal either, so we shall only have a couple of hours.

Vigo, with a population of some seventeen thousand, is a place of call for Mediterranean steamers, and a chief centre of the cattle trade. It is picturesquely situated, but its beauty is marred by railways, and the hand of the modern reformer has robbed it of much of its primitive simplicity.

On the sea-front may be seen a small specimen of its ancient walls, and between the town and the sea runs a newly planted "Alameda," or avenue of poplars.

Vigo Bay is memorable as the scene of one of Drake's dashing exploits. Somewhere between 1585 and 1589 he sailed into the bay with five and twenty ships of the line and attacked the combined fleets of France and Spain, and, in the teeth of batteries masking twenty thousand men,

Vigo.   Lazaretto de San Simon.

captured or sunk thirty-one of them—of the ships, not the men. This terrific loss is attributed, by historians, to the French convoys under Count Chateau Renaud having fled in mid-action, leaving the Spaniards in the lurch. But seeing that the joint loss of thirty-one consisted of six French and five Spanish captured, and twelve French and eight Spanish sunk, it is clear, unless the fleets were very disproportionate in numbers, that the French, in losing eighteen to the Spaniards' fifteen, had done more than bear their proportion of the punishment, and were fairly entitled to order their remnant to take the usual measures to ensure fighting

z

another day. Drake no doubt would have been only too glad if the little runaway convoy had remained, to increase both his victory and his prize-money. As it was, however, the Spaniards cast the bulk of their treasure into the sea, from which all manner of diving schemes have hitherto failed to redeem it.

The town of Vigo itself sustained a heavy bombardment in 1719, at the hands of Lord Cobham—that is, if one can say a place "sustains" that which causes its almost total destruction.

Five miles across the bay lies the delightful and ideal Spanish fishing village of Cangas. On the outward voyage the vessels of the Royal Mail make a little longer pause here, I believe, and, if so, then is the time to see Cangas, which is, I hear, well worth a visit. We did not call at Vigo going out, nor have we stayed long enough now to make the trip, but I know the best way to get there. Walk to Bongas—about two miles—and there hire a boat. The boatmen are rapacious, but if you bargain first they will take you safely and quickly for a mere trifle ; and if you keep cool there will be no disputing afterwards. It is safe to say they will land you or take you to Cangas for a third or a fourth of the sum they at first demand.

The port of Vigo is one of the finest in Spain. The bay has all the appearance of a lake, being hemmed in by rocky islands which, breaking the force of the Atlantic swell, make snug shelter for the shipping. Among the chief exports are sardines, boats laden with which may be seen in all directions wending their way to and from Gibraltar, Barcelona, etc.

From the entrance of the bay to the town, the country is rich and undulating, but only sparsely covered with white houses which serve to render more noticeable the rich green upon the hillsides behind them. One might do worse than spend a fortnight among such peaceful and pictur- esque surroundings, when one can reach the place in such a ship as the *Clyde* in about forty hours. Yet it has but few visitors. Is it because twenty-four out of the forty hours are spent crossing the Bay of Biscay? Perhaps.

10.30 a.m.—We are weighing anchor and off once more, and for the last time. Again we pass Cies Island, this time on the north side. Breakers are foaming round a reef which runs from the island two miles out to sea. The Second Officer tells me a big vessel was lost there not long ago.

Noon.—We are dashing along into the Bay of Biscay at sixty revolutions, twenty miles an hour. The sun is delightfully warm, and I take "Che" on deck for a sun bath, which is revivifying alike "for man and beast."

Vigo. General view of the port.

I intend no rudeness to " Che," who is, I may observe, a lady bird according to the best authorities on board ; I use the term " beast " as generic for all other creatures than man.

3.30 p.m.—We are off Cape Torinana, where the ill-starred iron-clad *Captain* heeled over suddenly, and went down with all hands. Mr. Childers' son was, if I remember rightly, a midshipman aboard her. Poor fellow! We are passing over his grave as I write. Between here and the next point, Cape Villano, the north coast of Galicia is considered very

Lost! (H.M.S. *Serpent.*)

dangerous and one of the worst bits of the Bay. It was there, as we have just heard, that the *Serpent*, only a fortnight ago, mistaking the Torinano for the Finisterre light, headed round the Cape, ran ashore in the Bay of Camarinas, and was lost with a hundred and thirty of her officers and crew. Their bodies are interred on the shores of the village of that name, whose inhabitants, we hear, rendered most kindly aid at the time of the disaster.

5 p.m.—We are well into the Bay and are feeling the full swell of the Atlantic. We even shipped some water just now, a rare thing for the *Clyde.*

A few moments ago I heard a young good-looking fellow, with bright eyes and brilliant complexion, who joined the ship at Vigo, talking to a lady about having had fever up the Amazon, and being invalided home. One of the passengers tells me he is a rich young "masher," resident on the south coast, who every now and then leaves by one of the ocean-going ships, goes ashore at Vigo or Lisbon, stops there eight or ten weeks, and then returns with thrilling accounts of his travels and hair-breadth escapes by flood and field. He is most at home when spinning yarns about his alligator-shooting in the Brazils; crossing the Andes on mule-back, with suitable local colouring; or "rounding the Horn," with its concomitant adventures. "Invalided!"— and with those cheeks—was "a little too, too!"

8 p.m.—There is really not a morsel of sea on, in this formidable Bay. It even looks smooth, and there are no "white horses" on the wave-tops. But the rollers are huge. Taking them broadside, as we do, if this grand ship, solid as an anvil, heaves so that as I write in my cabin the stool skates all over the place with me, and the luggage is playing at "touch and run away" in every direction—what must this Bay be in *bad* weather!

11 p.m.—There was a large and merry party in the "Smoking club" this evening, and songs and speeches were the order of the day. One gentleman, who had besought us over and over again to hear him sing "Paddy's Wedding," when at last he got his chance, couldn't remember the words. Another, however, did, as it happened, and came to the rescue, and so it ended in the song being given out a verse at a time, like a hymn in a Primitive Methodist chapel. But, to our further amusement, we found that the singer rendered this old Irish song in the very purest of

cockney accents. On his attention being gently drawn to
the incongruity, he explained that he did so because so
many people couldn't understand the words "when he sung
them *with the brogue.*" Upon this we challenged him to
try us, as his argument wouldn't hold now that the words
were being given out before each verse. Unable to escape
any longer, he consented, and sang us the most curious
jumble of Yorkshire dialect and Frenchman's broken English
I ever heard. It was simply delicious, and certainly
justified his plea for singing the song in English.

The chorus, " La, la, la, lalalala," etc., was Parisian, pure and
simple. But (style and all!) we joined in with an ecstasy I'm
sure beyond that which Sam Collins could have infused into
the original song.

Another friend getting first merry, then jubilant, and
finally generous, made a speech in which he invited us all
to his house—without saying where it was, which in the
circumstances was perhaps wise—in terms which precisely
reversed his predecessor's error, for he delivered English
in Irish fashion. He said we were welcome at any time,
any and all of us, to put our toes *under his table,* and he
hoped he would often have the pleasure of seeing many of
our *faces there!* This was received with volleys of " Later
on! Later on!" and unrestrained hilarity, amid which the
festivities closed.

December 18th.—8 a.m. At 2 a.m. this morning, one of last
night's revellers (who had been invited to go "under the table"
of the generous "universal provider"), having apparently
during the evening done his best to qualify himself for that
position, rang his bell violently. On my going to see what
was the matter, he peremptorily ordered me, pointing to the
corner, to remove "that man" who was "watching him."

In vain did I try to assure him that it was his own ulster
hanging harmlessly on its peg. He was obdurate. So, for the
sake of my own peace as well as his, I had to take it solemnly
down and carry it to my cabin. Whereupon he thanked me
effusively, and with the air of a duke, adding, thickly
somewhat, that he was sure in "calber bobents" I should
"ackdoledge-the-wis-dob-o-th-pre-caution." And with that
he turned on his face and I heard him addressing the rest of
his remarks to the bolster. This morning he is ringing his
bell again to know what's become of his coat, and is most
incredulous of my explanation, asserting that he was never
frightened of a coat in his life, at least (as a reservation), at
least, not of his *own* coat. From which last remark I incline
to think that he is still wool-gathering.

For myself, my chief beverage out and home has been
lemon squash. And very well it suited me. Now and then
I would venture on a single glass of whiskey; and occasionally
I indulged in a glass or two of champagne, but never except
at meals. To this moderation I attributed my ability to
sleep or wake, without fear, in the presence of *my* overcoat.

Last night I allowed myself to be tempted with a cigar
which a friend pressed upon me. He had but a couple—he
showed me his case—and he said they were 2*s.* 6*d.* each. This
decided me, and I smoked the thing. Hearing him afterwards
order "two more of those 6*d.* cigars," I opened my eyes at
him. "My dear sir," he said, "I only did it to induce you
to take one. What I said was strictly correct, if you think
my words over, only I didn't say a comma at two."

Noon.—Lat. and long. not announced by the Captain, but
we can't be more than a couple of hours off Cape Ushant,
passing which we are in the Channel.

This morning a pathetic little incident occurred. A poor

parrot on his wooden stand, one of the many braced to the bulwarks outside the cook's galley, was blown overboard. If he had sunk at once there would have been nothing very sad about the affair, for of course we could not stop to pick him up. But it was very touching to see poor Polly crawl to the perch and shake his drenched feathers as if he quite understood it was only some of our fun. And then to reflect, that it was only a reprieve from a speedy and merciful death to one of slow starvation, unless some friendly shark, seeing something alive, should invite him to dinner as the spider does the fly.

Even if a large dog, as occasionally happens, is swept

overboard, no efforts are made to save him, so what can a poor parrot expect ? Recently, however, I read of a case where the ship *did* lay-to when a fine Newfoundland dog was washed away. But it was his master's doing: for well knowing the rules on such occasions, he in an instant, and without pausing to think, sprang over the side too. This of

A gallant rescue.

course compelled the Captain to stop, and thus happily both the dog and his gallant master were saved.

While I was caressing my little " Che " this morning, and rolling him over and over on his back on my bunk, he attempted to extricate himself by fixing his beak in my nose. It was all my fault, but I reprimanded him in two or three strong Brazilian expletives I have acquired, and now that he sees me busily packing, with a view, as he seems to fear, of presently deserting him, he shows such contrition, and tries so hard to make reparation for his little fault by gentle ways, sweet notes, and attentions of all kinds, that I have had to let him sit on my head or shoulder despite the inconvenience to me. It is none to him, for he holds on to my coat-collar by his foot and sings most joyously while I blunder about the cabin among my many traps.

3 p.m.—It is raining hard, the sea is rough, and there is no walking on any of the decks, for the spray and rain are making a clean sweep of them. Only about twelve hours more and we shall be in Southampton, and the great trip of my life will be over and done. But its remembrance will feast me for the rest of my days, as at once the most delightful and wonderful experience I have known. It has made me fully five years younger in vitality, and a good ten years older in knowledge of the world.

8. p.m.—Getting up from dinner, Mr. Mervin went to the organ in the dining-saloon to play a favourite air on board, called " Daughters," with a chorus that has lately " caught on," as they say, so that everybody, even to the tiny ship's boys, are for ever singing it. The ship was rolling and pitching so that the getting there was no easy matter, and the stopping on the stool would have been simply impossible but for the assistance of one of these same ship's boys, whom Mervin employed to hold the seat steady. Now, the Doctor was having dessert with us, and wanting to send a message quickly, hailed this boy by name to carry it. For a moment a struggle went visibly on in the poor

The sliding scale.

lad's mind, between discipline on the one hand, and politeness on the other. Unfortunately for Mervin, the *former* triumphed; the boy went to the Doctor, and the organist to the uttermost ends of the earth, as represented by the ship's side.

11 p.m.—A select few of us have been having our last merry meeting. There were speeches, songs, and toasts galore, the Doctor, as usual, outshining us all. But most speeches had to be made from the speaker's seat, for standing—that is to say, *standing still*—was quite out of the question. One of our number sang a song in praise of the bonny ship that bore us over. Here are the words :—

A SONG OF THE CLYDE.

Air, " Sweet Kitty Clyde."

Oh " Sweet Kitty Clyde " my tune shall be,
  And I'll sing you a song, if you will,
Of one of her name that went to sea
  And is sailing the ocean still.
She is blithe and gay, as the sailor's wife
  When she welcomes her lad alongside :
And heart to my heart in the pulse of life
  Beats the breast of the bounding *Clyde.**

Chorus.

" Oh, the lovely *Clyde*, she's Ocean's bride,"
  Said Neptune, as he kiss'd her,
" And safe she shall ride, upon every tide,
  With the *Thames*, her sweet twin-sister."

Some people aver that she left her home
  On account of her well-known *slips*,

---

  * These words seemed to me to fit themselves to the rhythm of the lullaby of the engines. I have had to smooth them out, for they used to reach me in all sorts of queer assortments, such as—

    " And pulse to my life in the heart of bound,
    Heart the *Clyde* of the breasting beat."

—C. C. A.

And they say she is still inclined to roam,
   And they point to her *fast little trips.*
But I'll have none of their wordy strife,
   And whatever may her betide,
Still heart to my heart in the pulse of life
   Beats the breast of the bounding *Clyde.*

                Chorus.

Some say Old Neptune's a bit of a flirt,
   And is sweet on his sister-in-law.
But at that his wife will not feel hurt
   While his conduct's without a flaw.
And on the "deceased wife's sister" strife
   There will be no need to decide,
While heart to his heart in the pulse of life
   Beats the breast of the bounding *Clyde.*

                Chorus.

Oh, my pretty *Clyde,* 'twas a lucky chance
   That made us partners, dear,
In many a merry wavy dance
   In Neptune's ball-room here.
But oh, the thought stabs like a knife
   That I must leave thy side,
For heart to my heart in the pulse of life
   Beats the breast of the bounding *Clyde.*

                Chorus.

Thy gliding form will haunt my dreams
   In my home that is far away.
Ah me! How cruel this parting seems:
   "Good-bye!" is so sad to say.
One must not trifle with Neptune's wife,
   Yet oft I shall tell with pride
How, heart to my heart in the pulse of life,
   Beat the breast of the bounding *Clyde.*

                Chorus.

And now, dear boys, one parting word:
   To the *Clyde* your glasses raise,
And make your lusty voices heard,
   In one loud pæan of praise.
I'll stamp and whistle, for drum and fife,
   While each claps a hand to his side,

Singing, "heart to my heart, in the pulse of life,
   Beats the breast of the bounding *Clyde.*"

Chorus.

"Oh, the lovely *Clyde*, she's Ocean's bride,"
   Said Neptune, as he kiss'd her,
"And safe she shall ride, upon every tide,
   With the *Thames*, her sweet twin-sister."

The little party was a big success, and all I think enjoyed
it thoroughly; and as to our physical comforts, the cabin,
company, and concomitants left little to be desired. Thanks
to the hot-water pipes that skirt each cabin, we were all
as snug and cosy as heart could wish. But on deck how
different! I have had just one peep at it before turning in.
The cold is intense, the rain pouring in torrents, and the
sea sweeping the spar-deck from end to end. We are in the
" chops of the Channel," too, and the good ship tumbles
herself and us about as she has never done before, going
out or coming home. It was with the very greatest difficulty
I managed to get to Mr. Ritchie's cabin to say good-night,
his duties on such a night and in the Channel having kept
him from joining our farewell gathering. Indeed, poor
fellow, he will be up all to-night. The starboard (weather-
side) companion exit was shut and locked on account of the
violence of the wind, rain, and sea, and the only way to get
to the Chief Engineer was to go on the spar-deck by the
port side exit, and cross to the other side by the tunnel
behind the engines. The fight with the wind through that
tunnel I shall never forget. The distance from the port
side to his cabin is not more than twenty yards, but I
dare say it took me five minutes, moving barely an inch at
a time. While I was there, Mr. Mervin turned up also, but
it had cost him two shillings for a seaman to pilot him. It

is the wildest night that I have ever spent at sea. The rain
is blinding, and it is blowing a full gale. You can't sit,
stand, nor walk, and even lying is not easy except to
practised liars. A perfectly accurate phrase, I believe,
though it sounds strange.

December 19*th.*—6.30 a.m. Few on board can have slept
much, I think. What with the violent pitching and rolling,
and the thundering blows as each sea struck the ship, I have
been awake pretty well the whole night.

We expected to have been in by 3 a.m., but we are
evidently a considerable way from
home still.

8 a.m.—We were off Portland, I find,
at half-past six. Now we are nearing
the Needles, and in a blinding snowstorm. The Chief Officer has had
nine hours on the bridge in this bitter
weather, so that he was there when we
were toasting him below last night,
and wishing heartily, I warrant, that
he could *toast* himself. We have
been lying-to half the night, I hear,
unable to distinguish any "lights."

His watch.

10 a.m.—Breakfast has furnished me with my last meal
aboard the *Clyde*. Mr. Ritchie tells me there was no moving
all night for the dense snow that was falling. When once,
for a moment, the veil lifted, we found we were among a group
of vessels, all brought-to like ourselves, and one of them, a
North German Lloyd, not thirty yards off. He told me also
of the Doctor's narrow escape on leaving us last night.
Attempting to reach his cabin by the starboard or weather
side, on which it lies, a sea that swept the deck caught him,

lifted him off his legs, and hurling him the length of the deck, dashed him into the scuppers, where, holding on for dear life to the steps, he was nearly drowned with the volume of water, as wave after wave came crashing upon him.

The coast, which is for a moment visible, is thickly covered with snow, and the wind is piercingly cold. The glad tidings has just come, as the best of all Christmas messages of peace and good-will to the officers and crew of the *Clyde*, that the river Scheldt is frozen over and impassable, and the ship will not therefore proceed to Antwerp. The delight of every one at escaping that horrid trip across the North Sea, and getting in place of it a long Christmas holiday ashore in England and in their homes, is brightening every face, and noticeable in the cheery tones of every voice.

11.15 a.m.—We are still in a heavy snowstorm, fully as dense as a fog, and so have to keep on stopping and anchoring. Just now we weighed and moved five hundred yards, and are now stopping again.

Noon.—We have at last anchored finally, and the tender is alongside, and lunch has been considerately laid early, so I shall have one more meal.

1 p.m.—" Farewell my trim-built wherry," *Clyde;* I should say " my werry trim-built *Clyde!* " Good-bye, Ritchie, my generous friend, and Constantine, and Bamfield, and Dance, and Powell, and thou ever-merry Blandford. Good-bye! Good-bye!

Just as the paddles begin to move, up go three ringing cheers for each of them, and then three more, and lastly, as we steam away, the Captain gets his share.

At the Custom House all are busy despatching telegrams to relations and friends—telegraph officials being

there in the waiting-room to receive them. As to my boxes,
the authorities took my word and passed everything, and
so I was able to catch the 3.15 train to Waterloo, which
we reached at 6.30 p.m., to find London, as it had been, they
told me, for a month past, knee-deep in snow.

Home!
" Like a sheeted ghost the vessel swept."
LONGFELLOW.

L'ENVOI.

And now, before I say my last Farewell,
What is the outcome of the tale I tell?
Two months ago, I left these shores, to roam
In search of vanished " Health," and bring her home.
How have I brought her?   Like a truant wife,
To be more constant to our wedded life?
Or is her love, this second honeymoon,
To wane at our home-coming, all too soon?
Or shall we, like ill-mended china, hold
Together till our frail cement be cold,
And then, once more, upon the slightest strain,
At the old fracture, break and part again?
Well, these are speculations I must leave:
The web of Fate is not for me to weave.
'Gainst the lost *Past* I weigh my *Present* gain:
Who to the *Future* looks, shall look in vain.
You know the soldier's ancient boast, no doubt,
" I've caught a Tartar!"—" What are you about,"

Answered his comrade, "not to bring him home?"
" I would," replied the first, "*but he won't come!*"
And so we find too, in more recent days,
When Stanley, under Equatorial blaze,
At last discovered Emin Pacha's track,
He but contrived to bring him half-way back.
And then the wily prisoner slipped his chain,
And a-moth-hunting scampered off again.
After such warning voices, I confess,
There does seem such a thing as half-success.
Thus it appears, all I can fairly claim,
Is to have done what little was my aim.
To search for "Health" I went the *Clyde* aboard.
To find "Health"—somewhere—has been my reward
And, "How I *keep* Health" (if I do), in time,
May serve me for another theme or rhyme.
Meanwhile, if ever you my trip should try,
May my success attend you, friend, say I:
And may you have as happy a tale to tell.
Till then I bid you, from my heart—

Farewell !

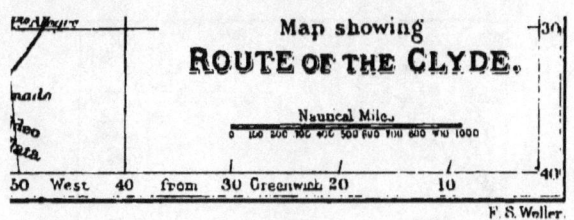

Map showing
ROUTE OF THE CLYDE.

Nautical Miles.
0   100 200 300 400 500 600 700 800 900 1000

50   West   40   from   30 Greenwich 20   10

F. S. Weller.

Map showing
ROUTE OF THE CLYDE.

London, Sampson Low and Company, Limited

INDEX.

2 A

Note to Page 122, Lines 28-30.—Since writing this, I have learnt. with great pleasure, that on the 13th of May, 1888, a Bill was passed for the immediate and unconditional emancipation of all slaves throughout what was then the Empire of Brazil.—C. C. A.

LONDON: PRINTED BY WILLIAM CLOWES AND SONS, LIMITED,
STAMFORD STREET AND CHARING CROSS.

2 B

A Catalogue of American and Foreign Books Published or Imported by MESSRS. SAMPSON LOW & CO. *can be had on application.*

St. Dunstan's House, Fetter Lane, Fleet Street, London,
October, 1890.

A Selection from the List of Books

PUBLISHED BY

SAMPSON LOW, MARSTON, SEARLE, & RIVINGTON,

LIMITED.

ALPHABETICAL LIST.

ABNEY (W. de W.) and Cunningham. Pioneers of the Alps. With photogravure portraits of guides. Small 4to, gilt top, 21*s.*

Adam and Wetherald. An Algonquin Maiden. Cr. 8vo, 5*s.*

Alcott. Works of the late Miss Louisa May Alcott :—
Aunt Jo's Scrap-bag. Cloth, 2*s.* ; gilt, 2*s. 6d.*
Eight Cousins. Illustrated, 2*s.;* cloth gilt, 3*s. 6d.*
Jack and Jill. Illustrated, 2*s.;* cloth gilt, 3*s. 6d.*
Jo's Boys. 5*s.*
Jimmy's Cruise in the Pinafore, &c. Illustrated, cloth, 2*s.*; gilt edges, 3*s. 6d.*
Little Men. Double vol., 2*s.*; cloth, gilt edges, 3*s. 6d.*
Little Women. 1*s.* ⎱ 1 vol., cloth, 2*s.* ; larger ed., gilt
Little Women Wedded. 1*s.* ⎰ edges, 3*s. 6d.*
Old-fashioned Girl. 2*s.*; cloth, gilt edges, 3*s. 6d.*
Rose in Bloom. 2*s.*; cloth gilt, 3*s. 6d.*
Shawl Straps. Cloth, 2*s.*
Silver Pitchers. Cloth, gilt edges, 3*s. 6d.*
Under the Lilacs. Illustrated, 2*s.*; cloth gilt, 5*s.*
Work : a Story of Experience. 1*s.* ⎱ 1 vol., cloth, gilt
—— Its Sequel, "Beginning Again." 1*s.* ⎰ edges, 3*s. 6d.*

Alcott. Life, Letters and Journals of Louisa May Alcott. By EDNAH D. CHENEY. Cr. 8vo, 6*s.*

—— *Recollections of My Childhood's Days.* Crown 8vo 3*s. 6d.*

—— See also LOW'S STANDARD SERIES.

Alden (W. L.) Adventures of Jimmy Brown. Ill. Sm. 8vo, 3*s. 6d.*

—— *Trying to find Europe.* Illus.. crown 8vo, 2*s. 6d.*

A

Alger (J. G.) Englishmen in the French Revolution, cr. 8vo, 7s. 6d.

Amateur Angler's Days in Dove Dale : Three Weeks' Holiday
in 1884. By E. M. 1s. 6d. ; boards, 1s. ; large paper, 5s.

Andersen. Fairy Tales. An entirely new Translation. With
over 500 Illustrations by Scandinavian Artists. Small 4to, 6s.

Angling. See Amateur, "Cutcliffe," "Fennell," "Halford,"
"Hamilton," "Martin," "Orvis," "Pennell," "Pritt," "Senior,"
"Stevens," "Theakston," "Walton," "Wells," and "Willis-Bund."

Arnold (R.) Ammonia and Ammonium Compounds. Ill. Cr.
8vo, 5s.

Art Education. See "Biographies," "D'Anvers," "Illustrated
Text Books," "Mollett's Dictionary."

Artistic Japan. Illustrated with Coloured Plates. Monthly.
Royal 4to, 2s.; vols. I. to IV., roy. 4to, extra emblematic binding,
Japanese silk, 15s. each.

Ashe (Robert P.) Uganda, England's Latest Charge. Cr.
8vo, stiff cover, 1s.

────── *Two Kings of Uganda.* New Ed. Cr. 8vo, 3s. 6d.

B̲ALDWIN (James) Story of Siegfried. 6s.

────── *Story of the Golden Age.* Illust. by HOWARD PYLE.
Cr. 8vo, 6s.

────── *Story of Roland.* Crown 8vo, 6s.

Barlow (Alfred) Weaving by Hand and by Power. With
several hundred Illustrations. Third Edition, royal 8vo, £1 5s.

Barnum (P. T.) Dollars and Sense. 8vo.

Bassett (F. S.) Legends and Superstitions of the Sea. 7s. 6d.

THE BAYARD SERIES.

Edited by the late J. HAIN FRISWELL.

Pleasure Books of Literature produced in the Choicest Style.

"We can hardly imagine better books for boys to read or for men to ponder
over."—*Times.*

*Price 2s. 6d. each Volume, complete in itself, flexible cloth extra, gilt edges,
with silk Headbands and Registers.*

The Story of the Chevalier Bayard.
Joinville's St. Louis of France.
The Essays of Abraham Cowley.
Abdallah. By Edouard Laboullaye.
Napoleon, Table-Talk and Opinions.
Words of Wellington.
Johnson's Rasselas. With Notes.
Hazlitt's Round Table.
The Religio Medici, Hydriotaphia,
&c. By Sir Thomas Browne, Knt.

Coleridge's Christabel, &c. With
Preface by Algernon C. Swinburne.
Ballad Poetry of the Affections. By
Robert Buchanan.
Lord Chesterfield's Letters, Sen-
tences, and Maxims. With Essay
by Sainte-Beuve.
The King and the Commons. Cava-
lier and Puritan Songs.
Vathek. By William Beckford.

The Bayard Series (continued.)

Essays in Mosaic. By Ballantyne.
My Uncle Toby; his Story and his Friends. By P. Fitzgerald.
Reflections of Rochefoucauld.

Socrates: Memoirs for English Readers from Xenophon's Memorabilia. By Edw. Levien.
Prince Albert's Golden Precepts.

A Case containing 12 *Volumes, price* 31s. 6d.; *or the Case separately, price* 3s. 6d.

Beaconsfield. See HITCHMAN.

Beaugrand (C.) Walks Abroad of Two Young Naturalists. By D. SHARP. Illust., 8vo, 7s. 6d.

Beecher (H. W.) Authentic Biography, and Diary. Ill. 8vo, 21s.

────── *Norwood; Village Life in New England.* Crown 8vo, 6s.

Beer Manufacture. See THAUSING.

Behnke and Browne. Child's Voice: its Treatment with regard to After Development. Small 8vo, 3s. 6d.

────── See also BROWNE.

Bell (H. H. J.) Obeah: Negro Witchcraft in the West Indies. Crown 8vo, 2s. 6d.

Beyschlag. Female Costume Figures of various Centuries. 12 reproductions of pastel designs in portfolio, imperial. 21s.

Bickersteth (Bishop E. H.) Clergyman in his Home. 1s.

────── *From Year to Year: Original Poetical Pieces.* Small post 8vo, 3s. 6d.; roan, 6s. and 5s.; calf or morocco, 10s. 6d.

────── *The Master's Home-Call.* N. ed. 32mo, cloth gilt, 1s.

────── *The Master's Will.* Funeral Sermon. 1s., sewed, 6d.

────── *The Reef, and other Parables.* Crown 8vo, 2s. 6d.

────── *Shadow of the Rock.* Select Religious Poetry. 2s. 6d.

────── *Shadowed Home and the Light Beyond.* 5s.

────── See also "Hymnal Companion."

Billroth (Th.) Care of the Sick, at Home and in the Hospital. Illustrated, crown 8vo, 6s.

Biographies of the Great Artists (Illustrated). Crown 8vo, emblematical binding, 3s. 6d. per volume, except where the price is given.

Barbizon School. I. Millet, &c. ⎱ 2 in 1,
────── II. Corot, &c. ⎰ 7/6
Claude le Lorrain, by Owen J. Dullea.
Correggio, by M. E. Heaton. 2s. 6d.
Cox (David) and De Wint.
George Cruikshank, Life and Works.
Della Robbia and Cellini. 2s. 6d.
Albrecht Dürer, by R. F. Heath.
Figure Painters of Holland.
Fra Angelico, Masaccio, and Botticelli.
Fra Bartolommeo, Albertinelli, and Andrea del Sarto.

Gainsborough and Constable.
Ghiberti and Donatello. 2s. 6d.
Giotto, by Harry Quilter.
Hans Holbein, by Joseph Cundall.
Hogarth, by Austin Dobson.
Landseer, by F. G. Stevens.
Lawrence and Romney, by Lord Ronald Gower. 2s. 6d.
Leonardo da Vinci.
Little Masters of Germany, by W. B. Scott.
Mantegna and Francia.
Meissonier, by J. W. Mollett. 2s. 6d.

Biographies of the Great Artists (continued.)

Michelangelo Buonarotti, by Clément.
Mulready Memorials, by Stephens.
Murillo, by Ellen E. Minor.   2s. 6d.
Overbeck, by J. B. Atkinson.
Raphael, by N. D'Anvers.
Rembrandt, by J. W. Mollett.
Reynolds, by F. S. Pulling.
Rubens, by C. W. Kett.
Tintoretto, by W. R. Osler.

Titian, by R. F. Heath.
Turner, by Cosmo Monkhouse.
Vandyck and Hals, by Head.
Van de Velde and the Dutch Painters.
Van Eyck, Memlinc, Matsys.
Velasquez, by E. Stowe.
Vernet and Delaroche, by J. Rees.
Watteau, by J. W. Mollett.   2s. 6d.
Wilkie, by J. W. Mollett.

IN PREPARATION.
Miniature Painters of Eng. School.

Bird (*F. J.*) *American Practical Dyer's Companion.*   8vo, 42s.
——— (*H. E.*) *Chess Practice.*   8vo, 2s. 6d.
Bishop (*E. S.*) *Lectures to Nurses on Antiseptics.*   With diagrams, crown 8vo, 2s.
Black (*Robert*) *Horse Racing in France : a History.*   8vo, 14s.
Black (*W.*) *Standfast Craig Royston.*   3 vols., cr. 8vo, 31s. 6d.
——— See also LOW'S STANDARD NOVELS.
Blackburn (*Charles F.*) *Hints on Catalogue Titles and Index Entries*, with a Vocabulary of Terms and Abbreviations, chiefly from Foreign Catalogues.   Royal 8vo, 14s.
Blackburn (*Henry*) *Art in the Mountains, the Oberammergau Passion Play.*   New ed., corrected to 1890, 8vo, 5s.
——— *Breton Folk.*   With 171 Illust. by RANDOLPH CALDECOTT. Imperial 8vo, gilt edges, 21s.; plainer binding, 10s. 6d.
——— *Pyrenees.*   Illustrated by GUSTAVE DORÉ, corrected to 1881.   Crown 8vo, 7s. 6d.   See also CALDECOTT.
Blackmore (*R. D.*) *Kit and Kitty.*   A novel.   3 vols., crown 8vo. 31s. 6d.
——— *Lorna Doone.*   *Édition de luxe.*   Crown 4to, very numerous Illustrations, cloth, gilt edges, 31s. 6d.; parchment, uncut, top gilt, 35s.; new issue, plainer, 21s.
——— *Novels.*   See also LOW'S STANDARD NOVELS.
——— *Springhaven.*   Illust. by PARSONS and BARNARD. Sq. 8vo, 12s.; new edition, 7s. 6d.
Blaikie (*William*) *How to get Strong and how to Stay so.* Rational, Physical, Gymnastic, &c., Exercises. Illust., sm. post 8vo, 5s.
——— *Sound Bodies for our Boys and Girls.*   16mo, 2s. 6d.
Bodleian.   See HISTORIC BINDINGS.
Bonwick.   *British Colonies.*   Asia, 1s.; Africa, 1s.; America, 1s.; Australasia, 1s.   One vol., cloth, 5s.
Bosanquet (*Rev. C.*) *Blossoms from the King's Garden : Sermons* for Children.   2nd Edition, small post 8vo, cloth extra, 6s.
——— *Jehoshaphat ; or, Sunlight and Clouds.*   1s.

Bower (*G. S.*) *and Webb, Law of Electric Lighting.* New edition, crown 8vo, 12s. 6d.

Boy's Froissart. King Arthur. Knightly Legends of Wales. Percy. See LANIER.

Bradshaw (*J.*) *New Zealand as it is.* 8vo, 12s. 6d.

—— *New Zealand of To-day,* 1884-87. 8vo, 14s.

Brannt (*W. T.*) *Animal and Vegetable Fats and Oils.* Illust., 8vo, 35s.

—— *Manufacture of Soap and Candles.* Illust., 8vo. 35s.

—— *Metallic Alloys. After Krupp and Wildberger.* Cr. 8vo, 12s. 6d.

—— *Vinegar, Cider, and Fruit Wines.* Illust., 8vo., 25s.

Bright (*John*) *Public Letters.* Crown 8vo, 7s. 6d.

Brisse (*Baron*) *Ménus.* In French and English, for every day in the Year. 7th Edition, with 1200 recipes. Crown 8vo, 5s.

Brittany. See BLACKBURN.

Brown (*A. J.*) *Rejected of Men, and Other Poems.* Fcp.8vo, 3s. 6d.

—— (*A. S.*) *Madeira and Canary Islands for Invalids,* Maps, crown 8vo, sewed, 2s. 6d.

—— (*Robert*) *Jack Abbott's Log.* 2 vols., cr. 8vo, 21s.

Browne (*G. Lennox*) *Voice Use and Stimulants.* Sm. 8vo, 3s. 6d.

—— *and Behnke, Voice, Song, and Speech.* 15s.; new ed., 5s.

Bryant (*W. C.*) *and Gay* (*S. H.*) *History of the United States.* Profusely Illustrated, 4 vols., royal 8vo, 60s.

Bryce (*Rev. Professor*) *Manitoba.* Illust. Crown 8vo, 7s. 6d.

—— *Short History of the Canadian People.* 7s. 6d.

Burnaby (*Mrs F.*) *High Alps in Winter; or, Mountaineering* in Search of Health. With Illustrations, &c., 14s, See also MAIN.

Burnley (*J.*) *History of Wool and Woolcombing.* Illust. 8vo, 21s.

Burton (*Sir R. F.*) *Early, Public, and Private Life.* Edited by F. HITCHMAN. 2 vols., 8vo, 36s.

Butler (*Sir W. F.*) *Campaign of the Cataracts.* Illust., 8vo, 18s.

—— *Invasion of England, told twenty years after.* 2s. 6d.

—— *Red Cloud; or, the Solitary Sioux.* Imperial 16mo, numerous illustrations, gilt edges, 3s. 6d.; plainer binding, 2s. 6d.

—— *The Great Lone Land; Red River Expedition.* 7s. 6d.

—— *The Wild North Land; the Story of a Winter Journey* with Dogs across Northern North America. 8vo, 18s. Cr. 8vo, 7s. 6d.

Bynner (*E. L.*) See LOW'S STANDARD NOVELS.

CABLE (*G. W.*) See LOW'S STANDARD NOVELS.

Cadogan (*Lady Adelaide*) *Drawing-room Plays.* 10s. 6d.; acting edition, 6d. each.

Cadogan (Lady Adelaide) Illustrated Games of Patience. Twenty-four Diagrams in Colours, with Text. Fcap. 4to, 12s. 6d.

———— *New Games of Patience.* Coloured Diagrams, 4to, 12s. 6d.

Caldecott (Randolph) Memoir. By HENRY BLACKBURN. With 170 Examples of the Artist's Work. 14s.; new edit., 7s. 6d.

———— *Sketches.* With an Introduction by H. BLACKBURN. 4to, picture boards, 2s. 6d.

California. See NORDHOFF.

Callan (H.) Wanderings on Wheel in Europe. Cr. 8vo, 1s. 6d.

Campbell (Lady Colin) Book of the Running Brook. 5s.

Carleton, City Legends. Special Edition, illus., royal 8vo, 12s. 6d.; ordinary edition, crown 8vo, 1s.

———— *City Ballads.* Illustrated, 12s. 6d. New Ed. (Rose Library), 16mo, 1s.

———— *City Ballads and City Legends.* In one vol., 2s. 6d.

———— *Farm Ballads, Farm Festivals, and Farm Legends.* Paper boards, 1s. each; 1 vol., small post 8vo, 3s. 6d.

Carnegie (A.) American Four-in-Hand in Britain. Small 4to, Illustrated, 10s. 6d. Popular Edition, paper, 1s.

———— *Round the World.* 8vo, 10s. 6d.

———— *Triumphant Democracy.* 6s.; also 1s. 6d. and 1s.

Chairman's Handbook. By R. F. D. PALGRAVE. 5th Edit., 2s.

Changed Cross, &c. Religious Poems. 16mo, 2s. 6d.; calf, 6s.

Chapin (F. H.) Mountaineering in Colorado, Peaks about Estes Park, Illus., 10s. 6d.

Chess. See BIRD (H. E.).

Choice Editions of Choice Books. (2s. 6d. each.) Illustrated by C. W. COPE, R.A., T. CRESWICK, R.A., E. DUNCAN, BIRKET FOSTER, J. C. HORSLEY, A.R.A., G. HICKS, R. REDGRAVE, R.A., C. STONEHOUSE, F. TAYLER, G. THOMAS, H. J. TOWNSHEND, E. H. WEHNERT, HARRISON WEIR, &c. New issue, 1s. per vol.

Bloomfield's Farmer's Boy.	Milton's L'Allegro.
Campbell's Pleasures of Hope.	Poetry of Nature. Harrison Weir.
Coleridge's Ancient Mariner.	Rogers' (Sam.) Pleasures of Memory.
Goldsmith's Deserted Village.	Shakespeare's Songs and Sonnets.
Goldsmith's Vicar of Wakefield.	Tennyson's May Queen.
Gray's Elegy in a Churchyard.	Elizabethan Poets.
Keats' Eve of St. Agnes.	Wordsworth's Pastoral Poems.

"Such works are a glorious beatification for a poet."—*Athenæum.*

(Extra Volume) Bunyan's Pilgrim's Progress. Illustrated, 2s.

Christ in Song. By PHILIP SCHAFF. New Ed., gilt edges, 6s.

Clark (Mrs. K. M.) Southern Cross Fairy Tale. Ill. 4to, 5s.

Clarke (P.) Three Diggers: a Tale of the Australian Fifties. Crown 8vo, 6s.

Collingwood (Harry) See LOW'S STANDARD BOOKS.

Collinson (Sir R.; Adm.) H.M.S. "Enterprise" in search of Sir J. Franklin. 8vo, 14s.

Colonial Year-book. By A. J. R. TRENDELL. Crown 8vo, 6s. Annually.

Cook (Dutton) Book of the Play. New Edition. 1 vol., 3s. 6d.

—— *On the Stage: Studies.* 2 vols., 8vo, cloth, 24s.

Craddock (C. E.) Despot of Broomsedge Cove. Crown 8vo, 6s.

Crew (B. J.) Practical Treatise on Petroleum. Illust., 8vo, 28s.

Crouch (A.P.) Glimpses of Feverland: West African Waters 6s.

—— *On a Surf-bound Coast.* Cr. 8vo, 7s. 6d.; new ed. 5s.

Cumberland(Stuart)Thought Reader'sThoughts. Cr.8vo., 10s.6d.

—— *Queen's Highway from Ocean to Ocean: Canadian* Pacific Railway. Ill., 8vo, 18s.; new ed., 7s. 6d.

—— See also LOW'S STANDARD NOVELS.

Cundall (Joseph). See "Remarkable Bindings."

Curtin (J.) Myths and Folk Lore of Ireland. Cr. 8vo, 9s.

Cushing (William) Anonyms, Dictionary of Revealed Author- ship. 2 vols., large 8vo, gilt top, 52s. 6d.

—— *Initials and Pseudonyms.* 25s.; second series, 21s.

Cutcliffe (H. C.) Trout Fishing in Rapid Streams. Cr.8vo, 3s. 6d.

*D*ALY *(Mrs. D.) Digging, Squatting, and Pioneering in* Northern South Australia. 8vo, 12s.

Dana (J. D.) Characteristics of Volcanoes, Hawaiian Islands, &c. Illus., 18s.

D'Anvers. Elementary History of Art. New ed., 360 illus., 2 vols., cr. 8vo. I. Architecture, &c., 5s.; II. Painting, 6s.; 1 vol., 10s. 6d.; also 12s.

—— *Elementary History of Music.* Crown 8vo, 2s. 6d.

Daudet (A.) Port Tarascon, Tartarin's Last Adventures; By H. JAMES. Illus., crown 8vo.

Davis (Clement) Modern Whist. 4s.

—— *(C. T.) Bricks, Tiles, Terra-Cotta, &c.* N. ed. 8vo, 25s.

—— *Manufacture of Leather.* With many Illustrations. 52s.6d.

—— *Manufacture of Paper.* 28s.

—— *(G. B.) Outlines of International Law.* 8vo. 10s. 6d.

Dawidowsky. Glue,Gelatine, Isinglass, Cements,&c. 8vo, 12s.6d.

Day of My Life at Eton. By an ETON BOY. New ed. 16mo, 1s.

De Leon (E.) Under the Stars and under the Crescent. N.ed.,6s.

Dictionary. See TOLHAUSEN, "Technological."

Diggle (*J. . IV.*) *Lancashire Life of Bishop Fraser.* With portraits; new ed., 8vo, 12*s*. 6*d*.

Donkin (*J. G.*) *Trooper and Redskin : N.W. Mounted Police,* Canada. Crown 8vo, 8*s*. 6*d*.

Donnelly (*Ignatius*) *Atlantis ; or, the Antediluvian World.* 7th Edition, crown 8vo, 12*s*. 6*d*.

—— *Great Cryptogram : Francis Bacon's Cipher in the* so-called Shakspere Plays. With facsimiles. 2 vols., 30*s*.

—— *Ragnarok : Age of Fire and Gravel.* Illus., cr. 8vo, 12*s*. 6*d*.

Dougall (*James Dalziel*) *Shooting.* New Edition. Crown 8vo, 7*s*. 6*d*.

> "The book is admirable in every way. . . . . We wish it every success."—*Globe.*
> "A very complete treatise. . . . . Likely to take high rank as an authority on shooting."—*Daily News.*

Doughty (*H.M.*) *Friesland Meres, and through the Netherlands.* Illustrated, new edition, enlarged, crown 8vo, 8*s*. 6*d*.

Dunstan Standard Readers. See LOW'S READERS.

*E*BERS (*G.*) *Joshua, Story of Biblical Life, Translated by* CLARA BELL. 2 vols., 18mo, 4*s*.

Edmonds (*C.*) *Poetry of the Anti-Jacobin. With Additional* matter. New ed. Illust., crown 8vo, 7*s*. 6*d*. ; large paper, 21*s*.

Educational List and Directory for 1887-88. 5*s*.

Educational Works published in Great Britain. A Classified Catalogue. Third Edition, 8vo, cloth extra, 6*s*.

Edwards (*E.*) *American Steam Engineer.* Illust., 12mo, 12*s*. 6*d*.

Emerson (*Dr. P. H.*) *English Idylls.* Small post 8vo, 2*s*.

—— *Pictures of East Anglian Life.* Ordinary edit., 105*s*. ; édit. de luxe, 17 × 13½, vellum, morocco back, 147*s*.

—— *Naturalistic Photography for Art Students.* Illustrated. New edit. 5*s*.

—— *and Goodall. Life and Landscape on the Norfolk* Broads. Plates 12 × 8 inches, 126*s*.; large paper, 210*s*.

—— *Wild Life on a Tidal Water.* Copper plates, ord. edit., 25*s*.; *édit de luxe,* 63*s*.

—— *in Concord. By Edward Waldo Emerson.* 8vo, 7*s*. 6*d*.

Emin Pasha. See JEPHSON AND STANLEY.

English Catalogue of Books. Vol. III., 1872—1880. Royal 8vo, half-morocco, 42*s*. See also "Index."

—— *Etchings.* Published Quarterly. 3*s*. 6*d*. Vol. VI., 25*s*.

—— *Philosophers.* Edited by E. B. IVAN MÜLLER, M.A. Crown 8vo volumes of 180 or 200 pp., price 3*s*. 6*d*. each.

Francis Bacon, by Thomas Fowler.	Shaftesbury and Hutcheson.
Hamilton, by W. H. S. Monck.	Adam Smith, by J. A. Farrer.
Hartley and James Mill.	

Esler (E. Rentoul) Way of Transgressors. 3 vols., cr. 8vo,
    31*s.* 6*d.*
Esmarch (F.) Handbook of Surgery. New Edition, 8vo,
    leather, 24*s.*
Eton. About some Fellows. New Edition, 1*s.* See also "Day."
Evelyn. Life of Mrs. Godolphin. By W. HARCOURT, 7*s.* 6*d.*
Eves (C. IV.) West Indies. Crown 8vo, 7*s.* 6*d.*

F̶ARM BALLADS, Festivals, and Legends. See CARLETON.

Fenn (G. Manville). See LOW'S STANDARD BOOKS.
Fennell (Greville) Book of the Roach. New Edition, 12mo, 2*s.*
Ferns. See HEATH.
Fforde (Brownlow) Subaltern, Policeman, and the Little Girl.
    Illust., 8vo, sd., 1*s.*
——— *The Trotter, A Poona Mystery.* Illust. 8vo, sewed, 1*s.*
Field (Prof.) Travel Talk in Italy. 16mo, limp, 2*s.*
Fiske (Amos K.) Midnight Talks at the Club Reported. 12mo,
    gilt top, 6*s.*
Fitzgerald (P.) Book Fancier. Cr. 8vo. 5*s.* ; large pap. 12*s.* 6*d.*
Fleming (Sandford) England and Canada : a Tour. Cr. 8vo, 6*s.*
Folkard (R., Jun.) Plant Lore, Legends, and Lyrics. 8vo, 16*s.*
Forbes (H. O.) Naturalist in the Eastern Archipelago. 8vo.
    21*s.*
Foreign Countries and British Colonies. Cr. 8vo, 3*s.* 6*d.* each.

Australia, by J. F. Vesey Fitzgerald.	Japan, by S. Mossman.
Austria, by D. Kay, F.R.G.S.	Peru, by Clements R. Markham.
Denmark and Iceland, by E.C.Otté.	Russia, by W. R. Morfill, M.A.
Egypt, by S. Lane Poole, B.A.	Spain, by Rev. Wentworth Webster.
France, by Miss M. Roberts.	Sweden and Norway, by Woods.
Germany, by S. Baring-Gould.	West Indies, by C. H. Eden,
Greece, by L. Sergeant, B.A.	F.R.G.S.

Foster (Birket) Some Places of Note in England.
Franc (Maud Jeanne). Small post 8vo, uniform, gilt edges :—

Emily's Choice. 5*s.*	Vermont Vale. 5*s.*
Hall's Vineyard. 4*s.*	Minnie's Mission. 4*s.*
John's Wife : A Story of Life in South Australia. 4*s.*	Little Mercy. 4*s.*
	Beatrice Melton's Discipline. 4*s.*
Marian ; or, The Light of Some One's Home. 5*s.*	No Longer a Child. 4*s.*
	Golden Gifts. 4*s.*
Silken Cords and Iron Fetters. 4*s.*	Two Sides to Every Question. 4*s.*
Into the Light. 4*s.*	Master of Ralston. 4*s.*

    *** There is also a re-issue in cheaper form at 2*s.* 6*d.* per vol.

Frank's Ranche ; or, My Holiday in the Rockies. A Contri-
    bution to the Inquiry into What we are to Do with our Boys. 5*s.*

Fraser (Bishop). See DIGGLE.

French and English Birthday Book. By K. D. CLARK. Imp.
16mo, illust., 7s. 6d.

French. See JULIEN and PORCHER.

Fresh Woods and Pastures New. By the Author of "An
Amateur Angler's Days." 1s. 6d.; large paper, 5s.; new ed., 1s.

Froissart. See LANIER.

*G*ASPARIN *(Countess) Sunny Fields and Shady Woods.*
6s.

Gavarni (Sulpice Paul; Chevalier) Memoirs. By FRANK
MARZIALS. Illust., crown 8vo.

Geary (Grattan) Burma after the Conquest. 7s. 6d.

Geffcken (F. H.) British Empire. Translated by S. J. MAC-
MULLAN. Crown 8vo, 7s. 6d.

General Directory of Johannesberg for 1890. 8vo, 15s.

Gentle Life (Queen Edition). 2 vols. in 1, small 4to, 6s.

THE GENTLE LIFE SERIES.

Price 6s. each; or in calf extra, price 10s. 6d.; Smaller Edition, cloth
extra, 2s. 6d., except where price is named.

The Gentle Life. Essays in aid of the Formation of Character.

About in the World. Essays by Author of "The Gentle Life."

Like unto Christ. New Translation of Thomas à Kempis.

Familiar Words. A Quotation Handbook. 6s.; n. ed. 3s.6d.

Essays by Montaigne. Edited by the Author of "The Gentle
Life."

The Gentle Life. 2nd Series.

The Silent Hour: Essays, Original and Selected.

Half-Length Portraits. Short Studies of Notable Persons.
By J. HAIN FRISWELL.

Essays on English Writers, for Students in English Literature.

Other People's Windows. By J. HAIN FRISWELL. 6s.; new
ed., 3s. 6d.

A Man's Thoughts. By J. HAIN FRISWELL.

Countess of Pembroke's Arcadia. By Sir P. SIDNEY. 6s.; new
ed., 3s. 6d.

Germany. By S. BARING-GOULD. Crown 8vo, 3s. 6d.

Giles (E.) Australia twice Traversed: five Expeditions, 1872-76.
With Maps and Illust. 2 vols, 8vo, 30s.

Gill (F.) See LOW'S READERS.

Gillespie (W. M.) Surveying. New ed., by CADEY STALEY. 8vo, 21s.

Glances at Great and Little Men. By PALADIN. Cr. 8vo, 6s.

Goldsmith. She Stoops to Conquer. Introduction by AUSTIN DOBSON ; the designs by E. A. ABBEY. Imperial 4to, 42s.

Gooch (Fanny C.) Face to Face with the Mexicans. Ill. roy. 8vo, 16s

Gordon (J. E. H.,B.A. Cantab.) Electric Lighting. Ill. 8vo, 18s.

—— *Physical Treatise on Electricity and Magnetism.* 2nd Edition, enlarged, with coloured, full-page, &c., Illust.2vols., 8vo, 42s.

—— *Electricity for Schools.* Illustrated. Crown 8vo, 5s.

Gouffé (Jules) Royal Cookery Book. New Edition, with plates in colours, Woodcuts, &c., 8vo, gilt edges, 42s.

—— Domestic Edition, half-bound, 10s. 6d.

Gounod (C.) Life and Works. By MARIE ANNE BOVET. Portrait and Facsimiles, 8vo, 10s. 6d.

Grant (General, U.S.) Personal Memoirs. With Illustrations, Maps, &c. 2 vols., 8vo, 28s.

Great Artists. See "Biographies."

Great Musicians. Edited by F. HUEFFER. A Series of Biographies, crown 8vo, 3s. each :—

Bach.	Handel.	Rossini.
Beethoven.	Haydn.	Schubert.
Berlioz.	Mendelssohn.	Schumann.
Cherubini.	Mozart.	Richard Wagner.
Church Composers.	Purcell.	Weber.

Groves (J. Percy) Charmouth Grange. 2s. 6d.; gilt, 3s. 6d.

Guizot's History of France. Translated by ROBERT BLACK. 8 vols., super-royal 8vo, cloth extra, gilt, each 24s. In cheaper binding, 8 vols., at 10s. 6d. each.
   "It supplies a want which has long been felt, and ought to be in the hands of all students of history."—*Times.*

——————— *Masson's School Edition.* Abridged from the Translation by Robert Black, with Chronological Index, Historical and Genealogical Tables, &c. By Professor GUSTAVE MASSON, B.A. With Portraits, Illustrations, &c. 1 vol., 8vo, 600 pp., 5s.

Guyon (Mde.) Life. By UPHAM. 6th Edition, crown 8vo, 6s.

HALFORD (F. M.) Floating Flies, and how to Dress them. New edit., with Coloured plates. 8vo, 15s.

—— *Dry Fly-Fishing, Theory and Practice.* Col. Plates, 25s.

Hall (W. W.) How to Live Long: or, 1408 Maxims. 2s.

Halsey (Frederick A.) Slide Valve Gears. With diagrams, crown 8vo, 8s. 6d.

Hamilton (E.) Fly-fishing for Salmon, Trout, and Grayling; their Habits, Haunts, and History. Illust., 6s.; large paper, 10s. 6d.

—— *Riverside Naturalist.* Illust. 8vo.

Hands (*T.*) *Numerical Exercises in Chemistry.*   Cr. 8vo, 2s. 6d.
and 2s.; Answers separately, 6d.

Handy Guide to Dry-fly Fishing.   By COTSWOLD ISYS, M.A.
Crown 8vo, limp, 1s.

—— *Guide Book to Japanese Islands.*   With Folding Outline
Map, crown 8vo, 6s. 6d.

Hanoverian Kings.   See SKOTTOWE.

Hardy (*A. S.*) *Passe-rose: a Romance.*   Crown 8vo, 6s.

—— (*Thomas*).   See Low's STANDARD NOVELS.

Hare (*J. L. Clark*) *American Constitutional Law.*   2 vls., 8vo, 63s.

Harkut (*F.*) *Conspirator; A Romance of Real Life.*   By
PAUL P.   8vo, 6s.

Harper's Young People.   Vols. I.-VI., profusely Illustrated
with woodcuts and coloured plates.   Royal 4to, extra binding, each
7s. 6d.; gilt edges, 8s.   Published Weekly, in wrapper, 1d.; Annual
Subscription, post free, 6s. 6d.; Monthly, in wrapper, with coloured
plate, 6d.; Annual Subscription, post free, 7s. 6d.

Harris (*W.B.*) *Land of an African Sultan: Travels in Morocco.*
Illust., crown 8vo, 10s. 6d.; large paper, 31s. 6d.

Harrison (*Mary*) *Complete Cookery Guide.*   Crown 8vo, 6s.

—— *Skilful Cook.*   New edition, crown 8vo, 5s.

Harrison (*W.*) *Memorable London Houses: a Guide.*   Illust.
New edition, 18mo, 1s. 6d.; new ed., enlarged, 2s. 6d.

Hatton (*Joseph*) *Journalistic London: with Engravings and*
Portraits of Distinguished Writers of the Day.   Fcap. 4to, 12s. 6d.

—— See also Low's STANDARD NOVELS.

Haweis (*H. R.*) *Broad Church, What is Coming.*   Cr. 8vo.

—— *Poets in the Pulpit.*   New edition.   Crown 8vo, 3s. 6d.

—— (*Mrs.*) *Art of Housekeeping: a Bridal Garland.*   2s. 6d.

Hawthorne (*Nathaniel*) *Life.*   By JOHN R. LOWELL.

Hearn (*L.*) *Youma, History of a West Indian Slave.*   Crown
8vo, 5s.

Heath (*F. G.*) *Fern World.*   With coloured plates, new ed.
Crown 8vo, 6s.

Heldmann (*B.*)   See Low's STANDARD BOOKS.

Henty (*G. A.*)   See Low's STANDARD BOOKS.

—— (*Richmond*) *Australiana: My Early Life.*   5s.

Herbert (*T.*) *Salads and Sandwiches.*   Cr. 8vo, boards, 1s.

Herrick (*Robert*) *Poetry.*   Preface by AUSTIN DOBSON.   With
numerous Illustrations by E. A. ABBEY.   4to, gilt edges, 42s.

Hetley (*Mrs. E.*) *Native Flowers of New Zealand.*   Chromos
from Drawings.   Three Parts, 63s.; extra binding, 73s. 6d.

Hicks (*E. S.*) *Our Boys: How to Enter the Merchant Service.*   5s.

—— *Yachts, Boats and Canoes.*   Illustrated.   8vo, 10s. 6d.

Hill (G. B.) Footsteps of Dr. Johnson. Ordinary ed., half-
morocco, gilt top, 63*s.* ; *édit de luxe,* on Japanese vellum, 147*s.*
Hints on Wills. See WILLS.
Historic Bindings in the Bodleian Library. 24 plates, 4to, 42*s.* ;
half-morocco, 52*s.* 6*d.* Coloured, 84*s.* ; half-morocco, 94*s.* 6*d.*
Hitchman. Public Life of the Earl of Beaconsfield. 3*s.* 6*d.*
Hoey (Mrs. Cashel) See LOW'S STANDARD NOVELS.
Holder (C. F.) Marvels of Animal Life. Illustrated. 8*s.* 6*d.*
—————— *Ivory King: Elephant and Allies.* Illustrated. 8*s.* 6*d.*
—————— *Living Lights : Phosphorescent Animals and Vegetables.*
Illustrated. 8vo, 8*s.* 6*d.*
Holmes (O. W.) Before the Curfew, &c. Occasional Poems. 5*s.*
—————— *Last Leaf : a Holiday Volume.* 42*s.*
—————— *Mortal Antipathy,* 8*s.* 6*d.* ; also 2*s.* ; paper, 1*s.*
—————— *Our Hundred Days in Europe.* 6*s.* Large Paper, 15*s.*
—————— *Over the Tea Cups, Reminiscences and Reflections.*
Crown 8vo, 6*s.*
—————— *Poems : a new volume.*
—————— *Poetical Works.* 2 vols., 18mo, gilt tops, 10*s.* 6*d.*
—————— See also ROSE LIBRARY.
Howard (Blanche Willis) Open Door. Crown 8vo, 6*s.*
Howorth (H. H.) Mammoth and the Flood. 8vo, 18*s.*
Hundred Greatest Men (The). 8 portfolios, 21*s.* each, or 4 vols.,
half-morocco, gilt edges, 10 guineas. New Ed., 1 vol., royal 8vo, 21*s.*
Hymnal Companion to the Book of Common Prayer. By
BISHOP BICKERSTETH. In various styles and bindings from 1*d.* to
31*s.* 6*d.* *Price List and Prospectus will be forwarded on application.*
*** Also a new and revised edition, 1890, distinct from the preceding
Detailed list of 16 pages, post free.

*I*LLUSTRATED *Text-Books of Art-Education.* Edited by
EDWARD J. POYNTER, R.A. Illustrated, and strongly bound, 5*s.*
Now ready :—
PAINTING.
Classic and Italian. By HEAD. | French and Spanish.
German, Flemish, and Dutch. | English and American.
ARCHITECTURE.
Classic and Early Christian.
Gothic and Renaissance. By T. ROGER SMITH.
SCULPTURE.
Antique: Egyptian and Greek.
Renaissance and Modern. By LEADER SCOTT.
Inderwick (F. A. ; Q.C.) Interregnum ; Studies of the Common-
wealth. Legislative, Social, and Legal. 8vo, 10*s.* 6*d.*
—————— *Side Lights on the Stuarts.* New edition, 7*s.* 6*d.*

Index to the English Catalogue, Jan., 1874, *to Dec.*, 1880.
　　Royal 8vo, half-morocco, 18*s.*
Inglis (Hon. James; "Maori") Tent Life in Tiger Land.
　　Col. plates, roy. 8vo, 18*s.*
Irving (Washington). Library Edition of his Works in 27 vols.,
　　Copyright, with the Author's Latest Revisions. "Geoffrey Crayon"
　　Edition, large square 8vo. 12*s.* 6*d.* per vol. *See also* "Little Britain."

JACKSON (J.) New Style Vertical Writing Copy-Books.
　　Series 1, Nos. I.—XII., 2*d.* and 1*d.* each.
———————— *St. Dunstan's Series,* 8 Nos., 1*d.* each.
———— *New Series of Vertical Writing Copy-books,* specially
　　adapted for the seven standards. 22 Nos., 2*d.* each.
———— *Shorthand of Arithmetic.* Crown 8vo, 1*s.* 6*d.*
———— *(L.) Ten Centuries of European Progress.* With maps,
　　crown 8vo, 12*s.* 6*d.*
James (Henry). See DAUDET (A.)
Janvier (T. A.), Aztec Treasure House: Romance of Contem-
　　poraneous Antiquity. Illustrated. Crown 8vo, 7*s.* 6*d.*
Japan. See "Artistic," also MORSE.
Jefferies (Richard) Amaryllis at the Fair. N. ed., cr. 8vo, 7*s.* 6*d.*
———— *Bevis: The Story of a Boy.* New ed., crown 8vo, 5*s.*
Jephson (A. J. Mounteney) Emin Pasha and the Rebellion at
　　the Equator. Illust. 21*s.*
Jerdon (Gertrude). See LOW'S STANDARD SERIES.
Johnson (Samuel) See HILL.
Johnston (H. H.) River Congo. New Edition, 8vo, 21*s.*
Johnstone (D. L.) Land of the Mountain Kingdom. Illus.
　　2*s.* 6*d.*
Julien (F.) English Student's French Examiner. 16mo, 2*s.*
———— *Conversational French Reader.* 16mo, cloth, 2*s.* 6*d.*
————*French at Home and at School.* Book I., Accidence. 2*s.*
———— *First Lessons in Conversational French Grammar.* 1*s.*
———— *Petites Leçons de Conversation et de Grammaire.* 3*s.*
————*Phrases of Daily Use.* 6*d. Leçons and Phrases,* 1 vol.,
　　3*s.* 6*d.*

KEATS. Endymion. Illust. by W. ST. JOHN HARPER.
　　Imp. 4to, gilt top, 42*s.*
Kempis (Thomas à) Daily Text-Book. Square 16mo, 2*s.* 6*d.*;
　　interleaved as a Birthday Book, 3*s.* 6*d.*
Kennedy (E. B.) Blacks and Bushrangers. New ed., Illust.,
　　crown 8vo, 5*s.*
Kent's Commentaries: an Abridgment for Students of American
　　Law. By EDEN F. THOMPSON. 10*s.* 6*d.*

Kershaw (S. W.) Protestants from France in their English Home. Crown 8vo, 6s.

Kingsley (Rose) Children of Westminster Abbey : Studies in English History. 5s.

Kingston (W. H. G.) Works. Illustrated, 16mo, gilt edges, 3s. 6d.; plainer binding, plain edges, 2s. 6d. each.

Ben Burton.	Heir of Kilfinnan.
Captain Mugford, or, Our Salt and Fresh Water Tutors.	Snow-Shoes and Canoes.
Dick Cheveley.	Two Supercargoes.
	With Axe and Rifle.

Kipling (Rudyard) Soldiers Three. New edition, 8vo, sewed, 1s.

——— *Story of the Gadsbys.* New edition, 8vo, sewed, 1s.

——— *In Black and White.* New edition, 8vo, sewed, 1s.
The three foregoing bound in one volume, cloth, 3s. 6d.

——— *Wee Willie Winkie, &c., Stories.* 8vo, sewed, 1s.

——— *Under the Deodars.* 8vo, sewed, 1s.

——— *The Phantom Rickshaw.* 8vo, sewed, 1s.

Knight (E. J.) Cruise of the "Falcon." New Ed. Illus. Cr. 8vo, 7s. 6d. Original edition with all the illustrations ; 2 vols., 24s.

Knox (Col.) Boy Travellers on the Congo. Illus. Cr. 8vo, 7s. 6d.

Kunhardt (C. B.) Small Yachts : Design and Construction. 35s.

——— *Steam Yachts and Launches.* Illustrated. 4to, 16s.

LANIER'S Works. Illustrated, crown 8vo, gilt edges, 7s. 6d. each.

Boy's King Arthur.	Boy's Percy : Ballads of Love and Adventure, selected from the "Reliques."
Boy's Froissart.	
Boy's Knightly Legends of Wales.	

Lansdell (H.) Through Siberia. 2 vols., 8vo, 30s.; 1 vol., 10s. 6d.

——— *Russia in Central Asia.* Illustrated. 2 vols., 42s.

——— *Through Central Asia ; Russo-Afghan Frontier.* 12s.

Larden (W.) School Course on Heat. Third Ed., Illust. 5s.

Laurie (A.) Conquest of the Moon : a Story of the Bayouda. Illust., crown 8vo, 2s. 6d. ; gilt edges, 3s. 6d.

——— *New York to Brest in Seven Hours.* Illust., cr. 8vo, 7s. 6d.

Leffingwell (W. Bruce; "Horace") Shooting on Upland, Marsh and Stream. Illust. 8vo, 18s.

Lemon (M.) Small House over the Water, and Stories. Illust. by Cruikshank, &c. Crown 8vo, 6s.

Leo XIII. : Life. By O'REILLY. Large 8vo, 18s.; édit. de luxe, 63s.

Leonardo da Vinci's Literary Works. Edited by Dr. JEAN PAUL RICHTER. Containing his Writings on Painting, Sculpture, and Architecture, his Philosophical Maxims, Humorous Writings, and Miscellaneous Notes on Personal Events, on his Contemporaries, on

Literature, &c. ; published from Manuscripts. 2 vols., imperial 8vo, containing about 200 Drawings in Autotype Reproductions, and numerous other Illustrations. Twelve Guineas.

Library of Religious Poetry. Best Poems of all Ages. Edited by SCHAFF and GILMAN. Royal 8vo. 21*s.*; cheaper binding, 10*s.* 6*d.*

Lindsay (W. S.) History of Merchant Shipping. With 150 Illustrations, Maps, and Charts. 4 vols., 8vo, cloth extra. Vols. 1 and 2, 11*s.* each ; vols. 3 and 4, 14*s.* each. 4 vols., 50*s.*

Little (Archibald J.) Through the Yang-tse Gorges. N. Ed. 10*s.* 6*d.*

Little Britain, The Spectre Bridegroom, and *Legend of Sleepy Hollow.* By WASHINGTON IRVING. *Édition de luxe.* Illus. Designed by Mr. CHARLES O. MURRAY. Re-issue, square crown 8vo, cloth, 6*s.*

Lodge (Henry Cabot) George Washington. 2 vols., 12*s.*

Longfellow. Maidenhood. With Coloured Plates. Oblong 4to, 2*s.* 6*d.*; gilt edges, 3*s.* 6*d.*

—— *Courtship of Miles Standish.* Illust. by BROUGHTON, &c. Imp. 4to, 21*s.*

—— *Nuremberg.* Illum. by M. and A. COMEGYS. 4to, 31*s.* 6*d.*

—— *Song of Hiawatha.* Illust. from drawings by F. REMINGTON. 8vo, 21*s.*

Lorne (Marquis of) Viscount Palmerston (Prime Ministers). Crown 8vo.

Lowell (J. R.) Vision of Sir Launfal. Illustrated, royal 4to, 63*s.*

—— *Life of Nathaniel Hawthorne.* Sm. post 8vo. [*In prep.*

Low's Readers. Specially prepared for the Code of 1890. Edited by JOHN GILL, of Cheltenham. Strongly bound, being sewn on tapes.

NOW READY.

FIRST READER, for STANDARD I. Every Lesson Illustrated. Price 9*d.*

SECOND READER, for STANDARD II. Every Lesson Illustrated. Price 10*d.*

THIRD READER, for STANDARD III. Every Lesson Illustrated. Price 1*s.*

FOURTH READER, for STANDARD IV. Every Lesson Illustrated. Price 1*s.* 3*d.*

FIFTH READER, for STANDARD V. Every Lesson Illustrated. Price 1*s.* 4*d.*

SIXTH READER, for STANDARDS VI. and VII. Every Lesson Illustrated. Price 1*s.* 6*d.*

Already adopted by the School Board for London ; by the Edinburgh, Nottingham, Aston, Birmingham and other School Boards.

In the Press, INFANT PRIMERS, In two Parts. PART I., Illustrated, price 3*d.* PART II., Illustrated, price 6*d.*

Low's Standard Library of Travel and Adventure. Crown 8vo, uniform in cloth extra, 7*s.* 6*d.*, except where price is given.

  1. **The Great Lone Land.** By Major W. F. BUTLER, C.B.

Low's Standard Library, &c.—continued.

2. **The Wild North Land.** By Major W. F. BUTLER, C.B.
3. **How I found Livingstone.** By H. M. STANLEY, 3s. 6d.
4. **Through the Dark Continent.** By STANLEY. 12s. 6d. & 3s. 6d.
5. **The Threshold of the Unknown Region.** By C. R. MARK-HAM. (4th Edition, with Additional Chapters, 10s. 6d.)
6. **Cruise of the Challenger.** By W. J. J. SPRY, R.N.
7. **Burnaby's On Horseback through Asia Minor.** 10s. 6d.
8. **Schweinfurth's Heart of Africa.** 2 vols., 3s. 6d. each.
9. **Through America.** By W. G. MARSHALL.
10. **Through Siberia.** Il. and unabridged, 10s.6d. By H. LANSDELL.
11. **From Home to Home.** By STAVELEY HILL.
12. **Cruise of the Falcon.** By E. J. KNIGHT.
13. **Through Masai Land.** By JOSEPH THOMSON.
14. **To the Central African Lakes.** By JOSEPH THOMSON.
15. **Queen's Highway.** By STUART CUMBERLAND.
16. **Two Kings of Uganda.** By ASHE. 3s. 6d.

Low's Standard Novels. Small post 8vo, cloth extra, 6s. each, unless otherwise stated.

JAMES BAKER. **John Westacott.**

WILLIAM BLACK.
> **A Daughter of Heth.—House-Boat.—In Far Lochaber.—In Silk Attire.—Kilmeny.—Lady Silverdale's Sweetheart.—Penance of John Logan.—Sunrise.—Three Feathers.—New Prince Fortunatus.**

R. D. BLACKMORE.
> **Alice Lorraine.—Christowell, a Dartmoor Tale.—Clara Vaughan.—Cradock Nowell.—Cripps the Carrier.—Erema. —Kit and Kitty.—Lorna Doone.—Mary Anerley.—Springhaven.—Tommy Upmore.**

E. L. BYNNER. **Agnes Surriage.—Begum's Daughter.**

G. W. CABLE. **Bonaventure.** 5s.

Miss COLERIDGE. **An English Squire.**

C. E. CRADDOCK. **Despot of Broomsedge Cove.**

Mrs. B. M. CROKER. **Some One Else.**

STUART CUMBERLAND. **Vasty Deep.**

E. DE LEON. **Under the Stars and Crescent.**

Miss BETHAM-EDWARDS. **Halfway.**

Rev. E. GILLIAT, M.A. **Story of the Dragonnades.**

THOMAS HARDY.
> **A Laodicean.—Far from the Madding Crowd.—Mayor of Casterbridge.—Pair of Blue Eyes.—Return of the Native.—Hand of Ethelberta.—Trumpet Major.—Two on a Tower.**

FRANK HARKUT. **Conspirator.**

JOSEPH HATTON. **Old House at Sandwich.—Three Recruits.**

Mrs. CASHEL HOEY.
> **A Golden Sorrow.—A Stern Chase.—Out of Court.**

BLANCHE WILLIS HOWARD. **Open Door.**

JEAN INGELOW.
> **Don John.—John Jerome (5s.).—Sarah de Berenger.**

GEORGE MAC DONALD.
> **Adela Cathcart.— Guild Court.—Mary Marston.—Stephen**

Low's Standard Novels—continued.

> Archer. —The Vicar's Daughter. — Orts. — Weighed and Wanting.

Mrs. MACQUOID. Diane.—Elinor Dryden.

DUFFIELD OSBORNE. Spell of Ashtaroth (5s.)

Mrs. J. II. RIDDELL.

> Alaric Spenceley.—Daisies and Buttercups.—The Senior Partner.—A Struggle for Fame.

W. CLARK RUSSELL.

> Betwixt the Forelands.—Frozen Pirate.—Jack's Courtship.—John Holdsworth.—Ocean Free Lance.—A Sailor's Sweetheart.—Sea Queen.—Watch Below.—Strange Voyage.—Wreck of the Grosvenor.—The Lady Maud.—Little Loo.

FRANK R. STOCKTON.

> Ardis Claverden.—Bee-man of Orn.—The Late Mrs. Null.—Hundredth Man.

MRS. HARRIET B. STOWE.

> My Wife and I.—Old Town Folk.—We and our Neighbours.—Poganuc People, their Loves and Lives.

JOSEPH THOMSON. Ulu : an African Romance.

TYTLER. Duchess Frances.

LEW WALLACE. Ben Hur: a Tale of the Christ.

C. D. WARNER. Little Journey in the World.—Jupiter Lights.

CONSTANCE FENIMORE WOOLSON.

> Anne.—East Angels.—For the Major (5s.).

French Heiress in her own Chateau.

Low's Standard Novels. NEW ISSUE at short intervals. Cr. 8vo. 2s. 6d. ; fancy boards 2s.

BLACKMORE.

> Clara Vaughan.—Cripps the Carrier.—Lorna Doone.—Mary Anerley.—Alice Lorraine.—Tommy Upmore.

CABLE. Bonaventure.

CROKER, Some One Else.

DE LEON, Under the Stars.

EDWARDS. Half-Way.

HARDY.

> Madding Crowd.—Mayor of Casterbridge.—Trumpet-Major.—Hand of Ethelberta.—Pair of Blue Eyes.—Return of the Native.—Two on a Tower.—Laodicean.

HATTON. Three Recruits.—Old House at Sandwich.

HOEY. Golden Sorrow.—Out of Court.—Stern Chase.

HOLMES. Guardian Angel.

INGELOW. John Jerome.—Sarah de Berenger.

MAC DONALD.

> Adela Cathcart.—Guild Court.—Vicar's Daughter.—Stephen Archer.

OLIPHANT. Innocent.

RIDDELL. Daisies and Buttercups.—Senior Partner.

STOCKTON. Casting Away of Mrs. Lecks.—Bee-Man of Orn.

STOWE. Dred.—Old Town Folk.—Poganuc People.

THOMSON. Ulu.

WALFORD. Her Great Idea

Low's Standard Books for Boys. With numerous Illustrations, 2s. 6d.; gilt edges, 3s. 6d. each.

Dick Cheveley. By W. H. KINGSTON.
Heir of Kilfinnan. By W. H. KINGSTON.
Off to the Wilds. By G. MANVILLE FENN.
The Two Supercargoes. By W. G. KINGSTON.
The Silver Cañon. By G. MANVILLE FENN.
Under the Meteor Flag. By HARRY COLLINGWOOD.
Jack Archer: A Tale of the Crimea. By G. A. HENTY.
The Mutiny on Board the Ship Leander. By B. HELDMANN.
With Axe and Rifle on the Western Prairies. By W. H. G. KINGSTON.
Red Cloud, the Solitary Sioux: a Tale of the Great Prairie. By Col. Sir WM. BUTLER, K.C.B.
The Voyage of the Aurora. By HARRY COLLINGWOOD.
Charmouth Grange: a Tale of the 17th Century. By J. PERCY GROVES.
Snowshoes and Canoes. By W. H. G. KINGSTON.
The Son of the Constable of France. By LOUIS ROUSSELET.
Captain Mugford; or, Our Salt and Fresh Water Tutors. Edited by W. H. G. KINGSTON.
The Cornet of Horse, a Tale of Marlborough's Wars. By G. A. HENTY.
The Adventures of Captain Mago. By LEON CAHUN.
Noble Words and Noble Needs.
The King of the Tigers. By ROUSSELET.
Hans Brinker; or, The Silver Skates. By Mrs. DODGE.
The Drummer-Boy, a Story of the time of Washington. By ROUSSELET.
Adventures in New Guinea: The Narrative of Louis Tregance.
The Crusoes of Guiana. By BOUSSENARD.
The Gold Seekers. A Sequel to the Above. By BOUSSENARD.
Winning His Spurs, a Tale of the Crusades. By G. A. HENTY.
The Blue Banner. By LEON CAHUN.
Startling Exploits of the Doctor. CÉLIÈRE.
Brothers Rantzau. ERCKMANN-CHATRIAN.
Adventures of a Young Naturalist. BIART.
Ben Burton; or, Born and Bred at Sea. KINGSTON.
Great Hunting Grounds of the World. MEUNIER.
Ran Away from the Dutch. PERELAER.
My Kalulu, Prince, King, and Slave. STANLEY.

New Volumes for 1890-91.

The Serpent Charmer. By LOUIS ROUSSELET.
Stories of the Gorilla Country. By PAUL DU CHAILLU.
The Conquest of the Moon. By A. LAURIE.
The Maid of the Ship "Golden Age." By H. E. MACLEAN.
The Frozen Pirate. By W. CLARK RUSSELL.
The Marvellous Country. By S. W. COZZENS.
The Mountain Kingdom. By D. LAWSON JOHNSTONE.
Lost in Africa. By F. H. WINDER.

Low's Standard Series of Books by Popular Writers. **Sm. cr.**
8vo, cloth gilt, 2s.; gilt edges, 2s. 6d. each.

Aunt Jo's Scrap Bag. By Miss ALCOTT.
Shawl Straps. By Miss ALCOTT.
Little Men. By Miss ALCOTT.
Hitherto. By Mrs. WHITNEY.
Forecastle to Cabin. By SAMUELS. Illustrated.
In My Indian Garden. By PHIL ROBINSON.
Little Women and Little Women Wedded. By Miss ALCOTT.
Eric and Ethel. By FRANCIS FRANCIS. Illust.
Keyhole Country. By GERTRUDE JERDON. Illust.
We Girls. By Mrs. WHITNEY.
The Other Girls. A Sequel to "We Girls." By Mrs. WHITNEY.
Adventures of Jimmy Brown. Illust. By W. L. ALDEN.
Under the Lilacs. By Miss ALCOTT. Illust.
Jimmy's Cruise. By Miss ALCOTT.
Under the Punkah. By PHIL ROBINSON.
An Old-Fashioned Girl. By Miss ALCOTT.
A Rose in Bloom. By Miss ALCOTT.
Eight Cousins. Illust. By Miss ALCOTT.
Jack and Jill. By Miss ALCOTT.
Lulu's Library. Illust. By Miss ALCOTT.
Silver Pitchers. By Miss ALCOTT.
Work and Beginning Again. Illust. By Miss ALCOTT.
A Summer in Leslie Goldthwaite's Life. By Mrs. WHITNEY.
Faith Gartney's Girlhood. By Mrs. WHITNEY.
Real Folks. By Mrs. WHITNEY.
Dred. By Mrs. STOWE.
My Wife and I. By Mrs. STOWE.
An Only Sister. By Madame DE WITT.
Spinning Wheel Stories. By Miss ALCOTT.

New Volumes for 1890–91.

My Summer in a Garden. By C. DUDLEY WARNER.
Ghost in the Mill and Other Stories. HARRIET B. STOWE.
The Pilgrim's Progress. With many Illustrations.
We and our Neighbours. HARRIET BEECHER STOWE.
Picciola. SAINTINE.
Draxy Miller's Dowry. SAXE HOLM.
Seagull Rock. J. SANDEAU.
In the Wilderness. C. DUDLEY WARNER.

Low's Pocket Encyclopædia. Upwards of 25,000 References, with
Plates. New ed., imp. 32mo, cloth, marbled edges, 3s. 6d.; roan, 4s. 6d.

Low's Handbook to London Charities. Yearly, cloth, 1s. 6d.
paper, 1s.

M*AC DONALD (George).* See LOW'S STANDARD NOVELS.

Macgregor (John) "Rob Roy" on the Baltic. **3rd Edition**
small post 8vo, 2s. 6d.; cloth, gilt edges, 3s. 6d.

Macgregor (*John*) *A Thousand Miles in the "Rob Roy"* Canoe. 11th Edition, small post 8vo, 2s. 6d.; cloth, gilt edges, 3s. 6d.
—— *Voyage Alone in the Yawl "Rob Roy."* New Edition, with additions, small post 8vo, 3s. 6d. and 2s. 6d.

Mackenzie (*Rev. John*) *Austral Africa : Losing it or Ruling it ?* Illustrations and Maps. 2 vols., 8vo, 32s.

Maclean (*H. E.*) *Maid of the Golden Age.* Illust., cr. 8vo, 2s.6d.

Macmaster (*M.*) *Our Pleasant Vices.* 3 vols., cr. 8vo, 31s. 6d.

Mahan (*Captain A. T.*) *Influence of Sea Power upon History*, 1660-1783. 8vo, 18s.

Markham (*Clements R.*) See "Foreign Countries," and MAURY.

Marston (*E.*) *How Stanley wrote "In Darkest Africa,"* Trip to Africa. Illust., fcp. 8vo, picture cover, 1s.
—— See also "Amateur Angler," "Frank's Ranche," and "Fresh Woods."

Martin (*F. W.*) *Float Fishing and Spinning in the Nottingham* Style. New Edition. Crown 8vo, 2s. 6d.

Maury (*Commander*) *Physical Geography of the Sea, and its* Meteorology. New Edition, with Charts and Diagrams, cr. 8vo, 6s.
—— *Life.* By his Daughter. Edited by Mr. CLEMENTS R. MARKHAM. With portrait of Maury. 8vo, 12s. 6d.

McCarthy (*Justin, M.P.*) *Sir Robert Peel* (*Prime Ministers*).

Mendelssohn Family (*The*), 1729—1847. From Letters and Journals. Translated. New Edition, 2 vols., 8vo, 30s.

Mendelssohn. See also "Great Musicians."

Merrifield's Nautical Astronomy. Crown 8vo, 7s. 6d.

Mills (*J.*) *Alternative Elementary Chemistry.* Ill., cr.8vo, 1s.6d.

Mitchell (*D. G. ; Ik. Marvel*) *English Lands, Letters and* Kings; Celt to Tudor. Crown 8vo, 6s.
—— *English Lands, Letters and Kings, Elizabeth to Anne.* Crown 8vo, 6s.

Mitford (*Mary Russell*) *Our Village.* With 12 full-page and 157 smaller Cuts. Cr. 4to, cloth, gilt edges, 21s.; cheaper binding, 10s.6d.

Mollett (*J. W.*) *Illustrated Dictionary of Words used in Art and* Archæology. Illustrated, small 4to, 15s.

Mormonism. See STENHOUSE.

Morse (*E. S.*) *Japanese Homes and their Surroundings.* With more than 300 Illustrations. Re-issue, 10s. 6d.

Motti (*P.*) *Russian Conversation Grammar.* Cr. 8vo, 5s.; Key, 2s.

Muller (*E.*) *Noble Words and Noble Deeds.* Illustrated, gilt edges, 3s. 6d.; plainer binding, 2s. 6d.

Mulready. See "Biographies."

Musgrave (*Mrs.*) *Miriam.* Crown 8vo, 6s.
—— *Savage London ; Riverside Characters, &c.* 3s. 6d.

Music. See "Great Musicians."

*N*AST: *Christmas Drawings for the Human Race.* 4to, bevelled boards, gilt edges, 12*s.*

Nelson (*Walfred*) *Five Years at Panama, the Canal.* Illust. Crown 8vo, 6*s.*

Nethercote (*C. B.*) *Pytchley Hunt.* New Ed., cr. 8vo, 8*s.* 6*d.*

New Zealand. See BRADSHAW and WHITE (J.).

Nicholls (*J. H. Kerry*) *The King Country : Explorations in* New Zealand. Many Illustrations and Map. New Edition, 8vo, 21*s.*

Nordhoff (*C.*) *California, for Health, Pleasure, and Residence.* New Edition, 8vo, with Maps and Illustrations, 12*s.* 6*d.*

Nursery Playmates (*Prince of*). 217 Coloured Pictures for Children by eminent Artists. Folio, in col. bds., 6*s.*; new ed., 2*s.* 6*d.*

Nursing Record. Yearly, 8*s.*; half-yearly, 4*s.* 6*d.*; quarterly, 2*s.* 6*d.*; weekly, 2*d.*

*O'*BRIEN (*R. B.*) *Fifty Years of Concessions to Ireland.* With a Portrait of T. Drummond. Vol. I., 16*s.* ; II., 16*s.*

Orient Line Guide. New edition, re-written by W. J. LOFTIE. Maps and Plans, 2*s.* 6*d.*

Orvis (*C. F.*) *Fishing with the Fly.* Illustrated. 8vo, 12*s.* 6*d.*

Osborne (*Duffield*) *Spell of Ashtaroth.* Crown 8vo, 5*s.*

Other People's Windows. New edition, 3*s.* 6*d.*

Our Little Ones in Heaven. Edited by the Rev. H. ROBBINS. With Frontispiece after Sir JOSHUA REYNOLDS. New Edition, 5*s.*

Owen (*Douglas*) *Marine Insurance Notes and Clauses.* 3rd edition, 8vo, 15*s.*

*P*ALGRAVE (*R. F. D.*) *Oliver Cromwell.* Crown 8vo, 10*s.* 6*d.*

Palliser (*Mrs.*) *A History of Lace.* New Edition, with additional cuts and text. 8vo, 21*s.*

—— *The China Collector's Pocket Companion.* With upwards of 1000 Illustrations of Marks and Monograms. Small 8vo, 5*s.*

Panton (*J. E.*) *Homes of Taste. Hints on Furniture and Decoration.* Crown 8vo, 2*s.* 6*d.*

Peach (*R. E. M.*) *Annals of the Parish of Swainswick, near* Bath. Sm. 4to, 10*s.* 6*d.*

Pennell (*H. Cholmondeley*) *Sporting Fish of Great Britain.* 15*s.* ; large paper, 30*s.*

—— *Modern Improvements in Fishing-tackle.* Crown 8vo, 2*s.*

Perelaer (*M. T. H.*) *Ran Away from the Dutch ; Borneo, &c.* Illustrated, square 8vo, 7*s.* 6*d.*; new ed., 2*s.* 6*d.*

Perry (*J. J. M.*) *Edlingham Burglary, or Circumstantial Evidence.* Crown 8vo, 3*s.* 6*d.*

Phillips' Dictionary of Biographical Reference. New edition, royal 8vo, 25*s.*

Philpot (H. J.) Diabe es Mellitus. Crown 8vo, 5*s.*

—— *Diet System.* Tables. I. Diabetes; II. Gout; III. Dyspepsia; IV. Corpulence. In cases, 1*s.* each.

Plunkett (Major G. T.) Primer of Orthographic Projection. Elementary Solid Geometry. With Problems and Exercises. 2*s.* 6*d.*

Poe (E. A.) The Raven. Illust. by DORÉ. Imperial folio, 63*s.*

Poems of the Inner Life. Chiefly Modern. Small 8vo, 5*s.*

Poetry of the Anti-Jacobin. New ed., by CHARLES EDMONDS. Cr. 8vo, 7*s.* 6*d.*; large paper, with special plate, 21*s.*

Porcher (A.) Juven le French Plays. With Notes and a Vocabulary. 18mo, 1*s.*

Portraits of Celebrated Race-horses of the Past and Present Centuries, with Pedigrees and Performances. 4 vols., 4to, 126*s.*

Posselt (A. E.) Structure of Fibres, Yarns, and Fabrics. Illus., 2 vols. in one, 4to.

Powles (L. D.) Land of the Pink Pearl: Life in the Bahamas. 8vo, 10*s.* 6*d.*

Poynter (Edward J., R.A.). See "Illustrated Text-books."

Prince Maskiloff: a Romance of Modern Oxford. New ed. (LOW'S STANDARD NOVELS), 6*s.*

Prince of Nursery Playmates. Col. plates, new ed., 2*s.* 6*d.*

Pritt (T. E.) North Country Flies. Illustrated from the Author's Drawings. 10*s.* 6*d.*

Publishers' Circular (The), and General Record of British and Foreign Literature. Published on the 1st and 15th of every Month, 3*d.*

QUEEN'S Prime Ministers. Edited by STUART J. REID. Cr. 8vo, 3*s.* 6*d.* per vol.

J. A. Froude, Earl of Beaconsfield.	G. W. E. Russell, Rt. Hon. W. E.
Dunckley("*Verax*"), Vis. Melbourne.	Gl dstone.
Justin McCarthy, Sir Robert Peel.	Sir Arthur Gordon, Earl of Aber-
Lorne (Marquis of), Viscount Pal-	deen.
merston.	H. D. Traill, Marquis of Salisbury.
Stuart J. Reid, Earl Russell.	George Saintsbury, Earl of Derby.

REDFORD (G.) Ancient Sculpture. New Ed. Crown 8vo, 10*s.* 6*d.* ; roxburghe, 12*s.*

Redgrave (G. R.) Century of Painters of the English School. Crown 8vo, 10*s.* 6*d.*

—— *(R. and S.) Century of English Painters.* Sq. 10*s.* 6*d.* roxb., 12*s.*

Reed (Sir E. J., M.P.) and Simpson. Modern Ships of War. Illust., royal 8vo, 10s. 6d.

—— (*Talbot Baines*) *Sir Ludar : a Tale of the Days of good Queen Bess.* Crown 8vo, 6s.

—— *Roger Ingleton, Minor.* Illus., cr. 8vo.

Reid (Mayne, Capt.) Stories of Strange Adventures. Illust., cr. 8vo, 5s.

Remarkable Bindings in the British Museum. India paper, 94s. 6d. ; sewed 73s. 6d. and 63s.

Ricci (J. H. de) Fisheries Dispute, and the Annexation of Canada. Crown 8vo, 6s.

Richards (W.) Aluminium : its History, Occurrence, &c. Illustrated, crown 8vo, 21s.

Richter (Dr. Jean Paul) Italian Art in the National Gallery. 4to. Illustrated. Cloth gilt, £2 2s.; half-morocco, uncut, £2 12s. 6d.

—— See also LEONARDO DA VINCI.

Riddell (Mrs. J. H.) See Low's STANDARD NOVELS.

Rideal (C. F.) Women of the Time, a Dictionary, Revised to Date. 8vo, 14s.

Roberts (W.) Earlier History of English Bookselling. Crown 8vo, 7s. 6d.

Robertson (T. W.) Principal Dramatic Works, with Portraits in photogravure. 2 vols., 21s.

Robin Hood; Merry Adventures of. Written and illustrated by HOWARD PYLE. Imperial 8vo, 15s.

Robinson (Phil.) In my Indian Garden. New Edition, 16mo, limp cloth, 2s.

—— *Noah's Ark. Unnatural History.* Sm. post 8vo, 12s. 6d.

—— *Sinners and Saints : a Tour across the United States of* America, and Round them. Crown 8vo, 10s. 6d.

—— *Under the Punkah.* New Ed., cr. 8vo, limp cloth, 2s.

Rockstro (W. S.) History of Music. New Edition. 8vo, 14s.

Roe (E. P.) Nature's Serial Story. Illust. New ed. 3s. 6d.

Roland, The Story of. Crown 8vo, illustrated, 6s.

Rose (F.) Complete Practical Machinist. New Ed., 12mo, 12s. 6d.

—— *Key to Engines and Engine-running.* Crown 8vo, 8s. 6d.

—— *Mechanical Drawing.* Illustrated, small 4to, 16s.

—— *Modern Steam Engines.* Illustrated. 31s. 6d.

—— *Steam Boilers. Boiler Construction and Examination.* Illust., 8vo, 12s. 6d.

Rose Library. Each volume, 1s. Many are illustrated—
Little Women. By LOUISA M. ALCOTT.
Little Women Wedded. Forming a Sequel to "Little Women."
Little Women and Little Women Wedded. 1 vol., cloth gilt, 3s. 6d.

Rose Library—(continued).

Little Men. By L. M. ALCOTT. Double vol., 2*s.*; cloth gilt, 3*s. 6d.*

An Old-Fashioned Girl. By L. M. ALCOTT. 2*s.*; cloth, 3*s. 6d.*

Work. A Story of Experience. By L. M. ALCOTT. 3*s. 6d.*; 2 vols. 1*s.* each.

Stowe (Mrs. H. B.) **The Pearl of Orr's Island.**

—— **The Minister's Wooing.**

—— **We and our Neighbours.** 2*s.*; cloth gilt, 6*s.*

—— **My Wife and I.** 2*s.*

Hans Brinker; or, **the Silver Skates.** By Mrs. DODGE. Also 2*s. 6d.*

My Study Windows. By J. R. LOWELL.

The Guardian Angel. By OLIVER WENDELL HOLMES. Cloth, 2*s.*

Dred. By Mrs. BEECHER STOWE. 2*s.*; cloth gilt, 3*s. 6d.*

City Ballads. ⎱ By WILL CARLETON. N. ed. 1 vol. 2/6.
City Legends. ⎰

Farm Ballads. By WILL CARLETON. ⎫
Farm Festivals. By WILL CARLETON. ⎬ 1 vol., cl., gilt ed., 3*s. 6d.*
Farm Legends. By WILL CARLETON. ⎭

The Rose in Bloom. By L. M. ALCOTT. 2*s.*; cloth gilt, 3*s. 6d.*

Eight Cousins. By L. M. ALCOTT. 2*s.*; cloth gilt, 3*s. 6d.*

Under the Lilacs. By L. M. ALCOTT. 2*s.*; also 3*s. 6d.*

Undiscovered Country. By W. D. HOWELLS.

Clients of Dr. Bernagius. By L. BIART. 2 parts.

Silver Pitchers. By LOUISA M. ALCOTT. Cloth, 3*s. 6d.*

Jimmy's Cruise in the "Pinafore," and other Tales. By LOUISA M. ALCOTT. 2*s.*; cloth gilt, 3*s. 6d.*

Jack and Jill. By LOUISA M. ALCOTT. 2*s.*; Illustrated, 5*s.*

Hitherto. By the Author of the "Gayworthys." 2 vols., 1*s.* each; 1 vol., cloth gilt, 3*s. 6d.*

A Gentleman of Leisure. A Novel. By EDGAR FAWCETT. 1*s.*

See also LOW'S STANDARD SERIES.

Rousselet (Louis). See LOW'S STANDARD BOOKS.

Russell (Dora) Strange Message. 3 vols., crown 8vo, 31*s. 6d.*

—— *(W. Clark) Nelson's Words and Deeds, From his Des-*patches and Correspondence. Crown 8vo, 6*s.*

—— *English Channel Ports and the Estate of the East* and West India Dock Company. Crown 8vo, 1*s.*

—— *Sailor's Language.* Illustrated. Crown 8vo, 3*s. 6d.*

—— *Wreck of the Grosvenor.* 4to, sewed, 6*d.*

—— See also "Low's Standard Novels," "Sea Stories."

*S*AINTS *and their Symbols: A Companion in the Churches* and Picture Galleries of Europe. Illustrated. Royal 16mo, 3*s. 6d.*

Samuels (Capt. J. S.) From Forecastle to Cabin: Autobiography. Illustrated. Crown 8vo, 8*s. 6d.*; also with fewer Illustrations, cloth, 2*s.*; paper, 1*s.*

Schaack (M. J.) Anarchy and Anarchists in America and Europe. Illust., roy. 8vo, 16*s.*

Schuyler The Life of Peter the Great. 2 vols., 8vo, 32s.

Schweinfurth (Georg) Heart of Africa. 2 vols., cr. 8vo, 3s. 6d. each.

Scientific Education of Dogs for the Gun. By H. H. 6s.

Scott (Leader) Renaissance of Art in Italy. 4to, 31s. 6d.
———— *Sculpture, Renaissance and Modern.* 5s.

Sea Stories. By W. CLARK RUSSELL.. New ed. Cr. 8vo, leather back, top edge gilt, per vol., 3s. 6d.

Betwixt the Forelands.	Sailor's Sweetheart.
Frozen Pirate.	Sea Queen.
Jack's Courtship.	Strange Voyage.
John Holdsworth.	The Lady Maud.
Little Loo.	Watch Below.
Ocean Free Lance.	Wreck of the *Grosvenor*.

Sedgwick (W.) Force as an Entity with Stream, Pool and Wave Forms. Crown 8vo, 7s. 6d.

Semmes (Adm. Raphael) Service Afloat: The "Sumter" and the "Alabama." Illustrated. Royal 8vo, 16s.

Senior (W.) Near and Far: an Angler's Sketches of Home Sport and Colonial Life. Crown 8vo, 6s.; new edit., 2s.
———— *Waterside Sketches.* Imp. 32mo, 1s. 6d.; boards, 1s.

Shakespeare. Edited by R. GRANT WHITE. 3 vols., crown 8vo, gilt top, 36s.; *édition de luxe*, 6 vols., 8vo, cloth extra, 63s.

Shakespeare's Heroines: Studies by Living English Painters. 105s.; artists' proofs, 630s.
———— *Macbeth.* With Etchings on Copper, by J. MOYR SMITH. 105s. and 52s. 6d.
———— *Songs and Sonnets.* Illust. by Sir JOHN GILBERT, R.A. 4to, boards, 5s.
———— See also DONNELLY and WHITE (R. GRANT).

Sharpe (R. Bowdler) Birds in Nature. 39 coloured plates and text. 4to, 63s.

Sheridan. Rivals. Reproductions of Water-colour, &c. 52s. 6d.; artist's proofs, 105s. nett.

Shields (C. W.) Philosophia ultima; from Harmony of Science and Religion. 2 vols. 8vo, 24s.
———— *(G. O.) Big Game of North America.* Illust., 21s.
———— *Cruisings in the Cascades; Hunting, Photography,* Fishing. 8vo, 10s. 6d.

Sidney (Sir Philip) Arcadia. New Edition, 3s. 6d.

Siegfried, The Story of. Illustrated, crown 8vo, cloth, 6s.

Sienkiewicz (H.) With Fire and Sword, Historical Novel. 8vo, 10s. 6d.

Sinclair (Mrs.) Indigenous Flowers of the Hawaiian Islands. 44 Plates in Colour. Imp. folio, extra binding, gilt edges, 31s. 6d.

Sinclair (*F.;* "*Aopouri;*" "*Philip Garth*") *Ballads from the* Pacific. New Edition. 3*s.* 6*d.*

Skottowe (*B. C.*) *Hanoverian Kings.* New ed., cr. 8vo. 3*s.* 6*d.*

Smith (*G.*) *Assyrian Explorations.* Illust. New Ed., 8vo, 18*s.*

—— *The Chaldean Account of Genesis.* With many Illustrations. 16*s.* New Ed. By PROFESSOR SAYCE. 8vo, 18*s.*

—— (*G. Barnett*) *William I. and the German Empire.* New Ed., 8vo, 3*s.* 6*d.*

—— (*Sydney*) *Life and Times.* By STUART J. REID. Illustrated. 8vo, 21*s.*

Spiers' French Dictionary. 29th Edition, remodelled. 2 vols., 8vo, 18*s.*; half bound, 21*s.*

Spry (*W. J. J., R.N., F.R.G.S.*) *Cruise of H.M.S.* "*Challenger.*" With Illustrations. 8vo, 18*s.* Cheap Edit., crown 8vo, 7*s.* 6*d.*

Stanley (*H. M.*) *Congo, and Founding its Free State.* Illustrated, 2 vols., 8vo, 42*s.* ; re-issue, 2 vols. 8vo, 21*s.*

—— *How I Found Livingstone.* New ed., cr. 8vo, 7*s.* 6*d.* and 3*s.* 6*d.*

—— *My Kalulu.* New ed., cr. 8vo, 3*s.* 6*d.* ; also 2*s.* 6*d.*

—— *In Darkest Africa, Rescue and Retreat of Emin.* Illust. 2 vols, 8vo, 42*s.*

—— *Through the Dark Continent.* Cr. 8vo, 12*s.* 6*d.* ; new edition, 3*s.* 6*d.*

—— See also JEPHSON.

Start (*J. W. K.*) *Junior Mensuration Exercises.* 8*d.*

Stenhouse (*Mrs.*) *Tyranny of Mormonism. An Englishwoman* in Utah. New ed., cr. 8vo, cloth elegant, 3*s.* 6*d.*

Sterry (*J. Ashby*) *Cucumber Chronicles.* 5*s.*

Steuart (*J. A.*) *Letters to Living Authors, with* portraits. Cr. 8vo, 6*s.* ; ed. *de luxe,* 10*s.* 6*d.*

—— *Kilgroom, a Story of Ireland.* Cr. 8vo, 6*s.*

Stevens (*E. W.*) *Fly-Fishing in Maine Lakes.* 8*s.* 6*d.*

—— (*T.*) *Around the World on a Bicycle.* Vol. II. 8vo 16*s.*

Stockton (*Frank R.*) *Rudder Grange.* 3*s.* 6*d.*

—— *Bee-Man of Orn, and other Fanciful Tales.* Cr. 8vo, 5*s.*

—— *Personally Conducted.* Ill. by PENNELL. Sm. 4to, 7*s.* 6*d.*

—— *The Casting Away of Mrs. Lecks and Mrs. Aleshine.* 1*s.*

—— *The Dusantes.* Sequel to the above. Boards, 1*s.* ; this and the preceding book in one volume, cloth, 2*s.* 6*d.*

—— *The Hundredth Man.* Small post 8vo, 6*s.*

—— *The Late Mrs. Null.* Small post 8vo, 6*s.*

—— *Merry Chanter,* cr. 8vo. Boards, 2*s.* 6*d.*

—— *The Story of Viteau.* Illust. Cr. 8vo, 5*s.*

—— *Three Burglars,* cr. 8vo. Picture boards, 1*s.* ; cloth, **2***s.*

Stockton (Frank R.) See also Low's STANDARD NOVELS.

Stoker (Bram) Snake's Pass, cr. 8vo, 6s.

Stowe (Mrs. Beecher) Dred. Cloth, gilt edges, 3s. 6d.; cloth, 2s.

———— *Flowers and Fruit from her Writings.* Sm. post 8vo, 3s. 6d.

———— *Life, in her own Words . . . with Letters, &c.* 15s.

———— *Life, told for Boys and Girls.* Crown 8vo.

———— *Little Foxes.* Cheap Ed., 1s.; Library Edition, 4s. 6d.

———— *My Wife and I.* Cloth, 2s.

———— *Old Town Folk.* 6s.

———— *We and our Neighbours.* 2s.

———— *Poganuc People.* 6s.

———— See also Low's STANDARD NOVELS and ROSE LIBRARY.

Strickland (F.) Engadine : a Guide to the District, with Articles by J. SYMONDS, Mrs. MAIN, &c., 5s.

Stuarts. See INDERWICK.

Stutfield (Hugh E. M.) El Maghreb : 1200 *Miles' Ride through* Marocco. 8s. 6d.

Sullivan (A. M.) Nutshell History of Ireland. Paper boards, 6d.

Szczpanski (F.), Directory of Technical Literature, Classified Catalogue of Books, Annuals, and Journals. Cr. 8vo, 2s.

TAINE (H. A.) "Origines." Translated by JOHN DURAND.
  I. **The Ancient Regime.** Demy 8vo, cloth, 16s.
  II. **The French Revolution.** Vol. 1. do.
  III. **Do.** do. Vol. 2. do.
  IV. **Do.** do. Vol. 3. do.

Tauchnitz's English Editions of German Authors. Each volume, cloth flexible, 2s. ; or sewed, 1s. 6d. (Catalogues post free.)

Tauchnitz (B.) German Dictionary. 2s.; paper, 1s. 6d.; roan, 2s. 6d.

———— *French Dictionary.* 2s.; paper, 1s. 6d.; roan, 2s. 6d.

———— *Italian Dictionary.* 2s. ; paper, 1s. 6d.; roan, 2s. 6d.

———— *Latin Dictionary.* 2s.; paper, 1s. 6d.; roan, 2s. 6d.

———— *Spanish and English.* 2s. ; paper, 1s. 6d.; roan, 2s. 6d.

———— *Spanish and French.* 2s.; paper, 1s. 6d. ; roan, 2s. 6d.

Taylor (R. L.) Chemical Analysis Tables. 1s.

———— *Chemistry for Beginners.* Small 8vo, 1s. 6d.

Techno-Chemical Receipt Book. With additions by BRANNT and WAHL. 10s. 6d.

Technological Dictionary. See TOLHAUSEN.

Thausing (Prof.) Malt and the Fabrication of Beer. 8vo, 45*s.*

Theakston (M.) British Angling Flies. Illustrated. Cr. 8vo, 5*s.*

Thomas (Bertha), House on the Scar, Tale of South Devon. Crown 8vo, 6*s.*

Thomson (Jos.) Central African Lakes. New edition, 2 vols. in one, crown 8vo, 7*s.* 6*d.*

—— *Through Masai Land.* Illust. 21*s.*; new edition, 7*s.* 6*d.*

—— *and Miss Harris-Smith. Ulu: an African Romance.* crown 8vo, 6*s.*

—— *(W.) Algebra for Colleges and Schools.* With Answers, 5*s.*; without, 4*s.* 6*d.*; Answers separate, 1*s.* 6*d.*

Thornton (L. D.) Story of a Poodle. By Himself and his Mistress. Illust., crown 4to, 2*s.* 6*d.*

Tileston (Mary W.), Daily Strength for Daily Needs. 18mo, 4*s.* 6*d.*

Tolhausen. Technological German, English, and French Dictionary. Vols. I., II., with Supplement, 12*s.* 6*d.* each; III., 9*s.*; Supplement, cr. 8vo, 3*s.* 6*d.*

Tompkins (E. S. de G.) Through David's Realm. Illust. by TOMPKINS, the Author. 8vo, 10*s.* 6*d.*

Transactions of the Hong Kong Medical Society, vol. 1, 8vo, sewed, 12*s.* 6*d.*

Tytler (Sarah) Duchess Frances: a Novel. 2 vols., 21*s.*

UPTON (H.) Manual of Practical Dairy Farming. Cr. 8vo, 2*s.*

VERNE (Jules) Celebrated Travels and Travellers. 3 vols. 8vo, 7*s.* 6*d.* each; extra gilt, 9*s.*

—— *Purchase of the North Pole, seq. to " From Earth to Moon."* Illustrated. 6*s.*

—— *Family Without a Name.* Illustrated. 6*s.*

—— *Flight to France.* 3*s.* 6*d.*

—— See also LAURIE.

Victoria (Queen) Life of. By GRACE GREENWOOD. Illust. 6*s.*

Vigny (A. de), Cinq Mars. Translated, with Etchings. 2 vols. 8vo, 30*s.*

Viollet-le-Duc (E.) Lectures on Architecture. Translated by BENJAMIN BUCKNALL, Architect. 2 vols., super-royal 8vo, £3 3*s.*

BOOKS BY JULES VERNE.

LARGE CROWN 8VO. WORKS.	Containing 350 to 600 pp. and from 50 to 100 full-page illustrations.		Containing the whole of the text with some illustrations.	
	Handsome cloth binding, gilt edges.	Plainer binding, plain edges.	Cloth binding, gilt edges, smaller type.	Coloured boards, or cloth.
	s. d.	*s. d.*	*s. d.*	
20,000 Leagues under the Sea. Parts I. and II.	10 6	5 0	3 6	2 vols., 1s. each.
Hector Servadac	10 6	5 0	3 6	2 vols., 1s. each.
The Fur Country	10 6	5 0	3 6	2 vols., 1s. euch.
The Earth to the Moon and a Trip round it	10 6	5 0	2 vols., 2s. ea.	2 vols., 1s. each.
Michael Strogoff	10 6	5 0	3 6	2 vols., 1s. each.
Dick Sands, the Boy Captain	10 6	5 0	3 6	2 vols., 1s. cach.
Five Weeks in a Balloon	7 6	3 6	2 0	1s. 0d.
Adventures of Three Englishmen and Three Russians	7 6	3 6	2 0	1 0
Round the World in Eighty Days	7 6	3 6	2 0	1 0
A Floating City	7 6	3 6	2 0	1 0
The Blockade Runners			2 0	1 0
Dr. Ox's Experiment	—	—	2 0	1 0
A Winter amid the Ice	—	—	2 0	1 0
Survivors of the "Chancellor".	7 6	3 6	3 6	2 vols., 1s. each.
Martin Paz			2 0	1s. 0d.
The Mysterious Island, 3 vols.:—	22 6	10 6	6 0	3 0
I. Dropped from the Clouds	7 6	3 6	2 0	1 0
II. Abandoned	7 6	3 6	2 0	1 0
III. Secret of the Island	7 6	3 6	2 0	1 0
The Child of the Cavern	7 6	3 6	2 0	1 0
The Begum's Fortune	7 6	3 6	2 0	1 0
The Tribulations of a Chinaman	7 6	3 6	2 0	1 0
The Steam House, 2 vols.:—				
I. Demon of Cawnpore	7 6	3 6	2 0	1 0
II. Tigers and Traitors	7 6	3 6	2 0	1 0
The Giant Raft, 2 vols.:—				
I. 800 Leagues on the Amazon	7 6	3 6	2 0	1 0
II. The Cryptogram	7 6	3 6	2 0	1 0
The Green Ray	6 0	5 0	2 0	1 0
Godfrey Morgan	7 6	3 6	2 0	1 0
Kéraban the Inflexible:—				
I. Captain of the "Guidara"	7 6	3 6	2 0	1 0
II. Scarpante the Spy	7 6	3 6	2 0	1 0
The Archipelago on Fire	7 6	3 6	2 0	1 0
The Vanished Diamond	7 6	3 6	2 0	1 0
Mathias Sandorf	10 6	5 0	3 6	2 vols., 1s. each.
The Lottery Ticket	7 6	3 6	2 0	1 0
The Clipper of the Clouds	7 6	3 6	2 0	1 0
North against South	7 6	3 6		
Adrift in the Pacific	6 0	3 6		
The Flight to France	7 6	3 6		
The Purchase of the North Pole	6 0			
A Family without a Name	6 0			

CELEBRATED TRAVELS AND TRAVELLERS. 3 vols. 8vo, 600 pp., 100 full-page illustrations, 7s. 6d., gilt edges, 9s. each:—(1) THE EXPLORATION OF THE WORLD. (2) THE GREAT NAVIGATORS OF THE EIGHTEENTH CENTURY. (3) THE GREAT EXPLORERS OF THE NINETEENTH CENTURY.

WALERY, Our Celebrities. Photographic Portraits, vol.
II., part I., including Christmas Number, royal folio, 30*s.*; monthly,
2*s. 6*d.

Wallace (L.) Ben Hur: A Tale of the Christ. New Edition,
crown 8vo, 6*s.*; cheaper edition, 2*s.*

Waller (Rev. C. H.) Adoption and the Covenant. On Confirma-
tion. 2*s. 6*d.

—— *Silver Sockets; and other Shadows of Redemption.*
Sermons at Christ Church, Hampstead. Small post 8vo, 6*s.*

—— *The Names on the Gates of Pearl, and other Studies.*
New Edition. Crown 8vo, cloth extra, 3*s. 6*d.

—— *Words in the Greek Testament.* Part I. Grammar.
Small post 8vo, cloth, 2*s. 6*d. Part II. Vocabulary, 2*s. 6*d.

Walford (Mrs. L. B.) Her Great Idea, and other Stories.
Cr. 8vo, 3*s.*; boards, 2*s.*

Walsh (A. S.) Mary, Queen of the House of David. 8vo, 3*s. 6*d.

Walton (Iz.) Wallet Book, CIƆIƆLXXXV. Crown 8vo, half
vellum, 21*s.*; large paper, 42*s.*

—— *Compleat Angler.* Lea and Dove Edition. Ed. by R. B.
MARSTON. With full-page Photogravures on India paper, and the
Woodcuts on India paper from blocks. 4to, half-morocco, 105*s.*;
large paper, royal 4to, full dark green morocco, gilt top, 210*s.*

Walton (T. H.) Coal Mining. With Illustrations. 4to, 25*s.*

Warner (C. D.) See LOW'S STANDARD NOVELS and STANDARD
SERIES.

Washington Irving's Little Britain. Square crown 8vo, 6*s.*

Wells (H. P.) American Salmon Fisherman. 6*s.*

—— *Fly Rods and Fly Tackle.* Illustrated. 10*s. 6*d.

—— *(J. W.) Three Thousand Miles through Brazil.* Illustrated from Original Sketches. 2 vols. 8vo, 32*s.*

*Wenzel (O.) Directory of Chemical Products of the German
Empire.* 8vo, 25*s.*

Westgarth (W.) Half-century of Australasian Progress. Personal
retrospect. 8vo, 12*s.*

Westoby (W. A. S.), Descriptive Catalogue of 50 Years' Postage
Stamps in Great Britain and Ireland. 8vo, 5*s.*

Wheatley (H. B.) Remarkable Bindings in the British Museum.
Reproductions in Colour, 94*s. 6*d., 73*s. 6*d., and 63*s.*

White (J.) Ancient History of the Maori; Mythology, &c.
Vols. I.-IV. 8vo, 10*s. 6*d. each.

—— *(R. Grant) England Without and Within.* Crown 8vo,
10*s. 6*d.

—— *Every-day English.* 10*s. 6*d.

—— *Fate of Mansfield Humphreys, &c.* Cr. 8vo, 6*s.*

—— *Studies in Shakespeare.* 10*s. 6*d.

White (R. Grant) Words and their Uses.   New Edit., crown
8vo, 5s.

Whitney (Mrs.)   See LOW'S STANDARD SERIES.

Whittier (J. G.) The King's Missive, and later Poems.   18mo,
choice parchment cover, 3s. 6d.

———— *St. Gregory's Guest, &c.*   Recent Poems.   5s.

William I. and the German Empire.   By G. BARNETT SMITH.
New Edition, 3s. 6d.

Willis-Bund (J.) Salmon Problems.   3s. 6d.; boards, 2s. 6d.

Wills (Dr. C. J.) Persia as it is.   Crown 8vo, 8s. 6d.

Wills, A Few Hints on Proving, without Professional Assistance.
By a PROBATE COURT OFFICIAL.   8th Edition, revised, with Forms
of Wills, Residuary Accounts, &c.   Fcap. 8vo, cloth gilt, 1s.

Wilmot-Buxton (Ethel M.)   Wee Folk, Good Folk : a Fantasy.
Illust., fcap. 4to, 5s.

Winder (Frederick Horatio) Lost in Africa : a Yarn of Adven-
ture.   Illust., cr. 8vo, 6s.

Winsor (Justin) Narrative and Critical History of America.
8 vols., 30s. each ; large paper, per vol., 63s.

Woolsey.   Introduction to International Law.   5th Ed., 18s.

Woolson (Constance F.)   See LOW'S STANDARD NOVELS.

Wright (T.) Town of Cowper, Olney, &c.   6s.

Written to Order ; the Journeyings of an Irresponsible Egotist.
By the Author of " A Day of my Life at Eton."   Crown 8vo, 6s.

London:

SAMPSON LOW, MARSTON, SEARLE, & RIVINGTON, Lp.,
St. Dunstan's House,
FETTER LANE, FLEET STREET. E.C.

www.ingramcontent.com/pod-product-compliance
Lightning Source LLC
Chambersburg PA
CBHW030949110726
47900CB00004B/1199